FICTION   Freemantle, Brian.
FREEMANT
          Kings of many
          castles.

KINGS OF MANY CASTLES

KINGS OF MANY CASTLES

A Charlie Muffin Thriller

Brian Freemantle

THOMAS DUNNE BOOKS

ST. MARTIN'S PRESS

NEW YORK

THOMAS DUNNE BOOKS.
An imprint of St. Martin's Press.

KINGS OF MANY CASTLES. Copyright © 2002 by Brian Freemantle.
All rights reserved. Printed in the United States of America. No
part of this book may be used or reproduced in any manner whatsoever without written permission except in the case of brief
quotations embodied in critical articles or reviews. For information, address St. Martin's Press, 175 Fifth Avenue, New York,
N.Y. 10010.

www.stmartins.com

Library of Congress Cataloging-in-Publication Data

Freemantle, Brian.
    Kings of many castles : a Charlie Muffin thriller / Brian
Freemantle.—1st ed.
        p.   cm.
    ISBN 0-312-30412-9
    1. Muffin, Charlie (Fictitious character)—Fiction.
2. Intelligence service—Fiction.   3. British—Russia—
Fiction.   4. Moscow (Russia)—Fiction.   5. Assassination—
Fiction.   6. Defectors—Fiction.   I. Title.

PR6056.R43 K45 2002
823'.914—dc21

                                            2002069280

First Edition: December 2002

10   9   8   7   6   5   4   3   2   1

For Roger and Glynis, with love

Author's Note

On August 19, 1991, a group of hardline Communists staged a vodka-fuelled coup against reforming Soviet president Mikhail Gorbachev. Among the plotters, who included the prime minister, the defense minister, and the interior minister, was Vladimir Kryuchkov, chairman of the Komitet Gosudarstvennoy Bezopasnosti, the KGB.

After the immediate failure of the coup, the KGB was broken up and redesigned between external and internal intelligence agencies in exactly the same way as America's CIA and FBI and the United Kingdom's MI6 and MI5. Russia's foreign intelligence organization is the Sluzhba Vneshney Razvedki, the SVR. Its internal service is the Federalnaia Sluzhba Bezopasnosti, the FSB.

All intelligence organizations commit murder, although all strenuously deny it. The topmost classified assassination division of the KGB was the Executive Action Department—Department V—of the First Chief Directorate.

Department V survived the reorganization and the redesigning and exists to this day. Both the SVR and the FSB deny that existence as they vehemently deny its purpose.

Winchester, 2002

Plots, true or false, are necessary things,
To raise up commonwealths and ruin kings

John Dryden,
Absalom and Achitophel

KINGS OF MANY CASTLES

1

The state visit was crucial for the political future of both leaders, which made maximum public and media exposure as important as the long ago concluded but unannounced nuclear missile defense treaty that was to be its triumphant, reelection assuring climax.

The apparent negotiations had been conducted with the surgical precision befitting the life-saving operation both considered it to be. To establish the impression of nation-protecting intractability, the American secretary of state had very publicly headed the three main delegations to Moscow and received the Russian foreign minister in Washington on a matching number of media-hyped occasions. After each of which they'd made dour-faced statements of insurmountable difficulties, left behind in the other's capital additional negotiators and on their returning flights personally given unattributable diplomatic briefings that success would be a miracle.

The public event preparations were as perfectly orchestrated. The leaked details—even suggested photographs—of what America's fashion-icon First Lady had chosen were balanced by those of the Russian president's equally fashion-conscious and vivacious wife, setting up couture competitions at the Bolshoi, the Tchaikovsky Conservatory and the Moscow Arts Theatre as well as at the intended official state banquets.

All of which were featured some way down the list of security considerations that had consumed the American Secret Service and the Russian Presidential Protection division of the Federal Security Service for as long as but far more actively than the time supposedly spent by treaty negotiators.

Both security groups—initially separately but soon in single, protesting voice—were appalled at the completeness of the intended open exposure.

Their argument that the major part of the arrival ceremony be in the totally-controlled inner courtyard of the Kremlin and not in the open, at the Moscow White House, was impatiently swept aside because of the Kremlin's most recent association with communism, whose reemerging official political party, the *Kommumisticheskaya Partiya Rossiiskoi Federatsii*, was seriously threatening the president's second term reelection. The symbolism of the White House, against which Boris Yeltsin sent tanks in 1993 to defeat the communist-led opposition of the Congress of Peoples' Deputies, better suited both presidents. It took a week of persistent argument, finally adjudicated by the chiefs of staff of both leaders, to get the arrival of Air Force One switched from Moscow's international Sheremet'yevo airport to a much more easily vetted and security-assured military airfield on the eastern outskirts of the city. There was an even more protracted dispute over the joint insistence that the two men, and their wives, should drive into the city in an open-topped car along a previously publicized route which Muscovites would be encouraged to line to cheer and wave pre-issued national flags.

It took a claimed terrorist bomb explosion in a car park just off the route, staged by the Russian security service and blamed on Chechen separatists, to gain the concession of a bullet-proofed glass bubble over the rear of the vehicle, which had to be changed from the intended Zil to an American-imported Cadillac because no such protective fitment existed for a Russian limousine. To compensate for the reluctant abandonment of open transportation both services acceded to an increase in the number of elevated TV camera positions but were again overruled by the chiefs of staff on their demand that the official cavalcade should drive at the traditional high speed along the government-reserved center lane of the approach roads.

A second officially planted bomb literally backfired when the two presidents decided to show their refusal to be cowed by terrorism— and gain the predictable headlines—by having their procession restricted to forty m.p.h. in the lane closest to the flag-waving crowds once they entered the built-up area. A request by three American Secret Service officers to be released from the Moscow detail was rejected with the warning that the protest gesture would be marked on their records. Twenty-four hours before the American president's arrival the designated route was, however, closed to vehicular traffic and all the drains and culverts checked by explosive-detecting sniffer dogs before all manhole covers were welded into place. By then all political dissidents and separatist group members with checkable police files had been detained in militia custody.

A cloudless, early summer day guaranteed the crowds. Maintaining the pretence of remaining treaty difficulties the American leader, Walter Anandale, declared at the airport arrival ceremony that a breakthrough in the negotiations to completely abandon his country's already suspended National Missile Defense project was only possible at president-to-president level. His wife was dazzling in pink, with a matching cloche hat. The Russian president's wife was in powder blue, her hair a blond, unruffled curtain to her shoulders on the windless day.

The immediately following car for the journey into Moscow carried three American and three Russian protection officers in constant telephone and radio contact with others lining the route ahead. One of the Russians was permanently patched through to the shadowing helicopters overhead. They left their car while it was still moving to be in position around the Cadillac when it stopped on Krasnopresnenskaya Naberezhnaya, despite the mixed, twelve-man detail already cordoning the podium from which the Russian leader was to respond to the American's arrival speech.

The ceremony was choreographed as perfectly as everything else. The two women left the limousine ahead of their husbands, to put them slightly at the rear when the two men turned to face the hedge of microphones and television cameras, some on their level and others stilted high above on elevated staging.

The sound of the first shot was only discernible from the sound-amplified replays and several commentators later remarked they were momentarily bewildered by the abrupt red splashes on the pink and blue suits of the First Ladies before seeing the Russian leader clutch his chest and realizing the redness was the man's blood.

Charlie Muffin, who was watching the live coverage on America's CNN, said: "Shit!" Natalia had only so far been peripherally involved but his immediate awareness was that it would all change now.

Charlie could never have imagined by how much.

2

The astonishing footage of the gunman's seizure was to win the CNN cameraman an international award, which confirmed the importance of being in the right place at the right time more than professional expertise: his elevated position was next in line and only seven meters away from the Russian TV gantry from which the shots were fired. All he had to do was swivel his camera forty-five degrees, point it and adjust the zoom.

There were only two wrestling men on the miniscule, swaying platform, one still clutching the telescope-mounted rifle, the other the Russian cameraman restricted by his equipment harness and the headset link to the control scanner unseen far below. The gunman was slim, eyes wild and virtually unfocused, already dishevelled long blond hair further matted by the fight. He wore soiled jeans and a creased, denim workshirt against which bounced, as they fought, a neck-chained identity disc that appeared the same as that around the cameraman's neck. The cameraman was an overweight but muscular man at least ten years older and much shorter. Despite the tussle his wispy remaining hairs stayed cemented in place over a reddish bald head. His face was mottled, too, by the frenzy and both arms were blackly tattooed.

They struggled for the weapon, torn at like a bone between two dogs. Each was yelling, snarling, kicking at the other but the words were lost because the witnessing CNN camera was mute, the commentary—a pointless, even inadequate description of what was obvious on screen—coming from the monitors in the ground-based American scanner. But the shouting would probably have been inaudible anyway beneath the roar of an escort helicopter which abruptly descended to within two meters of the pod, its downdraft threatening to blow both men off their narrow perch. It spun the tripod-mounted Russian camera wildly, smashing it once into its operator hard enough to teeter him against the edge of the guardrail and almost enabled the gunman to reclaim his rifle. The cameraman used his faltering hold to pull himself back to safety but the pummelling rotors tossed them around the platform more than the battle for the gun. At last the cameraman's hair was dislodged; that of the other man was an enclosing mask around his face.

A safety-belted marksman swung out of the helicopter into a practised crouch on to the port strut, his sniper's rifle moving smoothly to his shoulder, and for the briefest moment the brawling men paused, both looking upwards, and for the first time the American commentary made a contribution, reporting that from the Russian helicopter was being amplified an instruction for the two men to separate. The cameraman made as if to do so but immediately snatched for the disputed rifle when the berserk man began turning the barrel towards him. Above, the sniper sighted and abandoned the clear shot, sighted and lifted his rifle again in arm-jerking frustration.

Three men were climbing the gantry by now, the second two with Makarov hand-guns already out, making it difficult for them to pull themselves up the ladder rails. Both paused, trying for the unimpeded shot the sniper couldn't get from above but like the airborne marksman neither was able to distinguish between the locked-together fighters.

It was the first climbing Russian who ended it in what was practically an anti-climax. When his head became level with the pod floor the Russian simply reached up and jerked the younger man's feet from beneath him. For a moment he appeared to be supported entirely by his hold on his rifle. Then he crashed on both knees to the metal floor—his head thrown back, mouth wide, in an unheard cry of agony—finally releasing his hold upon the weapon. At once the leading security officer caught the back of the crumpled man's shirt and hauled him bodily through the gantry fence. For the briefest moment he was suspended, grabbing out for the cameraman then snatching to hold on to the platform edge before falling, arms and legs flailing, the fifteen meters to the ground where he was immediately lost beneath a scrum of other, waiting, security people.

Aware of the uniqueness of his pictures the CNN director had not switched cameras. Now he did, recapping with instant replay from the moment of the first blood splash. Charlie's initial impression was of the American First Lady bending to help the collapsed Russian leader, but she fell away from the man and Charlie realized she, too, had been hit. It was impossible to gauge how badly because everyone on the dais was instantly engulfed by security and the cameras were live here, so it was possible to hear the screams of fear and disorganized, unthinking panic, all the rehearsals for just such an eventuality forgotten, Russians and Americans jostling in total confusion. The one preparation that did operate smoothly was the instant arrival of the waiting-in-readiness ambulances, although their paramedics were delayed stretchering the victims into them by the crush of so obviously failed protection.

The siren-howling, militia-escorted journey to the Pirogov Hospital on Leninskaya Prospekt was this time along the centrally reserved carriageways and was recorded virtually throughout by the specially-installed cameras. An American reporter outside the hospital brought the coverage up to date, although the station kept cutting back to the TV gantry fight.

Few details had so far been made available, the reporter said. It was known that the Russian president, Lev Maksimovich Yudkin, was the most seriously hurt, with two separate wounds to the upper chest. He was currently undergoing surgery. So was America's First Lady, Ruth Anandale. Her injuries were not believed to be life-threatening. Her operation was being conducted by the surgeon and medical staff who routinely travelled with the President on overseas trips, although some Russian doctors and staff were assisting. The reporter understood that two other people had been hurt in the shooting, one an American Secret Service officer.

Charlie stayed until the last minute, flicking between local Moscow channels and the superior coverage of the American network and its fluke-of-positioning scoop, knowing precisely how long it would take him to get to the kindergarten to collect Sasha, to which he'd already agreed with Natalia before the attempted assassination. Their daughter greeted him with a model of a cardboard house puffed with cotton wool to represent snow for which she'd got a red star that reminded Charlie of those that still adorned the Kremlin towers. Sasha said it was a present for her mother but Charlie could share if he wanted. Charlie said he'd like to. He took the backroads to Lesnaya, sure the more direct main roads would still be blocked— maybe even pointlessly sealed off—by militia and Federal Security Service officers frantically pretending to fulfill the role they'd already so badly failed to perform. Don't be a smart ass, he told himself: there but for the grace of God and all that. Professionally able to guess just how much buck-passing and shit-shovelling there'd be, Charlie was caught by the mundane comparison of his meandering home on a school run with a chattering five year old beside him. There was no answering machine message from Natalia when he got to the apartment. CNN was still showing their extraordinary footage. The only update from the Pirogov Hospital reporter was that the American president had arrived and was waiting for his wife to emerge from surgery. It was difficult to see anything of the ground level of the hospital because of the hedge of Secret Servicemen.

It was almost nine o'clock, Sasha long ago bathed and asleep, before Natalia got to the apartment. She was sagged by tiredness and strain. The tone in which she said his name halted his automatically moving towards the waiting bottles, to make her the reviving drink.

"What?" he said, turning back to her.

"The gunman's name is George Bendall," she said, flatly. "His father was Peter Bendall, who defected from Britain nearly thirty years ago."

"Oh fuck!" said Charlie.

The adrenaline-surged panic was over. There were only two other men with the American president in the hurriedly-assigned office which still had the jacket of its normal occupant hanging from the inside door hook. The man's discarded salami sandwiches were in the waste bin. In the outside corridor the Secret Servicemen formed a solid, shoulder-to-shoulder wall.

"She's over the first hurdle," said Wendall North. "That's good."

"She's come through immediate surgery," qualified Anandale, who'd returned from the recovery room minutes before and was still in shirtsleeves after taking off his sterilized gown. "If it doesn't work she'll lose the arm. And there's going to be a lot of shock."

"It'll work," said the chief of staff, locked into empty reassurance.

"It sure as hell better," said Anandale, just as emptily. He was a big man, tall and heavily built. The Texas accent was very pronounced. "We need to get her out of here: back to America. The conditions here are Stone Age."

"What's Max Donnington say?" asked the chief of staff. North had expected the White House surgeon, a commissioned admiral, to come up from the resuscitation room with the president. The navy physician had to be concerned about Ruth Anandale's recovery not to have done so.

"He doesn't want her moved, not even to the embassy. He's bringing in some sterilisation equipment and more staff, to clean up the room that she's in. Liaise with him, Wendall. I want the best-equipped air ambulance brought in, ready the moment it's possible to move her."

James Scamell decided it was time to move the discussion on to practicalities. "I've spoken with the foreign ministry people who've arrived: Boris Petrin himself. It's touch and go whether Yudkin's going to make it."

Anandale was a consummate politician and it only took him seconds to refocus his mind. He nodded at the most obvious inference from the Secretary of State's remark. "Goodbye to a second term reelection for Lev Maksimovich."

"There's temporary provision but not a proper successor in waiting," said Scamell.

"What about the communist party candidate?"

"Petr Tikunov," identified Scamell. "A popular deputy in the Duma. The communists are well organized—better than Yudkin, even—and there's a huge number of people who've come to think that communism wasn't such a bad way of life after all. At street level everyone had some sort of job and some sort of income."

"Where's that leave us?" demanded Anandale, his reasoning in perfect synch with the circumstances.

"With a need to readjust," replied North, eager to get back into the discussion. He was an intense, quickly-blinking man anxious to share the president's reelection and the rarified atmosphere of being at the epicenter of World events.

"Easily possible," picked up Scamell. "No treaty's been signed; can't be now. We've still got our Star Wars preparations which we're sure as hell going to need if Yudkin dies and is succeeded by the opposition."

"The peacemaker becomes the iron man," headlined North. He decided to wait until there was a more positive prognosis about Ruth Anandale's recovery before hinting at the huge sympathy vote that could be manipulated.

There was another silence.

Anandale said, "We know who the son of a bitch is who did it?"

"The two bombs were Chechen," reminded North, uncomfortably.

"That's your job, Wendall. I've got a personal interest in knowing everything about whoever organized it and why. I don't give a damn about Russian jurisdiction or hurt feelings. And I want to know how people who were supposed to be protecting me—and my wife—let a guy with a godamned gun within kewpie doll shooting range of us."

"Yes, sir," said North.

"My wife might die," said the president, in near conversation with himself. "Someone's going to pay for that, pay for it personally. You hear me, Wendall?"

"Yes, Mr. President, I hear you."

In Washington CIA Director Jack Grech personally took the call from FBI Director Paul Smith.

Grech said, "We got a lot of problems here."

"You going over to head things up personally?" asked Smith.

"I need to speak to people first," evaded Grech. All the Secret Service precautions were based upon Agency—and Russian—advice, leaving the Agency in the clear.

Paul Smith decided an FBI director could do himself a lot of political good riding in with the cavalry, particularly when the gunman was already in custody. Smith said, "I think I'll start making plans."

"I guess I should, too," said Grech.

3

Charlie Muffin's office in the new British embassy on Protocnyj Pereulok was in complete contrast to the cobwebbed broom cupboard he'd been dismissively allocated in the old legation on Morisa Toreza, actually with an unobstructed view over the Smolenskaya embankment to the Moskva river and with a separate annex for direct, security-cleared telephone, e-mail and fascimile links to his London riverside headquarters at Millbank. He even had his own coffee percolator. Peter Bendall's complete file—together with separately wired photographs—had already been faxed through by the time Charlie arrived at the night-shrouded complex, carrying the video of the gantry struggle he'd recorded himself before leaving the Lesnaya Ulitza apartment. He was only three-quarters through the archive material when the querulous call came from Richard Brooking, the head of chancellery.

"This had better be justified."

"It is."

"We're on the coffee."

"Pass the mints and decanter around a second time."

The man sighed. "How long?"

"Fifteen minutes. Have you told the ambassador?"

There was another sigh. "I need to be sure there's a crisis first."

"Your decision," said Charlie, who hadn't given the diplomat the reason for breaking into his dinner party over an open telephone line from Lesnaya.

"Don't you forget that. My office. Thirty minutes."

Charlie finished reading in fifteen and spent the remainder of the time studying the fading photographs of one of Britain's most infamous post-war traitors. Peter Bendall had been a skeletally-thin man whose narrow face was dominated by a prow of a nose upon which balanced thick-lensed, round-framed spectacles. Every Old

Bailey trial, family and official government picture portrayed a fastidiously although cheaply dressed, aloofly-featured man bearing no similarity whatsoever to the fanatically staring, mop-haired figure who'd now been seen by every television owner in the world struggling in mid-air for possession of a sniper's rifle.

Brooking, a fleshy, overweight man assured an ambassadorial promotion on his next posting, was still wearing his dinner jacket and black tie when Charlie got to the man's office suite. He tried—but failed—to heighten the unspoken rebuke at having his evening interrupted by the contempt with which he regarded Charlie's shoespread, crumpled appearance. Charlie wondered if the man had told his guests to wait until his return. Around the man still hung a miasma of cigars.

"So what is it!" demanded Brooking, impatiently.

"Today's gunman is British, the son of a defector," announced Charlie. The theatricality was unnecessary—he should have warned Brooking during their internal telephone conversation earlier—but pompous assholes like Brooking had always irritated Charlie and he never had been able to resist the deflating pin-prick.

Brooking did visibly deflate. He shook his head, refusing the information, and several times said "No" as if to convince himself he'd mishead.

"George Bendall," insisted Charlie. "Son of Peter Bendall, an Aldermaston physicist who escaped from Wormwood Scrubs in 1970 after serving only two of a forty year sentence for betraying to the Russians over the previous fifteen years every British nuclear development, a lot of which was shared with America."

"Oh my God!" moaned Brooking.

Charlie hefted what had come from London. "Virtually nothing on George Bendall, who was only two when his father got caught. Brought to Moscow by his mother three years after his father arrived. She skipped sideways through Austria from what was purported to be a holiday in France using the same escape route as her husband. Gave the stiff finger to British counter-intelligence who were supposed to be watching her because hubby was rumored to have changed his mind and wanted to come back."

Brooking's recovery was as visible as his earlier collapse. "Why didn't you tell me this from the beginning!"

"It wasn't a secure line."

The man frowned. "Has this been officially announced by the Russians?"

"No."

"Then how do you know?"

"It's my job to know, the job I was posted here to fulfill."

"What's your source?"

"You know I can't tell you that." It was an inviolable rule that official diplomats were always separated from provable intelligence activities, and even though Charlie's function had changed it provided a very important personal protection for him and Natalia within Moscow. And the director-general in London hadn't pressed to learn his contacts. Observing his own even more inviolable personal rule Charlie already had a prepared escape if Sir Rupert Dean or anyone else ever became too curious or demanding.

"It could be wrong."

"It's not." Charlie belatedly realized that this was the very first time he'd directly acted upon—used—information from Natalia and her intelligence liaison directorship with the Interior Ministry. She hadn't tried to dissuade him because there was going to be an official announcement the following day but over the last few months he'd become increasingly aware how much of a strain their precarious situation was, far more upon her than him. He'd stopped talking about their getting married or of how easily they could live in England—anywhere in Europe—if their relationship did become known and he was inevitably expelled and she was just as inevitably dismissed her ministry position.

"You've told London?"

"Sir Rupert personally. He wants the ambassador informed ahead of the Russian announcement."

"Yes," agreed Brooking, briskly.

Pass the problem parcel time, Charlie recognized. "And lawyers."

"Yes," complied Brooking again, still brisk, aware of another layer of responsibility avoidance. "Their involvement is obviously essential."

Brooking's first telephone call was shorter than the second and Charlie wondered if the lawyer had already been in bed in the apartment block that formed part of the new British diplomatic compound. Charlie was one of a very few still living—because he clearly had to—outside the enclave, once more using as the reason the necessity to distance himself from official diplomacy, although since the post–Cold War re-alignment his was much more an FBI than a counter-intelligence function. Which was why, during his sleepy-voiced conversation with an awakened Sir Rupert Dean in London, the director-general had given the empire-preserving instruction that the embassy-attached MI6 be kept out for as long as possible.

Since that conversation Charlie had decided the delay, twelve hours at the most, would achieve little more than further alienating him from people who were supposed to be colleagues but who viewed him with the distaste that Brooking had evidenced minutes before. But it was a familiar experience for Charlie to find there was shit on every baton he picked up. He couldn't ever remember actually being part of a relay team but resisting inter-embassy association was a matter of professional necessity as much as self-protecting ostracism. Charlie never had been, nor ever would be, a team player. It made him reliant upon others and a further Charlie Muffin rule was never to rely upon anyone except himself.

An unsettling challenge came at once to mind. What about Natalia? Not a contradiction, he assured himself. He trusted Natalia implicitly and absolutely, trusted her more than she trusted him, with every justifiable reason for her doubt. He relied upon her, too, in equal proportion. But that trust and that reliance was personal, not professional. He would never, of course, have admitted it to anyone—most certainly not to Natalia, who would misunderstand it to be a lack of love, which it wasn't—but because Charlie Muffin knew himself so completely he acknowledged he'd never accept Natalia's professional judgment in preference to or above his own.

Sir Michael Parnell entered the room with vaguely hesitant authority. He was a thin man, although not as thin as Peter Bendall appeared in the file photographs, and any further similarity was smothered beneath the fullness of deeply black hair. Like Brooking, the ambassador wore a dinner jacket and black tie and to Charlie, who did not smoke, the cigar aroma smelled the same. Charlie's protocol-routed request, through Brooking, had been to meet Parnell immediately and he wondered if the man's initial refusal had been disinterest or the instinctive arms-length distancing of a regretted member of embassy staffing. Probably a combination of both. Moscow was a prestigious appointment and Parnell had only held it for four months and now he was about to confront his worst sleeping or waking nightmare.

Parnell looked undecided between the two men already in the room before settling on Charlie. "Do I really need to hear what this is all about?" The man's voice was unexpectedly high.

Instead of replying directly, Charlie looked at Brooking and said, "You thought so, didn't you? You got any second thoughts?"

Parnell's face stiffened. Brooking colored. The head of chancellery said, "Yes sir, you do."

"My director-general thought so, too." He wasn't going to improve any working relationship with these two men by showing the respect their condescension hadn't earned, so fuck them. He didn't want to spend any more time with them than they wanted to spend with him.

"What?" demanded the ambassador.

The lawyer's arrival delayed Charlie's reply. So well had he isolated himself against embassy staff contact that there was the briefest moment of surprise, although he was sure he didn't show it. She was tall for a woman, although not overly so, slim and small busted. If she were publicly to become known in what was to follow Charlie supposed willowy would be the English tabloid description. She wore a severe black suit that Charlie accepted to be her embassy-recognized uniform and he guessed the deeply auburn hair which now hung loose would during the day be more tightly pinned and controlled. She wasn't wearing make-up, either, apart perhaps from the lightest of lipsticks, and Charlie decided that she had been in bed and probably asleep when Brooking telephoned. She politely greeted the two diplomats by title and name and remained looking enquiringly at Brooking, who hurriedly introduced her to Charlie as Anne Abbott.

"Now I won't have to repeat myself a third time," greeted Charlie. Her handshake was firm, confident, and he liked her attitude towards the other two men, respectful of their embassy rank but not deferential. He put her at about thirty-eight, certainly not older.

"What is it?" demanded Parnell again, impatiently.

Neither the ambassador nor the woman openly gave the sort of disbelieving reaction Brooking had shown when Charlie told them, although Parnell at once asked if Charlie were sure and Charlie said he was.

"The nationality is the key," insisted Anne. "There's no doubt he's still British?"

Charlie handed her the London material. "You'll need to go through everything. It's Peter Bendall's entire archive. If he'd taken Russian nationality, it would have been logged. There was a lot of speculation that his refusal to adopt Russian citizenship showed an intention to return to England, despite the sentence he'd still have had to serve . . ." He looked to the other two men. "I've made copies of everything except the seizure video which needs the embassy facilities to duplicate."

"It's surely a moot point whether he had or he hadn't taken citizenship," challenged Parnell, objectively. "George Bendall is still *who he* is, the son of a British nuclear defector."

"Who's shot a Russian president hopefully about to agree to a Star Wars-banning treaty with America," picked up Brooking, assessing the diplomatic fall out.

Charlie hadn't considered the political symbolism. Completing it he said, "An agreement that won't now be reached. Might never be."

"And what's left is the mess, our mess, to clear up as best we can," said Parnell.

"What will the procedure be? Diplomatically, I mean?" asked the woman, practicably.

"In normal circumstances if a British national is arrested for an alleged crime the embassy applies for consular access," recited the ambassador, formally. "I don't consider this normal. I'll want guidance from London."

"What about legal representation?" Anne persisted.

Parnell shrugged. "That's usually made available."

"Are you criminal or civil?" Charlie asked the lawyer.

"Criminal."

"Recognized under Russian law?" pressed Charlie.

She shook her head. "I'd need guidance, like the ambassador. But I don't think I'd be accepted in open court as anything more than a qualified observer. I could probably get attachment to a Russian lawyer's briefing team if London wanted it. What are your instructions?"

"To investigate as much as I can as best I can," generalized Charlie. He went to the ambassador. "I'd like to be included in any access that's arranged. My director-general will be contacting you tomorrow."

"I'll definitely need Foreign Office guidance for that," warned Parnell.

"Sir Rupert expected you would," said Charlie.

The thin man's head came up sharply at the suspicion of condescension. Charlie stared back, blandly. Remaining fixedly upon Charlie, Parnell said, "It *is* a mess. I don't want it made worse by any mistakes from this embassy. I don't want anything—anything at all—initiated or done without prior reference to me. Is that understood?"

"Perfectly," said Charlie. Bollocks, he thought.

"Of course," said Anne, accepting her inclusion in the caution.

As she walked from the head of chancellery's office with Charlie, leaving the two diplomats composing their alert cable to the Foreign Office in London, she said, "It's illegal under the Copyright Act to duplicate videos."

"Let's not tell anyone we're going to do it." Charlie had never told anyone in advance what he was going to do. Or hardly ever afterwards. It was better that way for their propriety, ulcers, general state of health and overall peace of mind.

Charlie's mind as he emerged into the darkness of a slumbering Moscow night was anything but peaceful. He hadn't properly started yet and there were already things that worried him, one more obviously than the others. He didn't even need the warning ache from his talisman feet to tell him all was not right.

"We've got everything to consider, to protect ourselves against," protested Sir Michael Parnell, guiding the discussion.

"I understand what you're saying," agreed the about-to-be-promoted head of chancellery.

"We've got to be careful."

"Absolutely."

"If it gets to consular access, it'll be you, Richard."

"I know," accepted Brooking, uncomfortably.

"That intelligence fellow's a problem. I know he's not officially recognized here as such but that's what he is. Or was. And a confounded nuisance as well, from all the stories I heard before I arrived."

"He's caused a lot of problems in the past," confirmed Brooking.

"I won't allow him to cause any in the future. If London wants their own investigation, let them send someone from there to do it, separate us from that part of it. We're going to have enough difficulties as it is."

"Maybe we shouldn't ask for someone from London, for precisely that reason?" suggested Brooking.

Parnell allowed a half smile. "What's your thinking?"

"Muffin's already got the reputation in London as an uncontrollable troublemaker. Politically and diplomatically we couldn't be in a more unmapped minefield, with what's happened. There will be mistakes, no matter how hard we try to anticipate, mistakes we don't officially want to be associated with."

Parnell's smile broadened. "We'll have to watch the bloody man very carefully, of course."

"We might actually in the final analysis get rid of him altogether. It's still an experimental posting, despite his having tricked his way successfully so far."

"*That* would be good!" said Parnell, enthusiastically. There was a pause. "So! What do we tell London?"

"That we've inherited another intelligence embarrassment," insisted Brooking, at once. "Let's start from the very beginning preparing the way to distance ourselves."

The eruption was inevitable, the only uncertainty its timing, and Burt Jordan, the CIA station head, and the FBI Rezident, John Kayley—both of whom felt themselves safely beyond the endangered fall-out area—found much to occupy them in the initial file photographs of the shooting while Wendall North outlined the situation he'd just left at the Pirogov Hospital. They were in the *chef du protocol*'s office at the American embassy on the Novinskij Bul'var section of the inner ring road, even his desk surrendered by the local diplomat, David Barnett. Barnett considered himself the safest of them all in the aftermath and sat trying to guess when the explosion would occur.

"So that's it," concluded North. "A . . ."

"Total disaster," completed Jeff Aston, director of the White House Secret Service detail.

"We all know that," tried North. "The immediate need is to prioritize: evaluate and anticipate."

"Just how much do we all know to evaluate and anticipate, Wendall?" persisted Aston, who was black, six and a half feet tall, weighed two hundred and twenty-five pounds and had protected two previous presidents before Walter Anandale. "Give us an idea of your prioritizing. How would you assess the fall-out? Would you put a treaty that isn't going to be signed more or less important than the maiming of the president's wife? And where would you put the likely death of a Russian president against the possible resurgence of a communist government? And whereabouts in all of it would you put the fact that the shooting was allowed to happen in the first place because that's something that personally and professionally interests me a hell of a lot. . . ." Aston had hassled Barnett into including both the CIA and FBI, determined there should be witnesses. They'd already been waiting when the unsuspecting Wendall North arrived from the hospital, making it impossible for him to exclude them.

"I don't think that's very constructive, which is what we've got to be," protested North, conscious that he had no defense against the Secret Service chief's attack.

"Right again, Wendall," goaded Aston. "But I'm still a little curious about things being *de*structive. Which it's my job to prevent . . . providing, that is, I'm not prevented or obstructed from doing it."

"There'll be an enquiry," said North. He was red-faced and visibly sweating, despite the air-conditioning.

"I'm sure as hell glad to hear that, Wendall. Your office kept all the preparation and planning details for this trip, all the way back to when the negotiations first started? I don't want you or any of your staff to worry, if you haven't. We have, in the Secret Service. Every memo, notes of every discussion, telephone logs of every call and what the outcome was. And not just in English. Russian, too. I've already cabled Washington for it all to be handed over to counsel. Important, to keep everything intact. You know how these rumors start after something like this, suggestions of things getting lost or tampered with. So if you've got any problem finding anything, you just let me know because it's important that all the facts are established by whoever investigates the worst cockamamy screwup since God knows when . . ."

"I'll remember that," said North, tightly. "But at the right time. Which isn't now." He'd hoped having George Bendall's identity, which he'd learned at the hospital, would have deflected this obvious attack.

"Don't you worry about remembering, Wendall. I'll remind you often enough."

"There *are* other things to talk about," prompted the bespectacled, fair-haired diplomat whose office had been taken over and who had decided Aston had sufficiently established blame.

"Absolutely," agreed Aston. "Let's try to make sure we get it right this time."

"There's going to be a lot of balls in the air," warned the CIA's Burt Jordan. "From what Washington has rounded up so far this guy's father did a lot of damage to the American nuclear program as well as to the British. Which was bad enough at the time. This is a hell of a lot worse. My guess is they'll hunker down. Throw George Bendall to the wolves, which the bastard deserves anyway, and say he's Russia's problem by adoption, not theirs."

"There's some sound political reasoning in that," said North, relieved the inquest had moved on.

"Not for Moscow," challenged the locally-based diplomat. "Making them responsible for the man who's probably killed their president and badly wounding our First Lady throws detente right out the window."

"That's a fight between London and Moscow," challenged North, in return. "A fight we've got to stay on the outside of but do everything to make swing in our direction, to our president's benefit. There'll be a tide of sympathy now. And our missile shield planning is still in place, whatever happens here."

There was no reaction to the cynicism.

Kayley said, "So politically we don't need Russia or the treaty anymore?"

"Not as much as we did," qualified North. "What we do need is to ride shotgun on the British, particularly with whatever they do here . . ." He looked directly at Jeff Aston. "And to make damned sure there's no rebound on us."

"You mean get into bed with the British . . . ?" Jordan began.

". . . And fuck them every which way," completed Kayley.

Wendall North winced at the coarseness but said, "Yes, that's what I mean."

Charlie padded softly into the darkened bedroom, letting his clothes lie where they fell. He was careful easing himself under the covers to avoid any disturbing contact with Natalia, who lay with her back to him.

Natalia was fully awake but didn't turn. And remained so long after Charlie had settled into occasionally snuffled sleep.

4

The naming of traitor's son George Bendall was to bring a very changed world—some changes predictable, some not—to Charlie's door and for the first time in a permanently precarious life Charlie could rarely, if ever, remember the uncertainty he felt sitting in his river view office awaiting the first approach.

Natalia's giving him to within thirty minutes the timing of the official announcement ended, as far as Charlie was concerned, the futile pretense of keeping their professional lives entirely separate. Charlie's argument that morning had been that this attempted assassination *needed* their personal cooperation, but Natalia had equally insisted there should always be the mitigating defense of their never having colluded, which no tribunal would or could ever accept.

Charlie's confusion was not being sure where, if anywhere, it left he and Natalia. They both recognized the answer to the problem. It would, quite simply, be for one of them to quit their conflicting jobs. Which wasn't in any way simple. To both such a sacrifice was unthinkable. There was nothing else Charlie could do. Wanted to do. Was able to do. And he knew—as Natalia knew—that what was already stretched to near breaking point between them would snap beyond repair within weeks of Charlie becoming a house-husband, in title if not in legal fact.

Which put the onus on Natalia, upon whom the onus had far too often and far too heavily already been imposed in their uneven relationship, a burden Charlie readily recognized, just as he recognized her reservations after so much forgiveness and so many allowances.

She'd accepted as professional his first deceit, convincing her when she'd been assigned his KGB debriefer that his phoney operation-wrecking defection to Moscow was genuine. In those first, getting-to-know each other weeks and months she'd have turned him over to face trial as a spy if he hadn't managed to do so. Their problem—so much, unfairly, Natalia's problem—was in the direct aftermath. Although he'd maneuvered to avoid her being arrested for professional negligence, his return to London—essential professionally, wrong personally—had been an abandonment because by then they had been in love. Natalia had proved that love by being prepared, just once, to defect herself during an escort assignment to London. Trusted him more than he'd trusted her, despite loving her. He'd watched Natalia at their arranged meeting point but been unable to believe she wasn't bait—knowing or unknowing—in a repayment trap for the damage he'd caused Moscow. So he'd held back from the rendezvous and let her go, neither of them knowing then that she was pregnant.

It was a virtual miracle that she'd deigned even to acknowledge him—let alone be persuaded there was a second chance of finally being together—when, with the old, defunct KGB records necessarily self-cleansed to protect herself and their daughter and Natalia's elevating transfer to the ministry, he'd been officially accepted back by a totally unaware and unsuspecting Russian government too overwhelmed by organized crime to match an American FBI presence in the Russian capital.

There could be no blame—no surprise either—for Natalia insufficiently trusting him. He'd done nothing to deserve it. Little, indeed, to deserve Natalia. Which was a long-realized awareness that did nothing to resolve—help even—their escalating problem. Perhaps nothing could.

Charlie's irresolute reflections were broken by the first of the predictable announcement-prompted arrivals. MI6 station chief Donald Morrison flustered jacketless through the door, scarlet braces over monogrammed shirt, an unevenly torn-off slip of new agency copy in his hand. Offering it to Charlie, the man said, "Have you seen this!"

"I heard about it last night," said Charlie. "The ambassador knows. London too."

Morrison stopped abruptly halfway across the room, as if he'd collided with something solid. "How?"

"Contacts in the militia," avoided Charlie, easily.

"A call would have been appreciated," complained Morrison, cautiously. He was an enthusiastic, eager-to-please man at least fifteen years Charlie's junior whom Charlie guessed to have got the sought-after posting through family influence. His predecessor had been part of an inter-agency determination to get Charlie removed from Moscow, badly misjudged Charlie's thumb-gouging, eye-for-an-eye survival ability and now occupied a travel movements desk at MI6's Vauxhall Cross administration department. From the wariness with which Morrison had treated him since his arrival—and the immediate reaction now—Charlie suspected Morrison knew of the episode.

Charlie said, "It's a criminal investigation, more mine that yours under the redefining."

"It would still have been useful to know about in advance, if I'd got a query from London."

"Did you?"

Morrison shrugged, his argument defeated.

"So you haven't lost any credibility," Charlie pointed out.

"You intend running it as a one man show?"

Charlie hadn't yet decided how he was going to run anything, only that by the end of a long day there were probably going to be more people running about and getting in each other's way than in a whorehouse on pay-day when the fleet's in. Which Charlie philosophically accepted. Initially welcomed in fact. Despite his director-general's eagerness to control whatever involvement was achievable it was even possible London's edict would be for a jointly shared investigation, which would provide a sacrificial diversion if one became necessary. Which wasn't ultimate cynicism. It was an essential, practical rule of what the inexperienced or ignorant referred to as a game but which was not. Nor ever had been. Charlie actually liked the younger man and didn't want to cause him any disadvantage or harm. He hoped the need wouldn't arise if Morrison was accorded any part in what was to follow.

"I'll obviously get a call," pressed Morrison.

"I don't know anything more than what was on television this morning," said Charlie, which was almost true. Lev Maksimovich Yudkin had been described as critical after an operation to remove bullets from his abdomen and right lung and Ruth Anandale was stable after having a bullet removed from her right arm near the shoulder. The American president was still at the Pirogov Hospital, where he'd slept overnight. Ben Jennings, the American Secret Serviceman who had been hit, was on a life support machine with a bullet possibly too close to his heart to risk removing. The fifth shot had shattered the leg of a plainclothes Moscow militia officer, Feliks Vasilevich Ivanov, which might possibly need to be amputated. The only additional information, which Natalia had reluctantly provided, was that George Bendall had not regained consciousness after operations to rebuild and pin his left shoulder and leg, both of which had been broken in his fall from the TV gantry.

"It's not going to be an easy one," suggested Morrison.

"Very few are," agreed Charlie. It was like a dance to which he knew every stumbling step, which with his hammer-toed feet wasn't a good analogy.

"We're going to have to work together if London orders it," said Morrison.

"Of course," said Charlie, in apparent acceptance. He handed the other man a copy of Peter Bendall's file. "That's everything my people had. Might be an idea to see what's in your archives, to make a comparison."

Morrison smiled a relieved smile. "That's a good idea. I'll do that."

They both turned at Richard Brooking's arrival. The head of chancellery looked between them and said, "Yes. Of course. You obviously need to be together."

Why, wondered Charlie, had the diplomat come to him, rather than the other way around with a summons like the previous night? Surely their separation wasn't going to be as fatuous as worrying about which rooms they met in?

Morrison said, "That's what I was just saying."

"You heard from London?" demanded Charlie.

"I've been told to seek information," said Brooking.

"From whom or what?" asked Charlie, impatiently.

"The Foreign Ministry. That's our channel of communication."

Who'd simply repeat the official announcement, guessed Charlie. "What about access?"

Brooking shook his head, as if he were denying an accusation. "Nothing like that until we get an official reply from the ministry."

Needing to ride pillion with this man officially to get to George Bendall was going to be a wearisome pain in the ass, Charlie decided. "What about the Americans?"

Brooking hesitated. "Sir Michael is approaching their ambassador personally."

"Am I . . ." started Charlie but stopped. "Are *we* going to be told what's said?" It was important to establish ground-rule precedents.

There was another hesitation from the head of chancellery. "It would constitute a diplomatic exchange."

Charlie's direct-line telephone jarred into the room, breaking the conversation.

"What do you know, Charlie?" said John Kayley.

"Not enough," replied Charlie. "What about you?"

"Think we need to get together."

"Sounds like a good idea. I've got a room with a view."

"I got so much heat I'm getting blisters."

"Maybe I should come to you?"

"It would look better for me."

Charlie was glad he'd taken the trouble socially to meet Kayley at various U.S. diplomatic functions, although he was unsure of the man's by now familiar native American boast to be part Cherokee. It was fortunate, too, that he'd taken so many copies of Bendall's file. "On my way."

"Your contact?" enquired Brooking, hopefully, as Charlie replaced the receiver.

"FBI," said Charlie, shortly.

"You'll let me know what they say?"

"Not sure if it'll constitute a diplomatic exchange," said Charlie, straight faced.

There were several other titular generals in the Kremlin suite with her, although all were male, but Natalia acknowledged hers was probably considered the rank wielding the least influence. She wished she hadn't been included at all. But not as much, she guessed, as the general next to her. Lev Andrevich Lvov had gained his rank in the *spetznaz* special forces before his transfer to the White House to head the Russian president's bodyguard detail and still appeared vaguely uncomfortable in civilian clothes. It was an attitude reflected, too, by the man with whom he was drawn slightly apart from the rest of the group around the table. General Dimitri Ivanovich Spassky headed the counter-intelligence directorate of the FSB, the intelligence successor to the KGB.

"I want a complete assessment. I need to be fully prepared for the debate in the Duma," declared the prime minister, who under a decree issued by the now stricken Russian president assumed the emergency leadership he had, before the communist party resurgence, been predicted to get by democratic election upon Yudkin's second term retirement. Aleksandr Mikhailevich Okulov was a short, sparse-bodied man who, largely under Yudkin's patronage, had risen to the rank of premier in the ten years since leaving the St. Petersburg directorate of the KGB. His supporters praised him as the *eminence grise* of the current government. His detractors preferred the description of lackluster and uninteresting grey man of Russian politics.

The combined concentration in the room was on chief-of-staff Yuri Fedorovich Trishin, a rotund, no longer quickly-smiling man. "It's still too soon for any proper prognosis. The president's condition is critical, and likely to remain so for days. There is considerable trauma. Heart massage as well as mouth-to-mouth resuscitation had to be administered in the ambulance on the way to the hospital. There was substantial blood loss, maybe as much as half his body's capacity. There could be complications with the American president's wife, bad enough to make amputating her arm necessary . . ."

"What about prior to that?" Okulov interrupted. "How was it allowed to happen?"

The question was addressed to Lvov who hadn't broken the fixed stare he'd directed at the chief of staff. Accusingly, Lvov said, "There was too much interference in the security arrangements."

"By whom?" insisted Okulov, who was still trying to adjust and equate in his mind the full personal possibilities so abruptly thrust upon him by the attempted assassination. He'd already recognized his previous KGB career could be an embarrassment in view of Bendall's family history.

"The Americans," said Trishin, quickly. "The Americans made demands and after consultation we complied."

"Consultations with whom."

"Lev Maksimovich," said the plump man, quickly.

Who was too ill—might not even recover—to confirm or deny it, Natalia accepted, realizing she was witnessing a hurriedly conceived survival defense.

"Our own president agreed?" persisted Okulov. It was vital he didn't make a single mistake.

"With everything," insisted Trishin.

"Was there no professional argument?" asked the premier-cum-president. He was going to have to work with these men; decide who he could trust and of whom he had to be careful.

"A considerable amount," said Lvov. Some of the tension had gone out of the man.

"There is documentary proof?" demanded Okulov.

"Yes," said Lvov.

"Also that the pressure came from Washington?"

"Yes," said Trishin.

Okulov settled back in his chair, visibly relaxing, looking between Natalia and the FSB counter-intelligence director. "So! What do we know about the gunman?"

Okulov's KGB background was public knowledge—a target sometimes for attack—but in passing Natalia wondered if the man knew she had also once been a serving officer. In so short a time it was unlikely but it was the sort of preparation automatic for a trained intelligence operative. Ahead of Spassky, she said, "We're all aware of the reorganization and department divisions of the *Komitet Gosudarstvenno Bezopastosti* after the events of 1991. That included archives but it would appear that division was incomplete. I have . . ." she hesitated, bringing duplicated files from her briefcase and distributing them around the conference table of Okulov's office

". . . all that was available from the Interior Ministry files on the defector, Peter Bendall. There is only a two-paragraph reference to the son, at the time he was brought here by his mother. Bendall senior was paid a pension and was responsible to the former KGB until his death. You will see that the records are marked 'Some Retained.' Unfortunately I have not had the opportunity to discuss with General Spassky whatever files still presumably held by the Federal Security Service might contain . . . I hope he can help us with that now . . . ?" She had no alternative, Natalia assured herself. Spassky was one of the old school—proud of his continued membership of the Communist party—and would have tried to bulldoze her into the ground if she hadn't put the tank trap in his way first. Which she might not have done—not been alerted to do—if Spassky hadn't studiously avoided her four attempts to reach him before this meeting. The normally vodka-blotched face was redder than normal from what she inferred to be his fury at being anticipated and she decided the tank trap metaphor was appropriate. The iron-gray-haired bear of a man could very easily have physically crushed her and probably would have liked to have done at that precise moment.

In front of Spassky an ashtray was already half-filled with the butts from which succeeding cigarettes had been lit. There was a snatch of what was intended to be a throat-clearing cough that took several moments to subside and when he finally spoke Spassky's voice was initially threadbare. "We had insufficient time before this meeting . . . not enough indication from the Interior Ministry," flustered the man. "The search is being made now."

Okulov, intent upon identifying scapegoats, at once came back to Natalia, who was surprised at the obviousness of the intelligence general's confusion.

"The first written, advisory memorandum was personally sent by me to the Lubyanka at 8:33 last night, within an hour of the gunman being identified and after the FSB duty officer informed me there was no senior officer available to talk to me personally," she responded, quickly again. "That was followed by three more attempted telephone calls and two more memoranda, time-stamped copies of which are attached to what I have already made available."

"I mean we can't locate them," corrected Spassky. "Not in the time we've had so far."

"Are they lost?" pressured Okulov. The woman's competence made Spassky's inadequacy even more marked.

"We will have everything available later today," said Spassky.

"I personally issued the order to round up all known dissidents, extremists and possible terrorists," reminded Okulov. "Was the name George Bendall on any such list?"

"Not that I am aware of," said Spassky.

"Not that you're *aware* of!" echoed the politician. "Don't you *know!*"

"It was not on any list made available to the Interior Ministry," said Natalia.

"Nor to my service," insisted General Leonid Sergeevich Zenin, Moscow's militia commander, entering the discussion for the first time. "I have specifically re-checked, before this meeting."

"Are you telling me we don't know anything at all about a man who's tried—and might even have succeeded—to kill the president of Russia and seriously wounded the wife of the American president!" demanded Okulov, incredulously.

Not a question for her, Natalia decided.

"I have appointed an investigatory team. The senior colonel is by Bendall's bedside, waiting for him to recover from surgery," said Zenin, hurriedly responding. "His belongings included a workbook, in the name of Gugin, Vasili Gugin. He was employed, in the name of Gugin, by the NTV television channel. He was a gofer, a messenger who fetched and carried. He got the rifle up to the platform in an equipment bag. The address in the workbook is Hutorskaya Ulitza. . . ."

"Where did we get his real name?" interrupted Trishin.

"From his mother, at Hutorskaya Ulitza. She uses the name Gugin, too. But has kept her English given name, Vera."

"She in custody?"

"Of course," said Zenin. "So far she's denied knowing anything about what her son was doing or where he got the rifle. It is an SVD sniper's weapon. It's being forensically examined, naturally."

"The mother must have said something more about him!" demanded Okulov.

"He's been ill . . . mentally ill but she claims he got better."

"Do you believe her?"

"It's far too early to ask my people that."

Okulov went to the chief of staff. "What about the British?"

"There's been a formal approach through the Foreign Ministry, for information," said Trishin.

"The Americans?"

"They want access to Bendall. Full investigative cooperation from everyone involved here."

"Which we'll give them. The British too," decided Okulov. He was contemplatively silent for several minutes. "We have to emerge with unchallengable credibility. There will be maximum liaison between each and every investigatory department . . ." He smiled across the table. "And you, Natalia Fedova, will coordinate everything . . ."

Natalia's first realization was that she'd been made the most vulnerable of them all. Another awareness was that no one had asked—was bothered even—about the other two victims of the shooting.

"The trial must be totally open, a media event," declared Okulov, who'd insisted upon the chief of staff remaining after dismissing the rest. "I mean what I said about openness with the Americans and the British."

"Of course."

"There's no danger of the Americans refuting the security lapses being their fault?"

"They won't officially be *in* court," Trishin pointed out. "There'll only have observer status. We'll have the stage, they won't. And there really is a lot of confirming paperwork." This was the man with whom, initially at least, he was going to have to work with more than anyone else. The second realization was that Okulov's chances of being elected to the presidency was even more uncertain that Yudkin's had been.

"Good," accepted the other man, warming to the increasing personal possibilities. "We've got to discover a great deal more about this man Bendall or Gugin or whatever he calls himself."

"Whatever he calls himself isn't important," insisted Trishin, rebuilding his own bunker. "He *isn't* Russian. He's British, the son of a spy who was allowed to come here under the protection of an earlier communist government."

Okulov nodded, smiling, content for the other man to spell out the further personal advantage he'd already isolated. "Which he doubtless represents. We need to know if he's a supporter of the old ways. Anxious for their return. That could be useful."

Trishin was encouraged by the direction of the conversation. "I didn't get the impression from any of the hospital doctors that there's a possibility of Lev Maksimovich making a full and active recovery, if he survives at all. Which will be a tragedy."

"A great tragedy," agreed Okulov, refusing to respond too quickly to the obvious approach.

Bastard, thought Trishin. "Yours will be the mantle to continue the policies you've been so closely involved in formulating."

There's a power struggle whether Yudkin died or not, accepted Okulov. And he'd need allies who knew the keys to every locked hiding place. "Which I'll require help to do."

"The strength of the communists makes this a very uncertain time," said Trishin, comfortable with platitudes. "It's important to understand you have my complete trust and loyalty, Aleksandr Mikhailevich"

"That's good to hear," said Okulov. "It will be important to have someone like you, Yuri Fedorovich, upon whom I can rely completely."

"Which you can."

"You're quite sure the security lapses can be shown to be those of the Americans?"

"As I've just made clear, Alexandr Mikhailevich, you can trust me."

Until there's a political reversal, Okulov added, mentally.

John Kayley could very easily have had the native American Cherokee Indian ancestry he frequently—and proudly—claimed. He was saturnine with smooth, black hair. He was also indulgently fat and unconcerned about it. His footwear was neither moccasin nor molded into the shapelessness of Charlie's Hush Puppies, but the bagged, unpressed canopy of the button-strained suit could have come from a shared reject shop. The windowless office at Novinskij Bul'var was cloyed with the smell of the scented cigars the man smoked and on the table between them was a bottle of single malt already reduced by a third. It wasn't Islay, Charlie's favored choice, but he appreciated the gesture.

Kayley patted the Peter Bendall dossier with a pudgy hand and said, "I'm truly grateful for this. Like I told you, there's a lot of heat but very little to put on the fire."

"Thanks for this, too," said Charlie. The American had offered unasked the complete list of the failed security precautions, as well as the hospital update that the president's wife could lose her arm, which would be permanently impaired even if she didn't. Charlie liked the fact that the other man wasn't trying to disguise the exchange as anything more than the same give-to-receive shell game he was playing. It indicated—he hoped—that they were treating each other as professionals. He was still waiting for Kayley to point up the one incongruity that was so far troubling him. He wondered if the other professional omission was an oversight.

Kayley said, "Don't envy you the son-of-a-bitch still being British."

"It's a bastard," agreed Charlie. He nodded to his glass being topped up. He'd give the other man a little more time.

"You going to get access?"

"Not applied for yet. I expect it will be."

"We're asking for it, although I'm not sure of our legality. It's Russian jurisdiction and prosecution, even though it's the president's wife that got hit."

Kayley *was* professional, accepted Charlie. "You'll be allowed participation, though?"

"Limited's my guess. He's your national, you stand the better chance."

"I'm prepared to share, if you are." Surely Kayley would pick upon on that!

"Deal!" accepted the American, at once.

Perhaps Kayley was testing him. Charlie said, "Peter Bendall passed over a lot of your stuff to the Russians in the late sixties. There'll be an American dossier on him."

Kayley nodded, unembarrassed at being reminded of the obvious. "I guess. It would have been CIA, not the Bureau."

"Available to you now, though?"

"I'll check it out."

A professional like Kayley would have done so hours ago. If the American was trying to control the exchange, he'd failed. Charlie decided it was better to continue in the expectation of getting something but not all, which was the level at which he intended to work. "You getting any political playback this soon?" There might be a loose ball to play off against Brooking and Sir Michael Parnell and at the moment it was scraps he was scrabbling for.

"Nothing positive," said Kayley, shaking his head. "Washington's not comfortable about the Bureau's position here, if the communists get their man in."

Charlie's feet tweaked. "How's that?"

"We were accepted here by Yeltsin and the reformers, all part of the fight against crime," reminded Kayley. "State's thinking is that we'd be the first to be told to get out if the old regime was re-established. Guess that would apply to you, too."

"Yes," agreed Charlie. "I guess it would." What the hell sort of spin would that put upon the situation between he and Natalia!

"This could even be our last case. How's that for a thought?"

"Unsettling," said Charlie, honestly. About far too many things, he mentally added.

Senior Militia investigator Colonel Olga Ivanova Melnik was an attractive, even beautiful woman and knew it. What she knew even better was how to use it, in every way. She invariably wore civilian clothes instead of uniform, because dresses and skirts and blouses showed off her full-busted, narrow-waisted figure to her best advantage and always allowed distracting cleavage interrogating male suspects. She also adjusted her demeanor to every encounter, bullying when necessary, awkwardly stumbling sometimes to give her interviewees the dangerously misleading impression of their superior intelligence. It was an attitude strictly reserved for interview rooms. Outside she was a determined, supremely confident woman with an IQ of 175 that had academically taken her up the promotional ladder in balanced proportion to the occasions she'd climbed bedroom stairs with partners carefully selected more for her career advancement than their sexual prowess. Since attaining her detective seniority by the age of thirty-five prowess had taken precedence over influence among those invited to follow her up any stairs.

Olga Ivanova was politically as well as professionally adept and was more aware than anyone caught up in the immediate, twenty-four-hour aftermath of the shooting how totally successful she could emerge from the inquiry. How could she fail to get a conviction when the crime had been committed in front of a world-wide television jury?

It remained essential, of course, for Olga to be the hands-on focus of every facet of the investigation and that initially had obviously been for her to sit—fitfully sleeping in her chair when it was no longer possible to remain awake—just one whisper-hearing meter from George Bendall since his return from the operating theater.

But there hadn't been a whisper. Anything except the jagged peaks of the heart monitor and the in-out hiss of the ventilator and the silent blood and saline drip and increasingly dark brown filling of the catheter bag. While all the boring, unproductive time, in walking distance away in Lefortovo prison, Vera Bendall, alias Vera Gugin, had sat for virtually the same period unsuspectingly waiting to be broken.

Olga, a strongly featured, prominently-lipped woman, eased out of the no longer comfortable chair and stretched stiffly around the room, as she had several times before. She'd completed her first circuit and was about to begin her easier, cramp-eased second when the chief physician-administrator, Nicholai Badim, thrust into the room, for the first time in many visits uncaring of the noise. With him was an equally attentive pale-skinned, white-blond-haired psychiatrist, Guerguen Semenovich Agayan.

"We've got the brain scans," Agayan announced. "Look."

Olga did so, although she was unsure what she was supposed to be seeing.

"There!" demanded the surgeon. "At the base there. It's a hairline linear fracture. And here . . ." the finger went to a patch darker than the rest of the illustrated brain. "We did a spinal tap as part of the initial exploratory surgery. There's no blood in the fluid. So that darkening is suberachnoid bruising."

"What are you telling me?" demanded Olga.

"That he badly hit his head in the fall, in addition to all the other injuries," said Agayan.

"Is he brain damaged!"

"I won't know that until he recovers consciousness," said the psychiatrist.

"But I'm going to sedate him more deeply, to counteract any possibility of epilepsy," said Badim. "At the moment his medical condition is more important."

"When's he likely to recover sufficiently for any sort of interrogation?"

"I'm not going to allow him to open his eyes for at least another twenty-four hours and only then when I see some lessening in the bruising area. I'm sorry."

"Don't be," said Olga. "That's fine."

5

Lefortovo is the embodiment of terror—*The* Terror—that dominated Russia and its once Soviet Union for most of the twentieth century, initiated there before 1917 but quickly afterwards becoming the experimental laboratory in which was perfected every art and device of bone-crushing, mentally molding State oppression of State opposition.

The *Okhrana*, the intelligence service that so fatally failed to protect the ineffectual Czar Nicholas II from impending revolution, created it as the prison in which dissent and its advocates were literally snuffed out, like flickering candles. Within its uncleaned, blood-splattered walls the goatee-bearded Feliks Dzerzhinsky, who founded modern Russian intelligence by creating the succeeding *Vecheka*, installed his torturers and firing squads to maintain Lenin's rule. He didn't bother with wall cleaning. Neither did the terror-fuelled intelligence agencies of Stalin—the GPU and the OGPU and the NKVD and NKGB-NKVD and the MVD-MGB and the KGB—that followed, although occasionally spaces were scoured for official plaques proclaiming their chairmen as Heroes of the Soviet Union, psychopaths like Yagoda and Yezhov and Lavrenti Beria, the most psychopathic of them all.

There is an irony that in this glowering, barred-windowed mausoleum for a million—tens of millions—ghosts, such uncertified maniacs could unintentionally have left a psychological legacy making unnecessary their truncheons and electrodes and scalpels and syringes.

Fear is sufficient: fear of those truncheons and electrodes and scalpels and syringes and of the age-blackened gouts on the walls of bare cells without a bed or a lavatory hole or a bucket.

Olga Ivanova Melnik had learned to use that psychology of fear as successfully as she adopted—and adapted—her different questioning techniques. There were no bars at the sun-filled windows of the room into which Vera Bendall was escorted. There wasn't a desk, either. Easy chairs were arranged around a low table dominated by a display of bright yellow daffodils that had been moved slightly to one side for the tea thermos and cups. A cherry topped the sugar icing of each of the six cupcakes. The tape recorder was very small, unobtrusive.

Olga dismissed the escorts with a jerk of her head and gestured the other woman to a chair directly opposite. Vera Bendall remained just inside the door, terrified eyes flickering around the room. She was a gaunt woman, her uncombed gray hair straggled around a pinched, lined face. There had been no make-up to start with and her eyes were red, from recent crying. Her shoulders briefly heaved, with the closeness of more tears, but she managed to hold back. Although thin she was heavy-breasted and her unsupported bosoms sagged.

"Come in. Sit down," beckoned Olga, soft-voiced. This was

someone of the old Soviet, crushed, susceptible, malleable: a show trial puppet. From the preliminary interrogation Olga knew the woman was sixty-one years old.

Vera obediently did as she was told, although hesitantly, scuffing in pressed cardboard shoes from which the laces had been removed. There was a button missing from the badly knitted cardigan and the crumpled black skirt was stained and shiny from wear. The blouse was stained, too.

"They didn't hurt you?"

Vera shook her head.

"That's good. Most of them here only know one way of behaving." On Olga's instructions the initial arrest interrogator, in a windowless basement cell, had been a towering, brutish-featured militia sergeant in uniform. Olga unscrewed the thermos cap and poured. "Do you have milk?"

"No . . . thank you, no. Black." Vera needed two hands to pick up the cup but it still rattled in the saucer, spilling. "I'm sorry . . . so sorry . . ." She made a noisy slurping sound in her urgent need to drink.

"Have some cake." There'd only been one square of bread that morning and a small pitcher of water for the fifteen hours she'd been in custody.

The woman used two hands again, nibbling mouse-like. Her fingertips were puffed and swollen, from constant nail biting.

"You're here in Moscow—Russia—because of what your husband did. You know that, don't you?"

"Yes."

"You're allowed the apartment for the same reason."

"I know."

"I want you to tell me all about it. You'll do that, won't you?"

"Yes . . . please . . . I mean of course." The voice was frail, like the woman herself. The Russian was heavily accented.

"Would English be better?" asked Olga, who was fluent in that as well as French and Spanish.

"No. I understand. Is he . . . how . . . ?"

"Hurt, falling from the platform."

The woman stopped eating. "What . . . ?"

"Why did he do it?" asked Olga, her tone abruptly sharp.

"I don't know . . . didn't know . . ."

"What about the gun?"

"No! Believe me. I never saw it. Didn't know."

"He lives with you?"

"Most of the time."

"You must know about the gun then?"

"He never had it at home . . . brought it home."

"So where did he get it . . . keep it?"

"I don't know."

"Does he have anywhere else to live?"

"He stayed away sometimes . . . quite a lot, I suppose . . . I never knew where . . ." She tried individually picking up the cake crumbs that had fallen on to her greasy skirt.

"Don't do that! Concentrate on what I am asking!" ordered Olga, sharply again, and the other woman stopped at once.

"Sorry . . . I am . . ."

"You must know where he stayed when he wasn't at home?"

"I didn't!"

"Didn't you ask him?"

"He told me it was none of my business. He was always telling me that."

"Does he have a wife? A girlfriend?"

Vera Bendall shook her head. "He's not comfortable with women."

"Why?"

"I don't know. Frightened . . . doesn't know how . . ."

"Does he like boys?"

"Not like that . . . not how you're saying . . ."

"What about friends?"

"I don't know."

Olga poured more tea and pushed the cakes towards the woman. "Vera, you promised to help me. Tell me everything. Would you rather talk to the man who questioned you first . . . ?"

"No. Please no," broke in the woman.

"Then you have to help me, Vera. Do you understand what he's done?"

"Yes." The voice was a whisper.

"He shot the president."

"I saw, on television. What will happen . . . ?"

"He'll have to be punished."

"Yes."

Olga pushed the cakes further towards the other woman. "Let's think about you."

"Me?"

"What's going to happen to you, Vera? You're not Russian. You live here by permission . . ."

The woman nodded, dumbly.

"You get a State pension because of what your husband did?"

The shoulders started to heave again.

"I can only help you if you help me. Prove to me you weren't involved."

"I'm not . . . wasn't . . ."

"So who are his friends?"

"He's never told me . . . no one ever came . . ."

"But he did *have* friends?"

"He went out."

"Where?"

"I don't know."

"You asked him?" accused Olga.

"He wouldn't tell me. Said none of it was my business. Just his." There was a pause. "Is he badly hurt?"

"Is he political?" demanded Olga.

Vera Bendall shook her head, refusing to answer.

"I could take your apartment away. And your pension. Have you expelled, sent back to England."

"He wasn't right!"

Olga needed to pause. "How—what—wasn't he right?"

The woman hesitated, uncertain. "He hates Russia. Everything."

"Was he political?" Olga repeated.

"He read a lot of books when he was younger . . . books about England."

"Did he go to meetings?"

"He went out. I told you . . ."

"And he stayed away?"

"Yes."

"Often?"

"Yes."

"That wasn't what you told me earlier?"

Her lips quivered. "I'm sorry . . . I'm confused."

They were deviating, Olga realized. "I don't understand what you mean by saying he wasn't right?"

"He was in the army, had to be, of course. Went to Afghanistan in the beginning but they wouldn't let him stay. He had to leave. Sometimes he gets very angry."

"You mean he's mad?" demanded Olga, intentionally brutal. It wasn't such a personally advantageous case if Bendall was mentally ill.

"He loses his temper very easily. Particularly when he drinks."

"Does he see a doctor? Take medication?"

"He told me he was seeing a doctor recently. Not a medical doctor."

"Who!"

"I don't remember a name. I don't think he told me."

"Does he drink a lot?"

"Yes."

"Every day? Every night?"

"I suppose so."

"Peter, your husband, worked for the KGB when he came to Moscow?"

"Yes."

"Doing what?"

"He lectured for some years, in a scientific institute. In the last few years he used to read reports . . . English scientific magazines. Give an opinion about them."

"From an office in those latter years? Or from your apartment?"

"Both. Mostly from an office near GUM but sometimes from the apartment."

"So KGB people came to the apartment sometimes?"

"Sometimes."

"Did George ever meet them?"

"He would have been there when they came."

"How did George get on with his father?"

"Not very well. They argued."

"What about?"

"Everything. George said it was Peter's fault that we were here."

"What about you and George? How do you get on?"

"Quite well, except for when he gets angry."

"What does he do when he gets angry?"

"I told you, he fights."

"You mean he's violent."

"Yes."

"Has he ever hit you?"

"No. I've thought he was going to, sometimes. But he hasn't."

"Why didn't your husband take Russian citizenship? He chose communism, after all."

"No," denied the faded woman, strength in her voice for the first time. "He didn't do what he did for political ideology. He was ashamed of what he'd done—helped do—developing the West's nuclear capability. He gave it away to make things even."

Olga supposed there was some rationale in the convoluted justification. "But he used a Russian name?"

"No. That was George. He said he didn't want to have the name Bendall. He chose Gugin."

"Did George ever fight with his father?"

Vera Bendall looked down into her lap. "Sometimes. In the end George was bigger, stronger, than Peter."

Olga Melnik had expected more—a lot more—and the irritation was a combination of frustration and disappointment. She couldn't believe—didn't want to believe—the Bendalls' story could be as banal as this. "I'm not satisfied, Vera. Not at all satisfied."

"Please," implored the woman. "I've answered everything I can. I just don't *know!*"

"His friends, Vera. You've got to remember who his friends were. He must have said something, sometime. Given you some idea where he went. That's what you've got to remember and tell me . . . And the name of the doctor?"

Vera Bendall looked down at her drooped breasts. "Can I have my underwear back . . . my laces and belt. It's uncomfortable . . ."

"You're not going home, Vera. You're going to stay here, until you help me properly. Stay downstairs, in the cell that doesn't have a window . . . where a lot of other people have stayed, before you . . ."

"No . . . please . . ." begged the woman.

"Think, Vera. You've got to think very hard. Remember what I want to know and then tell me."

Charlie assembled video footage from America's NBC and CBS, Britain's BBC, Canada's CBS and Moscow's NTV to compare with CNN's unique and unparalled film. And worked with total concentration to parallel it, second for second, frame by frame. He did so muffled in earphones, stopwatch in hand, well aware even then he was not technically qualified to reach any conclusion. Which, being Charlie, he did. He was right: one hundred and one percent, fuck the doubters, diamond-hard right. The copies—the copies upon copies which Anne Abbott had protested to be illegal—were already in the diplomatic bag on their way to London for the scientifically provable tests Charlie specified but he was already personally sure he didn't need their confirmation.

What he wasn't so personally sure about was where in the name of Christ and His dog his conviction complicated an investigation already more than complicated enough.

As totally absorbed and externally soundproofed as he was, Charlie was initially, briefly, unaware of Anne Abbott easing herself beside him, physically starting at her touch on his arm.

"Shit, you frightened me!" admitted Charlie, who didn't like admitting fear or being startled. He depressed the remote control to stop the transmission as he took off the earphones.

"I've been looking for you!"

"What is it?"

Anne frowned at the obvious irritation. "I was hoping for an update."

"What's yours?" There hadn't been any contact messages from Donald Morrison or the head of chancellery when he'd got back from the American embassy.

"I'm to arrange legal representation—be part of whatever is set up—when we're allowed consular access."

"Has it been asked for?"

"You didn't know?"

"No."

"Brooking's already made the application. Maybe he had the same trouble finding you as I did."

"Maybe," dismissed Charlie.

"You got anything I should know about?"

Friend or foe? wondered Charlie, wearied that he had to pose the question. She'd have to be the first to know, if he were technically proved correct. He explained what he wanted her to listen for in advance of handing over the sound-enhancing earphones and gave her his clipboard and stopwatch, for her to make her own time comparisons.

Anne Abbott stopped after only twenty five minutes—only a third of the time Charlie had taken—and looked to him in astonishment. "You could be right!"

"So?"

"So I don't know what to say."

Olga Melnik snapped off the tape recording of her insufficient encounter with Vera Bendall and for several minutes the room was silent apart from the rewind whirr.

General Leonid Zenin said, "No one can be that unknowing. She's lying."

"She's of a type," balanced Olga. "A permanent victim."

"You believe her!"

"Not yet." On the recording her interview had sounded worse—unproductive, unprofessional—than she'd personally admitted it to be at the time.

"What have you done?"

"Asked the military for his army records, particularly medical. And the official reason—the papers—for his discharge. There's a team at NTV. He must have friends—acquaintances—there." Olga paused, regarding the tightly-bearded, hard-bodied man with whom she decided it might be pleasurable to ascend bedroom stairs. "There was certainly KGB control, after the father defected."

"Of course there was," said Zenin, who had told Olga of the emergency committee meeting. "That's why it doesn't make sense for Spassky to say they can't find files. In his time Peter Bendall would have been important."

There was another silence, longer than the first. Olga said, "You're surely not . . . ?"

"It's a question I'm going to ask if records aren't found," anticipated Zenin. "Spassky is KGB. Aleksandr Mikhailevich Okulov, already predicted to follow Yudkin as president, is former KGB. And the Federal Security Service—which is responsible for presidential protection—is nothing more than a convenient cosmetic name change, like all the others since Dzerzhinsky."

Olga felt a stir of unease. "We could be personally destroyed, trying to prove that . . . by even making the accusation."

"I wouldn't be making an accusation," insisted Zenin. "I'd be asking for an investigation into missing dossiers."

"Even if we could prove it, it wouldn't be politically acceptable."

"It would prevent us, the militia, being accused of any negligence or culpability."

"I suppose it would," agreed Olga, although doubtfully.

"What are you going to do about the Bendall woman?"

"Keep her as terrified as she is. She could still have her uses."

"So could the Britons and the Americans who've got to be officially involved."

6

It was performed as a political necessity, like so much else. Both Walter Anandale and Irena Yudkin wore deep black and posed for the Washington White House's official stills photographer against identifiably different backgrounds described in the accompanying caption as adjoining the emergency wards of their respective spouses, which neither were. Both Russian and American surgeons refused to allow the most minimal disturbance so close, which the protection services of both countries also argued against. The setting was, in fact, in the same room a block away from either victim, with a fifteen-minute interval to switch the medical equipment backdrop to make it look different. There were other stills of the American president and the Russian First Lady in an adjoining lounge, with Anandale holding Irena's hand, each consoling the other. Irena had frequently to use the handkerchief she kept in her free hand and Anandale was drawn and gaunt faced and had earlier dismissed the suggestion of camera make-up. The photocall was posed. Their visible, genuine anxiety was not.

Aleksandr Okulov was included in some of the lounge pictures but carefully kept out of shot otherwise, as were loosely paired entourages of matchingly ranked, soft-voiced politicians, diplomats and functionaries exchanging promises for undertakings and undertakings for promises. Wendall North and Yuri Trishin were joint ringmasters, moving smoothly between the groups, each enacting recovery operations of their own.

There was an instinctive American dominance, personified by the physical presence of the elected Walter Anandale against the emergency-elevated Russian premier, although there was no deference from Okulov since his security-cleared, back-door arrival at the Pirogov Hospital an hour earlier. It was the American chief of staff who orchestrated the final five minutes of the photo-shoot to just Anandale and Okulov, seemingly engrossed in deep continuity discussions. It was also North who directed the White House photographer and backed the protective services against admitting television. Only two organizations—CNN for America, NTV for Russia—were allowed within the precincts of the hospital to record Anandale briefly leaving the building for the first time since the shooting. He did so with a comforting hand on Irena Yudkin's elbow—Aleksandr Okulov followed slightly behind—and kissed her lightly on the cheek before personally handing her into her car.

Only Wendall North rode with Anandale in the lead vehicle of the American convoy to Novinskij Bul'var, sitting on the jump seat to face the president. The glass divide was fully raised between them and the driver and Secret Serviceman in the front. The rear section in which they sat was soundproofed and voice-cleaned.

"Spell it out for me," demanded Anandale.

"Additional communications were brought in as a matter of course, for the visit," reminded North. "Because of what's happened NSA is repositioning a geostationary satellite. We've got the Secretary of State and his people already here with us and a full secretariat. You've got the ambassador's office and a three-roomed suite in the embassy compound, already checked and cleared by the Secret Service. The embassy's a temporary but fully operational and functioning White House for as long as we need it to be."

"Donnington's lessening the sedation. If I can speak to Ruth I might sleep over at the hospital again."

"The ambulance plane's ready at Sheremet'yevo and we flew a fuel tanker in with it, for an unbroken flight back to Washington."

Anandale nodded approval. "What's the immediate schedule?"

"A meeting in an hour, to include the ambassador. That gives us time to set up a voice and visual satellite link with Washington, for a full cabinet session. I've called everyone in to Pennsylvania Avenue. And the CIA and FBI Directors."

"The Russians are talking total cooperation and exchange?"

"Absolutely."

Anandale looked briefly through the limousine window. They were using the cleared, intersection-controlled central lane again, with outrider escorts, moving so fast the buildings were blurred. Coming back inside the car he said, "Is it too early for any poll readings?"

North hesitated. "You're riding a sympathy wave. You're up fifteen points and rising."

"Anything about the other business."

North was glad he'd spent most of the early hours on the security-swept telephone link to the local party caucus in Austin as well as to Washington, bringing himself as up to date as possible on the independent enquiry by the hostile Texas senate into undeclared cash donations for Anandale's first term election from four separate corporations granted oil drilling and development contracts while

Anandale was state governor. "There's no irregularities showing in the audited accounts that were subpoenad."

Anandale smiled, fleetingly. "Much national coverage?"

"Paragraphs here and there, tagged on to the shooting here." The Moscow visit had been coordinated to overwhelm the Texas enquiry.

"What's the word?"

"That we're not to worry," said North, who'd been with Anandale from his days as Texas governor and worked as his campaign manager for that initial term success.

"That's good to hear," said Anandale. He looked out of the window again as the car swept over the Krymskij Bridge to get on to Zubovskij Bul'var for the final approach to the American embassy. "Okulov was KGB, right?"

"Right."

"You think there could be any link?"

"I've asked around already. The ambassador doesn't think so."

"They got the death penalty in Russia?"

"Yes, sir," said North, glad he'd anticipated that question along with all the rest.

"Good," said the other man. "I want the bastard who did this to fry."

North decided against pointing out that in Russia the death penalty was exacted by firing squad.

One of the larger reception rooms at the U.S. embassy was assigned for the gathering mainly because the satellite screen was large enough to encompass the seated, waiting Washington Cabinet members. It dominated virtually one entire wall, and most of a connecting corner overflowed with cameras and relay equipment to ensure the exchanges were simultaneous. Wendall North resolved the Washington hesitancy at the president's preoccupied, head-down filmed entry into the Moscow meeting by standing. Everyone followed, in both cities. Anandale waved them down, without speaking, and before sitting himself discarded his jacket and loosened his tie with another gesture for anyone to do the same if they wanted.

From Washington, Vice President Robert Clarke said, "I want to extend the sympathy of everyone here for what's happened, Mr. President. And wish the First Lady a very quick and full recovery."

There was a verbal scramble to be placed on record from others in the room, which Anandale curtly stopped with a series of "Thank you, thank you," after Secretary of Defense Wilfred Pinkton repeated practically word for word what the Treasury secretary had managed to say seconds ahead of him.

"I met with Acting President Aleksandr Okulov earlier today," announced Anandale. "He wants to continue the treaty negotiations. Suggested that at least we could agree a Protocol of Intent."

North said, "There needs to be a statement, to go with today's pictures. Trishin's proposing a joint press conference, you and Okulov together."

"Which establishes my supporting Okulov as the successor," said Anandale.

"He is, under their constitution," said the secretary of state. James Scamell was another old time ally from Anandale's governorship.

"Emergency," qualified Anandale. "Temporarily, until proper elections if Yudkin doesn't make it. If Okulov runs and loses against the communists, I'm shown to have endorsed the wrong guy."

"If he hadn't been shot and Yudkin had still lost to the communists you'd have been doing that coming here," Scamell pointed out. "We've got to say *something* about the treaty."

Anandale looked directly at the camera. "What's Defense's feeling on this?"

"The Joint Chiefs are nervous about a communist succession," said Pinkton. "We sure Okulov's got the following to take over?"

"Maybe we should have the local opinion on that?" avoided Scamell, turning to the ambassador.

Cornell Burton was a career diplomat who'd believed himself on the fast upward track the presidential visit could only further speed up but now he wasn't so sure. What he *was* sure about was that he couldn't afford one misstep. "Okulov's a closed-doors manipulator. Respected for it in the Duma but he's alienated some of the smaller parties he'd need for a coalition if the communists do anywhere near as well as is being predicted."

"So how well *will* they do?" demanded Anandale.

"Yudkin would have carried a peace vote, with a successful treaty. I'm not so convinced that Okukov will."

"What's the KGB story?"

The attention switched to John Kayley. The FBI man said, "Yudkin forced the reforms through and Okulov showed him how to do it. Word is among the old guard that Okulov's regarded as a traitor, turning against them."

"Which could be a very clever double-bluff," suggested Burt Jordan.

"Explain that," demanded Anandale.

"Okulov was the heir-in-waiting. What if he got too impatient to wait any longer?"

"Keep on top of that," ordered Anandale. "Okulov's KGB connections worry me."

"Aren't we leaving something hugely important out of the equation?" suggested North. "The guy who did it. And *why* he did it? If he turns out to be a protesting communist we've got a whole new picture to color in."

"Is he?"

Anandale put the question to those around him but the answer came too eagerly from Washington, from an FBI Director determined the American investigation should be Bureau-led. Paul Smith, a burly former circuit judge, said, "I've got twenty more agents on their way to Moscow, arriving later tonight. They're bringing with them all our files—Agency and Bureau—on Peter Bendall, the father. He was British counter-intelligence's disaster. I understand from John, who's with you there Mr. President, that their guy's let us have all he says they've got. The son's still unconscious, maybe even in a coma. The mother's in custody. We've been promised details of her interrogation but we've asked for our own access. And for the witnesses list. They were all rounded up by Russian security directly after the attack. We've asked for the rifle, for our own forensic examination here at Pennsylvania Avenue and . . ."

"We're not making our own, independent investigation!" cut off Anandale.

Smith unconsciously bit his lip, at once regretting not letting Kayley take the original question. "That's what I've got men on their way to do, under John's command. I think, though, it would be useful for me to come over personally."

Speaking with ominous quietness, Anandale said, "I want the attempted murder of the American president's wife investigated by Americans. Until I'm satisfied that's happening—satisfied that Aleskandr Okulov is keeping every cooperation promise he's made to me today—any treaty discussions are on the back burner, with the heat down low . . ."

North and the secretary of state exchanged brief, frowning looks. Scamell urged again, "There has to be a statement of some sort, Mr. President."

Anandale remained silent for several moments. "Here it is. We're in consultations with the emergency Russian leadership . . . need to consider the implications of the attack . . . our pledge to continued cooperation and detente unaffected . . . that sort of stuff. It'll fit the hospital pictures. We don't agree any joint media event with Okulov until we get all we want." He went to the secretary of state and the ambassador. "I want you to liaise with Wendall. *Really* find out the communist strength. It might play better back home to go hawkish and keep the defense system." He looked around the table. "Any thoughts?"

"Yudkin—or his successor—need the treaty to survive. That's why we're here," reminded Scamell. "We leave them with nothing, we're edging the door open to the opposition."

"We don't leave them with nothing," said Anandale. "You find the words, Jamie. The only thing they don't get is the final signature. We've surely blown enough smoke about how difficult it all is to make that totally believable!"

"I guess so," accepted Scamell.

Anandale went to Wendall North. "Get on to Yudkin's chief of staff." He stopped, snapping his fingers.

"Yuri Trishin."

"Trishin," picked up the prompted president. "I don't want him—or anyone he's got to tell—left in any doubt who's going to run this investigation as far as my wife is concerned. You clear on that?"

"Quite clear," said North.

"Would you like me to come over personally, Mr. President?" hopefully asked the FBI Director over the satellite link.

"No!" rejected Anandale, at once. "We've got enough chiefs here already. What we need is Indians."

John Kayley, with his early settler family legend of part-Cherokee ancestry, didn't like the smoke signals he thought he was reading.

The emergency Downing Street meeting was scheduled for the entire day but Sir Rupert Dean, the director-general, returned to the Millbank building with political adviser Patrick Pacey by early afternoon. The rest of the control group were already assembled.

"It's accepted to be an inherited problem but the decision is that it's *our* problem," announced Dean. Already his spectacles were working through his fingers like worry beads, a stress indicator the others had come to recognize. It was unfortunate that the man's receding hair rose from his head like a tidal wave, adding to the impression of startled nervousness.

"Because no one else wanted to come within a million miles of it," said Pacey.

"Hardly surprising," accepted Jeremy Simpson, the service's legal advisor. "I've heard from the Attorney General. We're arranging legal representation."

"We were told," said Pacey.

"Muffin was on, while you were at Downing Street. He thinks there's something odd about the shooting. But who better to imagine something odd than the man himself?" said Jocelyn Hamilton. The bull-chested, thinning-haired deputy director-general was more unsettled than Dean at the Russian crisis, although concealing it well. He'd supported the earlier effort to oust Charlie from Moscow and knew he had been lucky to escape with a formal censure when it had gone wrong.

Dean frowned at the obvious personal dislike. "What?"

"He's shipping over a selection of television footage. Wants an audio and timed comparison of the shots."

"Jesus!" said Pacey, in quick understanding. "His theory? Or Russian?"

"His, as far as I understand." Hamilton hesitated. "He's asked the ambassador to include him on any official access to Bendall. I told him he should have waited for official guidance from here. I'm assuming, of course, we're sending a team from here."

Dean let silence be the rebuke. Only when there were discomfited shifts around the table did the director-general say, "Why would you assume that?"

The deputy colored. "The magnitude of it. Surely too much for one man?"

"Swamping Moscow with people would be a panicked, knee-jerk reaction," rejected Dean. "Muffin alerted us to George Bendall hours before any official communication. He's obviously well established."

"And it *is* an inherited problem," repeated Pacey. "Bendall's been in Moscow for almost thirty years. Downing Street's thinking is that he's British by little more than a fluke. He's not ours anymore: never was. We'll do all we're asked but let Moscow and Washington take the lead."

"What about the technical checks Muffin wants?" persisted Hamilton.

"It could be a complication," admitted the director-general.

"There's invariably a complication with Charlie Muffin," warned the deputy.

Max Donnington was waiting for Anandale in the same lounge at the Pirogov Hospital that had earlier been used for the photo-call. The large, silver-haired naval surgeon still wore a sterilized ward coat and ankle-high theater boots.

Anandale said at once, "What's the change?"

"No worse. You can talk to her in a moment."

"To tell her what?"

"You'll understand better if you see the plates. I've set up a room along the corridor."

Anandale followed the surgeon further into the building. Cables from an unseen, inaudible generator were taped along the newly shined corridor lined every five meters by Secret Servicemen who came to attention as the president passed. The room into which

Donnington led the president was bright from newly installed neon strips and against one wall glowed an already lighted X-ray viewing screen. There was a heavy smell of disinfectant.

Donnington slotted the first plate into its clip and traced his finger around a large, completely black area at the end of the shoulder. "That's where the bullet hit Ruth. It's called the brachial plexus. Into it run the nerves from the neck, routed from between the fourth cervical and first thoracic. In layman's terms, think of it as a junction box. From the brachial plexus emerge three nerves specific to the arm, the radial, median and ulnar . . ." He changed plates, showing the arm. "The bullet that struck your wife destroyed those nerves at the branchial plexus. . . ."

"Does it have to be amputated?" demanded Anandale, hollow voiced.

"No," said the surgeon, immediately, putting the third plate into place. "I've had to wait this long to ensure that there is no interruption to the blood flow. There isn't. It missed the arteries. The First Lady will have a permanently numb and powerless arm but there is no risk of gangrene. The arm can stay."

"No use in it whatsoever?"

"None," said the surgeon, bluntly.

"Nerves can be reconnected. You read about it all the time," blurted Anandale.

"The damage here is too great," rejected Donnington.

"You could be wrong . . . there could be a medical—surgical— advance," insisted Anandale.

"Of course you need a second opinion . . . and a third and a fourth, every expert you can consult," acknowledged Donnington, unoffended. "I'm giving you my initial but at the same time considered, professional prognosis."

"*Initial!*" seized the president.

"I don't expect to change it. Believe me, Mr. President, I'd like to be proven wrong."

"When can she be moved back to America, to see other people?" asked Anandale.

"I don't want to risk disturbing anything for at least two days.

Maybe longer. Waiting isn't going to affect the arm in any way. It's the shoulder I want stabilized before we start thinking of getting on and off airplanes."

The president stared sightlessly at the X-ray for several moments. "What am I going to tell her?"

"Do you want me to?" offered Donnington.

"No," refused Anandale, quickly. "I'll do it."

There was a frame over Ruth Anandale's body, keeping off even the pressure of the bed coverings from her neck to her waist. Her face was sallow and shiny from how it had been swabbed and her thick, black hair was sweat-matted against the pillow because this early Donnington had refused even to allow the lightest of brushing to affect her neck. She lay with her eyes closed, mouth slightly open, her face occasionally twitching. Her uninjured arm was outside the frame, on top of the bed. A needle was inserted into a vein on the back of her hand through which pain killers could be administered. A catheter tube snaked from beneath the bedclothes and there were other leads connected to heart, respiratory and blood pressure monitoring machines across the screens of which tiny mountains peaked with reassuring regularity. The hair of the two uniformed attendant nurses was beneath sterilized caps. Both Anandale and the surgeon wore caps, too, and Donnington had changed his gown at the same time as the president had donned his. At their entry the two nurses withdrew close to the door but didn't leave.

One of the nurses said, "The First Lady's conscious," and at the sound Ruth Anandale opened her eyes.

It took several moments for her to focus and when she did there was a brief smile of recognition. She said, "I can't feel much. There's some sensation in my shoulder but nothing else. I don't remember . . ."

"There was a shooting," reminded Anandale. "You're under a lot of medication."

"Am I badly hurt?"

"We're going to get you home as soon as we can. Get you better there."

"I can't feel my right arm at all."

"It'll be all right."

"When can I go home?"

"Soon."

"I haven't lost my arm, have I? I'm going to be all right!" Her voice rose, cracking.

"You're going to be fine. We're going to find all the specialists and get everything fixed, I promise."

"Why . . . who . . . ?"

"We've got the man. It's all under investigation."

"Was anyone else hurt?"

"The Russian president. Some guards."

"They going to be all right?"

"We don't know, not yet."

The woman's eyes flickered and drooped and Anandale felt Donnington's hand upon his arm. As they scuffed out of the room Anandale said, "I didn't lie. I will find the surgeon to fix her arm."

"Yes, Mr. President," said Donnington.

Charlie didn't hurry responding to the internal messages that had finally arrived when he got back from the viewing theater. He first read what had come in from London and checked his e-mail and even then detoured to Donald Morrison's office, just for the hell of it.

"I know it's your assignment," greeted the MI6 man.

As Morrison grew older and wiser he wouldn't be so eager, Charlie thought. "It's not quite that definite." The assignment decision had been one of the waiting e-mail messages from Sir Rupert Dean.

"I'm to assist in any way necessary." The younger man offered a package. "Everything Vauxhall Cross has got."

Charlie took it. "Thanks, for getting it so quickly."

"You won't ask, will you?" anticipated Morrison, sadly.

"I don't know," said Charlie, honestly. "No one can guess which way this will go. It's better to limit any possible diplomatic damage by keeping it to one service."

"I expected them to send in a team."

"Limitation, like I said."

"I'd like to do something, if I can."

"I'll remember," promised Charlie, who was still digesting the London edict. It put him as much in the firing line as he would have been on the White House podium with the two presidents. He'd have to be bloody careful—more careful perhaps than he'd ever been—that he didn't become the fifth casualty.

Charlie hadn't bothered to tell Richard Brooking he was on his way. When he arrived the head of chancellery seemed lost in thought behind a desk totally clear of any activity—actually appearing polished—with blotter, pen set and telephones regimented precisely in place.

"No one knew where you were," accused the diplomat, abruptly aware of Charlie's presence.

"Making enquiries," said Charlie, unhelpfully. He had no intention of telling the man what he suspected and Anne Abbott had agreed it would be best to wait until the confirmation of the technical analysis.

"We've had Foreign Office instructions from London," announced Brooking. "We're formally requesting access . . ." The man paused, coming to unpleasantness. ". . . And you're to be included."

"I've been told that independently, from my people," said Charlie.

Brooking made obvious his head to toe examination of Charlie. "You'll have inferred diplomatic status. Do you have another suit? And some half decent shoes?"

Charlie grimaced. "I've got one for weddings and funerals."

"There's a chance for you to wear it," scored the other man. "We've just been officially informed that the American Secret Serviceman has died."

"So now it's murder," said Charlie, no longer glib.

"There was another message," continued Brooking. "A formal offer of investigating cooperation from the Russians. There's the name of the officer you're to liaise with. A woman . . ."

Charlie's hand was quite steady as he reached forward for the note that Brooking was proffering but his stomach dipped. Then he looked down and saw the name of Colonel Olga Ivanova Melnik.

7

It didn't begin confrontationally. Charlie actually set out to achieve the opposite—to convince her it was ridiculous for them not to discuss the case—by announcing he had brought Peter Bendall's records back to Lesnaya for her to read and was encouraged when Natalia said she had Vera Bendall's initial interview for him. She already knew about the meeting Charlie had the following day with Olga Melnik and said the FBI Rezident was also scheduled to meet the senior investigating colonel.

They'd established a routine of undivided, shared time with Sasha whenever it was possible, and the two dossiers remained unread on a lounge table for the hour they spent taking her slowly through an early reader book and discussing what Sasha referred to as going to grown up school. It wasn't until Natalia went to bathe and settle their daughter that Charlie got to the Vera Bendall interview. He read it twice before setting it aside, slouched with the second Islay malt resting on his chest, his mind more upon Natalia than upon what he'd just read.

He couldn't make any judgment on that evening's fifteen-minute conversation so far—although she had given him a head start identifying Peter Bendall the previous night—but he was encouraged by Natalia's apparently changed attitude. And not just professionally. That, for once, was a secondary consideration. The first need was for their personal erosion to stop. There'd been no thought of sex—thoughts of sex didn't seem to occur too often to either of them anymore—but he knew Natalia hadn't been asleep when he'd got into bed the previous night. Not something to challenge her with; he had to be careful not to challenge her about anything while he remained uncertain.

Charlie lifted his glass in invitation when Natalia emerged from

Sasha's bedroom. Natalia shook her head, taking the chair on the far side of the low lounge table. For several moments she stared down at Peter Bendall's waiting dossier and Charlie wondered if the seeming reluctance to pick it up was the final hesitation at committing herself. Wrong to say anything—to speak at all—he told himself. It was obviously much thicker than the interview and took Natalia longer to read. While she did, he made himself a third drink. That was almost gone, too, by the time she put the manila folder back on the separating table.

"Nothing about the son, apart from his existence," she said.

"The mother's disappointing, too, don't you think?" The question went beyond wanting to keep the conversation going. Natalia was amazingly intuitive, one of the best debriefers he'd ever encountered and he wanted her professional opinion.

She nodded. "I've also listened to the actual recording. I don't get the impression she was lying, holding anything back. But then again I've known some very clever liars." Natalia got up and poured herself a glass of the Volnay Charlie had opened for dinner.

"I offered you a drink," said Charlie.

"Half an hour ago. I didn't want one then. Now I do." Why had she snapped like that! "And no, I wasn't referring to you as a liar, when we first met."

Back off, thought Charlie. "So most likely George Bendall's a mentally unstable loner that no one knows anything about." In no way did he think himself a hypocrite. At the moment all he had was a suspicion about the sound of the gunshots. If it was confirmed, he'd tell her.

"Not the first high profile murderer to be just that, a total nonentity seeking his fifteen seconds or minutes of fame."

"But always the worst to try to investigate."

Natalia shrugged but said nothing. Why did it have to be so difficult for her to reach a compromise when their jobs overlapped! Because of the past: always the past which she could never completely forget no matter how hard she tried or how much she loved him. Charlie was making a very obvious effort. Couldn't she—shouldn't she—try harder?

Charlie didn't want to lose the flow. "We're talking?"

"Total cooperation is the instruction. You'd have got the transcript from Olga Ivanova tomorrow."

"Would you have shown it to me, if it hadn't been officially ordered?"

"Hardly the disclosure of the century, is it?" This wasn't helping.

"It surely makes our situation easier?"

Natalia shrugged again. "I don't know. Basically it doesn't change anything, does it?"

The confrontation had to come, sooner or later. It might as well be now. "Things aren't going to change, Natalia. This is it, the best it's going to get. I don't know anything more I can do to make it better for us . . . between us. What I do know is that I don't want everything to collapse and I think it is collapsing . . ."

"Meaning the concessions have to come from me!" Their relationship *was* crumbling. And it probably was more her fault than Charlie's.

"I'm not asking you to make any concessions. I'm asking you to acknowledge the reality . . . and the difficulty . . . of our being together."

"I hardly need reminding of that."

"You under any pressure?"

"I could be."

"Don't close me out as you have been closing me out."

The same argument, Natalia recognized: the same persuasive logic. And it was logical: Charlie was a better street fighter than she could ever be. "I know you're right."

"Then trust me."

Natalia allowed the pause. "That's what I've got to do."

"I won't let you down. I did before but I won't again."

"It's not just the two of us anymore. There's so much else that could go wrong. Sasha says they've been talking at school, about what parents do. Two kids said their fathers were in the militia."

"What did she say?" Big problems could easily come from innocuous innocence.

"She didn't know. That's how the conversation came up. She asked me."

"What did you tell her?"

"That we both worked in big offices, which will do for now. What are we going to tell her when she gets older?"

Charlie wished he had an easy answer: *any* answer that might come anywhere close to satisfying Natalia. It was ineffective and the last thing Charlie had ever been was ineffective. "We've got more important personal questions to answer."

"I know."

"It's not the jobs. It's the effect of them, perhaps. But not the jobs themselves . . ." He sniggered, in sudden realization. "We've come the full circle, haven't we? I screwed everything up the first time, by not being totally able to trust you—which was my terrible mistake—and now you can't trust me . . ."

"So now it's my mistake!" she pounced at once, regretting the words as they were uttered.

"No, darling," insisted Charlie, patiently. "You're justified. I wasn't."

Charlie filled the silence by refilling her glass, which she surrendered without protest. He thought about a fourth whisky but decided to change to wine himself. As he sat down again Natalia said, "You think there's still a chance we can make it work?"

"Yes," he said at once. When she didn't respond, he said, "What do you think?"

"I'm not sure."

"What do you *want*?"

"I want it very much. But I'm frightened there's too much in the way."

"Let's move it *out* of the way!" urged Charlie.

"Yes," she accepted, uncertainly.

"What's your pressure?"

"I've got to coordinate all the Russian agencies. Make everything work."

"The rock and the hard place," Charlie recognized. "Their successes are theirs, their failures are yours."

"Something like that." Should she tell him the old KGB files were missing?

"You're going to need my help, need someone to bounce theories off. I shouldn't have to say it but I guess I do. I won't take any advantage, put you—us—at risk in any way." For once in Charlie's life—probably the first time in Charlie's life—it wasn't a promise embroidered in easily expandable elastic.

"The FSB can't find Peter Bendall's records," blurted Natalia.

Charlie shook his head in professional refusal. "It would have been an ongoing, current file: assessments, surveillance, psychological profile not just of him but of his wife and son. It's the starting point for any investigation into George Bendall."

Why did she waste so much time—endanger so much—maintaining her obstructive integrity pretensions, Natalia asked herself, acknowledging the expertise. "What's your reading?"

"Immediate sanitizing, because of what's in them?" suggested Charlie. "Maybe about George particularly. It's clumsy but it's predictable panic. There's the excuse that the KGB isn't any longer the KGB, which it was when Bendall defected. Things do get misplaced in reorganization." It wouldn't help by reminding her that she'd destroyed his KGB dossier and sanitized her own of any original connection with him.

"Nothing more sinister?"

Charlie hesitated. She was being open with him at last and his offering something in exchange would show he was keeping his side of an unspoken bargain. "You had any technical discussion with anyone?"

Natalia regarded him intently. "About what?"

"I've got the soundtrack from four different television films covering the presidential arrival, as well as that of NTV," disclosed Charlie. "CNN were mute, remember. They're being scientifically tested now in London but I've carried out my own rough timing. According to my count five shots were fired in a time gap of nine point two seconds. That's very sharp sharp-shooting."

"We're getting George Bendall's army records."

"Are you?" demanded Charlie, pointedly.

"We've *asked* for George Bendall's—or Georgi Gugin's—army records," qualified Natalia.

"I'm particularly interested in what they'll say about his marksmanship."

"Or lack of it," accepted Natalia. "I was frightened enough to begin with. Now you've really scared me. I preferred the mentally unstable loner."

"Where's the mentally unstable loner get a sniper's rifle, which it very clearly was from the television pictures?" There was something else to check, he realized. It didn't fit this conversation. "Mosow—Russia—is awash with weaponry. You can buy a gun and ammunition for it in street underpasses. We can't even look after our nuclear arsenals!"

"Basic Kalashnikovs and Makarovs. Not something specialized like this."

"Do you intend saying anything tomorrow to Olga Melnik?"

Charlie shook his head. "Not without proof."

"Thanks for telling me."

"Isn't that the new deal?"

"Yes."

That night they did make love but for each of them it was more a duty than spontaneous passion and it wasn't good.

Charlie said, "We can get that back, too."

"I hope so," said Natalia.

Both appraised the other in the opening seconds.

Charlie hadn't expected Senior Investigating Colonel Olga Ivanova Melnik to be somewhere in her mid-thirties, which had to indicate a special ability he wouldn't have guessed at from the Vera Bendall transcript he'd read the previous night. He thought the cleavage interesting but a little too obvious: the unsecured button on her shirt didn't fit the pressed neatness of the perfectly tailored grey checked suit or the pristine orderliness of the high windowed, everything-in-its-proper-place office. And in any case the spider's web tightrope of his current high wire act with Natalia didn't allow any extramarital temptations. The cleared desk reminded him of that of Richard Brooking, who'd delivered the standard lecture on diplomatic conformity before he'd left the embassy that morning. The head of chancellery had been very pissed off at his ignoring the diplomatic dress code but Charlie didn't regard today's encounter as a fancy dress party. With luck it might be his first opportunity to start working properly.

Olga was disoriented, although she didn't allow any outward sign. Moscow was a prestige posting and Charles Edward Muffin had been knowingly accepted in Moscow as an FBI equivalent, a specifically chosen British contribution—like that of America—against Russia's virtually uncontrollable organized crime. From his physical appearance she wouldn't have believed the flop-haired, overweight man sitting opposite contributing anything more than a few kopeks to a charity rummage sale for down-and-outs for a suit to replace the sagged and pocket-bulged jacket and trousers and raft-like suede shoes that he was wearing now.

"Would you prefer English?" she offered, speaking it with little accent in a deep, oiled voice.

"Thanks but it's not necessary," Charlie replied, in Russian.

"I hope we can work well together?"

"I hope so too," said Charlie. Her territory, her speed. Until he chose otherwise.

She pushed across the uncluttered desk what was supposed to be his first copy of the Vera Bendall interview. "It's very preliminary." The discomfort at having this shambling man judge her was worse than it had been with Leonid Zenin.

He matched her offering with the heavier MI5 dossier. "All we have on Peter Bendall. Nothing on the son." He was not supposed to know Vera Bendall was in Lefortovo, he reminded himself. "My embassy was told today the official application for consular access has been granted." The information had been the only useful outcome of that morning's encounter with Brooking.

"The man was injured in the fall. It's not yet clear when he'll be well enough to be interviewed." There was obviously a diplomatic necessity for this charade but very little practical benefit, apart from hopefully recovering from the Vera Bendall debacle with an unsuspected transcript of this encounter. It was important to establish her supremacy on tape.

"The application extends to the family," persisted Charlie. "As far as we are aware Vera Bendall, like her son, hasn't applied for Russian citizenship." Charlie nodded to the Russian folder, already knowing the answer. "I presume her address is there?"

Olga looked steadily across her sterile desk. "She is in protective custody."

"Protected from whom?" asked Charlie.

"People who might take it upon themselves to exact revenge upon the mother of a man who shot their president."

"So she hasn't taken citizenship?" persisted Charlie.

It would be wrong to underestimate this shaman's monster, decided Olga, who had no religion but in whom was imbued the inherent Russian respect for witchcraft and Holy Men who could cast spells. "There is no trace of her having done so. Certainly not of it being granted."

Gently does it, thought Charlie. "I'm sure my embassy—my government—will appreciate that protection . . ."

"Thank you," intruded Olga, caught out by Charlie's inviting pause.

". . . Which of course in no way prevents our officially agreed access. I—and others from the embassy—can easily come to wherever she's being protectively held. Where is that, by the way?"

The criticizingly dismissive inference of her empty interview would be unavoidable on this transcript! "As I said, my initial interrogation is only very preliminary."

"Interrogation?" echoed Charlie. "You suspect she's in some way *involved*?"

Damn the man, thought Olga. He really did have a witchdoctor's split tongue. "It's too early yet to decide who might or might not be involved." She paused, reluctant to correct herself. "I meant my questioning has only just begun."

"We are cooperating fully, aren't we?" coaxed Charlie.

"Yes," agreed Olga, tightly, apprehensive of how Charlie Muffin could juggle such simple words but anticipating that he would.

"If we're sharing there's no order of priority?"

"It's become a murder enquiry," fought Olga. "Russian legislation must take precedence."

"I'm not an international lawyer," said Charlie. "It's something I'll leave to our legal attaché to handle through diplomatic channels. Under such international scrutiny we shouldn't go beyond our boundaries, should we?"

Olga wished the motherfucker wouldn't keep inviting her opinion, to turn against her. Why oppose him? There *was* enormous international scrutiny under which the claim that Vera Bendall required protective custody might become even more transparent than it was now. In Lefortovo Vera Bendall was very positively her prisoner, whose every encounter and movement she could control. And totally monitor. It was conceivable some indication of Vera Bendall's innocence or complicity might emerge if Britons were allowed access, access every minute and word of which could be taped and possibly even filmed. If there was something to be learned, she'd learn it, learn, too, from what the British offered whether their cooperation was genuine. And if the encounter was as unproductive as hers, there couldn't be any criticism—internally or externally—of what now lay on the desk between her and Charlie Muffin, like a taunt. Better apparently to concede—be persuaded, at least—to an unimportant audience of one than to a much wider and more influential theater. "Don't misunderstand me. I wasn't arguing priorities. As far as I'm concerned there's no reason whatsoever why you—and others from your embassy—shouldn't see the woman."

Charlie hadn't expected the turnaround so quickly, hadn't, in fact, expected it at all. "You haven't told me where she is."

He had a rat-trap, forget-nothing mind, acknowledged Olga. "Lefortovo."

How many had gone into "protective custody" in that bleak, icily-walled fortress never to emerge and certainly never for a moment to be protected? The first transcript was that of an already cowed, frightened woman. By now Vera Bendall would be terrified to the point of the insanity she was suggesting for her son. "That's conveniently central. Tomorrow would be good."

It gave her more than sufficient time. "Eleven?"

"Fine," smiled Charlie. "I could come here directly afterwards, to discuss anything that emerges."

"All right," agreed Olga, doubtfully, thrown off balance by the offer.

"None of the witnesses are in protective custody, are they?"

He was playing with her, his cat to her mouse! "No. Their statements are being translated."

"I'd prefer them in the original."

"Available tomorrow."

"Excellent! I can collect them after I've seen Vera Bendall."

"Yes." This was going to read even worse than it sounded. "What's the progress of the forensic examination?"

"Just that, in progress. Therefore incomplete." The satisfaction of the refusal was out of proportion to its effect: it was something she'd have to surrender eventually.

"Not available tomorrow?"

"I doubt it."

"We haven't talked about any positive lines of enquiry."

"It's too early to establish any."

"I suppose the most important thing we *haven't* talked about is the official record that would have been maintained upon Peter Bendall, throughout his time here. That would have included information upon the son, as he grew up."

Olga thought it was like being stripped naked in a Siberian winter. "That would be classified."

The already prepared excuse for their apparent loss? wondered Charlie. "You have officially asked for them, though?"

"Every investigatory procedure befitting the crime has been implemented," insisted Olga, regretting the formal pomposity the moment she began to speak but too angrily frustrated to find other words.

"That's encouraging to hear," said Charlie. "My embassy will feel that, too. On a personal level I'm sure we're going to work together extremely well."

I'm not, thought the woman.

As he was escorted from the building, Charlie decided that Olga Ivanova Melnik was not as good as she imagined herself to be. Perhaps that was why she found the need to have difficulty with blouse buttons. The hidden recording Charlie was sure would have been taken wouldn't do much for her, either.

Burt Jordan was already waiting at their reserved table when Donald Morrison entered the Arleccino, waving to attract the MI6 man's attention when he came in off Druzhinnikovskaya Ulitza.

"Sorry I'm late," apologized Morrison. "Couldn't get a taxi. Somehow it seemed easier when we were at the old embassy."

"But now you've got air con," smiled the CIA Rezident. He was a small, compact man made to look permanently doleful by the heavy moustache allowed to droop at either end. He gestured around the restaurant. "Italian OK for you?"

"Fine. I haven't been here before."

"The *saltimbocca alla Romana*'s the speciality." Jordan poured Valpolicella. "I figured it far better to get together like this, undisturbed. The embassy's a fucking mad house. How about yours?"

"Pretty calm, considering." It was unthinkable to tell the other man the virtually non-existent role to which he'd been relegated. He'd accepted the American's invitation in the hope of learning something with which to impress Charlie Muffin and get involved.

"It's good everyone's pulling with the same stroke."

"I guess it is."

"I get anything, it's yours."

"Likewise."

When the waiter arrived they both ordered the *saltimbocca*. Jordan held up the still half full bottle and ordered another.

Jordan said, "So what have you got?"

Morrison shrugged. "Very little. You've already got the counterintelligence stuff from Charlie. It was all internal—even the jail escape—so Bendall was their headache, not ours. When the rumors began that he wanted to come home the instructions to our man here then was to find him and help him back. If he'd had anything worthwhile from working with the KGB here we could have negotiated a little remission in the sentence he would still have had to serve. We couldn't get a lead. We even had some stories planted in newspapers here when the press got freer after 1991, hinting as much as we could. He never made contact."

"The KGB wouldn't have risked him with anything sensitive. They never treated defectors—even foreign nationals who'd worked for them—well or with any respect."

"Stranger things have happened," clichéd Morrison. "What about you?"

Jordan shook his head. "The Bureau made it a big operation. The stuff he leaked was from America, mostly Los Alamos. But as far as they discovered Bendall wasn't part of any cell. He was a solitary spy, a 'walk in' to the Soviet embassy in London, passing on stuff he received from us."

"What about when he got here?"

"Nothing," said Jordan. "There'd been the Bureau investigation by then, showing he'd worked alone. We didn't try to find him."

"You know," said Morrison. "Despite all the panic and chaos, when it comes down to it there's not a lot we're going to be able to do."

"We've still got to make the motions, though. That's why I thought we should meet like this. My word, about sharing anything I get."

"Mine too," said Morrison, enthusiastically. "Well met."

"It's murder now, Vera. The death penalty."

"Yes."

The acceptance was flat, totally without emotion. Olga Melnik had hoped for more, a collapse even. They were in the same room with the same flowers and there was tea again, with cake. The record light flickered on the unobtrusive tape machine.

"Drink your tea."

The woman did as she was told, gnawing at a cake between noisy sips. "Can I have my underwear back? And my shoes? It's really not comfortable without them."

"It's regulations," refused Olga. "What have you remembered?"

"Tuesdays and Thursdays."

"What about Tuesdays and Thursdays?"

"Those were the nights he seemed to stay out most often. Occasionally others, but mostly Tuesdays and Thursdays."

Better, thought Olga, hopefully. "You must have asked him about those nights?"

"I told you, he got angry."

"Particularly angry when you asked him about those nights?"

"I think so."

"He never told you, not once? Not even a word? Or a name?"

"No."

"What about the name of the doctor?"

"I can't remember."

"What did you talk about, when he was home?"

"We didn't, much. We watched television. Sometimes the programs he'd worked on. He made models."

"Models of what?"

"Cars. Boats. Planes. Things that moved. He liked things that moved."

"How did he make them? From wood or what?"

"Wood, sometimes, wood that he carved. And kits. The sort that children have."

"I don't remember the people who searched your apartment finding any models. It wasn't in their report."

"He broke them, as soon as he finished them. Said they were useless to him."

"What other hobbies did he have?"

"None."

"What about guns?" She had to improve on the original questioning.

"No . . . I told you . . ."

"Did he ever go shooting?"

"He doesn't have a gun."

"He could have borrowed one."

"I don't know."

"You are remembering things, aren't you?"

"I'm trying."

"Some other people are coming to see you."

"What other people!" pleaded Vera, immediately alarmed.

"From the British embassy. They want to help, like I want to help. That's why you're here, safe from people who might want to hurt you for what you son has done." It was imperative to get that on record, after the debacle with Charlie Muffin. She hadn't just underestimated the man, she'd even more badly miscalculated the collaboration that would be imposed upon her.

"Will you be here, with them?"

"No."

The woman looked down at her sagging bosoms. "Can I have my

underwear back, when they come? And the laces for my shoes?"

"Yes. But you will go on thinking, remembering, won't you?"

"I'll try."

Olga hurried from the prison warning herself that it scarcely provided a lead but it certainly justified going through the statements of the people and acquaintances with whom George Bendall had worked at NTV. And if there was no reference to something—anything—the man regularly did on Tuesday and Thursday nights, they'd all have to be re-interviewed and specifically asked.

"You had no right—no authority—to arrange access to the mother without reference to me!" protested Richard Brooking. "It should have been done diplomatically, through channels. You were specifically warned by Sir Michael himself!"

"Dick," said Charlie, intentionally using the name abbreviation for its ambiguity. "That's debatable and I'm not interested in debating it. I'm interested in finding out why a British national apparently tried to kill two presidents and when an opportunity presents itself, like it did today, then I'm going to take it without first asking your permission. You want to protest that to London, then go ahead. And while you're doing it, ask them how they feel about another British national—albeit one who's lived here for years—being banged up in a Stalin-era prison without charge."

"That's certainly questionable," agreed Anne Abbott.

"I thought you told me it was for her own protection."

"Bollocks," rejected Charlie.

Brooking looked embarrassedly to Anne, who smiled and said, "That's what I think, too."

"I'm not sure it would be proper for me to accompany you to a prison," said the diplomat.

"Don't then," accepted Charlie, relieved.

"It probably would be better left to us at this preliminary stage," agreed Anne.

"Thanks for the support," said Charlie, as they made their way along the corridor towards his office.

"Things are difficult enough without dicks like Richard Brooking," said the lawyer.

Charlie thought that it just might be that he and Anne Abbott were birds of a feather, which would be a welcome change from being surrounded by either vultures or cuckoos.

The information-starved international media thronged Petr Tikunov's press conference at the Duma. The Communist Party presidential candidate, a burly, beetle-browed man whose campaign managers tried to avoid facial comparison with Brezhnev, said that irrespective of any current investigation the new government he would be leading after the forthcoming elections would institute the most searching and thorough enquiry into the outrage.

8

It took the authority—and intervention—of Aleksandr Okulov's office for Natalia to reach the FSB counter-intelligence chief and by the time she did it was to announce the exasperated acting president had ordered her personally to the Lubyanka, which made her as uneasy as it clearly did General Dimitri Spassky.

The only delay when she entered the Russian intelligence headquarters from which she herself had operated for fifteen years was for the security formality of photographing, identification and official authorization. As she followed the required but unnecessary escort across the marbled and pillared hall to the elevator bank Natalia thought that Charlie was probably right that the sole difference between old and new was the name change. Not true, she corrected herself at once. She'd been transferred outside the service, a change she was certainly glad about. Or had been, until now. She'd recognized quickly enough the professional hazards of being appointed the crisis committee's coordinator but she hadn't expected to be sucked quite so quickly—and potentially deeply—into such obvious in-fighting. But she *was* here as the coordinator—the emissary of the acting president, in fact—not as a deputy director of the Interior

Ministry. It put her into a stronger position, despite Spassky's seniority. It had also been regulations when she worked there that visitors were searched, irrespective of their outside security clearance or whoever's emissary they were. So things weren't the same. She hoped her apparent advantage continued.

Natalia smiled at the care the escort took selecting the elevator bank, away from the lifts that went to the twelve basement levels—a subterranean township for the intelligence elite, with shops, roads and even a railway connection to the Kremlin on which Stalin once travelled by special carriage personally to witness the interrogations of purged Central Committee colleagues.

Spassky's smoke-fumed office overlooked one of the inner prison courtyards in which such victims were finally put out of their agony and Natalia wondered if there was an element of nostalgia in the old-time KGB general's choice.

He didn't rise at Natalia's entry, occupying himself lighting a fresh cigarette and having done so said, "It was unnecessary involving Aleksandr Mikhailevich."

"You weren't accepting my calls—as you didn't yesterday—or returning the messages I left." There was a recording being made: every Lubyanka office had been equipped within the first week of the invention of audio tape. She was glad—maybe fortunate—that this was such an old office. She still had to be alert to responses that could be edited to Spassky's advantage and her detriment.

"You mustn't question my authority here, Natalia Fedova."

"I am not questioning your authority. I am trying to fulfill the function I was given at yesterday's meeting." She'd probably cocooned herself in more protection than she imagined by protesting to Okulov's secretariat about Spassky's awkwardness.

"A meeting would have been arranged today." The man was perspiring as visibly as he had been at the previous meeting but Natalia didn't think that was the smell competing with the cigarettes. There was the sourness of alcohol, although she'd believed vodka to be odorless. Perhaps the old man was mixing his drinks.

"You promised the Bendall file in twenty-four hours. Twenty-four hours has elapsed. Aleksandr Mikhailevich has to address the Duma this afternoon."

"There are considerations."

"What considerations?"

"To whom it is going to be made available."

"Are you suggesting that the acting president of the Russian Federation—and a former regional director of the KGB!—has insufficient security clearance!"

Spassky's hands were shaking as he lighted another cigarette. "Of course I'm not!"

"Then I don't understand the objection you're making."

"It's not an objection."

"Have you found the Peter Bendall file!"

"Yes."

Too quick, gauged Natalia. What was she missing! "The *complete* file, covering everything he did after arriving here from the United Kingdom up to the time he died, to include his family?"

The hesitation of the bloated general was indicative. "That is what I am trying to establish."

"How!"

"Having the names of Bendall's case officers cross-referenced."

Spassky *was* an anachronism, the last stumbling dinosaur of an otherwise extinct species to whom it was instinctive to lie and evade. She supposed she should be grateful but she was abruptly determined not to be crushed when he finally fell. "Dimitri Ivanovich! Cross-referencing case officers on a Control that spread over thirty years could take *another* thirty years! You have three hours in which to provide our acting president with each and every recorded detail of George Bendall!"

"There is very little," finally conceded Spassky.

She had to guard against hurrying, Natalia recognized, in growing understanding. "The son *is* mentioned in the father's records?"

"Occasionally."

"Over what period?"

"Early."

"What do you mean by early?"

"When the family were first reunited here."

"How regularly?" There was a forgotten satisfaction at conducting an interrogation—being so sure of herself in an interrogation—after so long.

Spassky spilled butts on to his already burn-scarred desk stubbing out the existing cigarette. For once he did not attempt instantly to light another. "Every month or two I suppose."

"What sort of details?"

"Progress at school . . . assessments at assimilation . . ."

"Is it a complete stop or just interruptions?"

"Interr . . ." began Spassky before jerking to a stop, too late realizing he'd fallen into the easiest of interrogation traps, a question asked with the inference of the answer already known.

"They have been tampered with," accused Natalia, openly.

"They are incomplete," tried Spassky. "They were in disarray. The missing sections will be found."

"Not in time."

"I can let you have everything we have, up until the time the boy was maybe fifteen or sixteen."

"Not let *me* have," corrected Natalia, at once. "They are to be sent under FSB seal, by FSB courier, direct to Aleksandr Mikhailevich Okulov in the Kremlin." It was fitting, she supposed, that she should exercise such paranoid self-protection in the Lubyanka. "Please do it now, to avoid wasting any more time."

While Spassky made a flurry of telephone calls, culminating in his personally signing the dispatch note, Natalia sat comparatively relaxed reflecting how glad she was that there was now a sensible exchange between herself and Charlie. Refusing an over-interpretation, she supposed Charlie could have been right the previous night at omissions being caused by the chaos of reorganization. But just as quickly she remembered what he'd also said, about the Bendall family file being actively maintained until the defector's death, only two years earlier.

"It's the fault of Archives!" insisted Spassky, as the door closed behind the courier.

"You are ultimately responsible for internal security." Which she had, without too much difficulty, evaded long before Spassky's appointment, by cleansing the records of any reference to herself and Charlie Muffin.

"The missing sections could be found," suggested Spassky, more in hope than conviction.

"Or they could not." The man was introducing his own doubts now.

"It's the primary responsibility of Archives," persisted the man, his mind blocked by one defense.

There was no purpose in her staying any longer. "Has this meeting been recorded, Dimitri Ivanovich?"

"No," denied the man at once, concentrating upon another cigarette. "Why should you imagine it would be."

"It was once regular procedure."

"It isn't any longer." He smiled, in recollection. "A lot of memories, at being back?"

"None," insisted Natalia. She was, in fact, very eager to leave.

There was the ritual exchange of supposed information—together with the ritual offer and refusal of English—and another mutual appraisal.

Physically John Kayley was quite different from Charlie Muffin— much heavier, darker-skinned and with surprisingly long and thick jet-black hair—but Olga Melnik felt a similarity beyond the carelessness of the sagged suit and crumpled, yesterday's shirt. She was determined against letting this meeting get away from her, as it had done that morning with the Englishman, and felt more confident after the second encounter with Vera Bendall. The brief initial search of the statements of those who'd known George Bendall—or Georgi Gugin—at NTV had failed to discover any significance from his mother's Tuesday and Thursday recollection.

Kayley was as caught as Charlie had been by the woman's comparative youthfulness against the seniority of her rank and for the same reason. His first impression was that it wasn't going to be as easy maneuvring himself into the command role the president was insisting upon and which he'd initially chauvinistically hoped possible when he'd learned the Russian side of the investigation was being headed by a woman. He made a mental note to avoid hinting the sexism, although he wondered in passing if the cleavage valley was being offered for exploration.

"I'd welcome a brief run down in advance of reading what you've given me," he said.

"Bendall himself isn't yet recovered sufficiently to be interviewed," responded Olga, much better rehearsed the second time. "There are the two interviews I've so far conducted with the mother, who's in protective custody. She was evasive in the first. She began to break in the second, this morning. I don't believe Bendall could have done this alone. I think there's something significant in what you'll see about his regularly doing something on Tuesday and Thursday . . ."

"Meetings, do you think?"

"The mother made a point of mentioning it."

"You think she's involved?" He took out a packet of his scented cigars. "You mind?"

Olga did, but shook her head. "Perhaps not directly involved. But I think she knows more than she's telling me at the moment." Olga now had a very definite intention not just how to control this interview but how, from now on, to handle this bizarre troika. She was actually grateful—just—that the fortunately separate encounter with the Englishman had gone against her. She was alert now to what she might be up against and had had time completely to evaluate her situation. She had, she acknowledged, become arrogant, judging everyone by the inferior, graft-eroded standards all around her in the Militia. Into which, she decided, neither Charles Edward Muffin nor John Deke Kayley fitted. She didn't have the slightest doubt that both considered themselves superior—better able, better experienced, better resourced—to supervise the investigation. She wasn't frightened to compete with either in a one-to-one contest. With the Kremlin insistence upon total transparency, her undermining difficulties would come if the two Westerners combined to take side against her. Her answer—her protection as well as hopefully her advantage—was to play one off against the other to prevent such a combination.

"There would have been archives, on the father."

"Being assembled."

Kayley frowned, openly. "Still?"

"I'm expecting them later today."

"What about all the witnesses?"

Olga nodded towards the mini-barrier of stacked files between them. "All there. Nothing that connects with anything the mother said." The smell of the strange cigars made her feel vaguely nauseous.

"We'd also like the rifle, for forensic examination."

"It's still under tests here. You'll obviously get the full report."

"We'd still like physically to see the weapon. And there are the extracted bullets?"

"We'd also like to see the bullets that you have," countered Olga. Time to get a little harder, judged Kayley. "With our Secret Serviceman's death, we've got an American murdered within Russian jurisdiction by someone who appears still to be British?"

She couldn't see the point of stating the obvious but she could turn it back upon the man. "Complicated," she encouraged.

"Objectively—and quite obviously we always have to remain objective—the greater crime, the actual killing, is of an American." It was going far better than he'd imagined it might.

She shouldn't make it too easy. "It's good our three governments have agreed such total cooperation."

"But we have to decide upon a working structure," seized Kayley.

"The purpose of this meeting," announced Olga.

Was she jerking his chain? "How do you see us working operationally?"

She had to be extremely careful of the recording. "Together, I suppose."

"Charlie Muffin isn't here."

Charlie, not Charles, she noted. It was understandable that they'd know each other, but how well, how friendly? "Things still have to be organized, established."

"When are you seeing him?"

Olga hesitated, in apparent surprise. "I already have, this morning. The British have been granted consular access. That includes the mother, of course."

Now the hesitation was Kayley's, tilted momentarily off balance. "In view of what you've told me, ahead of my being able to read any of this, I need to talk to her."

"Of course," accepted Olga. "But I suppose now there's a diplomatic consideration. The purpose of consular access is primarily protection, which is after all why I placed her in custody. But she's not been charged with any crime: can't be, from anything we've got so far . . ."

"Are you denying me access!" demanded Kayley, overly forceful.

"Of course not! I'm simply suggesting there needs additionally to be some diplomatic consultations . . . I suppose between your two embassies . . . or maybe just with Charlie. . . ." She shrugged. "The sort of problems we're going to encounter . . ." She was losing her apprehension of the American. He was going to be far easier to manipulate than the Englishman, although for once she hoped there wasn't a need for that manipulation to become physical. He probably smelled like his cigars.

"You sure there's a need for her to remain in protective custody?"

Olga was completely prepared for that demand. "Most certainly, if the son had accomplices."

"But you've no objection to my interviewing her?"

"Not as long as the British have no objection." She paused. "We need to get together . . . establish some ground rules . . . don't we . . . ?"

"Very definitely," agreed Kayley. It had been a disastrous fucking meeting, achieving nothing. And he was scheduled to talk personally with the director in Washington in less than two hours.

Olga Melnik's only disappointment was the time it took to get rid of the traces of Kayley's presence, despite having the ashtray immediately removed and all her office windows opened. She was still reflecting upon the encounter when the courier arrived from the Defense Ministry, with George Bendall's army record.

At that moment, on the other side of the city, the diplomatic bag for which Charlie was impatiently waiting arrived at the river-bordered British embassy. He wasn't prepared for the disappointment it contained. If he had been he probably wouldn't have called Anne Abbott before he began reading.

The forensic evaluation for which Charlie had asked was divided into three parts—factual ballistic, the audio measurement from the

TV soundtracks and finally the expert assessment. Impatient though he was—sure though he was—Charlie decided to go through it in its prepared response to get the answers to his questions in the order in which he'd posed them.

The opening section only ran to two pages of little more than flat statistics. Dragunov was the Western identification for the telescope equipped SVD Russian sniper's rifle introduced into the Soviet army in the late 1960s. Based upon the Kalashnikov AK, to ensure its high degree of accuracy it fired an obsolete but essentially rimmed 7.62mm ball cartridge developed in the early part of the century for the bolt action Mosin-Nagant rifle, which was no longer issued to the Russian military. The SVD was gas operated, semi-automatic and carried a ten round magazine. There was also a commercial version, the Medved, which was usually chambered for a 9mm sports cartridge. Attached were photographs as well as sectioned illustrations detailing specific parts and Charlie at once identified the weapon over which Bendall and the cameraman fought to be the military model.

Anne came in smiling expectantly. "Well?"

"Not there yet," said Charlie, offering her what he'd already read.

The assessment of sound differences was longer than the opening and more technical. It had been made using both accepted accoustical measurements, the pascal variations of pressure according to newtons per square meter and the measurement of power creating the sound in terms of watts per square meter. The most positive register had been, unsurprisingly, from Moscow's NTV track. Two shots measured eighteen accoustical ohms, two were twenty and one was twenty-one. From both American stations, NBC and CBS, the highest resonance measured the first two at twenty ohms, one at twenty-eight and two at thirty-three. Canada's CBS came out at twenty-five, another twenty-six and two at thirty-five. The Canadian tape had needed to be sound enhanced to its maximum to detect the fifth shot, at forty-two.

Unspeaking, Charlie pushed across the desk towards the lawyer each page as he finished it. She shuffled them to one side, although in order, without looking up. Charlie had asked for as complete and as scientific an analysis as possible but he'd expected something before now. It had to be in the final summation, he decided, turning to it.

The five shots had been fired in the space of 8.5 seconds, not the slightly longer period he had amateurishly calculated. Using both versions of the Russian weapon, tests had been carried out on two separate British ranges by three Army marksmen, shooting at different times over the comparable distance and elevation of the NTV gantry from the White House podium at life sized models arranged as the presidential group had been. Each had completed firing in 6.75 seconds with positive kills of both presidents and the American First Lady. The figures representing the dead American Secret Serviceman and the Russian security officer were also hit in every test.

The conclusion was that the actual 8.5 seconds were fully consistent with the time it would take for one trained marksman to fire all five shots from the semi-automatic Dragunov. A misleading although understandable layman's interpretation had been drawn from the sound variations of the shots. It did not, in the opinion of ballistics scientists, indicate the presence of a second gunman firing from different positions. The positional difference was that of the five cameras from the pod from which all the shots had been fired. The sound variations had also been affected by the gunman shifting his stance to take individual aim, the NTV sound boom being the nearest although disengaged from its mute camera and that of the Canadian equipment having been the furthest away.

Charlie waited until Anne Abbott finished. She did so smiling up at him and said, "There goes the defense that was going to make me famous. Bad luck, Charlie."

"They're wrong," he stated.

She frowned at him. "Charlie!"

"The sound differences aren't from his shifting about on the NTV pod. There wasn't enough room."

"That's not their only scientific finding."

"It's the one that's their mistake."

"You gave them everything, even the five different camera points to calculate from. You can't argue with it."

He could, decided Charlie. And would. "The assumption is that George Bendall is a highly trained marksman."

"What if he is, or was?"

"He was a television station gofer!"

"Who'd been in the army." She was disconcerted by the thought that Charlie wouldn't let go of an opinion even when over-whelmingly proven to be mistaken.

"There's still a lot we haven't got from the Russians." Would he have to admit keeping his suspicion from Natalia to get it?

"Nothing that's going to affect this analysis," insisted Anne.

"Wait and see," said Charlie. Why, he wondered, was it so difficult to admit to the lawyer the possibility of his being wrong? He was relieved at the appearance at the door of Donald Morrison.

"I've just been lunched by the CIA," announced the younger man.

"And?" anticipated Charlie.

"Jordan told the truth about the *saltimbocca* being good but mostly he lied."

Olga Melnik decided that George Bendall's army record, under his assumed Russian name, would form an essential—and convicting—part of the man's prosecution. He'd served a total of eight years—a much longer period than she'd imagined and something else the stupid mother hadn't volunteered—two of them in East Germany and eighteen months in Afghanistan. He had been selected for specialist instruction after showing an aptitude for marksmanship in basic training and qualified, on an SVD rifle, as a Grade 1 sniper two years after enlistment. In Afghanistan he was credited with ten confirmed kills and three more had been judged to be most likely his. Four of the confirmed kills were listed as senior ranking leaders of the formative Taliban regime.

The first indication of a possible psychiatric condition emerged during his Afghanistan service. He served six weeks detention, in Kabul, for what was described as a frenzied and unprovoked attack in which the jaw was broken of a fellow member of his own squad. There were three other disciplinary report references to violence, one involving an Afghani, for which he was not imprisoned. He was named as one of four suspects in the fatal shooting of a Russian major, for which another soldier was eventually convicted, and after the investigation he was suspended from the snipers' detail. He was not reassigned to it. There were nine different charges of excessive drunkeness on two of which, with others, he was accused of drinking diluted diesel from military transporters which caused convulsions that required hospital treatment. He was based in an army camp in Odessa after leaving Afghanistan and it was there that he was finally court-martialed and jailed for six months, preceding his discharge, for the violent robbery of a civilian taxi driver who lost an eye in the attack.

Olga had just given orders for the multiple duplication of the dossier when Leonid Zenin called on the internal line from his office on the floor above. "The FSB can't find all the references to George Bendall in his father's KGB file. Looks as if there's a lot missing."

"A prosecution will hardly need it, from what I've just got from the army. Bendall's a raving drunken lunatic."

"That's not really the point though, is it?"

"No," agreed Olga, remembering their earlier conversation. "What are you going to do?"

"How's it going with the British and the Americans?" queried Zenin, not replying.

"Well enough." Olga felt a stir of uncertainty.

"Have they asked for KGB material?"

"Yes."

"The orders are to cooperate fully. They should be told why we—or rather the KGB replacement—aren't able to provide it."

But she'd be the identifiable person telling them, Olga realized, uncomfortably.

"You're right, Charlie. It's a hell of a view!" Beyond the embankment the summer sun was striking diamonds off the Moskva, churned by follow-my-leader pleasure boats.

"Did you manage to catch Okulov's Duma statement on TV?" Reciprocating the American's hospitality of the previous day, Charlie had Islay malt on the desk between them.

"I thought Petr Tikunov chewed him up and spat out the bits he didn't want."

That was Charlie's impression, too. "It was a pretty obvious inference that the security relaxations were imposed from Washington."

"He won't have made any friends with that."

"That your diplomatic playback?"

The American shook his head. "Personal view. You?"

"Not yet."

"Met the Russian gal this afternoon."

Moving towards it, guessed Charlie. Would Kayley play his hand any cleverer than Burt Jordan had, with Morrison? It had been stupid of the man to lie that the Agency hadn't tried to find Peter Bendall after his defection. What had amounted virtually to a joint operation would obviously remain on British file. Charlie said, "What do you think?"

"Attractive. Nice tits."

"Professionally?"

"Difficult to judge, from one meeting. We agreed we need a working structure."

"She suggest anything?"

"No. Gave me a whole bunch of stuff. Guess she gave you the same, when you met?"

"I hope so."

"Thought the second meeting with the mother was better than the first?" suggested Kayley.

Not bad, Charlie conceded. Should he admit to not having seen it or play the bluff? "What did Olga think?"

"That there might be something in it." The director had burned his ass for having so little to report about his conversation with the Russian colonel. It had been wise to hold back about the British access.

"You agree with her?"

"Difficult to say until I've gone through everything. You haven't told me what you think."

Time to try an ace, Charlie decided. "I'm keeping an open mind until I see her myself."

"That's best."

"I think so."

"Tomorrow, right?"

Correct on timing, wrong on tactics, gauged Charlie. "Right."

"It's good we're like that," said Kayley, extending a hand with his forefinger over his index digit.

"You'll get it all," promised Charlie.

"How's about me coming along with you?"

That was practically desperate! "It's British consular access! Diplomatic! *I'm* only being allowed in under protest." It hardly qualified as diplomatic without Richard Brooking. But Kayley wouldn't know that.

"You any idea what sort of pressure I'm under with the goddamned president sitting on my lap!"

"I told you, you'll get it all. I can't do more than that."

"I was looking for a favor."

Charlie recognized the inherent threat. "I'm going directly from the mother to Olga. Why don't we establish the working structure then?"

"I'm disappointed, Charlie."

Which was exactly what Colonel Olga Melnik intended the man to be, Charlie guessed.

Walter Anandale snapped off the remote control, blanking the screen upon which they'd watched the entire replay of Aleksandr Okulov's parliamentary appearance and said, "That's made me personally responsible for the whole fucking thing, including the maiming of my own wife, for Christ's sake!"

"That would be an extreme interpretation," said Wendall North, uncomfortable at the reappearance of security lapses he'd hoped safely swept behind him.

"We got people at home looking for extremes. You know that!"

"It certainly wasn't necessary," retreated the chief of staff.

"You get on to that guy . . . what's . . . ?"

"Trishin," helped the other man. Why did the president have such a problem with that name?

"Trishin. And you let him know I don't like what his guy's just

done . . . that I don't like it at all . . . And then you get on to our
public affairs people and tell them to start lobbying, not just among
the media travelling with us but back home in Washington, too. I
want it countered . . . Okulov wants to play dirty pool he's going to
get his knuckles crunched . . ."

"We could suggest it's the Russians trying to get out from under,
which it is," proposed North.

"Sounds good," agreed the president.

"Doesn't help the atmosphere," suggested North.

"There isn't any atmosphere to be helped, not anymore."

It remained essential to both sides that there was no suggestion
of an irreparable collapse but now wasn't the moment to start talking
of diplomacy and compromise, North decided. "I've spoken personally to the four orthopedic surgeons specializing in brachial plexus
injuries recommended by Max Donnington. He's made up complete case notes, together with the X-rays. We're shipping it all back
today. . . . And we're also flying Ben Jennings's body home."

"What's arranged?"

"Marines pallbearers from the embassy here taking the coffin to
the plane. Honor guard at Andrews."

"Is he married?"

North nodded. "Two kids, both at college."

"I should write personally."

"I've already made up a draft."

"What about the vice president attending the funeral?"

"It would look right."

"Fix it."

9

Vera Bendall's shoes were laced so Charlie presumed her bra had
been returned as well, although she was shapeless beneath a badly
knitted cardigan. The gray-streaked hair was straggled, no more than
finger combed, and there was no make-up. There was a dirt smudge

beneath her chin and her hands were soiled, blackly dirt-rimmed beneath the odd nail that hadn't already been bitten to the quick. Despite the laces, Vera scuffed into the interview room, stoop-shouldered, burdened by the unknown fears of whatever was going to happen to her next. She stopped apprehensively as Charlie stood, then gnawed in embarrassment at her lower lip when he held out the one remaining chair.

"Sorry," she said, quickly.

"You don't have to be frightened," said Anne Abbott, in English. "We're from the embassy."

"Please help me," pleaded the woman, at once.

"We'll try," promised Anne. "That's why we're here."

"We'd like you to help us, too," said Charlie. Vera Bendall had responded in English, so he did as well. He held out the small pocket recorder. "We're going to tape everything. Is that OK?"

She shrugged at the continued politeness. "I suppose."

Charlie hadn't bothered to look for the most likely position of the Russian equipment, although he'd shaken his head to stop the horrified lawyer bursting out aloud at the conditions inside Lefortovo while they'd waited for Vera to be brought to them. If the standard fish-eye-lensed camera was mounted somewhere in the overhead light surround, which was normal, the warning would probably have been picked up. It was a starkly functional room, entirely bare except for the center table and three stiff-backed wooden chairs. The door was metal, with a circular peephole. There was a summoning button set into the wall. It was strangely, almost disconcertingly, quiet, as if the room had been soundproofed against either internal or external noise. There was a prison smell, though—urine, sour food, un-washed bodies, decay—to which Charlie thought Vera was probably contributing.

"Tell us about George," prompted Charlie. He had to guard against showing he knew of Olga Melnik's first abortive interview or of the possibly improved second, which Natalia had shown him the previous evening, with other material the Russian investigator had not so far made available. It was going to be interesting to see how adept a questioner Anne Abbott turned out to be.

Vera Bendall's pent-up denials of anything her son had planned or done came in a babbled rush of protested innocence and uncaring admission of a totally dysfunctional relationship between mother and son but virtually everything she'd told Olga Melnik was included. The regular Tuesday and Thursday routine emerged in answer to a question from Anne.

"How did you feel about being in Russia?" explored Charlie, gently. "Did you hate it as much as George?"

"Not as much."

"But you didn't like it?"

"I've adjusted, after all this time. No alternative."

"You were a schoolteacher, in England?" remembered Charlie, from the English records.

"Yes."

"Were you forced to quit after Peter defected?"

"No."

"Why did you follow Peter?" came in Anne.

"I was his wife. It was my duty."

"He abandoned you. You and George?" persisted the other woman.

There was the familiar listless shrug. "I thought it was the right thing to do."

"George was only five?" picked up Charlie. Would Sasha hate being uprooted from Russia if the need ever arose?

"Not quite. Four and a half."

"So he knew virtually nothing of England; had no comparison against life here?"

Vera frowned, considering the question. "That's right."

"Why did he grow up to hate it?" said Anne, following Charlie's direction.

The faded woman didn't answer at once. "Peter and I, I suppose."

"I don't understand," said Charlie.

"We didn't get on, after I came here. Argued a lot about how much better it would have been if I hadn't come. I was close to George then. Not like it was later . . . he used to take my side . . . that's how it always seemed to be, how I remember it. George and me against Peter . . . every day. . . ." She trailed off, seemingly in bitter memories.

"There were stories . . . suggestions . . . in England that Peter wanted to return . . . ?"

"I wanted to. With George."

"What about Peter?"

"Maybe. I'm not sure."

"Why didn't you and George go back?"

"They wouldn't let us."

"They?" Charlie was dominating the questioning now, Anne silent beside him.

"The people Peter worked for?"

"The KGB?"

"Yes."

Charlie's bunched-up feet twitched. He'd spent more than an hour the previous night hunched over the recorder Natalia had protectively carried in—and out—of the Lubyanka, as surprised as she had been not just at getting past the reception area without being searched—prepared to insist upon the authority of the acting president—but also that Spassky's office hadn't been equipped with a "white noise" baffler to prevent tapes unknowingly being made. His instinct—as well as another foot spasm—told him the gaps in Peter Bendall's KGB files hadn't occurred accidentally. "Did Peter tell you that you couldn't go back to England? Or was it one of the Russians he worked for?"

"Peter."

Charlie instantly recognized the hesitation in her voice. He had to tiptoe, an inch at a time. "Only *ever* Peter?"

"As I told the Russian detective colonel, sometimes in the last few years Peter worked from home, at Hutorskaya Ulitza. The arguments got really bad around that time: that was when George was sixteen or seventeen. He said he didn't believe what Peter was saying and that he was keeping us prisoner. Once one of the people who came to see Peter took George into the room with them."

She looked at the water carafe alongside the tape and unasked Charlie poured for her.

"Did George tell you what went on in the room?"

"He said the man told him there were things he had to do but that he wouldn't do them."

"What things?"

"He didn't tell me."

"Didn't you ask him?"

"No."

Charlie felt a burn of frustration at Vera Bendall's constant, look-away acceptance of everything and anything that happened to her. "What did he say?"

"He said he wasn't weak, like Peter. That they were going to be surprised."

"Peter had been in the room?" persisted Charlie.

"Yes."

"So he would have heard whatever it was?"

"I suppose."

"Didn't you ask him?" said Anne.

"He said it was none of my business. That it was too late and that if I hadn't wanted to be here I shouldn't have followed him."

Would this be how his relationship with Natalia would finally—so disastrously—implode if she took Sasha away from Russia to live with him somewhere in the West, Charlie wondered again. No, he decided, just as quickly. The circumstances were far too different for there to be any conceivable comparison. "Did George accept it?"

The fatalistic shrug came again. "That was when the trouble started."

"What trouble?" asked the lawyer.

"Not going to classes . . . the beginning of the drinking . . . he was in an accident, in a stolen car. He wasn't charged with the theft because he couldn't drive. He started to use the Russian name around that time. Insisted I call him Georgi . . ."

"Used a Russian name but didn't like Russia?" queried Charlie, despite already knowing the answer: it was a logical question the eavesdroppers would expect to be asked.

"He said he didn't want to be known as George Bendall anymore."

"The behavior began suddenly?" pressed Anne.

"As I remember it."

"You must have thought about it, the reason I mean?"

Vera smiled, faintly. "I did. I think in some silly way he thought if he misbehaved badly enough he'd get thrown out . . . expelled from the country."

"Did you challenge him about it?"

"Not directly. I think I said once that it wouldn't work, that he'd just end up with a criminal record. He said he didn't know what I was talking about. That he didn't care anyway."

"Was there any more contact between him and the KGB people who came to Hutorskaya Ulitza?"

She nodded. "The same man came back. Peter didn't go into the room with them this time. Then others came and took him to a psychiatrist and for a while he got better, although he started to spend a lot of time away . . . not bothering to come home, I mean . . ."

"Who was the psychiatrist, Vera?"

"I never knew."

"But you knew he was seeing a psychiatrist?"

"Peter told me. He said it was best. That I'd given birth to an idiot and that it was my fault."

"Did George continue behaving himself?"

"I don't know. He would have been about eighteen then. He joined the army. After that we hardly saw him at all."

Charlie went to speak but suddenly remembered he wasn't supposed to know about the man's military record. "How long was he in the army?"

"A long time. He didn't contact me—it was always me, never ever Peter—for years at a time, two years was the longest. I don't believe he wrote more than ten letters, the whole time. When he did it was to ask for money. For a long time, towards the end, I thought he was probably dead. Then there was a letter from a prison in Odessa. He said he was being kicked out of the army. One day he just turned up."

"Was Peter still alive?"

"Yes."

"What did he say?"

"Accepted it. He wasn't well by then."

"Did the KGB still come?"

"Hardly ever."

"Did George ever meet any of the KGB people again, after coming out of the army?"

"I don't remember."

"What work did he do, after he came out of the army?"

"He didn't, not for a long time."

"How could he pay you to live at Hutorskaya Ulitza?" asked Anne.

"He didn't."

"He was still drinking?"

"Worse than ever, after the army. Every day. All day."

"Did you give him the money to buy it?"

The woman shook her head, positively. "There wasn't any. Not for drink. After Peter died, all I got was a 3,420 ruble-a-month pension."

She could count it to the last kopek, thought Charlie, less than sixteen pounds a month. "How did he get money to drink?"

"Stealing. He used to go out to Sheremet'yevo and steal suitcases from tourists. And the same at the railway stations, at the Kiev and Kazan departure terminals and at the central passenger bureau at Komsomol'skaya. There was always a lot of Western things at the apartment. I asked him not to because if he got caught we'd be thrown out of the apartment. . . ." She briefly trapped her lower lip between her teeth again. "That'll definitely happen now, won't it? The detective colonel said it could."

"I don't know," admitted Charlie, who thought it probably would. Hurriedly he went on, "Did he stop?"

She nodded. "Just under a years ago, when he started work at the television station."

"How did that happen?"

"I never knew how or why it happened, but George stopped stealing ever so suddenly. It was a long time before he told me he was seeing a doctor, a friend, who was helping him. I don't remember his name but I know you'll want to know it. I'll try. I'll really try."

"What about the job?"

"He said he'd met someone who'd helped him. I thought it might be the doctor."

Charlie felt a flare of hope. Don't rush, he cautioned himself. "Was he still drinking heavily?"

"I don't know about at work. Certainly at home. There were always bottles."

"What did he earn?"

"I don't know."

It should be easy enough to find out from the station. "But it was certainly enough to keep bottles at home?"

"It seemed to be."

"Who was the person he'd met who helped him get the job?"

"He never told me."

"Do you think it could have been the person he went out to meet on Tuesdays and Thursdays: perhaps stayed with on the times he didn't come home?" asked Anne.

"It could have been."

"Do you think this person worked at the TV stations, too?"

"It would have made sense, wouldn't it?"

"Was it a man? Or a woman?"

"I don't know. He didn't have girlfriends. It would most likely have been a man, I think."

"What were the names of the people who came from the KGB to see Peter?"

"They didn't have names . . . not names that they were introduced by. Peter never told me."

"Not ever?" demanded Charlie, disbelievingly.

"Not ever."

"What about Peter's papers after he died?" said Charlie, asking the question as it came to him. "Did Peter keep a diary . . . a journal . . . letters . . . ?"

"A diary. And other things. He was always writing."

Charlie was aware of Anne stirring beside him. He said, "What happened to it?"

"Taken," said Vera, shortly. "The day he died people came . . . they had security bureau identification. They collected up everything and said it would be returned when they'd finished with it."

"Was it?"

"No."

"Did you have the name of anyone to call . . . to ask . . . ?"

"No."

"Have you asked for Peter's things back?"

"I didn't want to upset anyone. I wouldn't be able to get another apartment . . . I can't survive without the pension . . ."

"Did George keep a diary . . . have things written down?"

"Maybe. He didn't let me go into his room. The militia searched the apartment when they came . . . brought me here . . . I don't know what they took . . . no one's told me."

Natalia hadn't mentioned anything about George Bendall's personal property taken from the apartment. Olga Melnik certainly hadn't, either. "I'll find out," promised Charlie.

"Get me out of here. Please," the old woman suddenly blurted. "I haven't done anything wrong. I'm in a cell. There's no toilet . . . nowhere to wash."

"I will," promised the lawyer. "You shouldn't be kept like this."

Charlie wished Anne hadn't been so positive.

"Now! Can I come with you now!"

"It'll have to be an official release. I have to arrange it," said the lawyer.

The older woman's face crumpled. "I don't know what else to tell you . . . what else I can do. I don't know anything that will help."

"I will do everything I can, as quickly as I can," said Anne.

Vera Bendall's lips quivered and her eyes flooded. "Don't abandon me . . . please don't do that."

"We won't," assured the lawyer.

Anne Abbott held back until they stepped through the prison gates. As they did she breathed out, theatrically, and said, "Jesus Christ! I don't think I've ever been in such a terrifying place in my life!"

"That's what it's supposed to be," said Charlie.

"You really believe there was a tape recording being made of us?"

"And a film."

"Jesus!" repeated the woman.

"Welcome to Russia."

"There's no justification for her being there."

"No," agreed Charlie.

"Do you think Sir Michael would agree to her being held some-where within the embassy?"

Charlie looked sideways in disbelief at the woman. "I wouldn't think so for a minute."

"She's British."

"The wife of a defecting spy—after whom she fled—and the mother of a murderer. Vera Bendall's going to be kept at the end of a very long barge pole," reminded Charlie. "The ambassador—and London—will want as little to do with her as possible."

"So much for compassion."

"So much for hard assed political reality."

"We've got to find somewhere better than that place."

"Good luck."

"How do you think it went, overall?"

She didn't yet know all that he did and he couldn't tell her, Charlie realized. "Overall we managed to raise more questions than we've got answers for." And there were more he still had to ask.

"That's what I think. I also think we made a pretty good team."

She had asked all the right questions, Charlie acknowledged. "Could be even better with practice."

"In fact, I was going to suggest buying you a celebration drink but I've decided helping Vera Bendall has higher priority."

"Let's take a rain check," agreed Charlie. Stealing an hour drink-ing with Anne Abbott would have been very pleasant but he sup-posed he had higher priorities, too.

"It *is* bad, isn't it? Worse than you've told me?"

Anandale looked down at his wife, one side of her body embalmed beneath her protective tunnel. They'd been married for twenty-two years—happily so despite his resisted temptations—and in their per-sonal life he'd always levelled with her, as she had with him. "The nerves in your arm have been damaged."

"Is that why I can't feel it?" Her hair had been lightly brushed and her face washed properly, not with an unguent, so that it didn't shine anymore but her pallor was still drained a deathly white. There was a saline as well as a plasma drip into her uninjured arm.

"Yes."

"Will I get the feeling back?"

"There's going to need to be treatment. We've already got the specialists lined up, for when we get back."

"What sort of treatment?"

"Re-connecting the nerves."

"The bullet smashed them?"

"Yes."

"What happens if they can't be re-connected?"

"We're going to the best people in the world to ensure that they can be."

"What if they can't," demanded Ruth Anandale, with the persistence of the criminal lawyer she'd been before their marriage.

Anandale hesitated, swallowing. "Then it will be permanent."

"No feeling at all?"

"No."

"No use then?"

"No."

Ruth Anandale didn't cry. Her face creased, once, as if there had been a spurt of pain but then she lay expressionless although not looking at him. "I broke my leg skating when I was a kid. About twelve, I guess. Even then all I could think about in the hospital was that it would be stiff when it got fixed, so that I'd have to limp—drag it maybe—for the rest of my life."

"I promise it'll be fixed."

"You'll have to help me, Walt. Help me a lot. I don't want a body that doesn't work right . . . look right . . ."

"We won't give up, until we get it fixed."

"No," agreed Ruth. "We won't."

The Russian Foreign Ministry is within walking distance of the American embassy, which was how Wendall North and the U.S. secretary of state finally completed their journey because Smolenkaja Sennaja Ploscad was gridlocked. The two Russians were waiting in Boris Petrin's office actually overlooking the traffic-clogged highway.

When North began to apologize for their lateness the foreign minister said, "We saw you, from the window. It's a perpetual problem." The floor to ceiling windows were double glazed, smothering any outside noise, but Petrin still led them deeper into the cavernous room, to where easy chairs and couches were arranged around a dead fireplace. There was an oasis of bottled mineral water and glasses in the middle of a low, glass-topped table. The Americans took the seats toward which the minister gestured and sat, waiting.

Trishin said, "We want formally to express our condolences about your dead security man." Local television had been dominated by footage of the coffin being loaded aboard the plane at Sheremet'yevo.

North nodded but didn't speak. Neither did James Scamell.

Petrin said, "I am glad you agreed there was no need for advisers or a secretariat."

The two Americans remained silent.

"Politically we've got to move forward now," said the Russian chief of staff. "I'm sure you agree with us on that, too?"

"I'm not clear what positive movement there can be in the circumstances," said Scamell, at last.

"The treaty was ready to be finalized," insisted Petrin.

"It had reached the final discussion stage," qualified the secretary of state.

"Easily resolvable points," argued Petrin.

"That's not our interpretation," said North. "Your elected president is alive but incapacitated . . ."

". . . And Aleksandr Mikhailevich Okulov is the legally acting president, empowered to make and take all presidential decisions under the conventions of the Russian constitution," interrupted Trishin, formally.

"Pending elections also required under your constitution in the event of that incapacity becoming permanent or the death of the legally incumbent president," finished the equally well-rehearsed North, just as formally.

"The pending elections are not specially convened," fought Trishin. "They were already scheduled."

"A circumstance of convenience," dismissed Scamall, briefed by the American embassy's constitutional lawyer. "Our advice is that it would be legally unsafe—as well as unfittingly hasty on the part of both sides—to consider any formal signing in advance of that election."

There was a visible stiffening from the two Russians.

"What do you consider appropriate?" demanded Trishin, tightly.

"A joint statement regretting what's happened, with the hope that those still surviving make a full recovery. And an assurance that the incident in no way endangers the treaty negotiations, which will continue," recited Scamell.

"To defeat the *Kommunisticheskaja Partiya Rossiiskoi Federalsii* there has to be a signed treaty," insisted Petrin. "That's been our understanding—our agreement—from the beginning."

"I can continue coming here during the lead up to the elections," offered Scamell. "There will only be one obvious inference."

"That the treaty will be agreed with us but not with the communists?" completed Trishin.

The scenario was North's and as he sat listening to it being spelled out he congratulated himself upon how well it suited both sides, although to a greater advantage to America than to Russia.

"We are disappointed," understated Petrin.

"Nothing is being withdrawn," insisted North. "Things are merely being postponed, which they should be."

"What about the joint statement?" queried Trishin.

"Which must *be* a joint statement," North said heavily and at once. "Strictly agreed between us, with no premature, unexpected announcements. I am giving you the American undertaking here and now that there will not be anything independent from us."

Petrin and the Russian chief of staff looked pointedly between each other. Trishin said, "I believe we see the point."

"If it is to be a joint statement, carrying the authority of both leaders, it should be made personally, not issued through spokesmen," demanded Petrin. "We'd consider that essential."

"There's the question of security . . ." North tried but Petrin overrode him.

"There is *no* question of security!" The man looked around the huge office, empty but for them, as a reminder that it was an unattributable meeting. Completing the unspoken threat he said, "A personal statement, by your president and Aleksandr Mikhailevich, would totally guarantee no premature, ill-judged comments, don't you agree?"

John Kayley was already waiting in the small conference room adjoining Olga Melnik's suite when Charlie arrived at Militia headquarters. For once the American wasn't fumigating the place with his cigar smoke, which was a welcomed relief.

As he passed over the transcripts of that morning's meeting with Vera Bendall Charlie said, "I've included copy tapes, as well."

There was a stone-faced, head-nod of acceptance from the American, which Charlie interpreted to be continued annoyance at his refusal to let the man in on the interview and thought, fuck you too.

"How did it go?" asked Olga, who'd already listened to her own eavesdropped recording and seen on film Charlie's warning head shake to the woman who'd gone with him to Lefortovo.

"One or two interesting points," suggested Charlie.

"Time to start work then!" she said, briskly.

"Exactly," seized Kayley. "And this isn't the place or the way."

Charlie looked at the other man in open surprise. Surely yesterday's rancor couldn't have remained as strong as this? Olga just as quickly discerned the American's irritation, hoping she'd succeeded in making the Englishman its focus.

Charlie said, "You've obviously got a point to make?"

"An obvious one," declared the American. "Maybe the three of us can get on well enough together . . . maybe not. None of us know yet. But passing around packages like this is ridiculous. We need a centralized operation: an incident room, with trained officers indexing and correlating everything. Computers. Telephones. Access to forensic facilities. Somewhere from which we can all work together, *be* together. Yesterday all those facilities were flown in from America. And have already been set up in a basement at the U.S. embassy. It's from there that I am going to head up the American side of the investigation, an American side which will be fully exchanged with both of you. But what I'm suggesting—inviting—is for both of you to join me there, have all your stuff filed there. It'll happen anyway, under the sharing agreement. But it'll be in three different locations, with no necessary centralization. This shooting is almost forty-eight hours old and we haven't got a damned thing properly off the ground yet . . ." He looked at Olga, smiling at last. "That's not a criticism, of anything you've done. But look . . ." He swept his hand towards the pile of dossiers in front of Charlie. "He hasn't had the opportunity to look at any of that yet . . ." He had to bulldoze them, be even more insistent if necessary. Paul Smith had made it a clear ultimatum when he'd spoken to the FBI director that morning. He had twenty-four hours to get everything on American terms under American control or he caught the direct Washington flight home the following night.

Charlie had recognized Kayley's point long before the American had got to it, his mind way beyond what the man was saying. The arrangement would suit him perfectly. Through Natalia he had virtually open access to the Russian investigation. And if he had entrée to the American facility he was confident he could discover whatever he wanted or needed, even if they didn't want him to.

Now it was Olga who was stone-faced. "You established all that without telling me—us—what you intended in advance!"

"It's the way I'm working the American part of the investigation!" repeated Kayley. "I'm inviting you both in, to be part of it. Like we're supposed to be, all part of the same thing. What do you say, Charlie?"

Yet again Charlie's mind was way ahead. Less than twenty-four hours earlier, Olga had been trying to drive a wedge between him and the American: how quickly what goes around comes around. "I think it's a good idea. It is, after all, what we're supposed to be doing."

"All those facilities exist here," insisted Olga.

Charlie was with him, which put her in the inferior bargaining position, calculated Kayley. "You don't want to come aboard, that's your decision. Charlie and I will operate out of Novinskii Bul'var, liaise and share everything with you from there. Not perfect but better than what we're doing at the moment."

She couldn't let it happen! They'd combine against her, cut her out. "It's a resolve to an operational difficulty. I'm prepared to give it a trial. If, for any reason, it doesn't prove functional we'll have to come to some other arrangement."

"Sure we will," smiled Kayley, allowing Olga her escape. Won! he thought.

"You're right," agreed Natalia, looking up from the transcript of Charlie's interview with Vera Bendall. "It throws up a lot of questions."

"Most of which I didn't follow through," conceded Charlie, self-critically. The day had continued unexpectedly but in Charlie's opinion far more productively than he'd anticipated. Kayley had used the fact that Charlie supposedly had to catch up with the newly produced information—as they did from his interview with Vera Bendall—to argue their first American embassy assessment should be postponed until the following morning and Charlie had gone along with it because the Russian forensic material, the incomplete KGB dossier and the preliminary medical report upon George Bendall were new, although then he couldn't have guessed how important he would judge one of them to be.

"When are you going to see her again?"

"Directly after the U.S. embassy meeting. I'll fix it there with Olga."

"You really think the embassy arrangements will be practical?"

"Between us we're covered from two sides. I'll take my chances getting what I want from America." At the moment all he wanted was one specific statistic.

From anyone else it would have sounded arrogant but from Charlie it didn't, thought Natalia. If only her professional trust could cross over to their personal situation. "You think from what Vera Bendall said the KGB were using him—had a use for him?"

Charlie shook his head. "It could be. But it doesn't fit! You were KGB. Can you imagine them taking on someone like George Bendall!"

"I wasn't operational," reminded Natalia. "He could have had his uses *because* he was unpredictable."

"Two other things that don't fit," itemized Charlie. "How does a drunken, unpredictable misfit like George Bendall, who made a living robbing tourists, suddenly get—and hold—a job in a TV studio? Any job, for that matter?"

"I was going to ask you that. I don't know."

"Try the second. George Bendall retained British nationality. How did he get accepted into the Russian army?"

"At the time the Russian army was made up of conscripts and volunteers from fifteen republics of the Soviet Union."

"The United Kingdom wasn't one of them."

"You think it's linked to what Vera Bendall said about the KGB?"

"The *Glavnoye Razvedyvatelnoye Upravleniye* is military intelligence," reminded Charlie. "What influence would the KGB have had?"

"Enough to get him in, if they'd wanted."

Charlie hesitated at the direct question but decided things were sufficiently relaxed between them now. "Did the instruction come from your ministry for Olga to tell Kayley and I that things were missing from Peter Bendall's dossier?"

There was no hesitation from Natalia. "No," she said at once. "It didn't come from the control group, either. So it's got to be internal Militia, blame apportioning."

It was an essential part of their self-imposed personal security that each had their own, independent telephone line into the Lesnaya apartment. Natalia rose hurriedly at the recognizable ring of hers, anxious that it wouldn't wake Sasha. Natalia's was the shortest end of the conversation and she spoke with her back to him so Charlie only picked up isolated words.

She remained by the telephone after replacing it, turning to him. "George Bendall's recovered consciousness. And the guards at Lefortovo found his mother's body an hour ago. They didn't take her bra away after she'd spoken with you. She hanged herself with it."

For once in her life Vera Bendall hadn't looked away, accepting everything and anything, thought Charlie.

10

From the upper stairway platform on to which he emerged from the lift Charlie had an elevated overview of the abruptly converted U.S. embassy basement and decided that all the stories he'd ever heard of plots of quicksand being turned overnight into fully carpeted, kitchen-gimmicked American estates of barbered lawns, helicopter emplaced matured trees and individual boat docks on canals really were true after all.

He was gazing down into a plasterboarded and sectioned beehive of criminal investigation, complete with its buzzing inhabitants of drones and worker bees. At its very center was the incident room itself, seried by mostly already occupied desks each with their own individual, screen flickering computer, telephone and individually dedicated fascimile terminal. At one end, dominated by a raised dais and a cleared desk larger than the others, were two only miniature electronic viewing screens flanked by four trestle-mounted static boards and at the opposing end a gantried projection camera. Linked by an open corridor was what Charlie recognized to be a mobile forensic laboratory. It was bisected by two long, metal-topped benches—each broken by suction-fitted sinks—upon which were mounted three more computers. There were four obvious although elaborate microscopes, each with two separate but comparison-capable viewing bases and four pieces of mysterious electronic machinery. On its own table, quite alone, was a large, bellow-middled piece of equipment which Charlie guessed to be a camera but wasn't sure. A third, corridor-connected separation had a inner battlement of gray filing cabinets in the very middle of which was a triptych of corner-to-corner archival computers, their screens already filling with type being entered by hunched operators.

Encircling everything was an appropriate honeycomb of individual outer rooms, each again with its momentarily dead-eyed com-

puter, filing cabinet, telephone and fax machine. Each had access to
the inner, communal area through a door.

The entire, unroofed complex was whitely illuminated by a sky
of fluorescent tubing and lifted from the basement concrete by an
artificial wooden floor—already covered by sound-deadening carpet—beneath which was concealed what Charlie calculated to be
literally miles of operating cable and wiring.

Like the wrongly sexed but omnipotent Queen Bee he'd clearly
appointed himself to be, John Kayley stood in the main room, ex-
pansive buttock perched on the large command desk. Charlie was
surprised to see Olga Melnik beside the American; he'd expected
her to be at George Bendall's bedside. In which order would she
choose to tell him? They both looked up at Charlie's entry and
Kayley waved, gesturing him down. Charlie was conscious of briefly
becoming the focus of everyone in the main room as he descended
into it and supposed Olga had been, earlier, even though there were
no forgotten shirt-buttons today. There wasn't, in fact, a shirt: the
business suit came right up to her neck, Mao-style. As he got within
hearing, Kayley said, "What do you think?"

Charlie said, "I liked it in the movie."

Kayley allowed himself a tight smile. "This isn't make-believe."

"I hope it isn't," said Charlie.

Kayley's smile went.

"Vera Bendall's dead. The son's come round." The words collided almost comically in Olga's eagerness to get them out.

Charlie allowed the apparent surprise. "Dead? How?"

"Hanged herself, with underwear that was returned to her for
your visit."

It was a poor attempt to spread blame. "Why wasn't it taken away,
afterwards?"

"It was a mistake," conceded Olga.

Should he hit them this early? The suspicion was justified, particularly in view of the incomplete KGB file and he'd forewarned
Natalia, for her to be ready. "Did she hang herself?"

"Her neck didn't break, if that's what you mean. She suffocated,
choked to death," said Olga.

"That wasn't what I meant," said Charlie. "Under whose administration does Lefortovo come, militia or FSB?"

"Jesus!" said Kayley, understanding.

Olga did, too. "The FSB," she said, flatly. It was a suggestion she had to pass on as quickly as possible to Leonid Zenin. The crisis committee were meeting that morning.

Charlie said, "She was, officially, accorded embassy recognition. We'd like a copy of the autopsy report. And for that autopsy to be as detailed as possible."

Olga wasn't sure a post-mortem was planned. One certainly had to be carried out now. "Of course."

"I listened to your meeting with her, read it, too," said Kayley. "She was upset, being kept there."

"Suicidally so?" demanded Charlie.

The American shrugged. "Who knows?"

Charlie talked looking around the prefabricated installation in apparent admiration, wondering how long it would take him to find what he wanted, if indeed it was here to be found. And then how to proceed. He was still working more from instinct than fact: the Russian forensic photographs were inconclusive and by themselves were insufficient. It was inevitable, he supposed, that the Russians would take offense at the questions that had to be asked. Others were necessary first. Or were they? Was he working—planning to work—for the possible benefit of George Bendall? Or to prove wrong experts who'd dismissed what he'd been so sure of? Wasn't it paranoia, in fact, to imagine he had to behave like this at all, saying nothing until he was sure in the belief he might prevent the convenient evidence of an open and shut case being tampered with, as the old KGB files in his opinion had clearly been tampered with? The self-doubt surprised Charlie. But it wasn't just self-doubt. It extended, as always, to Natalia. If his instincts were only half right she risked being caught up in open organizational warfare, even. She hadn't positively accused him of exaggeration but he knew that's what she was thinking, having warnings heaped upon her without having them fully explained. It was important, Charlie had determined, for Natalia to reach the conclusions for herself, without prejudging by having his opinions thrust upon her. Which didn't answer his immediate uncertainty. Follow the tried and tested instinct, he told himself. "What about Bendall? Can he be interviewed?"

"The recovery's intermittent," said Olga. "I'm going back to the hospital this afternoon."

"You've already seen him?"

"He wasn't aware of me, aware of anything. Didn't respond to anything I said."

There was no hurry for them to see the man, Charlie decided. He was aware of Olga moving from foot to foot, as if she was impatient to be somewhere else. He was probably more impatient, for other reasons. He looked around the room again. "So what's the set-up?"

"Heads up, everybody!" Kayley called. "Meet-the-folks time." The tour of the installation was conducted with the pride of a man showing off a new house. To most the acknowledgement was smiles and head nods, although the scientist controlling the forensic section and the man in charge of archives were introduced by name. The circuit finished at the side offices surrounding the main room, where two adjoining annexes were specifically set aside for Charlie and Olga.

"And I'm right behind you," declared the American, indicating the office directly after Charlie's.

I bet you are, thought Charlie. "Very hugger-mugger."

"You going to need any help with the computers?" Kayley asked, solicitously.

"If I do, I'll ask," said Charlie. All access would be monitored. So would telephone calls. The rooms were glass-sided, too. It was very definitely going to be a goldfish bowl experience. Olga was still shifting from foot to foot. Time to resolve both their impatience, he thought. "Everything already logged?"

"Just finishing off programming the witnesses' statements," said Kayley.

"Then we're totally up to date?" pressed Charlie. "Everything available to be accessed?"

Kayley was immediately attentive. "Unless you've got something additional?"

Charlie shook his head.

"Or have something specific in mind?" persisted the American.

"No," said Charlie. He smiled. "Guess I'd better familiarize myself."

It *was* impressive. There was no dust or debris from the hasty construction—rather there was the discernible and pleasant smell of the perfumed polish that had removed any—and in a corner beside his supposedly personal cabinet the operating lights of an air purifier glowed, although there was no noise. The answer to a prayer and Kayley's cigars, thought Charlie. The desk appeared to be genuine wood, although it probably wasn't, and the side table upon which the computer was mounted had an angled, padded rest upon which Charlie at once and gratefully eased his never comfortable feet. It was IBM hardware, predictably operating the latest—and same— Microsoft Word program installed on his machine at the British embassy. Charlie checked the drawers for back-up disks but couldn't find any and was unsurprised that he wasn't expected—or intended—to download anything to take away. As he took off his jacket—for which a convenient hanger was waiting on the coat pedestal—he saw Olga Melnik talking animatedly into the telephone in her adjoining office.

Mindful of his earlier expectation of any access being monitored, Charlie did not immediately boot up what he was most interested in but instead scrolled through the witnesses' statements already on disk until he found that of Vladimir Petrovich Sakov, the tattooed cameraman who had wrestled with George Bendall for possession of the sniper's rifle. It was the Russian transcript produced the previous day by Olga Melnik, with no additions from a second FBI interview, which meant the Bureau either hadn't bothered—which Charlie didn't believe—or didn't intend a meeting of their own, which he thought even more unlikely. The third possibility was that they hadn't got around to updating it, despite Kayley's assurances that everything was logged.

He didn't need the reminder but he pulled up the verbatim record of his own encounter with Vera Bendall, scrolling through the stumbling words. Again there were no additions—nor explanations for the obvious questions—cross-referenced from Russian sources.

Charlie felt an instant stir of excitement—a positive throb in his left foot, which was always the most sensitive—at the visual ballistic images of the bullets that shattered the shoulder of the American First Lady and caused the death of Secret Serviceman Ben Jennings. They were mounted against calibrated measuring grids in exactly the same way as the Russian evidence photographs he'd already studied of those extracted from the Russian president and his bodyguard and which Charlie had brought with him.

Charlie looked around through his glass-partitioned cell in feigned casualness. Olga was now engrossed in her own screen. John Kayley's room behind was empty. No one else appeared to be paying any attention to him whatsoever. He clicked on print, shielding the screen by lifting his briefcase on to his lap to take out what he'd brought from Protocnyj Pereulok. The comparison only took Charlie seconds: he didn't even bother to take the Russian pictures fully from his briefcase, instead putting into it what he was now convinced to be the confirming printout of the American evidence. He closed the image of the bullets, clearing his screen to call up the ballistics menu. What he wanted—hoped for—wasn't there, as it hadn't been in what Olga Melnik had given him.

Charlie pushed his chair back, although not far enough to lose the foot rest. How to do it? So far the interference had been to KGB archives and possibly with papers belonging to both father and son which had, according to Vera Bendall, been removed from the Hutorskaya Ulitza apartment by intelligence and militia officers. The challenge—a positive confrontation—was inevitable. And essentially it had to be in front of witnesses, to prevent anything else going missing. Why didn't he wait; persuade Natalia to guarantee that the complete Russian ballistic evidence be made available? Because it drew her too closely—too dangerously—into the active operational working of the investigation, which didn't fit—wasn't part of her remit and which, from what he'd just studied and compared, definitely was going to become more difficult. Would the actual, physical American evidence still be here, along the corridor? Or already back in Washington? Certainly something to discover.

Slowly, not wanting to attract Olga's attention, Charlie stood, stretched and made his way out into the main room, smiling back at the few who looked up and smiled at him. He still couldn't see

Kayley. He sauntered past the unoccupied command area into the forensic linking corridor, hands deep in his pockets, a man orientating himself to new and unaccustomed surroundings. The forensic controller—Bill Savage, Charlie remembered easily—saw him approaching and rose to meet him as Charlie emerged from the tunnel.

"How's it going?" There was no heavy, state-identifiable accent. Baldness—and the greyness in a compensating beard—made the man look older than he was.

"Good finally to be working in something of an organized system."

"Pretty unusual situation all the way round," agreed the man.

"How's it with you?"

"Truth to tell, we're kinda underemployed," admitted the scientist.

"Russians haven't given you the rifle? Or the recovered bullets, then?" anticipated Charlie. Looking beyond the American Charlie saw that two of the other four men in the improvised room were reading magazines and the other two appeared to be testing or tuning equipment.

"John's asked for it."

"You the ballistics expert?"

The other man shook his head, indicating one of the magazine readers. "Willie Ying's our gun man. Why?"

Charlie began moving, taking the controller with him, not responding until he got within the expert's hearing. When he did, Charlie said, loudly, "It struck me there was something missing from what's on the computer about the bullets."

The Chinese face came up abruptly from behind the magazine. It was *Soldier*, Charlie saw.

Aggressively Ying said, "What's the problem here!"

Charlie smiled, ingenuously. "Lack of facilities. Britain being the poor relation, as usual."

Neither American smiled back. Nor spoke.

Charlie said, "You got the bullets here that were taken from the First Lady. And Ben Jennings? Or have they already been shipped back to Washington?"

"Why?" demanded Ying, truculently.

"This is the scene of a crime," said Savage, in a half-answer. Maybe—just maybe—there was a God after all! "I must have missed it on the computer. I couldn't find the grainage. Could you show me where it is?"

"I'm waiting for the Russian exhibits," said the ballistics expert. "I need everything for a proper comparison."

"Something I need to know about?"

Fuck, thought Charlie, turning at John Kayley's voice. The FBI supervisor was coming out of the corridor like an elephant frightened of missing the sugar bun picnic, perhaps, remembering the ancestry, buffalo would have been a better analogy than elephant. He had to force it on, Charlie decided, risk the humiliation of being labelled the cocky Limey smart ass. Dropping the amiability—reckoning there might even be an advantage in antagonism—Charlie said, "Something we all need to know about, as quickly and accurately as possible."

"What!" demanded Savage, exasperated.

"You do something for me—*have* something done for me?" asked Charlie, only just according Kayley his authority. "You get Willie to weigh the bullets you're holding as evidence?"

"*What!*" demanded Savage, again.

The Chinese ballistics expert didn't immediately speak. Then he said, "I told you I was waiting. And why."

"Don't wait!" urged Charlie. "You've seen the photographs."

Ying look enquiringly to his supervisor who said to Charlie, "You got something?"

"Weigh the bullets," insisted Charlie.

Ying did so with the impact-distorted metal still encased in its plastic exhibit envelopes, the minuscule weight of which was known and easily subtracted to achieve the reading. He repeated the simple experiment three times before looking up directly at Charlie. The American said, "I won't offer it as empirical until I've tested what the Russians have."

"I wouldn't expect you to," said Charlie, as satisfied relief flooded through him. "But it's quite impossible for those two bullets to have been fired from the same rifle, isn't it?"

"Yes," conceded the Chinese, quietly.

There had been no prior indication that it would be a smaller gathering but Natalia decided that despite Charlie's ill-explained insistences she had no positive personal problem and from the previous evening's rehearsal she was quite confident she was totally prepared for anything that might arise. The only unexpected although quickly understood absence was that of General Lev Lvov, whose function was now to protect acting president Aleksandr Okulov, the other absentee. In the nuance and rumor-fuelled hothouse of Moscow political uncertainty it isolated General Dimitri Spassky as the man responsible for the security debacle, which Spassky had already and very obviously recognized. The ashtray in front of the man was overflowing and the hand with which he lighted the continual replacements was more visibly shaking than usual.

"There is some encouraging news," announced Yuri Trishin. "The president has recovered consciousness. The latest from the Pirogov doctors is that his condition is stable and that he is out of immediate danger, although still critical."

"Encouraging indeed, great news!" hurriedly coughed Spassky, anxious to have his name first on record.

The impatience of the presidential chief of staff for Natalia and the fourth member of the group, Militia Commandant Leonid Zenin, dutifully to respond was almost palpable and as soon as they had Trishin said, "So what's encouraging for me to hear in return?"

Nothing, conceded Natalia, accepting it was a question posed to her. According to the Lefortovo prison authorities, she said, there was nothing to suggest Vera Bendall had been likely to take her own life, although that did not excuse the oversight of not removing articles of clothing with which she could do herself harm. It was hoped to interview George Bendall later that day. The investigation had been centralized at the American embassy. Ruth Anandale continued to improve although the indications were that she had permanently lost the use of her right arm. A decision was being made in the next twenty-four hours whether to amputate the leg of Feliks Vasilevich Ivanov, the Russian security guard injured in the shooting. The likelihood was that it would be necessary.

Natalia hesitated as she came to the end. Everything on your terms, to your orchestration, Charlie had lectured: don't let anyone else get their explanations or excuses in ahead of you. Spassky had to be first. "Unless there has been a discovery in the last two or three hours that Dimitri Ivanovich has not shared with me there is the risk of considerable embarrassment. Substantial sections of former intelligence files containing information that could be important to this investigation remain missing. . . ." She turned to the militia commandant. "I also understand, from taped meetings involving Senior Investigating Colonel Olga Melnik, that the American and British investigators are aware of what's happened?"

It was Zenin who got in first. "I am not aware of the Americans or British being told. If they have been, I can only assume it emerged in answer to her being asked why the material was incomplete."

Spassky was quick to follow, surprisingly strong voiced in the chosen denial. "I am not, nor ever was, directly or personally responsible for archives."

"You are head of counter-intelligence—internal security—within Lubyanka," challenged Natalia.

"Exactly! We are talking of departmental mismanagement."

"Are we?" demanded Natalia. "I don't think we are."

"Are archives definitely missing?" asked Trishin.

"Yes," finally admitted the old man.

Natalia didn't want the impetus taken away from her. "Deliberately taken?"

"I have no evidence of deliberate interference," insisted Spassky.

"Has a thorough search been made?" pressed Natalia.

"Yes," said Spassky, again.

"Isn't it an unfortunate coincidence that Vera Bendall died in custody in a prison administered by the FSB?" leapt in Zenin. "I suggest that the most thorough, independent enquiry be held."

So Charlie had planted his suspicion in time for some contact between Olga Melnik and Leonid Zenin. Natalia's realization was fleeting, quickly replaced by near incredulity at what Zenin had just proposed. The militia commandant was actually pressing for the Russian intelligence service to be investigated by an outside organization, which was unthinkable. Even the supposed enquiry into the failed, KGB-supported coup against Mikhail Gorbachov in 1991 had been a strictly controlled, internal tribunal. Natalia's awareness continued, worryingly. Was this what Charlie had anticipated and really been preparing her for, a collision of nuclear proportions between Russian intelligence and presumably Russian civilian police, with herself inevitably—more inextricably than she'd ever feared—caught up in the middle? And she would *be* literally trapped in the middle, a former KGB executive now a department director of the Interior Ministry with ultimate authority over the militia.

The same analysis—although not necessarily in the same personal order—had obviously been made by the men in the Kremlin office with her.

Spassky's reaction was such open-mouthed disbelief that all he could initially utter was, "What?" so weak-voiced that he said it again, in louder outrage. *"What!"*

Trishin was no less surprised but more controlled. "You're virtually making an open accusation."

Surely, thought Natalia, the civilian commandant did not for a moment imagine the militia strong enough—able enough—to confront an intelligence apparatus developed over more than seventy years!

"I believe the gravity of what's happened demands a thorough enquiry," insisted Zenin. "I understand, too, that also to be the feeling of the Americans and the British."

Natalia was immediately, intently, alert. Charlie hadn't given her any indication of that. But then he hadn't properly—fully—explained all the guidance he'd given. And Zenin had clearly spoken to Olga Melnik at the American embassy, bringing him more up to date than she was. "What reason do you have for saying that?"

"The impression of my officers in direct contact with their investigators."

Impressions, isolated Natalia: there was only one officer, Olga Ivanova Melnik. The militia chief was railroading.

"The woman was in militia, not FSB, custody at Lefortova!" said Spassky, inadequately.

"Precisely why I think an enquiry justified," argued Zenin. "I do not want any innuendo—any innuendo whatsoever—directed at my service."

Was it as simple as that, not an attack at all but simply a defense, in advance of any accusation? Natalia said, "By whom, or what, do you consider such an investigation should be conducted?"

"What else but a presidential commission?" said Zenin.

A neat sidestep from direct confrontation, Natalia recognized. The unbelievable challenge had been laid but Zenin had separated himself from directly pursuing it.

"I think," said Trishin, "That this suggestion needs to be considered. Discussed with others."

Dimitri Ivanovich Spassky's hand was shaking very badly when he lit his new cigarette.

Like practically everything in Charlie Muffin's upwardly and onwardly mobile philosophy, the vindication was relegated to his mental trophy shelf for later burnishing—which none ever were—while he hurried on. Which, practicably, was not immediately possible because the bullets and George Bendall's rifle had physically—and finally—to be transported from the militia forensic laboratories, in the faraway Moscow outskirts of Chagino. There was coffee and separate reflection in their respective offices while they waited. From his Charlie saw both Olga and Kayley in gesticulating telephone exchanges but decided against calling his own embassy. There was no time difference urgency. Having satisfactorily proved his suspicions from a partial test, he now wanted the complete ballistics analysis before, fittingly, lobbing the bombshell into London's lap. Which wasn't, at that precise moment, his most pressing concern. They now had, unquestionably, two gunmen from which a neon-lit, flag-waving conspiracy emerged, which jigsawed with missing KGB archives and the death in custody of a potential witness who'd remembered the official removal of more papers and belongings—including those of the one seized gunman—that had not been mentioned in anything that Colonel Olga Melnik had provided. But far more importantly were not known about by Natalia, whom he'd specifically asked the previous night. Which, as muddied waters went, was thicker than pea soup, a mixed metaphor that Charlie was content with because it was so appropriate. There was something approaching a familiar comfort at being confronted by a situation totally different from that with which he'd begun: in Charlie's life, the obvious had never, if ever, turned out to be obvious.

Olga's sudden activity in the adjoining office alerted him to the arrival of the material evidence, which Kayley escorted her to the embassy reception area officially to receive. It was obvious that virtually everyone in the complex knew of a development, if not precisely what it was, but Kayley limited the audience in the forensic section to its specific staff, himself, Olga and Charlie. The much-filmed rifle as well as the medically-recovered bullets made up the Russian package but Willie Ying's concentration was again upon the distorted metal. The tests were as straightforward as those earlier, quadruple checked within thirty minutes.

The Chinese straightened, finally, and said, "There isn't any possible doubt."

Kayley said, "I need to have this spelled out, nice and easy. I've got a lot of curious people to tell."

Ying looked invitingly at Charlie, who said, "You're the expert."

The Chinese scientist said, "Western European and central European bullets are officially weighed in grains. Quite literally the measurement is the average weight of a seed of corn, one seven-thousandth of an avoirdupoidal pound . . ." He indicated the still unexamined sniper's rifle. "That's the Soviet—now Russian—military SVD, the Dragunov. It fires a 7.62mm cartridge, the bullets from which weigh 145 grains. The commercial version of the SVD, known as the Medved, fires a 9mm sporting cartridge that weighs 220 grains. It is technically impossible for the sniper's rifle recovered from the scene of the crime to fire 9mm bullets." He turned to the table, picking up two glassine sachets. "These are 7.62mm. According to their exhibit tags, one was taken from the Russian guard, Feliks Ivanov. The other killed our guy, Ben Jennings . . ." Ying swopped plastic envelopes. ". . . All these three—the two that hit the Russian president and the one that injured the First Lady—are 9mm. They were fired from a gun we don't have . . ."

". . . By someone we don't know," completed Charlie. "Now let's talk about other things we don't have, either."

"We talking Dallas, Texas, November 22, 1963!" demanded Walter Anandale, empty-voiced in disbelief.

"There's unquestionably another gunman, logically a group," said Kayley. It had only taken five minutes for him to come up from the basement and for Wendall North and James Scamell to be summoned to Cornell Burton's embassy office. The ambassador sat to one side.

"We've got to get out of here," decided the president. "Get Ruth out of here."

"I'll get on to Donnington right away, tell him the situation's changed," said North, moving towards the desk phones.

"Wait!" ordered Anandale. "Let's talk this through. You think this whole godamned thing's been a set up, right from the beginning?"

"No," cautioned Scamell. "What I do think is that quite early on, once we started to negotiate, people saw an opportunity—for what, exactly, I don't know—and began to plan."

"What people, whose people?" demanded the Texan. "Yudkin's? Or the communists? Or Okulov? Who, for Christ's sake!"

The secretary of state shrugged, helplessly, turning to the FBI Rezident. "I can't help there, sir. Not yet."

"Nor can I," said Kayley.

Anandale turned back to his chief of staff. "We don't make any more public appearances. I don't personally meet Okulov or anyone connected with Yudkin. We time a spokesman-issued statement about the hope to continue negotiations an hour after we're airborne, on our way to Washington. Everyone clear on that?"

"Clear," echoed Wendall North.

Anandale came back to the FBI man. "You did good, John. I'll remember that, make sure that the director knows it, too."

"So Charlie was right!" declared Sir Rupert Dean. He spoke looking at his criticizing deputy. Jocelyn Hamilton remained silent.

A copy of Charlie's Moscow fax lay before each of the control group.

"The bullet that killed the American still came from George Bendall's rifle," professionally pointed out Jeremy Simpson, the legal advisor.

"And now Bendall's part of a conspiracy," said Hamilton, choosing his time. "Our situation's worse, not better."

"We don't know *what* the situation is," rejected Patrick Pacey. Irritation at the deputy director's constant carping deepened the permanent redness of the man's blood pressured face.

"We know it's escalated," insisted Hamilton. "We need to start thinking—planning—proactively."

"There's certainly a need to withdraw Muffin for consultation," conceded Dean, his spectacles working through his hands.

"And for preparing contingency plans, to build up our investigation in Moscow," insisted Hamilton. "This service—maybe its future—could be decided by the outcome of all this. Since the end of the Cold War and the de-escalation of violence in Northern Ireland it's been difficult to justify a counter-espionage function apart from becoming even more of an anti-terrorism force. Defining an FBI role is still experimental, it can't be seen or allowed to fail."

"Replace Muffin, you mean?" directly accused the heavily moustached Simpson.

"Safeguard the department. And ourselves," qualified Hamilton.

11

Olga Ivanova Melnik felt as if she'd been engulfed by a flooded river—the swollen Volga of her Gorky birthplace at the start of the March thaw—swept helplessly along by swirling currents over unseen, snagging rocks. All—or any—of which was totally alien to Olga Melnik's until now carefully structured and even more carefully disaster-avoided career. She wasn't, of course, frightened of being sucked down. Olga Melnik wasn't the sort of person to sink beneath the first ripples of uncertainties. She just needed a momentary backwater; time briefly to tread water and examine—apportion and equate—everything swamping over her.

Olga accepted, objectively, that she should have anticipated Charlie Muffin's challenges; been readier, even, for the suggestion that Vera Bendall's death might not have been an accident. She shouldn't have needed the difference in the size of the Russian-recovered bullets to be pointed out to her, either. Nor been unprepared for the demand about the bullet casings, none of which had been found. The reason was obvious from the chaos and panic at the scene of the crime, there for everyone to see and understand from at least five different television films, but she should have offered the explanation instead of having the admission drawn from her. But perhaps her greatest embarrassment, close to positive humiliation, had been having to admit not knowing the whereabouts of any of George Bendall's personal papers the initial militia search squad—her officers!—had removed from the Hutorskaya Ulitza apartment. She'd heard Vera Bendall's eavesdropped claim within an hour of the stupid bitch making it and let more than another twenty-four elapse without even asking about it!

She would have got around to it eventually, she reassured herself; not eventually, almost at once. Tomorrow, certainly. How could she have been expected to cover everything, the smallest details, in such a short time! It was easy for the motherfucking Englishman, getting everything handed to him on a plate, not having to supervise an entire investigation and think about each and every political implication.

Those political implications—every implication—were too great properly to encompass now, this soon. But the escalation made it logical for Leonid Zenin to share this first interrogation of George Bendall. But that was all it was, the escalation, not any inferred criticism of her oversights. How could it be? The confrontation— the rock jarringly awkward question after awkward question from the motherfucking Englishman—in front of the fortunately limited audience in the American embassy basement hadn't been recorded. So there was no way Zenin could know. Would ever know. But she couldn't be caught out again: shouldn't have been caught out at all.

She'd identified Charlie Muffin for—and as—the danger he was from the very beginning. A mistake recognized is another mistake avoided, she reminded herself, calling to mind the appropriate Russian proverb. She felt firm ground underfoot, no longer jostled by conflicting currents.

She was impatient to begin the interrogation and hoped Zenin wasn't late, standing close to the window and looking up Gospital'naya Ulitza towards the blue domed church of Saints Peter and Paul, the direction from which she expected him to come. He'd sounded pleased, excited even, during the telephone conversation when he'd told her to wait for him and Olga was curious about the crisis committee meeting. Clearly it had gone better for him than hers had for her.

She almost missed Leonid Zenin when he did appear because she'd been looking for an official car and Zenin was on foot, striding past the small commemoration to Peter the Great's favorite general, Swiss-born Francois Lefort, who was never to know—and doubtless wouldn't have liked it if he had—that his was going to be the name given to one of the most infamous prisons in Russian history. Olga decided that the bearded militia commandant looked even more impressive in civilian clothes than he did in uniform and felt a pleasant stir of interest, wondering what the obviously athletic body looked like in neither.

She was well away from the window, to avoid hinting any impatience, when Zenin came urgently into the dusty waiting room, smiling as Olga imagined he smiled during their telephone conversation. Despite the white-coated Nicholai Badim beside him Zenin said, "God, what a place! An incentive never to become ill."

Affronted, the surgeon-administrator said, "Heroes of the Crimea were treated here!"

"Probably in beds that haven't been changed since," said Zenin, briskly careless of offense. "What's the situation with the prisoner!"

"You can have thirty minutes."

"I wasn't asking for a time limit. He's fully conscious?"

"Yes."

"And fully comprehending?"

"According to Guerguen Semonvich Agayan."

"What's Bendall said?"

"Your officers are with him."

"I meant to you."

"He's responded to our medical questions."

"Nothing else?"

"We haven't asked him anything else."

"It's about time someone did then."

The almost overbearing confidence surprised Olga. In official surroundings, only those in which she'd been with him until now, Zenin had always appeared more subdued.

Striving to achieve some of his dismissed authority, the doctor said, "I'll check with Guerguen Semonvich. Wait for me here."

Zenin said, "I've come directly from the Kremlin. Okulov's panicking, everyone's panicking. They've doubled the protection around Yudkin. Many more security people at the Pirogov hospital and they'll have to shift patients out to make room . . ." He smiled again. "And there's going to be a presidential commission into the missing KGB stuff. I suggested it at this morning's meeting: Okulov ordered it on the spot when the conspiracy was confirmed."

"The one person we've got to keep alive is George Bendall. I've permanently doubled the guard here." She had to find a way to tell him about the things missing from the Bendall apartment.

"Nothing's going to happen to him, believe me," said Zenin. "What's it like at the American embassy?"

"I don't know about stepped up internal security. The American ballistics man claims he'd recognized the difference but was waiting for our material."

"What's the excuse from our people at Chagino?"

"They hadn't got around to it yet."

"After more than two days!"

"They obviously thought they didn't have to bother."

"Log it, for it to be dealt with later."

"I already have."

"Is the Englishman crowing?"

Olga hesitated. "Not noticeably," she answered, honestly. It would be better if Zenin heard the other embarrassments from her. "He asked about the bullet casings. They were looked for, of course, after the area was cleared. We didn't find any."

"Would they have been automatically discharged from the rifle?"

"Apparently."

"We should have recovered some," complained Zenin.

"Further evidence of the conspiracy. How well planned it's all been." She wished that excuse had come to her in the embassy basement.

"Yes," accepted Zenin, doubtfully.

It *was* an acceptable excuse. "There's something else. You remember Vera Bendall saying militia officers took away her son's papers, among his other belongings?"

"Yes," said Zenin, cautiously.

"No written material is recorded among what was taken from Bendall's apartment. I've spoken to the squad that went there first, personally, to all three of them. Each insist there weren't any documents, nothing written down at all."

"The woman could have been wrong," Zenin pointed out.

"Or other people could have got to the apartment before our officers."

"Was there any indications of a search, ahead of them?"

"They said his room was a mess," Olga replied, honestly again.

"It should be laid before the commission," agreed Zenin.

Home clear! decided Olga, as the doctor reentered the room.

"Half an hour," stipulated the man.

"We'll see how long it takes," dismissed Zenin.

The walls of the corridor along which they followed the doctor were stained and in places adorned with uncleared graffiti—"fuck" and "hell hole" appeared several times—and narrowed by bed frames, once by two ancient, boat-shaped perambulators and unrecognizable scraps of metal and frame-like pieces of wood.

Zenin said, "This come up from the Crimea, too?"

The doctor ignored him.

Bendall's ward was identifiable some way off by the phalanx of guards outside it. Olga said, "Do you want to lead the interrogation?"

"You're the investigating officer, Olga Ivanova. I'll sit and listen." The feeling she experienced surprised Olga. It wasn't unease. It was, almost sexually, of anticipation. She didn't normally feel she had to impress a man. "I'd appreciate your input, if you think it's necessary."

"It'll be there, if it is."

The protective cordon stiffened, respectfully, at their approach, then parted for them to enter. It was an individual ward, further crowded inside by three more militia officers. Recording apparatus was already assembled. Its operator was late standing when they came into the room. The walls were streaked and discolored but there was no graffiti, at least none that was apparent. The sheets matched the grayness of the blankets, though, which also toned with the doubtful color of the bandages helmeting George Bendall's head and seeming to extend, unbroken, to the dressings trebling the size of the man's broken shoulder. A half-circular frame kept the bedding off the shattered leg but he was not connected to any monitors, although a catheter tube ran to a container beneath the bed. There was a perfect spider's web covering the inside of one of the upper-paned windows, complete with its spread-legged creator, and rivulets of long-past rain had tracked top to bottom patterns through the caked grime. The recording apparatus occupied the only table and its technician had the only chair. Militia-discarded cigarettes pebbled the floor. The cubicle stank, not just of cigarettes but of stale bodies. Maybe, thought Olga, indulging herself, patients from the 1850s really had been here.

"We think thirty minutes," said the psychiatrist.

"I think as long as it takes," said Zenin.

Olga, concentrating upon the prisoner, saw Bendall's eyes darting from person to person. When he became aware of her staring at him he abruptly stopped, gazing fixedly up at the ceiling. She said, "Everyone can go now. We need another chair." The recording technician looked surprised but then shrugged.

The doctor said, "I think I should stay."

"I'll stay too," announced Agayan.

"You won't," said Olga.

"No," agreed Zenin. "Neither of you will. Out!"

"We'll be directly outside," insisted Badim.

A chair was chain-passed in from outside by the departing inner squad, one of whom cupped the doctor's arm. Zenin took the chair and sat just inside the door. Olga realized the militia commandant would not have come into Bendall's vision: the man would believe she was the only person—the only possible interrogator—in the room. Bendall's virtually unbroken gaze remained fixed upon the ceiling. Olga glanced up, seeing it was as dirty as everything else.

Looking more towards the recording apparatus Olga said, "George Bendall—alias Georgi Gugin—you are charged with murder and attempted murder. There will be other charges officially proffered at a later date."

Bendall smiled, turning slightly towards her.

"But you failed," Olga declared, her tone at once sneering.

The man continued to stare at her, unresponsive.

"The person you killed was an American guard. You'll still get the death sentence."

Nothing.

"And we know there are others. They found the perfect idiot in you, didn't they? That was clever of them."

A blink. A throat-clearing swallow. The mummified head remained unmoving.

"Your mother's dead, too. She would have suffered, poor woman."

There was a spurt of blinking, swallowing. A nearly imperceptible—instantly corrected—head movement towards her.

"The story of your life, isn't it Georgi? Always failure. Failed father, failed mother, failed son. End result: total, miserable failure."

"How?" The voice croaked, dry-throated.

Now it was Olga who stayed silent.

"How?"

She allowed her eyes to flick to Zenin. The man was leaning forward with both arms on his knees but not looking directly at her, concentrating entirely upon the words.

"How did she die?"

The crack had been made in the dam; it had to be widened from inside, not out. "Hanged."

"Shouldn't have been hanged."

He'd have lost track of time, believed it to be official punishment. She'd let it go for the moment. "Why not?"

"Didn't know anything."

"I thought she did."

"No!"

"What didn't she know?" The crack was creaking apart.

"Anything."

"About what?"

The muscles stood out on Bendall's jaw, so tightly did he bite his mouth closed.

"Died for nothing then?" Bendall had sealed the crack. And she didn't know how to prise it open again.

Nothing.

"She knew you hated everything. Didn't believe you hated her though, after what your father did to her. Bringing her here."

"Fucking bastard!"

Another weakness in the wall, Olga recognized. "He was the one who should have died, not her."

There was the faintest of sounds from the doorway, where Zenin shifted in his chair. Bendall gave no indication of hearing anything.

"Should have been him."

"Did you want to kill him?"

"Yes." The word hissed out, emotion for the first time.

"Why didn't you?"

"Didn't."

This man was her only hope, thought Olga, the only one who could provide a lead. She had to break him. Trick or tilt the already unbalanced mind, however and whichever way she could. British consular protests were irrelevant, if there was a complaint. All she had to concern herself with was getting a Russian conviction in a Russian court and she could get a confession and evidence any way she liked to achieve that. "Frightened of him, were you?"

"No!" It was a shout. Proper anger.

"Of course you were."

"No!" He jerked his head around to look directly at her for the first time, wincing at the pain the movement caused. "Was going to kill him. Died first."

Olga shook her head theatrically, disbelievingly. "Why didn't you get the others to do it, like they killed your mother." It was convoluted but got her to where she wanted to be.

The eyes upon her noticeably focused, clearing. "What?"

"Why didn't you get the others in this with you to kill him, like they killed your mother?" repeated Olga.

"You said she was hanged."

"Not sentenced, by a court. Strangled. Murdered," invented Olga.

"She didn't know!" The denial this time wailed from him.

"They thought she did. The court won't believe you didn't know they were going to do that. I don't believe you didn't know they were going to do that. You'll be considered an accomplice."

"No!" Another wail.

"You're right to be frightened."

"Not frightened."

"They'll try to kill you, if they can."

"Not *frightened*!"

"They would kill you, if they could."

He was looking at the ceiling again, lips tight together.

Mistaken direction. He wasn't rambling, either. But then why should he? Mentally deranged people didn't necessarily ramble. Wrong to have started with that preconception. There was sudden noise from the door, a muffled voice. Olga saw the doctor gesticulating from beyond the wall of security men. Zenin turned at it, too, making waving away motions with his hand.

Olga went back to the embalmed man. "The other sniper was a lot better than you, Georgi. Should have practiced more."

"No one else."

The words jolted through Olga. She was aware of Zenin coming further forward on his chair, too. She said, "We know there was. Two different rifles, different bullets."

"Liar!"

Which way to go! "They couldn't leave it to you. Knew you weren't good enough to do it by yourself."

"Not true."

"You think you're a good sniper, Georgi?"

"Trained." For the first time there was an inflection in the man's voice, a whisper of pride.

Olga thought she saw a pathway. "You killed people before?"

"A lot."

"How many?"

"A lot."

"When was that?"

"In the army."

"Did you train every day when you were in the army?"

"Course I did. Had to." Now there was a hint of indignation.

"But you've been out of the army a long time now, haven't you?"

Bendall's face clouded, in an effort to understand. "Good sniper," he insisted.

"Do you still train every day, now you're not in the army?"

The smile was knowing, crafty. "Maybe."

"You do, don't you?"

Nothing.

"Who with?"

Nothing.

"Where did you get the rifle?"

The smile remained but he didn't reply.

"Did you fire as quickly on Wednesday as you did when you trained every day in the army? And since?"

"I'm good."

"Two shots, over eight seconds? That's not fast, not for a trained marksman."

"Less than eight seconds."

Got it with the wrong correction! snatched Olga, triumphantly. She actually looked at the slowly revolving tape spool. "There were five shots, Georgi. Not two. The other man really did do better than you. Hit our president twice. And the American First Lady. You were rubbish."

"No one else," He wasn't blinking anymore; the eyes were positively drooping now.

"We know there was. You know it, too."

There was fresh outburst from the corridor outside and Olga saw the doctor and the psychiatrist both arguing with the guards outside. She distinctly heard "enough" and "protest" over the barricading heads and shoulders of Bendall's protectors and this time Zenin stood up and gestured the two men through. Badim flustered into the room, still protesting, and Olga snapped off the recording just before he got to "outrage."

Zenin blocked the man just inside the door. "Shut up! We've stopped. He's OK."

"Stalin's not in the Kremlin anymore, this isn't a police state."

"You want to prove that enlightened opinion, doctor, you just go on shouting and yelling and making too much noise. I'll even give you your own choice of camp at Kolyma."

The professional anger seeped from Badim like air from a punctured balloon. "This man is still officially in intensive care!"

Olga saw George Bendall's eyes were shut, not twitching with feigned sleep. The man's chest rose and fell, evenly.

"Which is precisely where I want him kept," said Zenin, looking between the two hospital officials. "If anything goes wrong—if he dies under your intensive care—then neither of you will even get a choice of Kolyma camp. You hear me loud and clear?"

The small, stained-coated surgeon-administrator momentarily remained in eyeball to eyeball confrontation, his mouth and throat working with unspoken words. Finally, pitifully, he said, "You proud of what you do?"

"Hardly ever," said the militia commander. "It's something that has to be done."

Zenin led the hurried pace to get out of the hospital, trailing Olga with him. Short-breathed she said, "I was almost there! I could have broken him!"

" 'The only person we've got to keep alive is George Bendall,' " Zenin quoted back at her. "You did brilliantly. But we pushed him. Keep him the right side of sanity, we'll get the others. Push him over, we've got what you said he was, a chosen idiot. George Bendall isn't important. I want the people who manipulated him. The conspirators."

Minutes, thought Olga, infuriated, in just minutes Bendall would have given them the lead. "The British are invoking their access agreement tomorrow. I want to see him again, before they do."

"Good idea," agreed Zenin. They were nearing the exit on to Gospital'naya Ulitza. "I am going back to the Kremlin. They're waiting."

"Yes?" she said, curiously.

"We need to talk more. Please wait for me, at headquarters."

"Of course."

"I meant what I said, Olga Ivanova. You did brilliantly."

"I told the militia everything," said Vladimir Sakov. "I told the Yanks to go to hell. Now I'm telling you. You want to be helped out, I'll help you."

A bravado—and vodka—fuelled bully, thought Charlie. But definitely able to fight, from the evidence of the television struggle with George Bendall that the world had watched. The NTV camera room was cluttered with equipment, discarded cups and food containers, cigarette debris and protective outdoor clothing.

Charlie said, "I've read what you told the militia." It had occupied less than one page. The man had been jolted by Bendall, knocking the camera off focus, turned to yell at him and seen the rifle. He'd thought Bendall was going to shoot him and fought him for the gun. No one liked Bendall and Bendall didn't like anyone in return. He tried not to work with the man.

"So fuck off!" Sakov was lounged in an ancient armchair leaking its stuffing into the rest of the mess, glass in hand, wearing only a sweat-stained singlet hanging over even dirtier jeans. There was a lot more of the crude tattooing along each arm than Charlie had seen on film and Charlie was sure he was right, although he didn't put the Russian older than thirty-five, despite the near baldness.

He was probably gambling with his front teeth. But Charlie was in no mood to be told to fuck off. He'd ascended floor by floor the former Comecon skyscraper and two smaller towers blocks from which the second gunman could have got an elevated firing position before abandoning the chore to the recognized FBI group outside the fourth possible location. The pain from his feet had reached his knees and was climbing. "You're not old enough."

"What?" frowned the man.

"You're not old enough to have been in a gulag. And those are gulag tattooes, aren't they?" identified Charlie. "And if you had been you wouldn't have got this job. Your workbook would have been marked."

"Smart fucker." The man lifted a clear, unlabeled bottle Charlie hadn't seen from beside the chair and added to his glass.

It was the yellow of street-distilled potato vodka, harsher—and stronger—than that sold in shops. All part of the macho image. But the remark was less belligerent. And his teeth were still intact. Charlie said, "Father? Grandfather?"

The man shrugged. "Father."

"Pretty dramatic testimonial," said Charlie, in apparent admiration.

"He wasn't guilty of anything. None of them were."

Family suffering explained a hostility to authority or officialdom. Continuing the flattery Charlie said, "Still a brave—unusual—thing to do."

Sakov shrugged, not speaking.

Having eased past the barrier Charlie didn't want to lose the momentum. "Quite a difference from Georgi. He hated his father."

"Bastard hated everyone."

"Can't imagine that worrying you."

"It didn't."

"Why didn't you like working with him then?"

"Morose fucker."

"He drank."

"Not properly with the rest of us."

"Not with anyone?"

"Maybe."

"He did have friends here, didn't he?" chanced Charlie.

"Vasili Gregorevich, I suppose." The man made a vague gesture, crossing himself.

A religious gesture? "Vasili Gregorevich who?"

"Isakov," completed the Russian. "He was a good guy, never understood what it was with him and Gugin. No one did."

Was, picked out Charlie. "What happened to Vasili Gregorevich?"

Sakov looked surprised at the question. "Dead."

Charlie felt a stir of satisfaction. "Dead how?"

"An accident. His car got hit by a train on the level crossing near Timiryazev Park. That's where he lived, near the park."

Association with George Bendall seemed to bring with it a high mortality rate, reflected Charlie. "When was that?"

"A few months back. Four, five maybe."

"How'd it happen?"

"Don't know. Tried to race the train, that's what they said."

"Who said?"

"People here. Talk. You know."

"What did Vasili do here?"

"Senior cameraman, like me. That's what I am now—why I got the White House position—since Vasili Gregorevich died."

"They were good friends?"

"Couldn't understand it," repeated Sakov. He lifted the bottle again. "You want a drink? Private stuff. Good."

Charlie had never refused a drink in his life and wasn't going to now, because it marked his acceptance, but he mentally apologized to his liver. The Russian poured almost three fingers into an already print-smeared tumbler, added yet again to his own and said, "To the witches being kindly ones."

Charlie touched glasses to the traditional Russian toast, wishing the witches had been kinder when he was tramping pointlessly around the high rises. The liquid burned and went down his throat like a clenched fist. "They work together a lot, Vasili and Georgi?"

"Permanent team, most of the time."

"Is that usual?"

"Suited everyone else."

"Did they know each other, before Georgi started working here? I heard someone helped Georgi get a job? Vasili maybe?"

"That's the story I heard. I never asked."

Charlie wetted his lips with the drink. It stung. "There a favorite bar everyone drinks in around here?"

"Elena's, on Tehnicskij."

"Did Georgi and Vasili use it?"

Sakov took his time. "Sometimes."

"They spent time together outside of work, then?"

"Seemed to."

"What about Tuesdays and Thursdays?"

The Russian looked blankly at Charlie. "What?"

"His mother said Georgi used to do something every Tuesday and Thursday but she didn't know what it was."

Sakov shook his head. "Neither do I."

"How'd it come about that Georgi was your gofer on the day of the shooting?"

"Rostered, I guess."

"He didn't ask for it particularly?"

"Not that I heard. You're not drinking?"

Charlie brought the glass to his lips again. "You didn't like working with him?"

"I already told you that."

"Why didn't you ask for a roster change?"

"It wasn't that bad! He fetched and carried OK."

"How many days ahead were the rosters fixed?"

"A week. This was regarded as a big job."

"He brought the rifle up to the gantry in an equipment bag?"

"That's what they say."

"You decide what equipment you want?"

"Of course."

"What was it supposed to be?"

"Spare tripod stand."

"You didn't check it?"

"I told you, he did the job OK. You told him what you wanted and he did it."

"So that's what happened? You told him what you needed and left him to get it ready?"

"Yes. Nothing wrong with that!" The belligerence was back.

"Nothing wrong at all," agreed Charlie, quickly. "How many trips did he need, to get everything up?"

"Two. He took the camera and mount up first and put down a line to gather up the leads. Then went back for the rest of the stuff."

"What about security checks?"

The man shook his head. "We had our identity discs, of course.

But we arrived in an NTV van. The security people saw us: knew who we were."

Charlie sighed. "He would have got the rifle up on the second trip?"

"Yes."

"What did he have to do, when you were filming?"

"Keep out of my way until I asked for something."

"Tell me what happened, from the time you heard the cavalcade was coming."

"Got the warning from the scanner . . . from other cameras along the route . . . Picked the cars up as soon as they crossed the Kalininskij bridge on to Krasnopresnenskaja nabereznaja. Tracked them all the way to the White House. Refocused, for the tight shots, as they got out of the car. Saw the president go. The blood splashes. Then the fucker went into me. That's when I saw the gun. He was bringing it towards me, I thought, so I grabbed at it . . ."

"I saw the fight," broke in Charlie. "What did he say, when you were fighting. You were saying things, both of you? I saw you!"

"I don't remember, not properly . . ." Sakov cupped a hand to each ear. "I still had the cans on at first, to the scanner. Then they got knocked off. We were swearing. Calling each other cunts. I think I said what the fuck was he doing and he said it was right. That he had to. He said he'd kill me, to get me out of the way. Tried to turn the gun. I couldn't hear much when the helicopter came over, only to get away from him but I couldn't. When I tried, he started to turn the gun."

"How many shots did you hear?"

"None." He cupped his hands to his ears again. "I told you I had earphones on, to the scanner."

"Did you know Georgi was trained as a sniper, in the army?"

Sakov snorted, disbelievingly. "No."

"Did he ever talk to you about himself . . . about the army . . . what he did in his spare time . . . ?"

Sakov shook his head. "Didn't even know his father was a spy until I read it in the papers."

Bendall would have absorbed the language from the age of four, remembered Charlie. "What about politically. Did he talk about hat-ing the new regime . . . the Americans . . . anything particular?"

"No."

"Why do you think he did it?"

"Because he's fucking mad . . . useless."

Mad maybe, thought Charlie. But not useless.

"Is it a long way away?"

Not by Russian distances but Sasha would probably think it was. "Yes. A long way," said Charlie.

"Do you have to go by aeroplane?"

"Yes."

"Will you be gone a long time?"

"No more than two days."

"Will you bring me back a present?"

"Sasha!" corrected Natalia, sharply.

"Maybe if you're good," said Charlie. There was a tightness about Natalia but they hadn't had chance to talk yet. "And being good is going to bed."

"It's not time yet," protested the child.

"It will be when you've finished your milk and cleaned your teeth."

"Not fair," pouted the girl.

"Bed," insisted Charlie. "I'll be back by the weekend. We'll do something. You choose."

"The circus!"

"The circus," agreed Charlie.

Charlie had drinks ready—his Islay malt, her Volnay—when Natalia returned from Sasha's bedroom.

She said, "You spoil her."

"That's what fathers are supposed to do."

Natalia didn't smile. "Don't buy her anything expensive."

"What would you like?"

"Nothing."

"What's tonight's problem?"

Natalia's disclosure of a presidential commission was hurried, disjointed, but Charlie let her talk herself out. "I'm being dragged in, deeper and deeper. We'll be discovered, you and I," she concluded.

Charlie regarded her for a moment in total bewilderment. "Natalia! It's a commission into how—and why—things disappeared from old KGB archives! How can that extend to us! You cleared all the records of anything to do with us."

"It's possible."

"It's not!" She could make monsters from every shadow; sometimes from no shadows at all.

"It's a risk!" she persisted.

"It's not."

"I'm more in the middle—more the object of everyone's attention—than we ever anticipated. I'll be seen an an enemy of the KGB successors."

"Nothing's changed!" Charlie insisted. But it had, he thought.

"What have you been called back to London for?"

"People wanting to appear to be doing something. It's called consultation." He paused. "Do you wish it was for something more permanent?"

"No," denied Natalia.

Charlie didn't believe her. He'd been wise not to tell her that Anne Abbott was being recalled with him.

"I didn't expect things to end like this," said Olga. That wasn't true. By the time they'd got to the brandy—French at his insistence—they'd both known they were going to sleep together. There hadn't even been any conversation about it on their way to his apartment. What she hadn't expected was the dinner invitation—of course impossible to refuse—or that he'd choose the Mercator, which really did have to be the best French restaurant in Moscow. Most unexpected—and pleasurable—of all was how good he'd been once they'd gone to bed.

"Sorry?"

"Of course not." His body—and his performance—had been even more athletic that she'd fantasized about, looking down at him approaching the hospital earlier that day. She turned sideways, pleased that he'd kept the light on. "You?"

"Of course not. There's something I haven't told you, until now."

"What?"

"I played your interrogation tape at the Kremlin."

"To Okulov himself?"

"And Trishin. Their opinion was the same as mine, brilliant. But we decided we don't want you to question Bendall again until after the British."

"Why?"

"There might be something they're holding back we can use to break him."

"I can break him by myself."

"We'll do it this way," said Zenin.

He hadn't allowed her to take control in their lovemaking, either, but she hadn't minded that as much as she did this.

12

Charlie got the jump seat, which jammed his knees beneath his chin so tightly he couldn't have jumped anywhere, difficult anyway after the exertion of already shuttling between the British and American embassies to ensure they were completely up to date before their encounter with George Bendall. At least, Charlie consoled himself, he was opposite the slender-thighed Anne Abbott and not the fat-assed Richard Brooking. They travelled initially unspeaking, the lawyer and the diplomat exchanging transcripts of Olga's interrogation of Bendall and Charlie's meeting with the NTV cameraman. As Brooking finished Vladimir Sakov's account of the gantry struggle he looked uncomfortably to the woman, who'd read it first, and said, "Appalling language!"

"Dreadful," agreed Charlie. "Shouldn't be allowed."

Anne smiled at Charlie. "A lot of openings."

"We'll do it as we did with the mother."

"You lead," said Anne.

"We need to talk about that," interjected the head of chancellery.

"About what, exactly?" demanded Charlie. He didn't want the man buggering things up.

"This is not something I'm accustomed to," admitted Brooking. "In fact, I haven't ever done anything like it before."

"All good for the CV," said Charlie. "Better to let Anne and I handle it, though, don't you think?"

"I've the ranking authority!"

It was an embassy car, with the ambassador's chauffeur. Charlie was surprised the pompous prick hadn't insisted on flying the British pennant from the bonnet masthead. "What's the book say you've got to do." There'd be a guidance book. There always was.

"Ascertain the full facts. Establish the nationality is genuinely British, obtain the passport number if possible. Offer consular assistance. Obtain all United Kingdom residency details to advise next of kin. Make clear any repatriation advance is a loan that has to be repaid and get the applicant's signature to that agreement," quoted the man.

Anne covered her mouth with her hand and looked determinedly out of the window at the glued-together traffic.

Jesus! thought Charlie. "Let's work our way through all that. London's already established he's British, with a British registered birth, although he doesn't hold a British passport as such. There aren't any United Kingdom residency details and I don't think, whatever happens, we've got to think about repatriation. Agree with me so far?"

"Yes," said Brooking.

"Ascertaining all the facts is what Anne and I are here to do, right?"

"Right," accepted Brooking.

"So there we are!" said Charlie, triumphantly. "All you've got to do is offer the consular assistance, tell him Anne and I are it, and leave the rest to us."

"It doesn't sound much," said the man, doubtfully.

"It's your *being* there, as the ranking diplomatic representative, that's important," urged Charlie.

"Yes, of course." Brooking still sounded doubtful.

Charlie said, "It's all a great deal more uncertain—more complicated—than it seemed to be at first?"

"Yes," agreed Brooking.

"Everything's going to be recorded, that's part of the cooperation
agreement."

"I understand that."

"I'm not trying to teach you your job, of course—heaven for-
bid!—but on something that's going to be circulated around the
highest levels of the Russian and American government it might be
better if you waited to ask about anything that's not immediately
clear from our questioning, rather than putting it on tape at the
time."

"Quite! Good thinking." Brooking smiled, relieved. "All quite
straightforward really, isn't it?"

"The best way's always straightforward," sighed Charlie.

"My feelings exactly," said the man.

One of the several reasons for Charlie's early morning trip to the
centralized incident room had been to ensure with Olga Melnik their
acceptance at the Burdenko hospital. They were fifteen minutes
ahead of the agreed time but the first security check point was at
the ground floor reception. Brooking hurried into the lead, produc-
ing his Russian diplomatic credentials and standing vaguely to attention to be compared against an identification photograph that
Charlie had given Olga, and in the temporary separation Anne
squeezed Charlie's hand and whispered, "That's my dinner table
anecdote: you try to steal it, I'll serve an injunction."

Charlie said, "There'll be more."

Virtually as he spoke the protest erupted ahead of them—"I am
an accredited representative of Her Majesty's government, I must
not be physically touched!"—and Charlie turned to see Brooking
pushing away an attempted body search.

Softly, for only Anne to hear, Charlie said, "Oh fuck, what did
I tell you!" Louder Charlie said, "If there'd been that sort of security
five days ago, people wouldn't be dead and maimed and we wouldn't
be here."

More quietly Anne said, "It's still not diplomatically permissible."

The awareness seemed to be registering at the checkpoint. There was a huddled conversation and Brooking was ushered through, untouched. There was no attempt to body search either Charlie or Anne, although all their documentation—as well as their photographs—was compared and their briefcase contents examined. There was an insistence upon testing the tape recorder to confirm that's what it was. To get further into the hospital they had to pass through an airport-style electronic, metal-detecting frame.

When they caught up with him Brooking said, "That was outrageous! I'll file a protest!"

"What's the point?" pleaded Charlie. "They're doing their job!"

"Authority is the point."

"It might well be," acknowledged Charlie, with a meaning Brooking didn't comprehend. "There are times usefully to invoke it and there are times when you are going to fuck everything up, like now . . ."

"I don't think . . ." broke in Brooking, in fresh outrage, only to be interrupted in turn by Anne Abbott.

"I do, Richard! If this all degenerates any worse and I'm asked why, I'm going to have to say you weren't any help at all. In fact, that you got in the way. And we're having a row within the hearing of Russians one, if not more of whom, I am sure speaks very good English. I'd also expect there to be CCTV cameras, with sound, and for every moment of this totally unnecessary nonsense to be recorded. Which I deeply regret, as I'm sure Charlie regrets. I thought we'd talked about this, on the way here."

Brooking's face burst crimson. "I . . ." he started, then abruptly stopped, his eyes searching the vestibule and the corridors leading from it for the threatening cameras.

"My name is Badim," said a voice, behind Charlie. "Nicholai Iliach Badim. I am the surgeon-administrator. I can escort you, if you're ready?" He spoke English.

"And I am Guerguen Semonovich Agayan, psychiatrist-in-charge," said a second man. He spoke English, too.

"We're ready," said Charlie. Fucked up before we start, he thought. Then he thought, no *I'm* not. It was unsettling to realize he'd begun to think of himself as part of a team, although while he was in England it had obviously been necessary to designate the eagerly accepting Donald Morrison as the local British contact with the now supposedly centralized investigation and to duplicate all the Russian witness interviews. Perhaps, for once, there needed to be a team.

The photo-comparison and briefcase check was repeated outside the guard-blocked ward but there was no attempt at body searching.

"Strictly half an hour," said Badim. "We'll stay with you."

Brooking nodded in smiling agreement. Charlie thought how fortunate his earlier visit to the American embassy had been and said, "This is officially a British embassy interview, without the presence of any foreign nationals. We respect, of course, your medical restrictions. Which we'll observe. But you cannot remain with us. Everything that is said is being recorded and will be made available to your authorities."

Brooking made no move to speak.

Anne said, "That's international law, once you've agreed he's medically and mentally capable of being interviewed. Which you have."

Badim said, "I'll register a protest, as I did yesterday."

"So will I," threatened Agayan. "We'll be directly outside, from where we can see the patient."

"And we'll abide to your time stipulation," undertook Anne.

Charlie wished she hadn't, standing back for Anne and Brooking to go into the cramped room ahead of him. There were again four men inside, all of whom looked expressionlessly at them but made no move to leave. The gray-bandaged George Bendall lay gray faced on his gray bed, eyes closed.

Charlie said, "We'll be half an hour."

A surprisingly slight, bespectacled man said, "Our instructions are to remain at all times in the room with the prisoner."

Charlie saw the record light was rhythmically throbbing on the heavy, antiquated Russian equipment beside the bed. "We want you to go."

"We have our orders."

Charlie moved to the dirt-fissured window to get a better signal on his cell phone and dialled the direct line into the American embassy incident room. Olga was very quickly on the line. Charlie said, "I'll put you on to your people," and passed the telephone to the clerk-like man, who listened without responding until the very end, when he said, "I understand." He handed the telephone back to Charlie as he stood and still not speaking led the other Russians from the room.

Charlie was careful to place their recorder on a table on the opposite side of the bed to the still operating Russian machine, to avoid conflicting disturbance, gesturing Anne to the solitary chair vacated by the Russian recordist. There were two other chairs waiting at the door by the time he went to fetch them. Both Badim and Agayan lurked in the corridor. Charlie accorded Brooking the seat closest to the eyes-tight man, depressed the start button of their machine and nodded for the diplomat to open the encounter.

It was several moments before Brooking did so, not initially anticipating the invitation. He stumbled, several times calling Bendall by name in the hope of waking him. He looked sideways in confusion when the bandaged man remained with his eyes closed. Charlie made rotating movements with his hands for Brooking to continue, which the diplomat awkwardly did although limiting his contribution to setting out the consular representation. By the time he'd finished Brooking was visibly sweating and his starched, cut-away collar had garrotted an unbroken red line around his nervous throat.

"Do you understand everything I've said, Mr. Bendall?" concluded Brooking.

The feigned sleep continued. Brooking looked helplessly at Charlie and Anne.

Charlie said, "Vladimir Petrovich Sakov calls you a fucking idiot. Useless with it." Although Charlie was concentrating intently upon the man in the tunnelled bed he was aware of Brooking's wince. Bendall's eyes remained steadfastly closed. Thirty minutes, remembered Charlie. "Vasili Gregorevich wouldn't have said that, would he?"

There was a lid flicker, a stirring.

"You think Vasili Gregorevich died in an accident? I don't. I think he was killed, probably by the same people who murdered your mother." Olga Melnick should easily be able to recover all the details of the Timiryazev railways crossing crash by the afternoon. Hopefully with all the other officially tracable queries he'd raised earlier that morning. Charlie was aware of Anne's uncertain frown across the raised bed covering.

Bendall's eyes opened. At once Charlie said for the benefit of the tape, "George Bendall—Georgi Gugin—appears to have recovered consciousness," and nudged Brooking into a repetition of the consular guarantee. Brooking reacted as if he were waking up too, but echoed virtually verbatim what he'd earlier registered on tape. Anne Abbott picked up the moment he finished, identifying herself as a lawyer there to formulate a defense, which would have to be presented in court by a Russian attorney.

"I don't want any help from the British embassy. From the United Kingdom," announced Bendall. His voice wasn't as weak as it had been on the previous day's tape to which Charlie had listened.

"Why are you going down for everyone else?" demanded Charlie, ignoring Anne's fresh look of concern at what amounted to their dismissal by the man.

"No one else."

"When did you get together?" asked Charlie. "It was the army, wasn't it?"

Bendall began to hum, very softly, a tuneless wailing dirge that reminded Charlie of Middle Eastern music. Or Afghan, he reminded himself. "That where you met Vasili Gregorevich, in Afghanistan? Was he in the army with you?"

Bendall said something Charlie didn't hear, his head turned, but Anne did. "Brother?" she queried.

There were no brothers! thought Charlie.

It was Anne who carried it on, understanding. "Is that where you formed the brotherhood? Joined it in Afghanistan?"

There was a moment's more humming, then "Never knew."

"You must have laughed at the officers, their not knowing?" said Charlie, taking Anne's lead. The army record was one of drunken loutishness. It didn't fit.

Bendall didn't reply but he sniggered.

"You sure they didn't know?" pressed Charlie. "You got punished a lot."

"Didn't understand."

"What didn't they understand, Georgi?" He didn't like his English name, Charlie remembered.

"Didn't understand."

"Were you tricking them in the army . . . pretending . . . ?" suggested Anne.

"Didn't know."

"That was clever," said Anne, persuasively. "Good to stay together afterwards, too, when you left the army."

"Meeting old friends . . . old comrades . . . every Tuesday and Thursday?" added Charlie. He was conscious of Brooking frowning in bewilderment between himself and Anne.

"Comrades," said Bendall.

"Not at first, though," prompted Charlie, recalling Vera Bendall's account. "You didn't meet up with them at first when you left the army, did you?"

The wailing hum rose and fell.

"Was that your song, what you sang when you were all together?" asked Anne.

It stopped, abruptly.

"Tell us the words, Georgi? It does have words, doesn't it?" Fifteen minutes left, Charlie saw. He checked that their recorder was revolving smoothly.

"No one knows."

No one knows what? thought Charlie, desperately. "Secret, like the brotherhood?" he guessed.

Bendall smiled. "Special."

"You were, weren't you Georgi?" said Anne. "A special person in a special group . . . special, secret group that noone knew about."

"Shan't tell you."

"Did you swear an oath, Georgi?" asked Charlie. "Promise to be loyal to each other . . . protect each other?"

Bendall smiled but didn't speak.

He said that it was right. That he had to, remembered Charlie. Bendall's words when he was struggling for possession of the gun, according to Vladimir Sakov. "Was that what you were doing when you shot at the president, protecting the brotherhood?"

Bendall's face clouded. "Had to."

"Why did you have to?" pressed Anne. "What was the president going to do to hurt you and your friends?"

"I knew."

"Tell us what you knew," urged Anne.

"Right to do it."

Even the same words, isolated Charlie. "Who told you that?"

"Someone who helped."

"*Who* helped you?"

"Friend."

"How many shots did you fire?" Another of Charlie's reasons for going first to the U.S. embassy had been to discover how many cartridges had remained in the rifle's ten-round magazine when it had been recovered, an obvious questions he was irritated at himself for not finding out earlier that it had been empty when it had been picked up after the fall.

"All of them." The man's eyes were becoming heavy.

"How many's that?"

"Two."

"Only two?"

"Special bullets. All they had."

"Who's 'they' Georgi?" came in Anne.

"Special," said the man again.

He wasn't referring to the cartridges, Charlie decided. "They'll be very proud of you."

"Yes."

"Are you proud of them, to be one of the brotherhood?" asked Anne.

The smile was of a satisfied, proud man. He didn't speak.

Brooking was sitting back in his chair, legs extended full length in front of him, mind obviously elsewhere. Probably up his ass, thought Charlie.

"It's good to belong to something: a proper—special—family, isn't it?" coaxed Charlie.

The eyes closed, didn't open.

"Georgi!" said Charlie, sharply. "Who are we? Why are we here?"

The eyes flickered open, although slowly. "Not going to tell you anything."

"If I'm going to help defend you, you've got to tell me things I have to know," said Anne, urgently.

"Too tired."

"There's a lot more time, as much time as you need," said Anne. "All we need. We'll come back again. For as long as it takes."

Charlie didn't totally believe Bendall was too tired to go on, but there was no way—no time because he was already aware of the doctors at the door—it could be challenged. Nor should it be. Over a life-time which seemed to begin when people had dinosaurs for pets Charlie believed he'd perfected an untrained ability to out-psychologize most psychologists. And the amateur Freudian diagnosis—even with the essential Freudian sexuality—encompassed wombs, although not physical ones, family dysfunction and surrogates, with generous outlets for mentally disturbed violence and an already beer-hall tested philosophy of foot-stamping marching songs and a lot of alcohol. Bendall had performed as much as he intended. And had unquestionably given away more than he wanted or imagined he had. It was important to leave Bendall thinking he'd controlled the encounter but with an eroding worm of doubt. "After you did it, how were they going to get you away, get you back safely among them?"

There was no obvious physical reaction but Charlie was sure Bendall wasn't asleep and had heard him.

"Thank you, for being properly considerate," said the waiting Badim, when they emerged. "I don't after all think there's anything officially to complain about."

"This is probably the first of several sessions," said Charlie. "One visit obviously isn't enough."

"I suppose not," said Agayan, walking with them back through the cluttered corridors.

"You typed his blood when he was admitted, of course?"

"Of course," confirmed Badim. "He needed transfusions. It's AB."

"Were there any other tests?"

Badim's head came around sharply. "The only concern was to find the right blood group, for a safe transfusion."

"You've still got some of the sample?"

"Yes?"

"Could we have some, now?"

Badim stopped. "Why?"

"We want to test for alcohol." That was sufficient for the man to know, thought Charlie.

"It could be tested here."

"And I'd appreciate a copy of those tests, just as I'm sure you'd like to know the result of our analysis. Which I'll guarantee, for comparison."

"I'm not sure I'm authorized."

"It's a medical request. I understood you to be the surgeon-administrator, the responsible authority?"

"I am!" said the easily offended man.

"A sample wouldn't need any specific control. We could wait," said Charlie, wanting to stop short of the heavily guarded vestibule. "And you know our authority is from the Kremlin."

For several moments the man hovered, uncertainly. Then he gestured them into a room about two meters further along the corridor which they were never to know was from where Olga Melnik had the previous day gazed down upon the approach of her new lover. Agayan walked away with the other Russian.

Immediately inside Brooking said, "This has all been absurd, a total waste of time. The man is obviously mentally unwell. That will have to be the plea!"

"Obviously," agreed Charlie. There was no way it could have been anticipated they'd be in this room so it wouldn't be wired or cameraed but he still looked intently around.

Ignoring the diplomat, Anne said, "I told you we were a good team, didn't I?"

"And I agreed," reminded Charlie.

"What do you mean?" demanded Brooking.

"Just technical stuff," said Charlie.

"I want a copy of that tape, to take with us to London," said the lawyer. "It probably won't be admissable in court but I want a psychiatric assessment."

"So do I," said Charlie.

"It's much less of an embarrassment to the government if he's certifiably insane, someone not mentally responsible for his actions," offered Brooking. "That and the fact that he *has* lived here for twenty-six years."

Charlie had to force himself to talk to the man. "Luck all the way along the line."

Mikhail Badim reentered the room alone carrying a phial in his outstretched hand. "We're testing for alcohol, too."

"A comparison is essential, for an empirical result," accepted Charlie. He was contributing more towards a mitigating defense than to the continuing investigation, but then that was the primary purpose of today's interview.

In the car on the way back to the embassy Anne said to the diplomat, "Do you feel there's any reason for you to come with us, for the next meeting?"

"Not at all," said Brooking, hurriedly. "I think I fulfilled everything I had to do in today's visit. I thought it all went very well, despite the unfortunate fellow's obvious madness."

"Very well indeed," echoed Charlie.

Walter Anandale ended the urging of both Wendall North and the secretary of state for a diplomatic compromise by rejecting their suggestions in preference to his own, which didn't include acting Russian president Aleksandr Okulov, and just as curtly ordered them to fix it.

Jeff Aston, the now unquestionably-obeyed head of presidential security, insisted they needed a highway-cleared, intersection-controlled route from the embassy to the hospital but gave the embassy as the return destination in the demand to the GIA traffic police. The Secret Service chief also insisted upon being in total media charge, once more restricting the still picture and television coverage of Anandale's meeting with the Russian leader to American White House cameramen. It also guaranteed his being in total control of their release, which was to be timed to give the impression that the American leader, his wife and entourage were still in Moscow when the intention was for them to be already high over the Atlantic, on their way to Washington.

The American president spent the first thirty minutes at the Pirogov hospital being reassured beyond the already promised reassurance from Admiral Donnington and a support group of Russian physicians that Ruth Anandale was sufficiently fit and recovered to be medevacced back to America. Only then did he go, completely encircled by agents and with the towering Aston by his side to the other wing of the hospital where North and Aston had spent those same thirty minutes hurriedly arranging the photocall with the Russian president's protection squad.

Lev Maksimovich Yudkin was fully conscious, although still attached to drip-feeds and line-waving monitors—which made for fittingly dramatic pictures—but too weak for any conversation, which was not the intention anyway. Anandale was, however, posed as if they were in discussion as well as solicitously standing by the man's bedside. It only took fifteen minutes.

As they made their way back to the American-commandeered wing James Scamell said, "This is going to be interpreted as a snub to Okulov."

"Fix it with the statement we're going to issue," demanded Anandale. "Abrupt departure for urgent medical treatment for the First Lady . . . no time for official farewells apart from seeing the president whose recovery we're delighted about . . ." He looked sideways at the secretary of state. "And your staying here—plus the unattributable briefings you'll give—establishes that everything's still on track."

"You know what we've just shown by being allowed in like that?" demanded Aston, rhetorically. "That Russian security is godamned awful and that they haven't learned a thing. Even you, Mr. President, shouldn't have been allowed in. I wouldn't have permitted it, if the situation had been reversed."

Unseen, behind the president's back, Wendall North gave the Secret Service chief the stiff middle finger.

In his wife's room Anandale said, "We're going home."

"To get my arm fixed?" said the woman.

"To get your arm fixed," agreed Anandale.

Olga Melnik had already heard the Russian tape but went through the pretense of reading the transcript Charlie took back to the embassy incident room, together with his original recording to become part of the evidence collection. While she did—with John Kayley in his room absorbing it for the first time—Charlie studied the autopsy report on Vera Bendall.

He skipped the normal medical introduction, although noting that the woman was described as generally under-nourished, eager for the specific findings. The cricord cartilage of the larynx had been crushed but the odontoid peg of the second cervical vertabrae was intact, which it would not have been if she had succeeded in properly hanging herself. There were three lesions in the neck caused by the support metal breaking through the left bra cup. There was pre-death bruising to her shoulder blades and to the back of the head, which the pathologist attributed to the back of her body hitting the cell door, presumably in her death throes or in the agony of strangulation. No photographs had been taken of the body before it was removed but according to the prison guards' reports the woman had been virtually in a sitting position, with her back against the door. There were mortuary photographs of the body, naked, showing strangulation bruising completely encircling the neck. There was bruising on the finger endings of both hands which the medical examiner suggested were caused by the woman's instinctive efforts to loosen the ligature in the final moments before death. The pathologist described as lividity the discoloration to Vera Bendall's knees and thigh and to both buttocks, all of which was clearly visible on other post mortem photographs. In the opinion of the Russian pathologist the medical evidence was as consistent with a choking person's failed, last minute change of mind when an attempted suicide hanging went wrong as it was with any suggestion of foul play, which made it too inconclusive for either definitive finding.

"But not for me," declared Charlie, carrying the report out into the larger room as Kayley and Olga emerged from theirs.

"I think I hear you," welcomed Kayley.

"And I've heard John's opinion," continued Olga.

There was an inherent moment of reluctance, not actually at sharing but at the worry of not knowing how it would be interpreted and acted upon by people whose minds worked so much differently from his. This was a static evaluation of something that had to be carried on, Charlie reminded himself. Which Kayley had obviously already decided. "As the pathologist remarks, there unfortunately aren't any photographs of Vera Bendall in the position in which she actually died. Three guards—and the prison doctor—have sworn statements that she choked herself, by twisting her bra around her throat, attaching it to the cell's protruding locking mechanism and then dropping in the expectation of breaking her neck. Which wasn't ever possible. We know the precise measurements of the lock, from the ground, is only a meter. Her neck didn't break, couldn't have broken. She was suspended—according to what the guards' evidence suggest—with her legs and buttocks virtually against the ground, slowly to suffocate . . ."

"Which is what the pathologist describes," broke in Olga, playing Devil's Advocate.

"There are too many things that don't click together," came back Charlie. "Lividity is *after* death bruising, when the blood puddles at the lowest possible point in the body, where it's no longer being pumped because the heart's stopped. Medically—provably—Vera Bendall has blood puddling in both knees *and* both buttocks. She can't have died in two positions. She either died on her knees. Or on her back, which accounts for the much more substantial blood collection in her buttocks . . ." Charlie offered the series of mortuary photographs showing the continuous, unbroken pre-death bruising around Vera Bendall's throat. "That marking isn't possible if she half-suspended herself, with her back against the door and her calves and buttocks against the ground. The strangulation line would have been continuous in the front but not at the back: her weight would have kept the ligature *away* from the nape of her neck, leaving it unmarked. Vera Bendall was choked to death from behind, on her knees, her neck totally encircled *from* behind until she died. The bruising to her head and shoulders came from her struggling against the knees, pressed hard up against her, of her killer like the bruising to her fingers came from trying to prise the ligature away. She was held like that, throttled on her knees, long enough for the blood to begin to puddle in the front. Which it did even more obviously in these pictures when she was turned on to her back and the bra attached to the door lock."

Olga turned to Kayley. The American said, "I didn't get the total neck encirclement. It makes it even stronger."

"I want to take all the autopsy material back to England, get independent pathology opinions," said Charlie, talking to the American. "You doing the same?"

Kayley nodded, lighting one of his aromatic cigars. "You want to tell us about England?"

Charlie wasn't aware of any air extractors in the main room, feeling the passive fumes at the back of his throat. "Consultation, with my directorate. Bullshit bureaucracy. The usual stuff. You're both set up here: no need. I'm not."

There was obvious disbelief on the faces of both Olga Melnik and John Kayley. Charlie humped his shoulders, exaggeratedly. "That's all it is. There isn't anything more." He was glad of the precaution of taking his packed case to Protocnyj Pereulok that morning: he had hoped to go back to Lesnaya to say goodbye again to Natalia and Sasha but this was taking longer than he expected.

The American matched Charlie's shrug, exhaling a wobbling smoke ring at the same time. "If you say so, Charlie."

"I say so." Why the fuck didn't anyone believe him when he was actually *being* honest!

Kayley made a flag of the transcript Charlie had just delivered. "You sure as hell got under his skin."

"Opened some doors, maybe," allowed Charlie. To Olga he said, "Is there anything on the Isakov death at Timiryazev?"

"Accepted—until now—as an accident," replied the woman. "All I've been able to get so far is the basic militia report. It's an ungated crossing. His car stalled, straddling the line. Hit by the Kalininin express so hard it virtually broke in half . . ."

"Autopsy?" interrupted Charlie.

Olga shook her head. "And of course he's been buried. I'll apply for his exhumation."

"What about a military record?"

"The detailed request has gone to the Ministry of Defense."

"And an organization . . . a brotherhood . . . ?" pressed Charlie. He'd definitely run out of time to get back to Lesnaya.

"That too, as soon as we find, if we can find, whatever service Vasili Isakov was in."

"I bumped into a lot of your guys checking vantage points for the second gunman?" Charlie told Kayley. "There were more of them than me so I left them to it."

"Four possible high rises, the tallest the Comecon building," recounted Kayley, wearily. "They even checked the Ukraina Hotel across the river. Between the most obvious buildings there's a total of forty-two positions, eight more if you want to include the almost impossible hanging-out-of-the-window points. No one heard anything, saw anything, although most were looking from their windows at the presidential arrival. No shell casings found by my guys or handed in, before they asked. Two more high rises that could conceivably have been used. They're being checked because everything's being checked."

It was like climbing Everest backwards, wearing skis, thought Charlie, who'd never dreamed of risking his feet in such contraptions. "I'll only be away two days, tops. Donald Morrison's taking over."

"I want to see Bendall for myself," announced Kayley. "It's the murder of an American that's going to be the major charge. You've had your consular access."

"He's Russia's prisoner," said Charlie.

"But you're no official problem?"

Charlie supposed he should have checked legally with Anne Abbott. Richard Brooking never came into his thinking. "None at all."

Kayley said, "Thanks for that at least."

Charlie let it go. "Luck with the interview." He already knew how he would pursue the next meeting with Bendall but had no intention of prompting the American. It was always possible John Kayley might nerve-touch something far more productive than what he'd so far achieved. It would be interesting—although hopefully not ultimately demoralizing—to see.

"I intended to get back, to say goodbye, but we over-ran."

"OK." There even seemed to be a distance in the sound of her voice on the telephone.

"I think the Bendall interview is good. It's on file in the incident room, if you want to access it."

"OK."

"Any problems today?"

"No."

"I'll only be gone a couple of days."

"You said."

"Tell Sasha I love her."

"Remember what I said about a present."

"I love you."

"I love you, too."

"Keep safe."

On their way to Sheremet'yevo in the embassy car Anne Abbott said, "I'm back to thinking there's a dramatic defense."

"We're a long way from finding it."

"You sure the accountants will stand our staying at the Dorchester?"

"By the time they get the bill we'll have been and gone. They won't have any alternative."

"Do you go out of your way to upset people?"

"Do I upset you?"

"You make me laugh. And curious."

"You ever see Liberace perform?"

Anne exploded into laughter. "I only just know who Liberace *was*! What the hell are you talking about?"

"They've got his glass piano in the Dorchester bar. It's pure kitsch. You'll like it."

Charlie answered the car phone, on the central reservation beside the driver. Morrison said, "Moscow Radio has disclosed the second gunman. There's been an official Russian government enquiry; Brooking's going around in circles. Olga Melnik's been on, demanding to know if it was us. I told her we hadn't broken the agreement."

"Who did it?" asked Anne, when Charlie relayed the conversation.

"Something else on the long list of what we don't know," said Charlie.

"It worked letting the British have the second interview," declared Zenin.

"It was a good idea," agreed Olga.

It had been his idea for her to cook at his apartment that night and she was nervous because in this ridiculously short time it had become overwhelmingly important to go on impressing him, the unfamiliar need for which made her even more nervous. She'd chosen pasta with clams and mussels and squid—trying for the joke by insisting the Black Sea fish were a Crimean souvenir she'd collected from the hospital the previous day—and he'd seemed to think it funny as well as continuing the Italian theme with Chianti.

"The Englishman's very good. The woman, too."

"What did the Defense Ministry say?" asked Olga. The request for anything known about Vasili Gregorevich Isakov and brotherhoods had been made with Zenin's superior authority to ensure a matchingly authoritive response.

"That secret societies aren't permitted in any of the services. I told them that wasn't the question."

"What about my—our—interrogating Bendall again?"

"We'll see if giving the Americans as well as the English their turn is the good idea it's proved to be so far. The Americans can go ahead of us; we can use whatever they get, when we go again. Waiting will also give us time to hear back from the military. That's where the conspiracy is, what we've got to find."

"What about the second gunman leak?"

"It was anonymous. A telephone call."

"Which they reported without trying to check?"

"I've got people looking into it."

He leaned across the table, touching his glass to hers. "The pasta's wonderful. This is wonderful."

"I'm glad," she said, responding to both remarks.

"I haven't asked you yet if you're married?"

"I'm not," she said. She looked around the apartment. "I suppose your wife could be away, although speaking as a trained investigator there isn't any obvious evidence of anyone else living here."

"If there was one she could be away," Zenin agreed, smiling back. "But there isn't."

"I'm embarrassed now to have said that! Shit!"

"Don't be. I'm not."

Olga thought it couldn't be happening so soon, so quickly.

13

Charlie Muffin's tightly structured timetable—most specifically his intention to get back to Moscow in two days—began to unravel before his first appointment. That was scheduled for ten thirty. He was at Millbank before nine, to set up the various tests and analyses he wanted upon the material he'd brought with him. No longer with an office or any working facility within the building, everything had to go through Sir Rupert Dean's personal assistant, a dedicated spinster whose christian name remained unknown and who had long ago decreed she should be universally known and addressed simply by her surname—Spence—without the courtesy of Miss. He had to negotiate his way past two junior secretaries to get into her sanctum and having done so reflected—and passingly mourned—the transition from Roedean-accented, experimentally-eager debutantes with legs that went all the way up to their shoulders to unsmiling, business-like practicality from women whose legs looked as if they'd been carved from solid oak by a man with a blunt hatchet. Spence herself needed such support for a granite body formidable enough to have single-handedly repelled a Special Forces invasion of the director-general's office. The woman listened in intimidating silence to everything Charlie wanted—even asking to ensure he'd finished— before bluntly declaring it wasn't possible in two days. He should have known there were no laboratory resources in the headquarters building: the ballistics people worked from Woolwich Arsenal and she very much doubted psychiatrists and psychologists would drop everything to put him at the top of their lists. It took Charlie thirty wheedling minutes to persuade her personally to try to arrange the mental assessment from the tapes and their transcripts and to dispatch the ballistic and blood samples to their respective testing centres.

"It's still not possible," she insisted.

"I've heard everything's possible backed by your authority."

"And I've heard bullshit and how good you are shovelling it."

But she'd enjoyed it, Charlie decided. "I brought you a souvenir, to thank you in advance." Charlie took the joke *maestroika* set from his briefcase doll by doll, identifying each Russian leader depicted in succeeding order of leadership. Whose face would be the next in line, he wondered, reassembling the figures one inside the other.

The smile—finally—broke the professional shell in which she clearly existed within the building, illuminating a surprisingly young face. "Don't expect two days. But I'll try to get it done as quickly as I can."

Still with time to spare before the meeting with Sir Rupert and his advisors, Charlie took his time shuffling along nostalgically familiar corridors to the cafeteria in which he recognized no one and where no one recognized or acknowledged him in return. The coffee was as he remembered, like a long-term alcoholic's urine sample, and all the riverview tables were occupied. So were those in the middle section. Charlie found an empty, single-seated table near the clattering service entrance. One of its legs were uneven, so the coffee spilled the moment he put it down. Why nostalgia? he demanded. Familiarity perhaps—even to being shunted to the worst table in the room—but there shouldn't have been the smallest iota of remembered regret. So why was there? Why had he enjoyed the innocent flirtation of being with Anne Abbott in the Liberace-pianoed Dorchester bar the previous night and the cab ride through the flower dazzling Green Park and actually looked at and liked, for the first time, the hump-shouldered statue of Churchill glowering at the parliament buildings? *Just* remembrance: not nostalgia and certainly not regret. He never thought—reminisced—of any of this in Moscow. It was a freak of *deja vu* or something he couldn't find a better phrase to describe. He *had* enjoyed being with Anne Abbott the previous night. Not in any silly, dangerous way: not even flirtatious. They'd just made each other laugh and in his case he'd been able to say things, make jokes, without balancing every word for hidden, misunderstood or misconstrued meaning before uttering it. Relaxed, he thought, surprised. Despite the impending encounter and whatever it was in which he was professionally involved in Moscow, for this brief returning moment he felt relaxed. At ease. Would Natalia be feeling that, with his not being in Moscow? Unburdened; briefly, gratefully, unendangered?

When Charlie got back to the top, executive-level floor Spence said, "Everything's gone off and I've got calls in to those who can read our minds."

Charlie wished he had a mind reading facility. He said, "I knew you could make it work for me, Spence."

"I haven't, not yet. Everyone's waiting for you in the conference room."

It adjoined Sir Rupert Dean's office and was necessary for a full gathering. They were assembled at a long table, with the director-general in the center, their backs to the Thames. From where Charlie was directed to sit he could see the yellow and green, antenna-haired MI6 building on the other side of the river. It reminded him to call Donald Morrison sometime that day.

It was not Charlie's first encounter with the control group and Dean didn't bother with reintroductions. Instead he said, "We've kept ahead until now. So well done, so far. But now it's all changed. The only thing that isn't changed is our need to stay ahead."

"Which is why you've been withdrawn," announced Jocelyn Hamilton, brusquely eager. "We need to know the extent of the conspiracy: how much more deeply we might become involved."

His adversary, Charlie knew, from the past; there always seemed to be one. As he looked directly to the burly deputy director, Charlie caught the sharp, sideways look from Dean and thought, shot yourself in your stupid mouth, asshole. Charlie said: "I know what we need. At the moment I can't provide it."

"Then perhaps you need help, supervision even," seized Hamilton, at once.

"Perhaps what we all need is to hear what Charlie's got to tell us before we start offering suggestions," said Patrick Pacey, irritably.

An ally, Charlie recognized. He remained unspeaking, using the silence against his attacker until Dean came in, supporting him too.

"Let's hear that, Charlie. What is there to add to what you've already shipped back, which we've all seen?"

"I'm having our own ballisic confirmation, obviously, but it's already come from the Americans," said Charlie. "There were definitely two gunmen and it was the second one who hit the Russian president and Ruth Anandale. I believe Vera Bendall was murdered, inside Lefortovo. I'm hoping our pathologists will agree with me on that: the Russian autopsy verdict is that the evidence is inconclusive . . ."

". . . Why would she have been killed?" broke in Jeremy Simpson, the group's legal advisor. "The statements you've given us don't read as if she knew anything?"

"I don't have answers for most of the questions you're going to ask," admitted Charlie, reluctantly. "Maybe she did know something but didn't realize it, had to be silenced before it emerged."

"Maybe she *did* know, was part of the conspiracy but hadn't expected to be put in jail. Committed suicide because she couldn't withstand the interrogation?" said Hamilton.

"Which would be the worst imaginable scenario," unnecessarily reminded the permanently red-faced political officer. "Assassin son of a British defector is bad enough: assassin son with British defector's wife as an accomplice is appalling."

Charlie shook his head. "Vera Bendall was neither clever nor strong enough to have been actively involved or included. What she knew—if anything—she knew accidentally. Or was killed for an entirely different reason."

"Prove it, any of it!" demanded the deputy director-general.

"I can't," said Charlie. This wasn't how he'd expected it to be. He was appearing to have reached far too many conclusions upon far too little evidence.

"If Vera Bendall *was* murdered the conspiracy has in some way to involve disaffected factions among highly placed Russians with access to Lefortovo," said Sir Rupert Dean.

"Which points to the FSB, formerly—or alias, even—the KGB, whose files have disappeared," completed Charlie. He added, "An intelligence service, irrespective of whatever its name is now, that was in the forefront of the 1991 coup against change."

"We're going around and around in unresolved circles!" protested Hamilton.

"Maybe that's the intention," suggested Charlie. Another "maybe" he recognized, uncomfortably.

Hamilton sighed. "Off we skip down another yellow brick road! I can't wait to hear this theory!"

In Charlie's mind everything made sense: was supported by known, established facts. But as he paraded them—analyzed them—in his mind he stumbled over too many maybes. "It's too clumsy. George Bendall is mentally unstable, possibly alcoholic. If the intention was to kill one—possibly two—presidents, no conspiracy group would trust George Bendall to carry it out. Or only allow him just two bullets to do it. Or put him in a position where it was inevitable that he would be seized. . . ." Charlie paused for breath, wondering if his parting question to Bendal—*how were they going to get you away?*—had properly registered with the man. There were various expressions on the faces of the men opposite him, none which Charlie judged receptive. Pressing on determinedly, he said, "It was the second gunman who put two bullets into Lev Yudkin. And hit the American First Lady, most likely in mistake for the American president. They didn't *need* George Bendall . . ."

"Except to be caught?" queried the bald, moustached Simpson, following Charlie's argument.

"Except to be caught," agreed Charlie.

"Why!" demanded Hamilton. "What for?"

"I don't know," Charlie was forced to admit. "To create a confusion, send everyone the wrong way."

"They've certainly succeeded here, if that was the intention!" jeered Hamilton.

Charlie didn't feel relaxed anymore. He felt exposed—wallowing—and he didn't like it.

"We've all read your hospital interview with the man," said the director-general, his spectacles moving back and forth between his hands like the preparation for a conjuring trick. "Give us your analysis of that."

"Again, I'm having it assessed by experts," assured Charlie, grateful for the escape. "But I think Bendall fits a mold. He comes from a totally dysfunctional family, hates everything and everyone. He'd got a predilection to violence, usually under the influence of drink. The army doesn't help him; appears—I repeat *appears*—to make it worse. But there seems to have been a group, a brotherhood to use his word, that admitted him. His first—only—acceptance. They had a song. If you've listened yet to the tape I sent, along with the transcript, you heard him humming it. You also heard—and read— him several times use the word 'special.' There were a lot of mentally questionable, often drunk, violence-inclined men in beerhalls in Munich from the 1920s onwards who had their own particular song and thought themselves part of a special, select brotherhood. . . ."

"I don't believe this . . ." broke in Hamilton, shaking his head in exaggerated incredulity.

Charlie wasn't sure that he did anymore. Before he could continue, Simpson said, "Do you think that's where the conspiracy is, among this so called brotherhood?"

"Yes. And I think I can establish it, in time," insisted Charlie. "It's a question I want to put to a psychiatrist or psychologist but I don't infer that first encounter with Bendall as obstructive, a refusal to talk. He thinks he's clever: there *is* often a deceptive cleverness in madness. I believe Bendall imagines he's playing with me, being cleverer than me, but that he *wants* to tell me about whoever or whatever it is he was a part of."

"I'm trying to work it out," mocked Hamilton. "Are we following the theories of Freud here? Or could it be Jung? Or there again could it be the teachings and crystal ball of Madam Maud, the clairvoyant in a gypsy tent at the bottom of a pier somewhere?"

Jocelyn Hamilton clearly wasn't aware of the profound Russian belief in clairvoyants and superstition, Charlie decided. Ignoring the ridicule, he said, "I'm hoping to get some sort of psychiatric or psychological report within twenty-four hours."

"We accept a conspiracy," conceded the director-general, slowly. "There's forensic proof, at least, of that. It succeeded in removing the Russian president from the political scene, possibly forever, if it didn't actually kill him. Hurt—in one instance killed—others. Why should a well organized group in any way involve someone as unstable as Bendall who, if you're right, will eventually expose them? It doesn't make sense."

"That's my point!" pleaded Charlie, only just avoiding the exasperation being obvious. "Not yet it doesn't make sense, far too little does. It might when the Russians trace Bendall's army medical records . . . find evidence of a special group in the units in which Bendall served. And there's a proper investigation into the death of the NTV cameraman Vasili Isakov."

"But then again, it might not," sneered Hamilton.

Every other face remained blank, unconvinced, and unimpressed. Patrick Pacey, whose function as political officer was to liaise with the Home Office and Downing Street, said, "I want a positive answer. Is there any possibility of another Briton being involved in this?"

"I can't give a positive answer," apologized Charlie. "I don't know."

"Is there any possibility of the mother being found to be involved?"

"I don't personally believe she was, but again I can't give a positive answer." Charlie couldn't remember any debriefing being as bad, as humiliating, as this.

There was an echoing silence.

The permanently red-faced political officer said, "There was an overnight Note from Sir Michael Parnell that the Russians are furious at the leak about a second gunman. That makes it an official diplomatic enquiry."

"I wanted it kept back as much as they did," said Charlie.

"So it didn't come from you?" persisted Hamilton.

"Of course it didn't!" said Charlie, careless of the indignation.

"What about from someone you're dealing with in Moscow, one of your sources?" asked Dean.

It was more of a strident klaxon than a warning bell that sounded in Charlie's mind. If there'd been a diplomatic enquiry it *was* official. And could easily become annexed to the presidential commission into the missing intelligence dossiers. "It would not have come from any of my sources."

"How good is liaison between you, the Americans and the Russians?" persisted Hamilton.

Would Donald Morrison have told MI6 across the river of being lied to, by the CIA's Burt Jordan? Charlie said, "Good enough, I think. Everything's fully computerized in the American incident room."

"Which means that anything one or the other—or both—doesn't want put on the computer isn't logged in the first place," dismissed Hamilton. "Have you been totally open, with whatever you've obtained independently?"

"Those were my instructions, from here," reminded Charlie.

"Which isn't the answer to my question," said Hamilton.

"Yes, I've shared everything." It was more or less true: the qualification came down to timing.

"If the leak didn't come from you—or any of your contacts—and it didn't come from the Russians, then the Americans must be the source," said Jeremy Simpson. "What's their benefit in doing that?"

"There isn't one, as far as I can see," said Charlie. When the hell was there going to be a question to which he did have an answer! Addressing Patrick Pacey, he said, "I'm surprised—perhaps even more curious—that so quickly there's been diplomatic traffic from Moscow about a criminal investigation, certainly about something that happened less than twenty-four hours ago. Aren't you?"

"Yes," agreed the political officer, reflectively. "What's your point?"

"Something along the lines of protesting too much."

"More convolution," sighed Hamilton.

"I think it's a valid observation," contradicted the director-general. "But the question remains, why? What's the Russian benefit?"

"There's going to be an investigation by a presidential commission into the missing KGB files," reminded Charlie, reminding himself in turn of the possible personal implications. "This could deflect some of the pressure on their successors, the FSB. A lot of whose senior officers—Dimitri Spassky most definitely—*are* former KGB."

"There's a logic there," agreed Dean.

"A rare commodity!" derided Hamilton.

"We need a lot more to move this discussion on," said the director-general.

"I could make some calls," offered Charlie. Donald Morrison would obviously be first—maybe even Brooking—but dare he risk telephoning Natalia?

"I think we'd benefit from a group discussion, too," said Hamilton, balefully.

Spence was waiting when Charlie emerged into the outer office. "Woolwich Arsenal say it'll take three days for the ballistic confirmation you want. They're miffed at being caught out on the acoustical assessment. And three days is the earliest for any psychological profile. The blood tests will be ready by tomorrow."

"What I can't take back with me will have to be sent in the diplomatic bag," said Charlie.

The formidable woman shook a permed head. "The psychologist didn't want to do it at all; called it working from a distance. He wants to see you to answer whatever questions he might have."

He wouldn't be back to take Sasha to the circus, Charlie realized.

"That was appalling!" pounced Jocelyn Hamilton, at once. "Muffin's clearly out of his depth, unable to handle this."

"He proved there was a second gunman," Simpson pointed out.

"It would have come out through ballistics," insisted the deputy director.

"But he suspected it first," said Simpson, equally insistent. "And he was the first to learn of Bendall's involvement."

"If we keep him on the investigation—which I personally don't think we should—Muffin needs to be supervised," argued Hamilton. "Somebody else definitely should be put in charge."

"That would look as if we believed he was the source of the second gunman disclosure," said Pacey.

"Are you sure he wasn't?" demanded Hamilton.

Sir Rupert Dean said, "I prefer Muffin's theory of it being an FSB leak. They're the only beneficiaries, although not by much."

"So do I," said Simpson.

"I propose that Muffin is taken off the case entirely," said Hamilton. "And that we send in better qualified investigators from here."

"What do you imagine someone from here could have achieved better than Charlie Muffin in just five days!" demanded Simpson. "We're not in fantasyland—your yellow brick road—we're in murderous reality, maybe even more murderous than we yet know."

"That's theatrical!" protested Hamilton.

"No!" refused Simpson. "It's what I called it, murderous reality. Charlie lives there, knows the place. Speaks the language. And as he's proved, has got useful contacts. Sending someone from here at this stage, cold, would be stupid."

"Quite apart from the reason I've already given, I see no purpose whatsoever in side-tracking Charlie Muffin, supervising him," agreed Pacey. "There's nothing to show Muffin isn't doing everything he should be doing. There's no *reason* to replace him."

"How many times did he say, in answer to anything he was asked, 'I don't know'?" demanded Hamilton.

"Probably not as many times as the Russians or the Americans with whom he's working," said Simpson.

"Aren't we losing sight of the fact that with the uncertainty that surrounds this department, we can't *afford* to take a chance with Charlie Muffin!" said Hamilton.

"It's a matter of opinion whether or not we're taking a chance," said the director-general, belatedly joining the exchange.

"I think I've expressed my opinion," said Hamilton.

"You've certainly done that," said Simpson. "I think we should leave things as they are."

"I'd like to get more guidance from the ambassador in Moscow," said Pacey. "This Russian Note has diplomatic implications."

"We'll give it twenty-four hours, to see what the guidance is from the ambassador and what Charlie gets from his calls to Moscow," decided Dean.

"And then?" pressed Hamilton.

"Then we'll talk again," said the director-general.

The spare room Spence found for him reminded Charlie of the cell he'd occupied for so many years when he'd been permanently attached to the Millbank building. It was at the rear, the one dirty window overlooking a clutter-filled courtyard and other dirty windows. But it had a reasonably dust-free desk and a chair and a secure telephone and Charlie was totally uninterested in anything else.

He reached Donald Morrison immediately. Richard Brooking was still spinning in circles, reported the MI6 officer. The head of chancellery was blaming Charlie personally for what he complained to be criminal intelligence wrongly crossing the boundaries into diplomacy: the ambassador had sought Foreign Office instruction how to respond to the Russian Note. Morrison had spoken personally to John Kayley, who insisted the leak had not come from any American source. Olga Melnik had reminded him it was she who had demanded the second gunman remain secret. They, too, were therefore blaming the leak on Britain and in particular upon Charlie. Morrison was slowly working his way through the witness re-interviews. So far there was nothing new although other colleagues at NTV described Bendall as a loner, with Isakov his only friend.

"Doesn't help your being there instead of here," said the younger man.

"You denied it, of course?"

"No one believes me." There was a pause. "It wasn't you, was it, Charlie?"

"Thanks a fucking lot!" It most certainly didn't help his being in London.

"You'd have asked the same question."

It was true, Charlie conceded. "What else?"

"Isakov's exhumation is scheduled for tomorrow. I'll go, as our representative."

There wasn't a lot of purpose but Charlie supposed it was necessary. "What about Bendall's medical records: psychiatric particularly?"

"Colonel Melnik says they haven't heard back from the Defense Ministry."

This was a wasted call, Charlie decided. "That it?"

"Brooking said he wanted to talk to you if you called."

That would be an even greater waste of time. "Don't tell him I called."

"You haven't told me what's happening back there?"

"Not enough," said Charlie.

"Anything more you want me to do?"

"Keep safe."

Charlie asked for—and got—John Kayley first when he telephoned the U.S. embassy incident room and at once initiated the conversation about the second gunman, arguing the only beneficiary could be the FSB.

"It's a possibility," allowed the American. The reluctance was palpable.

"A damned sight more likely than me—or you—doing it," insisted Charlie.

"You left out Olga," accused Kayley.

"What's she say?"

"That she was the one who insisted it be withheld."

A carosel of denials, thought Charlie. "What's new?"

"Technical guys came up with something," said Kayley. "Got hold of a complete TV film of the presidents and their ladies from the moment they got out of the Cadillac until Yudkin got hit. They slowed it, virtually frame by frame. At that degree of slow motion you can see that Ruth Anandale moved—instinctively I guess—as Yudkin was shot. That movement put her in front of Anandale himself. She took the bullet which would otherwise have hit the president. Killed him, maybe. It was just a fluke that it didn't."

"Who have you told?" anticipated Charlie.

"You. Olga. Washington, obviously."

As a leak test it was a pretty poor effort, Charlie decided. "When are you seeing Bendall?"

"Later today."

"I might be here longer than two days."

"You going to tell me what you're there for?"

"I already did."

"Yeah."

"I'd better speak to Olga."

Kayley brought her to his telephone rather than transferring the call. Charlie listened for the echo of the recording device but didn't detect it. He couldn't hear anything of Kayley in the background, either. Olga listened with matching, unspoken disbelief to his denial of the leak and to his FSB suggestion. Before he was halfway through Charlie asked himself why he was bothering and then abruptly realized there was an expanded question that should have occurred to him long before now. The awareness took away the pointlessness of establishing contact.

"Anyone Bendall knew—who might have been part of the group—failed to turn up at the television station?"

"No."

"Anything else?"

"You know of the exhumation?"

"Yes."

"What else were you expecting?"

"It was a general question," sighed Charlie.

"No, there's nothing else to tell you."

"I won't bother to repeat what I told John."

"No," the woman accepted.

The blinds were down and the lights were out, Charlie recognized. "What more do we know about Vasili Isakov?"

"I've got people on it. Nothing yet."

"I'll call again tomorrow. See how John's interview with Bendall went."

"Yes." The Russian put down the telephone without saying good-bye. When Charlie got back to the upper floor Spence said the interrupted meeting had been further postponed until the following day, although Sir Rupert was available if there was anything he should know from Charlie's contact with Moscow.

"There isn't," said Charlie, dejectedly.

Burt Jordan was with Kayley. So was the embassy lawyer, whose name was Modin and whose Jewish grandparents had fled from Kurybyshev to escape the Stalinist pogroms. On their way to the ward, after the security check, Nicholai Badim said that Bendall seemed greatly improved from the previous day and Guerguen Agayan agreed. Knowing of Charlie's earlier confrontation Kayley had insisted Olga phone ahead and the inner security guards left the room unasked. There were chairs already waiting. The tunnel support was still over Bendall's legs but the bed had been raised, propping the man up into a near sitting position. The lawyer identified the three of them more for the recording than for Bendall's information.

Kayley said, "Good to hear you're feeling better."

Bendall smiled but didn't reply.

Kayley took a pack of Kent cigarettes from a sagging jacket pocket and said, "You want a smoke?"

"I don't," said Bendall. The voice was far stronger than it had been on any previous recording.

"I won't then."

Jordan said, "Why'd you try to kill the American president, George?"

"My name is Georgi."

"Why'd you try to kill the American president, Georgi?"

"Reasons."

"What reasons?"

"Good reasons."

"We'd like to hear them," said Kayley.

"None of your business."

"It is, Georgi," said the FBI man. "The president's wife got hit but we think you really tried to kill him. That's what you did, didn't you? Aimed to kill the American president."

Bendall smiled again but didn't reply.

"You know you were set up?" said Jordan. "You were meant to get caught while the other guy got away."

"There was no one else."

"You only had two cartridges. There were five shots."

"Liar."

From his briefcase Kayley took a copy of that day's *Trud*, which led with the disclosure of the second gunman and held it up for the man to read. Bendall frowned but said nothing.

"Why are you frowning, Georgi," Jordan demanded. "Didn't you *know* there was a second shooter?"

"It's a fake," said the bandaged man.

Kayley swapped *Trud* for *Moskovskaya Pravda*, *Izvestiya* and *Nezavisimaya Gazeta*, all three dominated by the same coverage, and laid them out side by side on the bed in front of the man. "We'll have a television brought in. You can watch your own network. It's their lead story, too."

"Not true."

"They really made a fool out of you, didn't they?" said Jordan. "Jesus, how they must be laughing!"

"I don't want to talk to you anymore."

"Can't understand why you're taking the rap for people who set you up like this," said Kayley. "They're not doing anything to help you."

"Need to think."

"Let's think it through together," said Kayley.

Bendall began to hum the wailing dirge.

"That song got words?" asked Jordan.

The man hummed on, appearing oblivious of them.

"It'll help you if you tell us about the others," said Kayley.

"Comrades," said Bendall.

"Comrades who deserted you, cheated you," said Kayley.

"No! Go away!"

"Tell us what we want to know and we'll go away," said Jordan.

"GO AWAY!"

The roared demand was so unexpected that all three Americans actually jumped and there was a scuffed arrival of the two doctors at the door. Bendall screamed it again and tried to lash out at Jordan with his uninjured arm. He missed but swept the tape recorder off the bedside table, laughing when the cassette hood broke as it hit the floor. He threw his head back and shouted "GO AWAY" over and over again, breaking the words occasionally with a cackling laugh. He finally stopped shouting, exhausted, and when he did the hysterical laughter turned to tears. They streamed, unchecked, down his face and his nose ran, too.

Agayan hurried in from the doorway, pushing past the lawyer. "What did you do to him . . . ! Say to him?"

"We didn't do anything," said Kayley, defensively. "Just tried to get answers to some questions."

"Go away," mumbled Bendall, his voice a hoarse whisper.

"Yes, go away," agreed the psychiatrist. "This is bad."

Badim had his fingers at Bendall's wrist, checking his pulse. "Bad," he echoed.

In the car on their way back to the embassy Jordan said, "We hit a nerve."

"And maybe broke it," said Kayley.

"It's being overemphasized," insisted Charlie.

"For what reason?" demanded Natalia.

"To create precisely the situation that's arisen: to spread suspicion and distrust among us." The way to prevent any official curiosity about Natalia's dedicated Interior Ministry telephone number appearing on his hotel bill was to pay it—and then destroy it—himself. It would only represent a temporary out-of-pocket expense.

"So we're back to KGB—of FSB—disinformation?"

"Doesn't it fit better than anything else?"

Natalia didn't reply for several moments and when she did it wasn't an answer. "The leak's been added to the presidential enquiry remit."

"We'll be OK!"

"We'll be found out."

"I'm not able to get back as soon as I thought I would."

"How long?"

"Three, maybe four days."

"Don't call me direct again, like this. It could be traced."

"You haven't told me if there's anything new."

"Bendall had a mental collapse when he was with the Americans."

Why had she waited until now to tell him! Because her personal concerns were overwhelming her professionalism, he answered himself. Forcing the calmness, Charlie said, "He's all we've got!"

"We all know that."

"What do the psychiatrists say?"

"They haven't been able to talk to him properly yet."

"There'll be a tape. That's the system we're working with here."

"The transcript hasn't got up to my level yet."

"And you haven't got a prognosis, of his condition?"

"I told you, psychiatrists haven't been able to talk to him yet! Medically he seems OK."

"I'll call . . ." began Charlie but Natalia said, "I told you I don't want you to."

"I'll see you in a few days."

"Yes."

"Tell Sasha I'm sorry about the circus. We'll go next weekend."

"Yes," she said again, almost uninterestedly.

For several moments Charlie sat hunched on his hotel bed, reaction colliding with reaction. What the fuck had Little Big-Foot-in-the Mouth said to tip Bendall over the edge! More importantly, what was needed to pull him back? And at this moment he couldn't . . . Yes, he could. Kayley had told him about the intended meeting. Again Charlie got at once through to Donald Morrison.

"You heard how Kayley's meeting with Bendall went? He told me earlier it was to be this afternoon."

"Not a word."

"I'm having all the meetings analyzed, by people here. So I need not just a transcript but a copy tape. Can you chase Kayley up, get one shipped over in the diplomatic bag?"

"As quickly as I can," promised Morrison.

"If not quicker," encouraged Charlie. He actually thought it was the MI6 man coming back to him when his phone rang five minutes later.

Instead Anne Abbott said, "How's your day been?"

"You don't want to know about it," said Charlie, his mind not fully on the woman.

"I do, Charlie. I've got to know about everything, remember?"

14

Leonid Zenin insisted they personally confirm the extent of George Bendall's collapse by going to Burdenko hospital which Olga had intended to do anyway. She was irritated at not having initiated the suggestion ahead of the man it was becoming practically automatic—or did she regard it as essential?—to try to impress as much *out* as *in* bed. Among the ground floor and ward level security men there was a discernible foot-shuffling uncertainty that they were in some way going to be blamed which Zenin did nothing to allay by sweeping autocratically past both contingents, shaking his head against any verbal explanation from either group. The warned-in-advance Nicholai Badim and Guerguen Agayan were waiting outside Bendall's room.

"There's no purpose in going in," said Badim. "There's a room along the corridor . . ."

"We came here to see for ourselves," said Zenin.

"There's nothing to see! Do!" protested the doctor.

"Please open the door; let us in."

It wasn't a request and Olga felt a sexual flicker at the authority. She said, "There were some sounds, like scuffling, on our dedicated tape?"

"Your people got to the door before I did. I understand he was trying to hit one of the Americans . . . lashing out at them."

"You mean he was fighting them off?" asked Zenin, at once.

"No one was watching, even from outside," said the doctor. "He was wildly out of control by the time I got here. My impressions was that he was trying to hit—to hurt—the nearest person."

Zenin put himself closest to the deeply snoring, comatose man. "Difficult to believe someone as heavily bandaged as this would even think of trying to hit out at anyone."

"Think is the operative word," said Agayan. "Bendall wasn't *thinking*. He was reacting."

"To what?" demanded Olga. The tape was permanently revolving and she wanted to be featured on it as much as possible.

Agayan shook his head. "To something he didn't want to confront."

"By tomorrow I want to know what, in your considered, analytical opinion, went wrong today," insisted Zenin.

"That sort of opinion is not possible overnight."

"Do you really need reminding of the importance of this! Of everything connected with it!"

"Of course not!" protested Agayan, in matching indignation.

"Good!" said Zenin. The smile was a lip-withdrawn grimace. "So you'll know how essential it is to help us, in every way you can. And I look forward to getting that help by tomorrow. . . ." He looked to Badim. "What's wrong with him medically? Is he unconscious?"

"Deeply sedated. He had to be quietened."

Olga said, "Could he be rational again when he comes around?"

"I don't consider he's ever been totally rational," intruded Agayan, bringing both militia officers around to him at once.

"He's said things we've believed to be important, things we're trying to work on, work *out*," said Olga. "Are you telling us it could all well be fantasy!"

"Quite easily," said the psychiatrist. "He might well not even remember what he did."

"Every taped conversation indicates that he knows perfectly well what he did," rejected Zenin.

"In your judgment, perhaps." said Agayan. "Your judgment isn't necessarily mine."

A smile at the psychiatrist's refusal to be intimidated was flickering at the corners of Nicholai Badim's mouth. It was out-matched by another of Zenin's teeth-baring grimaces.

"I *knew* it wouldn't take you long to help with a diagnosis," said the militia commander.

"We can X-ray an arm, to find a break," patronized Agayan. "We can brain-scan a hemorrhage or a tumor, because they're physical manifestations; we can visually see the problem, on a screen. We can't photograph—visually *see*—mental illness. We can conduct outward observations and attempt verbal analysis and try to fit our conclusions into general and wide guidelines and every time we do it we know those guidelines are far too general and far too wide and that we could be wrong by a margin of one hundred percent. Precisely because I know the level and importance of what I'm being asked to do I don't want to be wrong by a margin of one hundred percent. That's why you're going to have to wait for my opinion of this man's mental condition and health. If you think anything he's said gives you something to follow up, follow it up. But don't expect it to materialize. If it does, you're lucky. If it doesn't, you've encountered the problem I meet every day of my life. The day you start solving a one hundred percent of all crime, I'll be hoping to reach a twenty-five percent success rate with my patients."

The only sound in the room was the sonorous rumble of George Bendall's drugged breathing.

Trying to come to the aid of her lover, Olga said, "When will you be able to give us a firm diagnosis?"

The man shrugged, shaking his head at the same time. "I don't know. I haven't been able to get past you people for a proper conversation yet."

"He said he understood me, when I charged him," remembered Olga.

"He might equally have said he knew how to land a space vehicle to the moon if you'd asked him," said Agayan.

"You both told me he was medically *and* mentally able to be interviewed; charged even!" Olga accused the two doctors.

It was the psychiatrist who continued to answer. "At the time we agreed that, we both considered he was. Today he suffered a mental collapse. Which proves everything I've tried to make clear to you, about reaching mental opinions."

"When will the sedation wear off?" asked Zenin.

"Sometime during the night," said Badim.

"What happens then?"

"We see how he behaves, how rational he appears to be, and then try to decide what else to do."

"Might he need to be further sedated?" pressed Olga.

"Quite possibly."

"Could he never properly recover to what until now we've believed to be a rational level of comprehension?" asked Zenin.

"Yes, that's possible too."

"For all our sakes, I hope you're wrong," said Zenin.

"You don't have to concern yourself about my career," said Agayan. "Only your own."

"We need a new—a better—psychiatrist," insisted Olga. She hadn't liked seeing Zenin so openly opposed.

The man shook his head, not looking at her across the car in which they were driving, again without discussion, back to his apartment. "This will go to trial, whether Bendall's got a mental condition or not. The caliber of every Russian witness will be important in front of an international audience. Agayan will look good in a witness box."

Olga's embarrassment became admiration. "I still think he's hiding behind psychiatric mumbo-jumbo. Bendall's understood what's been going on."

"I want you to talk very closely to Kayley, see if Bendall was trying to fight them off."

"From doing what?"

"Something being done to him physically."

Olga twisted in her seat to stare directly at Zenin. "You surely don't imagine . . . !"

"Kayley's FBI, a counter-intelligence agency, probably the other man, too. Maybe even the supposed lawyer," argued Zenin. "Scopolamine is a known part of their lie detection equipment, just like it is with our people. Pentothal too. In similar circumstances the FSB would use them: the KGB certainly did."

"We should have asked Badim to check for puncture wounds," said Olga, reflectively.

"What?" Now Zenin looked at her.

"Supposing the Americans did inject Bendall," suggested Olga. "The violence—the mental collapse even—might be the result of their drugs against whatever other medication he's on."

Zenin made the call from his apartment. Badim said he hadn't looked for injection marks on Bendall's free arm, which would now be punctured by the sedatives he'd had to administer to calm the man. There was one failed injection, which would have left two marks. Reluctantly he agreed to take a blood sample to test for any drug other than those recorded on Bendall's hospital log. Even more reluctantly he agreed there could possibly have been a violent reaction if Bendall had been given an unauthorized drug.

Zenin remained on the line for both security group leaders to be brought to the telephone. Each man insisted that the briefcases of the three Americans had been thoroughly examined but that their orders had been that no body searches could be carried out upon accredited diplomats. Those orders had been reemphasized after such a search was attempted upon the British embassy visitors.

"A prepared syringe would have been no more obtrusive than a pen," said Zenin, as he replaced the receiver.

An hour later Nicholai Badim called back, as instructed. There was what could be a puncture mark on Bendall's uninjured arm where no hospital doctor would have attempted an injection. Blood had been taken for tests that would take at least twenty-four hours.

"They'll deny it," said Olga.

"They won't be able to if we can prove he's been drugged," said Zenin.

"So!" demanded Anne. She'd chosen the Italian restaurant in Wilton Street because it had memories. Charlie hadn't asked. She hadn't offered.

"The British—which seems to come down to me—are being blamed for the leak. The ambassador or Brooking—probably both—have made it political. My people here don't see things the way I do: there's one trying to dig my burial pit. The scientists and professional experts can't break away from other things to do what I've asked. The psychiatrists or psychologists—Christ knows which or who—are demanding I stay, to answer their questions. Which means I can't get back to Moscow, where I need to be . . ." He couldn't tell her about George Bendall's collapse. There was no way he could officially know.

"That all?"

"That's all that comes instantly to mind," said Charlie, allowing the cynicism.

"So you're pissed off?"

"Thoroughly fucked off." He sipped the Barolo he'd ordered in preference to her Chianti suggestion, glad she'd conceded. "But curious." It had taken a long time coming, too long. But now the feet were throbbing and he was sifting the wind-strewn intrusions.

The lawyer sipped her own wine. "Curious about what?"

"The cleverness of it all," offered Charlie. "It never was about a mentally unstable man with a gun. We were *intended* to realize there was a second gunman. And believe we were uncovering other scraps . . ."

Anne frowned at him. "I'm not sure what you're telling me?"

Charlie's reply was delayed by the arrival of their food, guinea fowl for Anne, wine-cooked veal escalope for him. As the waiter left, Charlie said, "You ever personally experienced a sandstorm?"

Anne's frown remained. "No."

"You can't see where to put your feet, the direction in which to go."

"In which direction should we be going?"

"If I knew I'd take it." This wasn't any better than it had been at Millbank, earlier. At least Anne appeared to be taking him seriously.

"In which direction should I be going?"

"Which way have you been told to go?" asked Charlie.

"Mental instability, up to and including unfit to plead. I'm being kept back, too, for consultation with psychiatrists. Looks like you're stuck with me."

"Or you with me."

"I'm not complaining."

In which direction was *this* going? "Did the engagement become a marriage?" he finally asked, guessing the earlier reference to the restaurant's particular memories.

"Two years, four months and three days."

"Very specific?"

"Prison counting: scratching off the sentence on the cell wall."

Not his business—or his interest—Charlie decided, remaining silent.

"He wouldn't compromise his career—he was a lawyer, like me—and I wouldn't compromise mine. We met at week-ends but there were others in between that didn't really mean anything. After two years, four months and three days we realized that we didn't mean anything, either."

Almost precisely the time he'd been permanently in Moscow with Natalia, thought Charlie. At once he stopped the reflection, irritation burning through him, making him physically hot. There wasn't the slightest comparison! It was ridiculous even attempting—imagining—to make it. He and Natalia had to do something, though, to resolve their problems—real or otherwise—before they got any worse: before they ceased to mean anything to each other too, inconceivable though that was. Perhaps it was personally a good thing the London visit was being extended, giving them both time and space to realize what it was like to be without each other, even for a short period. Straw-clutching, Charlie recognized, objectively. There'd been other short breaks since they'd been together—intervals longer than this one would probably be—so nothing was likely to be different when he got back. Weren't both of them allowing a self-deceit—an hypocrisy invoking Sasha as a bond—in prolonging their staying together?

"Have I said something awkward?"

"I'm sorry," apologized Charlie. "My mind went off at a tangent."

"I could practically see the cogs moving. Want to talk about it?"

"No!"

"Sorry!"

"No, I am," said Charlie. "That was rude."

"You're quite a mystery man at the embassy, you know?"

Charlie felt a stir of concern. "That's what I'm supposed to be."

"Story is that you've got an apartment in what used to be a royal palace?"

"A minor grand duke was supposed to have lived there before the revolution." He had to stop this: divert it.

"Is there such a thing as a *minor* grand duke!"

"It's diplomatically better for me to be physically separate from the embassy."

"Morrison doesn't live outside the compound."

"I'm officially recognized by the Russian government, like Kayley and the FBI. Morrison's accreditation is as a diplomat." It was getting threadbare.

Anne frowned. "You lost me on the logic of that. There doesn't seem to be any."

Charlie gestured for the waiter to clear their plates, needing the interruption. She shook her head against anything more and so did Charlie. He said, "Is this the Anne Abbott courtroom technique?"

"You offended?"

"No."

"What then?"

"Curious, at the interest." With luck the joking flirtation of the previous evening might just be the diversion.

She smiled. "I like to get to know as much as I can about people I work with, particularly when it's as close as we seem to be thrown together. *That's* an Anne Abbott technique."

"What you see is what you get," said Charlie, inwardly cringing at the B-movie dialogue.

"Now I'm curious. It'll be interesting to find out."

They walked back towards the Brompton Road along Beauchamp Place, pausing to window shop after Anne said she could use the extra time in London to restock her wardrobe, reminding Charlie he'd have a longer opportunity to buy Sasha's promised present. And something for Natalia, too, despite her insistence that she didn't want anything. Anne walked easily, familiarly, with her arm looped through his, pleasantly close. Natalia wasn't tactile like that: too long by herself, caring for herself, he guessed. Charlie halted determinedly at the main road, demanding a taxi. It was Anne who suggested the brandy nightcap, which became several. There were only stools at the bar, which brought them close together again. Charlie didn't try to move away. Neither did Anne.

She said, "I ever tell you my philosphy about sex?"

"No."

"It's the obvious—logical—progression of friendship."

"What about love?"

"That's different. That's letting things go too far."

"Very free spirited," said Charlie. With whom had she philoso-phied in Moscow? he wondered.

"I don't want any more brandy."

"OK."

"Do you?"

"No."

"Time to go to bed then?"

They stayed close together walking to the elevators and got a car to themselves and kissed and Charlie enjoyed the uncommitting, uninvolving excitement of it, shutting his mind to everything except the woman he was holding and who was holding him back without any resisting stiffness or over-her-shoulder hesitation. They went to his room because it was the nearest along the shared corridor but there was no first-time urgency, which heightened the pleasure. They undressed each other, savouring the unhurriedness of it and when Charlie was naked she held him at arm's length and giggled that he looked better without his clothes and his feet were a reve-lation all of their own and Charlie held Anne the same way and said he liked everything he saw, without any qualification. They led each other, matched each other, her preference, his preference and burst together and Charlie didn't allow himself the surprise that he was able to do it—all of it—so quickly again.

Anne said, "I won! The second time I had a multiple orgasm."

"That's a whole new definition of friendship," said Charlie, still breathing heavily.

"That's all it is though, ultimate friendship. No confusion."

"It'll be the only thing that isn't confusing so far," said Charlie.

"So it was meant for me?" said Walter Anandale. The White House showing of the slow motion TV film of the shooting had been de-layed until that night because of the time the president had spent at the conveniently close Walter Reed Army Medical Center on Washington's Georgia Avenue, to which Ruth Anandale had been immediately admitted. Secretary of State James Scamell was the only cabinet member absent from the meeting.

"I don't think there can be any doubt, sir," said Wendall North.

"She took my bullet," said Anandale, more to himself than anyone else in the room.

Wendall North decided against pointing out that the intercession had been totally accidental. "Yes, sir, she did."

"Wouldn't that have been a hell of a coup, wiping out both presidents at the same time!"

"Unthinkable," said Defense Secretary Wilfred Pinkton.

"We any closer to understanding it?"

FBI Director Paul Smith shifted uncomfortably at the anticipated question. "We're running the investigation, just like you ordered, Mr. President. The incident room's ours, totally under *our* supervision at *our* embassy. Bendall had some kind of relapse when Kayley was interrogating him today. Everything had to be suspended."

"That isn't an answer to my question!"

"We don't so far know who else is in the conspiracy."

"I want ass kicked, Paul. I want each and every son of a bitch involved in this either in the chair or behind bars for the next hundred years and I'm disappointed you're not telling me you're there already. You tell Kayley from me I don't care how it's done. Just do it!"

It was three A.M. Moscow time when Paul Smith's e-mail, couched in even stronger terms, was taken by the director's personal assistant to the communication section of the FBI's Pennsylvania Avenue headquarters.

"Ass-burning time," the man told the transmissions operator. "Make sure it's not yours." The remark, only marginally misquoting the president, was intended as a joke. It didn't become one.

Two address lists had been defined in Microsft Outlook for the Russian investigation. "Kayley" was the back-channel, eyes-only route for information and messages restricted to the Bureau Rezident, not to be shared under any circumstances. "Kayley+" was the block address automatically distributing Washington traffic to Olga Melnik and Charlie Muffin, to maintain the impression of complete cooperation.

The FBI operator was new, being introduced into the job on the normally less stressful evening shift. It was the first personal director's message he'd ever handled and he agreed with the assistant that it was very much ass-burning. In his nervousness he clicked the cursor on Kayley+.

Paul Smith's do-whatever-it-takes instruction was waiting in Olga Melnik's e-mail box when she arrived in the incident room that morning, intentionally earlier than usual in her determination to confront John Kayley. Obeying Zenin's telephone instructions she called Donald Morrison before leaving the American embassy.

The time difference also benefited Charlie Muffin, in reverse. It was still only seven in the morning, London time, when he got the call from Morrison. Charlie awakened instantly and his interrupting questions finally awoke Anne Abbott beside him. Still sleepily voiced, she said, "What is it?"

"If I knew—understood it—I'd tell you," said Charlie.

15

Charlie Muffin's reception was very different from the previous day. Within minutes of his beginning to speak at the reconvened meeting even Jocelyn Hamilton straightened from his overly-theatrical, shoulder-slumped affectation and hunched as attentively as everyone to the tape of George Bendall's collapse. Charlie finished with the verbatim transcript of the FBI director's cable that Morrison had relayed that morning. No one spoke, unwilling to offer an opening opinion. It was the director-general who did, finally.

Sir Rupert Dean said, "No! They quite simply *wouldn't* have tried to drug him! It's inconceivable!"

"Kayley's under enormous pressure," said Charlie.

"I don't think it's inconceivable," said Patrick Pacey. " 'All and every investigatory means,' " he quoted, from the bureau director's misdirected e-mail. " 'Earlier and explicit orders . . . clear understandings from the highest level . . .' There's very obviously been instructions we don't know about that fits what could have happened in Burdenko hospital . . ."

"At the moment it's only an unidentified although possible puncture mark on Bendall's arm, which has no medical explanation or purpose to be there," cautioned Charlie. "There's no proof it was an unauthorized, invasive injection until they get the results of the blood tests."

"Where, legally, does that leave us—the United Kingdom?" asked the subdued deputy director.

Jeremy Simpson hunched uncertain shoulders. "Totally uninvolved, particularly with Charlie here in London, which probably turns out to be very fortunate. Going beyond that, if it's true, legally—technically—it constitutes a physical assault upon George Bendall. That's according to our law and as Bendall, again technically, is still a British subject I suppose there are grounds for us to protest. But I don't see any practical purpose in our doing that. I don't know what it qualifies as in Russia, even if there's any competent statute. But is that what we should be talking about? If the Americans have done this, it surely blows any honest cooperation—any cooperation honest or even limited—completely out of the water?"

"Absolutely," quickly agreed Hamilton, gratefully seizing the lawyer's lead.

"But it doesn't affect a legal prosecution for murder, does it?" argued the director-general, just as quickly.

"It might affect Bendall's ability—competence—to plead if the damage is permanent," said Simpson. "It could, possibly, be part of a defense plea in court."

That had been Anne's first reaction, as they lay side by side immediately after the telephone call from Donald Morrison in Moscow. Charlie decided against saying anything, despite the fact that Anne was known to be back in London for consultations.

"What's the Russian response?" asked Dean.

"I don't know, not yet," said Charlie. "Olga Melnik told Morrison she'd been withdrawn from the incident room—which means from the American embassy—for discussions. It wasn't clear with whom."

"What did you tell him to do?" asked Hamilton.

"To get to the incident room as quickly as possible. Find out everything he can. I'm calling him there later. If there's anything he doesn't want picked up on the American monitor, he'll go back to our embassy after we've initially talked and we'll speak on a secure line from there."

"The Americans are monitoring our calls!" demanded Hamilton.

Everyone in the room looked at the man in varying degrees of surprise. Charlie said, "Of course they are! I'd do the same, in their circumstances."

The deputy flushed and shook his head but said nothing more.

Pacey said, "Sir Michael Parnell's guidance from Moscow was that it was a serious diplomatic breach if it were proved we were responsible for the second gunman leak but that they'd been embarrassed as it is by the accusation. What's happened since diminishes the leak problem, I suppose, although that was public and this isn't."

"Yet," qualified Charlie, in another caution. "But what's happened now helps us. I wasn't responsible for the leak. So a denial would have been the truth. After today's developments—the FBI director's cable in particularly—the leak looks far more likely to have come from America."

"If Parnell wants to be told what to do, tell him to deny it in the strongest terms," said Dean, almost impatiently. "Which America will do about this injection business, of course. What's the chances of the Russians suspending their part in the supposed cooperation?"

Charlie accepted he'd be able to answer that better after he'd spoken to Natalia, which it was now essential he do, despite yesterday's insistence that he shouldn't. After a lifetime of professional truth paring, convenient deception and ingenuous, open-faced lying, Charlie didn't have the slightest doubt he could smother any guilt—certainly over a three thousand mile telephone link—but at that moment he was surprised, disappointed even, that there was no self-recrimination about the previous night's unfaithfulness. There hadn't been any awakening with Anne beside him that morning, either, and certainly she'd exemplified her own unique philosophy, doing nothing, saying nothing, to make their being together anything but totally unremarkable. Morrison's telephone call had been the only conversation at breakfast. To his parting arrangement to meet at the bar that evening she'd smilingly queried whether it was intended only to be a friendly drink and he'd asked what else it could be and seriously she'd said, "Nothing, remember?" There hadn't been any embarrassing pretence of kissed farewells or lingering hand touching, either. So why didn't he feel any shame or guilt, if he loved Natalia as much as he was always telling her—and himself—that he did? Because it wasn't any more than Anne's special philosophy. He wasn't going to pretend to fall in love with Anne and she wasn't going to pretend to fall in love with him. Each knew where they stood or—perhaps more appositely—exactly where things lay. No confusion. No problems. A perfect unencumbering, unendangering ultimate friendship.

Finally addressing the question, Charlie said, "I don't know about positive suspension. They might, although by cutting themselves off they'd be cutting themselves out. . . . ." The speculation thrust into his mind but he chose not to introduce it until he'd thought more fully about it. "I guess things will remain in limbo until the results of the tests for any non-prescribed drug."

"So I ask again," said Hamilton. "Where does that leave us?"

"In a reasonably good position, as Charlie's already pointed out," suggested Pacey, the political manipulator. "It's not our argument; it's for the Russians and the Americans to fight out. Hopefully we could work between both camps, if there is a positive split."

"That's how I see it," agreed Charlie.

"When did you plan to go back?" asked Pacey.

"Tomorrow, hopefully. As soon as I've seen the psychiatrist."

"Wouldn't there be an advantage in keeping out of it for a little while longer?"

Charlie very positively shook his head. "We've got a murder conspiracy to uncover . . . understand. This is yet another side-track I don't want to go down."

"I think you're right," said Dean.

Simpson said, "Quite apart from whether or not Bendall was drugged, where can we go if his collapse is irrecoverable?"

"That's what's worrying me most of all," conceded Charlie. "Probably nowhere." Which was, he decided, the side-track down which he *did* want to go. And a journey upon which he had already been far too long—and far too effectively—prevented from taking. But he thought, at last, that he could see some signposts.

Leonid Zenin collected the coincidences like unwelcomed souvenirs. The car taking him to the Kremlin swept past the White House on Krasnopresnenskaya naberezhnaya at precisely the time of the shooting eight days earlier and entered the ancient citadel by the most traditional "pine grove" Borovitskiye Gate through which the security detachments had so vainly argued would have brought both presidents to an arrival ceremony in a totally safe inner courtyard. Zenin didn't hurry crossing the square, gazing around at the easily patrolled castellated ramparts and gated internal labyrinth, acknowledging how utterly protected everyone would have been. Hindsight instead of foresight. Some had it, some didn't. What, he wondered, would be shown today?

Those summoned had been personally selected by Aleksandr Okulov, primarily to exclude not just General Dimitri Spassky but to keep any awareness of the gathering from the suspected FSB. Yuri Trishin, who'd adeptly adjusted to being chief of staff to the emergency president, was automatically included. The Foreign Minister, Boris Petrin, was an essential figure hurriedly added because of the overnight developments and Federal Prosecutor Pavl Yakovlevich Filitov was there for the same reason. Zenin and Natalia guaranteed both the complete, liaising knowledge as well as the necessary continuity of the investigation.

Okulov was the last to enter the suite which came close to overwhelming the small number assembled, despite being only an anteroom to the much larger main chamber, and Natalia's immediate impression was how much more physically confident Okulov appeared to have become in such a short time, no longer the shadowy *eminence grise* but the positively striding—imperious almost—man very definitely to be seen, determined to be judged, in black and white leadership terms. He even seemed to dominate the baroque, echoing surroundings. Confirming that perception the short, hardbodied man said, "Things have come to light in the last twenty-four hours that need to be discussed to decide the future of the shooting investigation . . ." He looked to Zenin. ". . . General?"

Zenin had been given no indication of how many would be attending and had copied twice as many transcripts of the FBI director's message as were necessary. It took him slightly longer to distribute them around the table than to disclose the discovery of the possible but unauthorized injection mark on Bendall's arm.

Filitov, a white-haired, pedantic lawyer, came up from his e-mail print-out and said, "This is outrageous—verging on the hysterical—but the puncture mark is only a *possibility*, according to what I've understood you to say. We need to be absolutely sure."

Zenin made a deferring head movement towards Okulov. "If there's a positive pharmacology result from the tests during this meeting, I shall be informed."

Okulov, still smarting from what he considered the personal insult of Walter Anandale leaving—virtually fleeing—the country without any contact, said, "Whatever the outcome of the medical tests, where does this leave any future cooperation?"

"That's a political decision, far beyond my responsibility," said Zenin. "What I would ask this meeting to confirm is my immediate decision that under no circumstances can Bendall be seen without our people being present, in the same room. He's our prisoner, under our arrest. The British have the right of diplomatic access but there's no legal requirement for the Americans to see him again."

Physically an even more charismatic figure than the emerging Okulov and also someone extremely sure of himself, judged Natalia. With everything predicated by personal as much as professional considerations, she said, "It was an American who died."

"And the man who killed him will be tried by full and open judicial process, not according to the cowboy justice obvious in this Washington message," seized an unexpectedly outspoken Filitov.

"Which is *exactly* what this message is!" agreed Okulov. "An invitation to cowboy justice: lynch law. Or whatever the FBI contingent here—an FBI in this country at our invitation and permission—arrogantly considers they can do."

Natalia at once saw beyond the remark. Charlie was in Moscow because of the FBI presence. If the Americans were expelled, his remaining was thrown into doubt. Which took the decision about their continuing future . . . Natalia stopped the thought, finishing it differently from how it began. It didn't take any decision about her and Charlie out of her hands. Rather it thrust it forward, *for* her to decide. Her choice—her avoided, refused, head-in-the-sand choice—would be whether to go with him if he were ordered to leave. Or stay. It was important for her to remain objective, to concentrate upon the immediate positive rather than the negative of an uncertain future. "How tight is the security that Bendall's been under since the moment of his arrest, the moment of his hospitalization, in fact?"

All attention switched to her, Zenin's most curious of them all. The closely bearded police chief said, "Total. I thought that's been made clear?"

"To the extent of a detailed log being kept of everyone—including doctors—who've had access to him?"

Zenin said, "Of course," but Natalia thought she detected a whisper of doubt.

"Everyone listed—including doctors and hospital staff—are being questioned?"

"Of course," said Zenin, again.

"What's your point?" demanded the Federal prosecutor.

"Premature, unsubstantiated reaction, which I thought you'd already warned against," said Natalia. "I accept there is strong circumstantial evidence against the Americans. But look at the timing of their director's instructions—twelve hours *after* their encounter with Bendall and the discovery of an apparent puncture wound in the man's arm. Let's not accept the obvious. I want to be sure we don't over-respond to be proved wrong, at some later date. There's been very little practical progress so far in the murder and conspiracy investigation."

"I'd welcome the general's suggestions how it could have progressed any quicker or more practicably!" said Zenin, in stiff, personal indignation.

"It was not a criticism! It was an observation," said Natalia. "Of course the American director's instructions is ill considered and reprehensible and I am not arguing against a protest if the feeling is that our making it is justified. But it also shows impatience, which I think is understandable. Let's not forget that it is our FSB that can't find files that could be important. Or that according to Vera Bendall, unknown people—people we can't trace—took from her apartment what could be other evidence that might be equally, if not more, important. Or that the military still haven't provided anything more than the most basic of George Bendall's records. Or that in Russian custody Vera Bendall died in what could, at least, be suspicious circumstances . . ." She was going on too long, Natalia realized; almost appearing to offer a defense for the Americans, which she hadn't set out to do. "Certainly this latest episode with George Bendall—coupled with our awareness of what would appear to be the official American attitude towards the investigation—should be our most direct concern. But I think there would be a benefit considering it in context with the other things I've set out."

There was a momentary silence, heightening Natalia's discomfort.

It was the rotund chief of staff who moved them on. Yuri Trishin said, "There is a further purpose for this meeting: the establishment of the presidential commission . . ."

"I had already decided it should be concentrated upon the FSB . . ." took over Okulov. He smiled towards Natalia. "But which I'm now persuaded should be expanded to include the points you've just raised . . . perhaps others, as well . . ."

". . . Which will provide an answer to any complaints Washington might make against us for how the investigation is going," said Trishin, completing the double act.

This was hardly the emergency meeting Natalia had believed it to be. From the expression on Zenin's face, it wasn't what he'd anticipated either. The police chief said, "When will that commission convene?"

"That's a matter for its members," said Okulov. He smiled again. "I'm appointing you, Natalia Fedova, to be its chair. I'm aware, of course, of your previous connection with the KGB, just as I am even more aware of the constant public reminders of my previous association. But I consider that a benefit rather than a disadvantage: you don't have to be introduced into its workings nor, hopefully, will it be as easy to keep things from you as it might from someone unaware of those workings. I think speed is of the essence and you won't need to be briefed on the progress of the investigation you've been monitoring and liaising since it began. And you've given us ample evidence this morning of your impartiality . . ." The man switched his attention. "You, Pavl Yakovlevich, are obviously necessary for the legal application of the enquiry. The third member of the tribunal will be Yuri Fedorovich, which ensures I am fully aware of everything at all times. Yuri Fedorovich has the terms of reference. Quite simply they are that you have the presidential authority to bring before you whatever witnesses and material you demand, with physical imprisonment at your disposal for anyone who fails fully to cooperate. And I want a preliminary report within a week, sooner if that's possible. Any questions!"

Natalia was sure there would be a lot but at that moment so complete was her astonishment that she couldn't isolate one from another, her thoughts like dust swirls in the wind. Was she more exposed? Or better protected? Was her ability being recognized—rewarded—or was she being made a target? Did she really have the authority? Would it be acceded to her by Filitov and Trishin and whoever else she might now have to confront? Or was she a puppet, a totem? And—inevitably, the ghost always hovering in the corridors of her mind—would it, could it, endanger her and Charlie as much as she'd feared when she'd first learned there was going to be such an enquiry? The immediate positive, she urged herself again: all the other uncertainties could wait. "I appreciate the confidence. I will do everything I can to fulfill it."

"If I hadn't believed you capable, I wouldn't have appointed you," said Okulov.

The transition, from gray to black, *was* remarkable, Natalia decided. Answering—for the moment at least—one of her own questions she decided the appointment strengthened rather than weakened her.

Zenin said, "How will this affect Natalia Fedova's liaison role, with the existing group of which I am part?"

"Not at all," said Okulov. "For the reasons I thought I'd already made clear."

Zenin's face imperceptibly although only briefly tightened at the public rebuff. Before there could be any further reaction, one of Trishin's aides came quickly into the ante-room and gave an obviously pre-arranged signal to the militia chief, who'd started getting to his feet at the secretary's entry.

There was a hiatus after Zenin's departure. The Federal prosecutor said he would be pleased to serve on the tribunal, as if he had a choice, and Natalia sat trying to get her thoughts into order, deciding that while her appointment carried with it power—full access to the acting president himself—and prestige, it was also the path into an unmapped minefield in which she risked making many enemies, both known, which would be unnerving, and unknown, which could be potentially disastrous. And forcing the examination further, she honestly acknowledged that for once Charlie was not a primary, endangering factor. She'd been pushed farther across the swaying bridge between professionalism and politics. The reverie was broken by Zenin's reappearance, the shoulders-back march to the table almost a parody of Okulov's earlier entry.

"Well?" demanded the standby leader, before Zenin properly sat.

"There was provable traces of thiopentone in Bendall's blood," declared the militia commandant, stretching his announcement for its maximum effect.

"What's that?" said Okulov.

"Pentathol," identified Zenin. "A truth drug in common use in American agencies." He extended a further pause. "But not available as such in this country." He came sideways to Natalia. "Perhaps not as circumstantial as it was an hour ago?"

"Evidence, not proof," refused Natalia, dogmatically. She wasn't concerned at Zenin not being an ally. She hoped, though, that he didn't become an enemy.

"Proof or not, we have to react in some way," insisted Okulov. Consciously bringing the American expression to mind, he decided that whatever the outcome of the investigation—and long after—the FBI director's message was going to be a smoking, quickly reloaded gun.

"And there's a way readily to hand," suggested Foreign Minister Boris Petrin. "Let's not forget the American secretary of state stayed on, after the president's hurried exit. I propose that I summon the American ambassador, and James Scamell, and ask them to explain their director's message. And at the same time ask how they think an unprescribed drug—a truth drug—was found to be in George Bendall's system so soon after his interview with American officials."

"Perfect," accepted Okulov. He allowed a pause as theatrical as Zenin's, earlier. "And make it clear we will do our utmost to prevent it being leaked to the media, which we were unfortunately unable to do about a second gunman."

The Home Office pathologist was a nervously moving, distracted man named Geoffrey Robertson whose strained and bulged laboratory coat had clearly been bought before the weight gain from the sort of overflowing, doorstep-thick sandwiches he was eating when Charlie arrived. There was a dab of mayonnaise on the man's chin. He frowned, seemingly unable to remember Charlie's confirming telephone call before saying, "The Russian business!" and leading Charlie to a side table in his office on which everything that Charlie had provided was laid out in meticulously neat order, dominated by the Russian photographs.

In advance of any professional protest Charlie said, "I accept the difficulties, asking you to work like this. I'm looking for something a bit more positive than the Russians are prepared to agree."

"I need properly to examine the body, of course," said the pathologist. "And there's virtually no scene-of-crime material whatsoever, but I'm prepared to agree with you that she was much more likely to have been manually strangled than suffocated by her own hand in a botched attempt to hang herself. . . ." He paused, looking down at the photographs with Charlie beside him. "Look at those closing sutures, after their examination! She's almost been nailed back together. I'm always offended by the lack of respect in stitching like that."

"Vera Bendall was someone who didn't get any respect in life, either," said Charlie. "But you were saying . . . ?"

"The post lividity bruising, as you said in your notes, is the most obvious. That and the complete neck-encircling bruising, with the crushing of the cricoid cartilage of the larynx. But look here . . ." he demanded, isolating four photographs. "I've done a comparison between the bruising on either side of the neck. See, it's heavier on the right side than it is on the left. To have garrotted her as totally as this, her killer would have had to stand behind her pulling right to left, left to right. That heavier bruising, to the right of the neck, shows in my opinion that her killer was left handed: that's the stronger pressure. And here . . ." He picked out two more photographs. "See those two slight, side-by-side bruises, above the ligature mark? I've seen those before, in these sort of strangulations. They're made by the killer's thumbs, where he drove them into the neck for additional leverage. And you're right, in my opinion, about the shoulder blade markings. That's where she was pulled back against the knees of the man strangling her . . ."

"Can you give me that, in a report?"

The man shook his head, dislodging the mayonnaise to add to the stains on his already marked coat. "Not to be produced in any court. I haven't personally examined the body. There is *no* scene of crime material . . ."

"Not to be produced in court," interrupted Charlie. "All I want is a contrary, more positive opinion than the Russian pathologist is giving."

Robertson remained doubtful. "I'd have to qualify it, make it clear that it was entirely an opinion based upon the photographs."

"But that opinion would be what you've just told me?"

The man nodded, slowly. "I suppose I could say that."

"Please say it," encouraged Charlie. "And there was the blood sample?"

"It showed 200mg," said the bulged man, too glibly and without consulting his side-desk preparation.

"Spell it out," insisted Charlie, satisfied more than surprised.

"The legal alcohol limit beyond which someone is incapable of being in charge of a moving vehicle is 80mg per 100ml of blood," said the doctor, literally responding to Charlie's demand. "Bendall was two and a half times over that limit."

"Drunk?" persisted Charlie.

"By our legal driving standards, yes."

"Those readings are incontrovertible?"

Robertson appeared surprised. "They're scientific!"

"Which I can have, in written analysis, to take back with me to Moscow?"

"I don't know what the legal alcohol limit is to drive in Russia," protested the man.

"I'd guess it's nonexistent but I'm not investigating a drunk driving offense," said Charlie.

Robertson's laboratory was in north London but Charlie still managed to get back to Millbank by mid-afternoon. Spence told him the director-general did not want to see him unless there was a positive development and that he could use the same temporary inner courtyard office that he'd been allocated the previous day. Charlie reached Donald Morrison on the basement incident room extension.

The younger man said, "A lot seems to be happening, but I don't know what it is. When Kayley and I got to the cemetery the exhumation had already taken place. There was just an empty grave and a militia guard who wouldn't talk to us. Kayley said he wanted to speak with you but he was called upstairs about an hour ago and hasn't come back."

"So the investigation's stalled?"

"Has it ever started?"

Charlie smiled at the cynicism. "Our pathologist's just agreed Vera Bendall was murdered. And George Bendall was drunk when he fired."

"Surprising that he hit anyone."

"That's what I'm thinking." It had been automatic professionalism for Charlie to bring back from Moscow not just the Russian ballistic evidence but actual firing tests conducted by the Americans using the rifle recovered from George Bendall. Now he was glad he had. It was probably fortunate, too, that offended prima donnas at Woolwich Arsenal had staged their go slow.

"Can I tell Kayley?"

"No!" refused Charlie, at once. "I need to discuss it with others first." Not others. Only Anne Abbott preparing George Bendall's seemingly impossible defense.

"Nothing's come from re-interviewing the witnesses but the personnel director at NTV confirms it was Vasili Isakov who got Bendall the job. Anything else you want me to do? I feel a bit like a spare prick at a wedding, hanging around with nothing to do."

Charlie smiled again, this time at Morrison's too obvious, one-of-the-street-boys' ribaldry. Aloud he said, "There aren't supposed to be any spare pricks at a wedding."

It wasn't a convenient—safe—time to call Natalia. There was more than enough time, though, to go present-buying. Charlie actually thought he'd received a few presents himself that day. But they were in kit form, he had to assemble them himself.

Petr Tikunov's second press conference since the shooting was again overwhelmed by the international media. The burly communist presidential candidate accused Okulov of stealing his party's idea of an investigatory commission. But Okulov's enquiry would be a cover-up, he insisted, conducted by puppets personally selected by Okulov himself. In answer to repeated questions about Okulov's former association with the KGB, Tikunov said he left the public and the voters to judge the man's previous connection with the intelligence service, the majority of whose officers, he knew, resented the disbandment and reorganization imposed by the existing government, disbandment and reorganization which had allowed the rise in crime culminating in the attack upon the two presidents. After his reelection, fighting crime—and seeking the FSB's assistance in doing so—was going to be his immediate priority.

"If the need was for someone intimately aware of all the facts to bridge the two situations I should have been the one appointed!" protested Zenin.

Olga wondered if she would ever get properly to know this man. "You weren't for the very reasons Okulov gave: it needs someone knowing every facet of the case but factionally above it. She is. You're not, you're the one who initially *proposed* an enquiry into the FSB!"

"Are you sure she's factionally above it all?"

"Aren't you?"

"She *was* KGB, before all the changes! Just like Okulov."

"Which Okulov specifically referred to, from what you've told me. Referred to as a benefit." Olga wished she were with him, instead of talking on the telephone. But everything was far too new to make demands upon him. The very thought surprised her. When had she ever been the one to seek and hope in a relationship! Lovers danced to her tune, not her to theirs. Until now. Exactly the time to get things in proper—normal—balance then. Spend at least one night apart: they weren't, after all, rutting teenagers, discovering sex for the first time. But was it only—just—sex? That thought didn't even deserve an answer.

"I think we should be extremely careful we don't in some way fall victim," said Zenin.

Precisely what she'd warned him about in the very beginning! remembered Olga. "We can be."

"How did the exhumation go?"

"I advanced the timing, as you suggested. It was over before anyone else arrived. The tissue samplings were delivered to the laboratory by mid-afternoon. Kayley called six times during the day, trying to make contact."

"What about the British . . . their new man?"

"Nothing."

"Let's talk tomorrow, early."

"I'm missing not being with you," she blurted and at once regretted it, wishing she could bite back the words.

"What . . . ?" he started, just as unthinkingly but instantly recovered. "Yes! I'm sorry. There's things . . . tomorrow? Tomorrow night, I mean. If you're free?"

"I'm free," said Olga.

As always, Charlie let Natalia talk first, knowing her need was greater and afterwards kept his account brief and factual.

"Well?" she prompted, when he'd finished. She hadn't mentioned the inference of the FBI possibly being expelled, not wanting to trample over ground already muddied by being walked on too many times before.

"You couldn't be better protected, against our situation becoming known," assured Charlie, sure that was the point of her question.

"You're spanning everything, knowing everything."

"And attracting enemies in doing so," she said. "I've convened the first session for tomorrow. Summoned the FSB chairman himself, along with all the rest."

"*Above* any enemies, looking down at them," out-qualified Charlie. "You can dispose of them before they can endanger you. You're ahead, whichever which way you want to look at it."

"You're actually taking things forward professionally, as a criminal investigation," Natalia allowed.

"I wish I'd known about the Pentathol before seeing the pathologist." It would mean a second visit, he supposed. "What state is Bendall in now?"

"Still sedated."

"It was a good suggestion you made about a visitor's log," praised Charlie. "I hadn't thought of that."

"What's it like, being back there?"

The moment for guilt, Charlie recognized. Nothing came. "I've been too busy to do much else but work and appear before committees. I did get time to buy Sasha a doll. It wets itself and has to have its nappy changed."

"She'll like that." He'd forgotten buying Sasha the same on a previous recall to London.

"I hope you're looking after her," he said, with insufficient thought.

"I was looking after her very well a long time before you reappeared on the scene," came back Natalia, at once.

His mistake, Charlie accepted. "Best of luck for tomorrow."

"Yes."

"I hope to get back the day after."

"You told me already."

"Goodnight then."

"Goodnight."

She hadn't told him she loved him, thought Charlie. But then he hadn't told her, either. He was still by the telephone when it rang.

Anne said, "That was a hell of a long call! I'm in the bar, waiting. Liberace's look-alike ghost is about to make a pass at me."

"If it's Liberace's ghost, you're safe," said Charlie.

———

Charlie had again to filter what he could tell the lawyer from what he shouldn't have been in a position to know but there was sufficient for Anne to remark that he seemed to be working hard to provide her with a TV soap opera defense. Short of that being available, however, the decision had been made to have Bendall examined by two independent Russian psychiatrists to formulate a plea of mental impairment or even outright insanity, depending upon their diagnosis. But all that hinged on what sort of recovery the man made. It would also help if the court psychiatrists had access to Bendall's previous psychiatric history that Vera had mentioned. A Russian lawyer necessary to lead Bendall's defense had been engaged by fax that afternoon from the list Anne had brought to London with her.

"So you've finished?"

"Everything discussed and decided," she agreed.

"You going back tomorrow?"

She frowned, in mock offense. "You in a hurry to get rid of me?"

"No," said Charlie. "Not at all."

"Good. And I haven't done any shopping."

They'd eaten again at a restaurant of Anne's choice in Notting Hill and they had a nightcap again in the hotel bar and went unquestioningly to his room. Afterwards she said, "We're getting very good at this. Maybe we should take it up professionally."

Charlie said, "I thought we had."

The bag containing Sasha's doll was by the wardrobe, "toys" prominently printed against the name of the shop in which Charlie had bought it. Anne said, "You've already managed to do your shopping?"

"Some," said Charlie.

He waited for the obvious question but she didn't ask it.

16

Natalia Fedova had triumphed in a jungle of human animals for a long time before Sasha's birth and for three years afterwards and in doing so, like Charlie, had perfected a number of survival rules. One—unknowingly again like Charlie, with whom she'd never discussed it—was never to be pulled down by the mistakes and misjudgments of people who imagined they knew better than she did. Which she anticipated, without needing proof, would be the attitude of both Yuri Fedorovich Trishin and Pavl Yakovlevich Filitov and why she set out from the very beginning to impose the control inherent in her appointment. She recognized the danger of the strategy and hoped Charlie was right in his assessment of her strength.

Befitting their presidential credentials they were allocated a suite of rooms, with a five-strong secretariat, within the Kremlin itself and Natalia summoned both men to it an hour before their scheduled start supposedly to brief them upon everything that had come before the crisis committee. She did so with two of their secretaries at the prepared apparatus, determined that everything be recorded. Filitov was just slightly ahead of the chief of staff with the authority-challenging protest that he'd thoroughly assimilated all that had come before the committee, with which he'd been provided overnight but Natalia talked them both down, insisting upon her agenda that their initial concentration be upon the missing KGB dossiers, extended only to what the succeeding FSB might have taken from the Bendalls' Hutorskaya Ulitza apartment. Because of her intimate knowledge of the former KGB structure—as well as her personal knowledge of the crisis committee discussions which might not be reflected in its written material—she intended leading the questioning but of course expected them both to contribute. It was not until Natalia said she would seek Filitov's advice before invoking their imprisonment provisions that she got the impression they were beginning to defer to her, although the prosecutor's reaction at first was more one of undisguised surprise.

"I don't think we should lose sight of the rank and importance of people with whom we're dealing," cautioned the lawyer.

Nor, suspected Natalia, of the clear threats Petr Tikunov had made at yesterday's press conference. "It's precisely because I'm aware of the rank and importance that we're discussing the provision now."

"An opinion surely based upon a personal experience which ended several years ago?" suggested Trishin. "I don't believe the acting president intended the recourse to be used lightly."

"It won't be," assured Natalia. "We won't forget, though, that it exists."

Trishin attempted to restore his prerogative by querying Natalia's full understanding of the other terms of reference, which she'd anticipated and not only answered without hesitation but corrected two that he misquoted. Filitov remained silent until that day's witness list was brought in by the registration clerk.

The Federal prosecutor said at once, "We were not consulted about the summoning of the FSB chairman himself!"

"Do you have a problem with it?" Natalia was glad she *hadn't* discussed it.

"Of course I do."

"Why 'of course'?"

"Yesterday you talked of premature reactions," reminded the lawyer. "This is inappropriately premature until we've had the opportunity to judge the compliance."

"Do you feel it's inappropriately premature?" she asked Trishin.

The chief of staff looked uncertainly towards the recording bank. "I think prior discussion would have been advisable."

Now Natalia indicated the silently turning apparatus. "Your dissent has been noted."

"I didn't say I dissented," Trishin quickly insisted. "If we are to reach a combined opinion, which *is* in the terms of reference, we've got to come to combined decisions upon the conduct of the enquiry."

Perfect politico-speak, Natalia recognized. "Combined decisions? Or majority decisions?"

Their exchanged looks answered Natalia's question before Filitov did. The lawyer said, "Our primary term of reference is speed. Which requires majority opinions, in my judgment." The man paused, to establish the mockery. "Dissent can always be noted."

After politoco-speak, legal-speak, acknowledged Natalia. And each—rarely—as illuminating as the other. She hadn't expected to benefit so much—be warned so quickly—from this pre-session encounter. She was glad she'd orchestrated it as precisely as she had. She hoped she could continue the momentum, although again she didn't foresee the quickness with which that would come about.

There was still ten minutes to go before the official opening when their registration clerk reentered the chamber and initially bent to Natalia's ear with his copy of the witness list.

"We all need to hear," demanded Filitov.

"An unscheduled witness whom we'll hear at once," announced Natalia. "First Deputy Director Gennardi Nikolaevich Mittel."

"I don't understand," protested Trishin, his frowned confusion matching the other man's.

"It won't take long," promised Natalia, at Mittel came confidently into the room. The FSB deputy was a young man with an indented scar grooving the left side of an otherwise unlined face. His deeply black hair was helmeted directly back from his forehead in greased perfection and his civilian, uncreased gray suit was just as immaculate. The smile, as confident as his easy entry, showed sculptured dentistry. He took the fronting chair Natalia indicated and crossed one razor-sharp leg across the other.

"You are not on the list of witnesses whom this commission has asked to help it, Gennardi Nikolaevich?" invited Natalia. It was predictable, she supposed, but she'd thought there would have been a written protest, not a patronizing emissary.

"You summoned my chairman," said Mittel, as if in reminder. He remained smiling.

"Viktor Ivanovich Karelin is indeed among those whom we wish to question," agreed Natalia. Beside her she was conscious of Trishin and Filitov shifting, in belated understanding.

"Whom you will understand is an extremely busy man," said Mittel. "I am here to represent him. I am sure I shall be able to help you with any questions you might have."

Natalia let a silence chill the room. "Viktor Ivanovich fully understands that this is a presidential commission?"

The smile faltered. "Of course."

"As you do?"

"Yes."

"You have discussed it with Viktor Ivanovich?"

"He personally—officially—appointed me to represent him."

"Tell us, for the record, what you and Viktor Ivanovich understand a commission established by the acting president to be?"

The man was no longer smiling. He unfolded his legs. "It is an enquiry into some irregularities that appear to have arisen in the *Komitet Gosudarstvennoy Bezopasnosti*, an organization that no longer exists."

In her former chief interrogator's role within Special Service 11 of the KGB's First Chief Directorate, Natalia had invariably found conceit—condescension—the easiest shell to crack. She wondered if the man knew how much of the FSB's defense he'd given away in that one reply. "That wasn't an answer to my question. So I'll make it easier for you. Do you—and your chairman—understand the authority of this commission?"

"Of course." Mittel was wary now, his hands forward on tight-together legs.

"An authority not lessened by the fact that Aleksandr Mikhailevich Okulov is at the moment *acting* president?"

"It is the authority of the office," said Mittel.

"An authority and an office that your chairman is too busy to observe?"

"I can assure this commission that no disrespect was intended to it or to the acting president."

"I think that is important to be established on the record," said Natalia, indicating the secretariat. "Let's see what else can be established. You have been deputed as the highest official of the FSB to help this enquiry?"

"Yes."

"So help us."

Mittel gazed back at her, blankly. "I'm sorry . . . I don't . . ."

"Where are the complete files of Peter Bendall, a British physicist who defected to the Soviet Union in 1972, the corollary details that would have been maintained upon his family, after they joined him in Moscow, the information that would have been kept separately upon the son, George Bendall—also known as Georgi Gugin—and everything that was taken from the family apartment at Hutorskaya Ulitza upon Peter Bendall's death and again upon the seizure of George Bendall, nine days ago?" Natalia wondered how long it would be before Trishin or Filitov came into the exchange. Or were they remaining gratefully quiet, leaving what was clearly an immediate and dangerous confrontation entirely to her?

Mittel remained unmoving for several moments. There was the faintest hint of the earlier smile, quickly gone. "As I pointed out a few moments ago, the KGB no longer exists as an organization. It has been largely disbanded, its functions, manpower and archives greatly reduced. What remained was absorbed by the FSB, which I represent here today on behave of its chairman. And on behalf of its chairman I have to assure this enquiry that the most rigorous search has been made, among archives that the FSB inherited, to locate the material you've asked for. I regret to say—regret to tell this commission—that nothing has been found."

"Which is what we are going to be told by everyone else from the FSB whom we have called here today?"

"I am afraid so." One leg was crossed easily over the other again.

The reforms and supposed new democracy *were* still fragile, the more so in the uncertainty of the rapidly growing communist strength. And the FSB remained a megalith, waiting in the wings to reemerge as an unchallenged government within a government. To protect herself there had to be provable discussion, with the other two on the panel. Even that might not be as protective as she hoped. "Would you retire, Gennardi Nikolaevich? But don't leave the anteroom. We'll need to call you back."

"The intention is to reduce us—and by inference the acting president—to a laughing stock!" insisted Natalia. "The man's actually told us what each and every witness we've called is going to say!"

"We need to consult," said Trishin.

"We *are* consulting, right now!"

"I meant with the president."

The *president*, noted Natalia: not Aleksandr Mikhailevich or *acting* president. "If we do that, we're making a laughing stock of ourselves: proving ourselves totally inadequate for the function for which we were appointed."

"It's directly confrontational," judged Filitov.

"Apparently," cautioned Natalia. Could she bring them with her, convince them? Their knowledge that she'd once served in the KGB—a service to which Trishin had already referred—might help. Both men were looking at her, waiting. She didn't continue.

Finally Filitov asked, "What's that mean?"

"It's classical textbook, whatever name or acronym or initial letter designation you want to choose. They're elite: above reproach, question or examination," said Natalia.

"I still don't follow," protested Trishin.

"Our reaction is their test of strength: the strength of Aleksandr Mikhailevich Okulov if he succeeds to the presidency against those who will oppose him." How much of a two edged sword was it to have maintained the secretariat recording? She was committed now: not a sword carrier, more a solitary standard bearer stranded in the no-man's-land between opposing forces.

"That's your professional judgment, based upon your knowledge of the organization?" demanded Filitov.

"Yes," said Natalia, at once.

"Which makes it essential to consult Aleksandr Mikhailevich before we do react," declared Trishin, relieved at the decision being taken from them.

"No," refused Natalia, quickly again. "That *is* the test. You, Yuri Fedorovich, are the president's—the acting president's—chief of staff, the man who reflects his thinking, speaks for him, *acts* for him. You, Pavl Yakovlevich, are the judiciary: for the first time in more than seventy years the supposedly independent-of-government law. I—more tentatively although more specifically—represent civilian law enforcement, one of the few functions that has really been lost to the FSB by the cosmetic disbandment of the KGB. In microcosm, who we represent is the new order in Russia."

"Aren't you over-stressing the symbolism?" challenged Filitov.

"I don't think so," said Natalia, as forcefully as she could.

"Are you inferring FSB *complicity* in the attack upon the presidents?"

"You know, from the crisis committee's discussions that have been made available to you, that complicity hasn't been excluded, although there's no proof whatsoever to support an accusation," reminded Natalia. "At this stage I'm suggesting nothing more than the Lubyanka moving to turn a potentially embarrassing weakness—their loss of records—into a positive strength-testing benefit. We have, now, not just to match but outmatch that strength: or, if you prefer, out-bluff them."

"How?" demanded Trishin, forehead creased in his effort to keep up.

"If we accept the arrogance of First Chief Deputy Gennardi Mittel—and all those who are going to recite the same denials after him—then we destroy ourselves on our first day," insisted Natalia.

"I suppose we do," allowed Trishin, uncertainly.

Filitov nodded agreement, but didn't speak.

"So let's play the hand," urged Natalia. "Let's confront their confrontation now, only harder. Let's face the arrogance down, at least for today. That allows you, Yuri Fedorovich, all the time you need to consult and discuss with the acting president . . ." She nodded to the secretariat. ". . . with the advantage of every word that's been exchanged. If we haven't responded as we should then tomorrow we back down under the bullying of the FSB, which effectively ends any purpose in our being empanelled. The only humiliation will be ours, which it will be anyway if we collapse now under FSB pressure."

"Not quite," contradicted Trishin. "The humiliation will be that of acting President Okulov, as well."

"Which it will be if we cave in now."

Filitov said, "It's a convincing argument."

"I'd welcome a better one," admitted Natalia.

"I don't have one," said the federal prosecutor.

"Neither do I," said Trishin.

The spring had gone out of Gennardi Mittel's step when he was recalled and there was no languid crossing of legs.

Natalia said, "We do not think you or your chairman fully understand the importance of what this commission is charged and authorized to inquire into. Which is unfortunate. We will not accept your deputizing for Viktor Ivanovich Karelin. You will return to the Lubyanka, with a copy of our terms of reference and with the request from us to chairman Karelin to make himself available, before this commission, tomorrow. We will continue today to examine the other FSB officials in the very sincere hope that they will not repeat the explanation that you seemed to think adequate. But as you indicated that would be their response, we would have you advise chairman Karelin that it is unacceptable and have him bring with him tomorrow people better able to answer our questions. Do *you* have any questions, First Chief Deputy Mittel?"

The man's throat was working, in his astonishment, but no words came at once. When they did, they were strained in disbelief. "I would respectfully ask this commission to reconsider."

"This commission does not believe there is anything to reconsider," said Natalia. "We look forward to seeing chairman Karelin before us at the scheduled time tomorrow." She'd imposed her will, Natalia accepted. But at what cost or purpose?

They used the satellite transmission installed for Walter Anandale visually to conduct the Washington cabinet meeting when he'd been in Moscow, although this time the exchange was far more restricted in numbers although not in emotion, which went through the whole gamut from implacable fury to benign unconcern. There were three, in each capital. In the specially adapted embassy room on Novinskij Bul'var James Scamell sat between John Kayley and the ambassador, Cornell Burton. In Washington the president was flanked by Wendall North and the FBI director, Paul Smith. The guilt-apportioning, one-to-one encounters had been conducted behind closed doors before the link-up but the recriminations still simmered, like summer heat off a tarred road. Paul Smith's humiliating inclusion was a continuing part of the man's punishment.

"We were roasted alive," complained the secretary of state, voice still tight with the memory of their summons to the Russian Foreign Ministry. "Petrin actually used the word 'arrogance' and 'cowboy'. And we didn't have a position to come back from. How the hell did it happen!"

"A mistake that shouldn't have occurred," said Anandale, still gripped by the anger with which he'd flayed the FBI director, towards whom he intentionally looked sideways as he spoke. "What's the proper story of this damned injection?"

"We categorically denied knowing anything about it, which we don't," quickly came in Kayley, outwardly grave-faced like the rest of them but inwardly the happiest man involved, knowing that from now on he was absolutely fireproof, double-coated in Teflon. Whatever went wrong could be squarely—irrefutably—blamed on the director's stupid instructions even more stupidly wrongly directed, for everyone to read. "None of us touched the guy; it's absurd imagining that we would."

"Except for the e-mail," said Scamell, who two hours earlier, standing in the Russian ministry being treated like a miscreant schoolboy, had finally seen disappear any publicly acknowledged diplomatic credit for almost a year's commuting between Washington and Moscow. "We can swear on a stack of bibles a mile high that it wasn't us and they'll laugh in our face just like Boris Petrin laughed in my face. There's no purpose in my staying here anymore but for the fact that by coming home I'd be inferring we *did* do it. We're screwed here, Mr. President. We couldn't be in a worse position if we tried to invent one."

"What about the practical, on-the-ground operation?" asked Wendall North.

"There isn't one," dismissed Kayley. "The Russians have withdrawn from our combined incident room. Switched the timing of an exhumation that might be important, so I wasn't able to be there. It's the autopsy that's important and I've no way now of getting that . . ." He hesitated, wanting to build his self-protecting barricade as strong as he could. "We were told, at the Foreign Ministry, that we wouldn't in future be allowed any access whatsoever to Bendall. Effectively, we've been closed down."

"Jesus!" said Anandale, stretching the word in his exasperation.

"We didn't do it . . ." started Wendall North.

It was a rhetorical remark but Kayley's day had begun facing Scamell's suspicion. The dishevelled man said, "Can we get this straight, the first and last time! We-did-not-drug-the-goddamned-man!"

"Appreciate you making that so clear to us," continued the chief of staff. "So who did?"

Kayley shook his head, discomfited by his over-reaction. "God only knows!"

"What about the British?" persisted North.

Kayley shook his head again. "Too long an interval, from the time they saw him."

"Which only leaves the Russians," isolated Smith, desperate to make some sort of recovery. "How about it being a set-up? Injecting the guy and pointing the finger at us, to break up the cooperation?"

"What's the point of their going to all the effort?" demanded Scamell.

"Resentment, at our leadership," answered Smith.

Everyone waited for someone else to make the point. It was Anandale who did. "We made a pretty good job of screwing that up for ourselves." The president let the repeated criticism settle before he said, "OK, what can we do to restore the situation?"

"It'll need a substantial gesture," advised the secretary of state. "Something like getting the treaty back on track."

"I agree," said the ambassador. "Diplomatically we're looking pretty bad here. I can't remember so bad."

"I don't want to go that route," rejected the president. "OK, we've got to play pull-back. But as it wasn't us and it couldn't have been the British, the Russians did it themselves and are using it to force us into treaty concessions. I'm not going to do that."

"That's my only idea," said the secretary of state.

"What about my talking to Okulov direct?" suggested Anandale.

"That's the one thing I don't think you should do, get *directly* involved," warned Scamell. "I think you've got to remain above the actual recrimination."

"So do I," said Wendall North, at once.

"I want to get the damned thing back on course. Find the son-of-a-bitch who did what he did to Ruth," insisted Anandale.

"It's got to be right, first time," said Scamell. "Thought out, from every which way."

"So let's do just that," agreed Anandale. "Let's you and I think about it from every which way over the next hour or two, Jamie. Call me at four, your time. I want a recovery idea by then."

Olga Melnick pushed herself back in her chair, waiting for Zenin's lead. She didn't feel dependent; inadequate. The feeling was of being comfortable, able for the first time to rely on someone. She wasn't ready yet to start thinking of love, because she wasn't sure she knew how to recognize the emotion, but it was something she had to confront soon.

The militia commandant said, "There's just no way of telling how big this conspiracy is, is there?"

"It doesn't look like it," she agreed. She picked up the autopsy report on the exhumed remains of Vasili Isakov. "For this much pentobarbitone still to be tissue traceable in the body he would at least have been too deeply unconscious to have felt anything when the train hit him."

"I read the opinion," reminded Zenin. "He couldn't have been forced to take it all orally. It would have been injected. Probably mixed with alcohol, too."

"And that couldn't have been the Americans!" said Olga.

"So we're back to the FSB." Now Zenin took up and let drop the official security log of everyone admitted to George Bendall's ward. It lay among the other reports on the table between them in Zenin's top floor Moscow Militia headquarter office, a starkly functional, bakelite-tiled Brezhnev era memorial to personal, bribe-bolstering aggrandisement and boxed awfulness. There were already cracks fissuring from the dried-out, water-and-dust glued bricks of the outer rooms into the man's inner suite in one corner of which the floor was already too uneven to support anything heavier than a triangular stand for Zenin's exchanged momentoes—mostly unhung plaques—of foreign police visits. "So how did they do it! Not Isakov, on the level crossing. They could have managed that a dozen different ways, particularly if he had been drinking the night it happened and was already incapably drunk. I mean at Burdenko. I've personally questioned every squad leader: each one is adamant no one who isn't recorded on that log entered Bendall's room. And apart from the British, us and the Americans, it's just doctors and nurses."

"One of whom has to be an FSB plant," declared Olga.

"Obviously," agreed Zenin. "I want every member of the hospital staff on that list investigated, until we find out who it is."

"I'll personally organize it," Olga promised. She hesitated, unsure whether to make the suggestion, remembering Zenin's annoyance at what he considered his being overlooked. Their relationship allowed her to do it, she decided. "Don't you think we should pass this on to the presidential commission?"

"It's negative, at the moment," said Zenin. There was no irritation in his voice.

"There'll be a lot of FSB people altogether in one place at the same time, people who could be questioned to shorten the time it'll take us to find the FSB operative at the hospital; if, indeed, we ever do find who it is."

"That's a constructive point," agreed Zenin. "We'll pass it on, ahead of my seeing Natalia Fedova at our next group assessment." He tapped the third folder on the table, the finally arrived and complete military medical record on George Bendall, listed however as Georgi Gugin. "There's nothing constructive about this. Liver enlargement, through excessive drinking. A stomach ulcer, probably from the same cause . . ."

". . . But no psychiatric evaluation," broke in Olga.

Zenin wearily shook his head. "He might have been selected as a sharpshooter but he was still only an ordinary soldier, like one of the twenty million sacrificed during the Great Patriotic War. Which is what men like George Bendall are. Sacrifices, to be offered up whenever the need arises. There's no concern about their *mental* health; the less they can think—rationalize—the better."

"That's exactly what George Bendall is, isn't it!" seized Olga. "A sacrifice, selected when a need arose."

"He's all we've probably got," said Zenin. "My fear is that we're not going to be able to get beyond him, to discover the rest, to understand the true story."

Olga was surprised at the unexpected depression. "We're making progress."

"No we're not, Olga Ivanova!" refused the man. "We're being directed further and further into a maze. And I don't know how to avoid our going deeper into it or how to get out, from where we are now."

Reluctantly—for the first time making herself face the total reality of it—Olga acknowledged that Zenin was right. "We can't let it happen. Fail, I mean."

"What's the way to stop it happening?"

Olga didn't have an answer.

The Botanic Gardens on Moscow's Glavnyy Botanicheskiy Sad, with their enormous, tunnel-shaped glassed exhibition halls, had been the secret tryst for Charlie and Natalia after he'd been sure enough of her love—which he wasn't any longer—to admit his supposed defection to the then Soviet Union was phoney but that because of that love he was refusing to trigger his KGB-wrecking return to London until he'd guaranteed her safety from suspicion or recrimination.

There was a twitch of recognition when he was ushered into the presence of the psychiatrist who'd analyzed the tapes and the transcripts of the George Bendall encounters. A slipper-shuffling housekeeper—or maybe even the man's elderly and totally disinterested wife—led Charlie through an echoing mausoleum of a Hampstead house directly into a carbuncle of a glass greenhouse, abandoning him at its tropically-heated entrance. From there he found his own, sweaty way through giant fronded plants and ferns and sharp quilled, brilliantly technicolored cacti to locate, along the third path he followed, the shoulder-stooped, cardiganed professor. Arnold Nolan was in conversation with himself, narrow-spouted watering can in one hand, snipping secateurs in the other, his canopy of white hair more tangled than the foliage he was tending. His patchwork-patterned slippers matched those of the elderly woman and Charlie envied their obvious trodden-into-comfort shapelessness.

The man showed no surprise at Charlie's arrival beside him, just slightly raising his voice above the earlier self-conversation. He said, "Plants have an intelligence, you know. They feel discomfort, injury."

"So I've been told," said Charlie. Perspiration was rivering his face and forming into tributaries down his back.

"Restful things, plants."

"I've come about the Moscow tapes."

"I know. See that plant there? *Dionaea Muscipula*. Have to feed it flies and insects. Isn't it pretty?"

"Do you mind if I wait outside? I find it very hot in here."

The man turned for the first time, fixing Charlie with pale blue eyes. "Hot? You think so?"

"Very much so." Nolan wasn't sweating at all, Charlie saw. The man's cardigan was thick, all the buttons secured.

"If you need to. Shan't be long."

Charlie returned gratefully to the outside corridor, feeling the sweat dry upon him, wondering if he'd make his second meeting with Geoffrey Robertson. When he'd telephoned the pathologist the man had said he could only give him ten minutes and insisted Charlie be on time, an hour from now.

Charlie heard the shuffled scuff of Nolan's approach before he saw the man. He was talking to himself when he finally appeared. Or maybe, Charlie thought, he was talking to the plants. He'd read that people did.

"Come on," said Nolan, as he past, and Charlie obediently followed. Over his shoulder Nolan said, "Like to meet your man. Interesting."

"I appreciate the difficulty of what I'm asking, your not being able to do that."

"Awkward but not a problem," said the psychiatrist. "Some things are fairly obvious, others not."

Although he'd never actually seen one Charlie decided Nolan's office looked like the inside of a bear's cave after a winter's hibernation. It was a completely shelved cavern of books which overflowed on to the floor and on to overstuffed leather chairs and a couch, interspersed with apparently discarded papers and magazines and occasionally skeletal newspapers from which articles had been clipped. The debris was so great that there were clearly delineated paths through it, the most obvious to the overwhelmed, leather-topped desk, with side alleys to the bookshelves.

"There's a chair . . ." said Nolan, waving to his right with a distracted arm, as if he'd forgotten where one might be. When the man snapped his desk light on Charlie saw his tapes and their transcripts were neatly—surprisingly—stacked next to a pocket-sized replay machine.

"I'm only able to give you—to suggest—a general picture," began Nolan, abruptly professional. "There are clear indications of a schizophrenia, which is too often used as a catch-all when people like myself can't think of a more positive diagnosis. We're not going to go all Hollywood and suggest there are strange voices telling Bendall what to do. I suspect, though, that he's obsessional. He'd be very susceptible to being told what to do, particularly if he loved or felt particularly close to the person giving the instructions . . ."

"What about more than one person? A group?" interrupted Charlie.

Nolan pursed his lips. "Possible but there would still need to be one person in that group upon whom he would need to focus. But certainly a group could be important to him. Your notes were helpful. He's classically dysfunctional, alienated from a splintered home. That's why the army might have been attractive to him: somewhere in which he might have felt embraced, a family he did know or have. But I think it would have been too big, too amorphous. But a group, a brotherhood, wouldn't have been. And let's get a correction in here, because it's important. All the interviews so far have been wrongly directed, the Americans most of all. Bendall needs to be encouraged—praised, admired, loved if you like, not ridiculed which has been the tone of everything I've listened to so far, with yours as a possible, partial exception. From what you've said in your notes, there's certainly more than one person—a conspiracy—involved here but Bendall did what he did to become admired by his friends, in the same mentally disturbed way that loners have attacked—killed—famous people, to become famous themselves . . ."

"Did he—does he—know what he was doing?" broke in Charlie again.

"Very much so. That's part of it, a very important part. That's your way forward, when you talk to him again?"

"How can I get him to tell me who the others are?"

Nolan gestured uncertainly. "From your interview, more than any of the others, I got the impression that he *wants* to tell someone: after all his life being discarded and down trodden he's suddenly *someone*, the object of everyone's attention. He wasn't just being used physically, to fire a rifle. He was being used—manipulated—mentally. Those short, staccato replies to you are indicative. He believed he was playing with you: testing you out. Let him go on thinking that. Let him think he's superior, in charge."

"There's something that wasn't in my notes, that I've only just discovered," said Charlie. "Somehow—I don't know how—Bendall was administered with an unauthorized drug, thiopentone. It could have been during the American interview when he broke down. Could that have any long term effects, combined with the other drugs with which he's being treated: affect, in fact, how he might be in any future sessions?"

Nolan humped his shoulders. "You know what the prescribed drugs are?"

Charlie felt a burn of embarrassment. "I'm sorry."

"Now he's well out of surgery I guess it'll just be some type of sedative," suggested the psychiatrist. "Thiopentone shouldn't react against any of the barbiturates."

"So it wouldn't have caused that outburst, during the American session?"

The psychiatrist shook his head. "That was far more likely to have been caused by the way he was being talked to. He was being ridiculed, which was how he's been treated all his life. He simply closed himself down."

"Why did he break all the models he made, which his mother told me he did?"

"Models of things that moved, could have taken him away from an existence he hated, had they been real," Noland judged. "That was his physical way of showing that hatred of his surroundings—

making his imagined escape and then smashing it—before he began showing the actual violence towards others."

"Can I send you other tapes?"

"I'd like you to. I've never worked like this before: as I said, it's interesting. And remember something else I told you. Let him think he's superior: cleverer. You going to find that difficult?"

"Not at all," said Charlie. "I've been doing that all my life."

The pathologist was wearing a clean laboratory coat but it was again at least two sizes too small. Geoffrey Robertson gave the same answer as the psychiatrist when asked about thiopentone but promised to get a definitive assessment from a pharmacologist if Charlie sent back from Moscow George Bendall's complete medication list.

"Can't understand the point of it being done," said the man.

"That *is* the point of it being done," said Charlie. "For people not to be able to understand why. And it's working brilliantly."

With the need—minimally productive though it turned out—for a second meeting with the pathologist Charlie had put back for an hour his appointment with the ballistics expert at the Woolwich Arsenal. But he was still late and knew at once from the man's demeanor that Archibald Snelling had fantasized for the further delayed thirty minutes about the toothbrushed lavatory cleaning sentence he would have imposed in a much mourned earlier army career. From the man's disapproving, top to toe and sideways examination, Charlie guessed his appearance would probably have got him denied the toothbrush and that he would have had to scour with his bare hands, if not his own toothbrush. Snelling had to be almost two meters tall and although there was a slight stomach sag in the parade ground rigidity his voice retained the come-to-attention bark. Into the man's office, which actually did overlook a parade ground, came the occasional and distant sound of a weapon being discharged. The only chair available was straight-backed and wooden-seated and Charlie turned and sat with one arm crooked over its rear rail, just for the hell of it. Snelling was sitting to attention, shoulders squared, ramrod straight.

"You got something more to tell me!" demanded Snelling, at once.

"I'd hoped you'd have something to tell me," retorted Charlie. The aggressiveness was an abrupt contrast with the attempted helpfulness of the other specialists that day but then, remembered Charlie, he had shown the man—or his colleagues—to be lacking. Charlie was more irritated than offended; he certainly wasn't intimidated.

"I don't understand," complained the man.

"I don't, either," said Charlie. "It might help if you explained in more detail what the problem is."

"You don't have another Dragunov? Photographs?"

Charlie's feet twitched, in aching unison. Slowly he said, "Why would you expect me to have another Dragunov?"

Color began to prick out on the man's already red face. "You're still only considering two rifles: the one recovered from the arrested man and the unknown, different caliber Medved?"

"Yes."

"Let's go into the workshop."

It was a march more than a walk along a connecting corridor and Charlie's feet hurt with the effort of keeping up. It was a long room, with what was obviously a firing range leading off to the right, some with unmarked targets, others with bullet-recoverable butts for analyses and comparison. Deeper into the room were benches equipped with vices and calibrating machinery and enhancing cameras. Snelling led past it all to the far end, where there were the sort of backlighted viewing screens against which X-rays are normally examined. Upon the entire bank were clipped what Charlie realized, when he got closer, to be the hugely enlarged photographs of the bullets recovered from the Moscow victims. Closer still he saw each was identified against the victim's name. Separated by a gap was what were marked to be pictures of bullets test fired from Bendall's gun by the American ballistics team.

"We're not interested in the 9mm bullets, from the Medved," dismissed Snelling, a blackboard pointer now in his hand. "This . . ." he tapped the third print "is the bullet recovered, according to your notes, from American Secret Serviceman Jennings. This . . . " the pointer went farther to the right "is from the Russian security man, Ivanov. And these . . ." Snelling moved over the division, to the American prints "are pictures described to me as being three separate test firings, from the SVD recovered from the gunman, George Bendall . . . ?"

"Yes?" said Charlie.

"The SVD bullet from Ivanov is a better comparison than that from Jennings, although there's still just enough," said the ballistics expert. "Look at them. There's no marking. But look at the American test firings. See it!" The pointer tapped impatiently. "There's a groove line, on every one. You know was rifling is?"

Charlie did but he said, "No."

Snelling sighed. "The barrels of rifles—particularly snipers' rifles—are bored like the thread of a screw. It increases accuracy and velocity. There's a fault, a snag, in the rifling of the SVD you say was used by George Bendall. Any bullet fired from it would be scored, like these three pictures of the American test firings show them to be identifiably marked."

"But the bullets that hit Jennings and Ivanov are not?"

"There's substantial impact damage," qualified Snelling. "But they don't appear to be from the photographs with which I've been provided."

"So they weren't fired by George Bendall?"

"I'll go as far as saying that in my professional opinion it's highly unlikely."

Anne Abbott was again waiting in the bar when Charlie got back, late, to the Dorchester. "What would you say if I told you the bullets that killed Ben Jennings and cost Feliks Ivanov his leg weren't fired by George Bendall?" demanded Charlie.

"I'd say holy shit and then I'd ask you to convince me."

In Moscow the American embassy incident room quieted at John Kayley's entry. Kayley said, "The president has accepted the resignation of Paul Smith as Bureau Director."

"Will it be enough?" queried someone in the room.

"As far as I know there isn't anything else."

17

Sir Rupert Dean said, "Are you telling us George Bendall didn't shoot anybody!"

It was the first interruption since Charlie had started to speak fifteen minutes earlier in the riverview conference room at Millbank and he was enjoying the unqualified attention. Even Jocelyn Hamilton hadn't found anything to attack. Charlie said: "In the opinion of one ballistics expert, with fifteen years of specific forensic experience matching bullets with guns, it is highly unlikely from the photographs he's seen that the two bullets thought to have come from Bendall's rifle were in fact fired from it. He's now submitted what he examined to two other specialists, for their independent assessment. He also wants to examine the physical evidence: all the recovered bullets and Bendall's rifle. Until he's able to do that, he says he can't be categorical."

"Will the Russians release them?" demanded Hamilton, at last.

"I won't know that until I get back," said Charlie. "At the moment they're in the incident room at the American embassy. It could be that their ballistics people have come to the same opinion and carried out the tests our man wants to conduct. Reached a definitive conclusion, in fact."

"You had this overnight, known about it for fifteen hours!" protested Hamilton. "What's wrong with the telephone!"

"All sorts of things if the call's made to the wrong place and number," said Charlie, savoring being able to puncture the man's attempts so easily. "I spoke to Morrison at our embassy, on a secure line, first thing this morning. Got him to check what's been made generally available by the Americans on the incident room computers, which are supposed to hold all the evidence we have. It's convenient our two embassies are so close. It didn't take him long to come back to me, again on our own secure line. There was nothing about this, as of an hour ago. So if the American have picked it up, they're not sharing it."

"How do you read that?" asked Jeremy Simpson.

"I don't," said Charlie. "They might not have found it yet. If they have, they might be holding it back to be some sort of bargaining counter, to recover with the Russians. Or they think it's something only they've discovered and don't intend sharing it at all. If they haven't got George Bendall they haven't got anyone who really matters."

"Neither have the Russians," Simpson pointed out.

"Let's talk about that!" demanded Patrick Pacey, more to the lawyer than anyone else. "How clear are we, if what the director said is provable: that Bendall didn't shoot anyone?"

They were aware of Anne Abbott, Charlie reminded himself. And there seemed no longer any reason why he shouldn't refer to her. Charlie said, "A lawyer from the embassy's legal department came back from Moscow with me. She's postponed her return, because of this, to discuss it and possibly get different instructions."

"Those instructions will have the advantage of Russian law, which I don't know in sufficient detail," said Simpson. "We accept there's a conspiracy, which Bendall has in some way to be part. He was at the scene, he had a gun and he fired it, even if he didn't hit anybody. If the bullets aren't his I think it helps greatly with a mitigation plea, like the fact that he was drunk and that there's a mental problem. If we get the real conspirators in the dock we could possibly show Bendall to be the totally manipulated dupe."

"And if we don't get the real conspirators in court?" persisted the political officer.

"We've got a defendable not guilty plea to murder, a guilty plea—with the mitigation I've talked about—to conspiracy to murder," assessed Simpson. "But let's not lose sight of the fact that under English law *conspiracy* to murder—premeditatedly planning a killing rather than committing the act in a moment of anger or passion—is held to be worse than the actual crime itself."

"So we're not a great deal further forward?" said Hamilton.

"I'm not qualified to offer a legal opinion," said Patrick Pacey. "What I can assess is our ability to offer a political and diplomatic defense and I think that's gone up tremendously."

"And in so doing continues to justify this department," agreed the director-general, looking pointedly at his deputy.

And his continued posting in Moscow, Charlie recognized. He wondered how Natalia would feel about that when he told her. *If* he told her. He probably wouldn't. He hadn't talked to her in any detail about the initial criticism in London which was now virtually immaterial anyway. It had been a more conscious decision to withhold the uncorroborated ballistic findings even before she'd told him of the FSB confrontation during the previous evening's call. Despite getting the unintended admissions and concessions from the insufficiently programmed secondary witnesses, she'd gone farther than he would have liked or suggested in summoning the chairman of the FSB, particularly with the presidential uncertainty and it surprised him. He was even more anxious now to get back to Moscow and talk to her about it. What else was there for the two of them to talk about? Nothing, Charlie decided at once; no commitment, no recriminations therefore no guilt.

Jocelyn Hamilton said, "Are we in any way affected by the dismissal of the FBI director?"

"I don't see why we should be," said Pacey. "It's obviously a political gesture, a pretty dramatic attempt to recover by the Americans; desperate, almost."

"Might that not indicate that they haven't got the ballistic analyses yet?" queried Dean.

"I don't think so," Charlie came in quickly, always aware that Sir Rupert was an academic, not a sewer soulmate. "You want to burst a dam, you set a heavy enough charge to ensure everything's engulfed. The entire responsibility for the breakdown between America and Russia has been dumped upon their director, who's blown away; charged, convicted and sentenced if not to death then to career oblivion. Washington's adopting Russian precedent—purging—is easier for Russian to understand. And, hopefully, to be enticed back into the sharing, communal fold."

"We do need to be part of a sharing, communal fold, don't we?" suggested Sir Rupert Dean.

Charlie was way ahead of the older man's reasoning—why, in fact, irrespective of today's discussion, he'd never intended sharing the Woolwich Arsenal doubts until he got back to Moscow—but showing the deferential diplomatic awareness that would have surprised everyone in the room, he said, "I think so, sir, for all the reasons we've already discussed."

"So we've got the way to achieve it, haven't we?" said Dean.

Charlie smiled, as if in initial understanding. "Yes we have, haven't we?"

Viktor Ivanovich Karelin was someone who strove—and succeeded—to be the sort of man crowds were made of, inconspicuous, unrecognized and unknown. He actually cultivated the amorphous grayness—gray face, gray hair, gray suit—traditional for an intelligence head but which was all the more necessary in the current leadership flux. He was a KGB-era bureaucrat, politically—and willingly—promoted by the president as a hopeful bridge across which the old would cross to the new in attitude and allegiance. Which some, although not all, attitudes and allegiances had and which added to what the pliably adaptable Karelin viewed as a major personal problem, his now being stranded in the middle of the bridge without knowing which side visibly to head for. Sending Gennardi Mittel in his place had put him on the traditional side of the divide. He had never, in a million years, expected the unthinkably direct—humiliating—challenge. Which had to mean that the intelligence he had so far had analysed on the likely succession—and Aleksandr Mikhailevich Okulov's strength—was questionable. In which case there had potentially been a very bad miscalculation—a mistake for which professional analysts would be called to explain—and from which he had to recover. Or at least put himself back in the middle of the bridge. The problem was getting back there, without losing any further face. The truth—or what he believed to be the truth—would actually add to the humiliation.

There was none of the arrogant strut of his previous day's emissary when Karelin entered the Kremlin room, although there was a self-enclosed confidence about the man when he sat, folded his hands in his lap and waited to be addressed. I've come this far—reluctantly—now you come to me. Only Yuri Trishin knew what the FSB chairman looked like, so completely did Karelin preserve his anonymity and that recognition came from an unpublished photograph on presidential record, not from any personal meeting. The photograph had been badly lit, to be intentionally misleading. Natalia's immediate impression was of a self-assured professional. She hoped she was right. It would mean—*should* mean, if she were right—that he wouldn't be taking this personally. It would have been worrisome that he looked intently and undividedly at all three of them—herself last and most intently of all—as if identifying them had she not earlier that morning received the acting president's signed congratulations for her previous day's handling of the FSB opposition.

The moment for their meet-in-the-middle diplomacy, decided Natalia. "Thank you, Chairman Viktor Ivanovich, for coming today."

"I'm afraid there was a misunderstanding," said Karelin. There was a slight sibilant speech impediment.

"Which is what we believed it to have been," said Natalia. Hands extended, hands touched: no embarrassment.

"I would like to help the commission, if I could."

"We hope you can," said Natalia, more positively. Nudge him off the prepared path, she thought. "Was the FSB actively involved in the attempted assassination of the Russian and American presidents?"

Karelin gave no facial or physical reaction whatsoever. Neither did he artificially hesitate, as if surprised or offended by the question. "No."

Not a hard enough push, Natalia decided, remembering the telephone call from Leonid Zenin. "Has the FSB any assets within the Burdenko Hospital?"

"I don't understand that question," said Karelin, again without hesitation. He'd demanded briefings on every possible question but the hospital hadn't been mentioned.

"It's a very simple one," said Natalia. "Is there someone on the medical staff of the Burdenko Hospital who is an informant or operative of the FSB?" There would have been, when the organization was the KGB. There hadn't been a government body, civilian institution or supposed independent organization that hadn't been infiltrated.

"Not to my knowledge."

"You are the chairman, Viktor Ivanovich. Such awareness would be far below your personal knowledge, wouldn't it?"

Karelin's concentration was absolute, the two men either side of Natalia non existent. "Yes."

"This is a presidential commission. We have the highest security clearance."

Karelin was churning inwardly, bewildered by the questioning. "I acknowledge that."

"The FSB has taken over the responsibilities of the KGB?" Beside her Natalia was conscious of Pavl Filitov shifting, noisily, and decided the Federal Prosecutor was communicating with Karelin in sympathetic body language. It was going to be a surprise for him and Trishin when she stopped allowing both to hide behind her skirts. Knowing as they did of Okulov's congratulatory letter, both men were noticeably deferential.

"In a greatly reduced and publicly accountable way."

Natalia could not have anticipated that response and for a moment she needed to recompose herself—adjust her mind—to the maximum benefit. "Does the Fifth Chief Directorate still exist?"

"I had forgotten you were once a KGB officer," said Karelin.

A weak response—weak threat—Natalia decided. "Does the Fifth Chief Directorate still exist?"

"With greatly reduced functions. And no longer under that designation."

She had to be careful not to demean the man. "Will you undertake to have the former Fifth Chief Directorate, whose responsibility was to emplace KGB agents and informants in all public services, checked to see if your succeeding organization has an asset within Burdenko Hospital?"

"Not without knowing the reason for such an enquiry." Karelin listened expressionlessly, still physically unmoving, to Natalia's explanation and didn't speak for several moments after she'd finished. When he did he said, "I will have that search made."

"We appreciate your cooperation," smiled Natalia. She gave herself pause, to anticipate the moment. Then she said, "I'll now hand the inquiry over to my colleagues."

There was a deafening silence, more disconcerting for both Filitov and Trishin by the way the FSB chairman visibly moved his head between them, in expectation. It was the federal prosecutor who finally verbally stumbled into the exchange and almost at once Natalia was conscious of Karelin relaxing, settling more obviously—comfortably—into his chair. Filitov—and occasionally Trishin—recited their questions never once pressing the man. Nor did they pick up from the concessions that had been prised out of the previous day's witnesses after their dismissal of Gennardi Mittel. Karelin *was* clearly a professional, so he would be reading the encounter—particularly Trishin's part in it—as she was. The presidential chief of staff was nervous, deferring to the other man. So he was uncertain of the current political situation, according the organization Karelin represented—and Karelin himself—the respect of fear Russia's intelligence apparatus had always commanded. There was another, more personal—and disconcerting—conclusion to be drawn. She hadn't properly succeeded in including either Trishin or Filitov in the difficult questioning so she was very obviously isolated. It would be wrong for her to show the unease of the men sitting on either side of her.

Natalia chose a hesitant gap from Filitov and said, "We yesterday took evidence from four officials of the Registry and Achives department, which appears to have remained unchanged in the reorganization?"

"That is so."

"It was agreed that the records of Peter Bendall—and those upon his family—would have been specially assigned to be retained, not disposed of."

"That is so," repeated Karelin.

"None of the witnesses we questioned yesterday could account for their disappearance. Can you help us about what might have happened to them?"

"There was clearly an unauthorized removal."

"Stolen, you mean?" pressed Natalia.

"Yes," confirmed Karelin. "The reorganization since the early nineties has been substantial: something in the region of 22,500 personnel have been released. Ill feeling was inevitable. The Bendall dossier is not the only instance of interference and tampering, of sabotage. Is it the wish of this commission that I have investigated every one of the 22,500 people who have been dismissed?"

Condescension invited by the deference of Filitov and Trishin, recognized Natalia. "I'm sure we can bring that down to manageable proportions. Registry would have the names of every Control under whom Peter Bendall operated after his arrival here, people who would know the existence of everything involving the family. They'd also know which, if any, officer associated with the Bendalls is among those discharged from the service and likely to be disaffected . . ."

"That's a very constructive suggestion," said Karelin.

"It would help all of us involved now to be able to talk to the officer described by the mother as having spoken specifically to George Bendall when he was being disruptive at home," pressed Natalia.

"It's noted."

"It was suggested by the mother that during that disruptive period the KGB arranged psychiatric counselling for George Bendall. Registry would have the identity of that psychiatrist?"

"Wasn't that put to Registry personnel yesterday?" queried the man.

"They said they were not aware of the treatment. We'd like the question reemphasized, with your authority."

"It will be."

"And I think we can even more tightly confine the search for officers who removed material from your archives," said Natalia. "It was only positively decided in the last four months that the American president was actually coming here for the summit, so it was only in the last four months that the conspirators would have had any need for the Bendall files. No one to whom we talked yesterday from Registry and Archives was seemingly able to help but if called upon by you, personally, I would have hoped they could have even *remembered* people showing an interest in the material, wouldn't you?"

Karelin's smile could only have been of admiration, for her laser-like paring of possibilities, but it was still glacial. "I would have hopes so, too."

"I think we might have made considerable progress today, chairman Karelin."

"I trust that we have."

"We can look forward to hearing from you very soon then?"

"You will hear from me," promised Karelin. The smile was glacial again.

Guerguen Agayan limited the attempt to fifteen minutes but Bendall's response to every question either Zenin or Olga put to him was to hum the wailing tune and Zenin gave up after only ten. They withdrew to the cluttered office of Nicholai Badim.

Zenin said, "So he's worse?"

"I don't think there's an actual deterioration," said the psychiatrist. "I think that was today's game."

"Has he spoken coherently to you?" asked Olga. There hadn't been a chance to listen to the permanently maintained recording.

"Barely. But he understands what I'm asking him."

"What's he say about the injection?"

"He can't remember it being done. Whether or not it was the Americans."

"I'm surprised he's out of bed?" said Zenin, turning to Badim.

The surgeon said, "Physically he's healing remarkably well. I didn't want any lung congestion from his being kept in bed."

"How long will he be confined to a wheelchair?" pressed Olga.

"The problem is the conflicting injuries," said Badim. "His shoulder isn't strong enough to support his weight on crutches and he can't use his fractured leg unsupported."

"So how long?" insisted Zenin.

"Several weeks; three at least," said the surgeon.

"But he's recovering well?"

"Very well," said Badim, although doubtfully, knowing there was a point to the questioning.

"And he understands what's being said to him?" demanded Zenin, of the psychiatrist.

"I believe so," said Agayan.

"So there's no reason why he shouldn't be arraigned in court, in a wheelchair—appear in public and be formally charged?"

Badim looked uncertainly to the psychiatrist and then back to Zenin. "No medical reason," allowed the doctor.

"The public don't know what's going on," Zenin said to Olga. "So it's the militia who are getting all the media criticism for the investigation making no progress. I'm going to move for a court appearance."

The British Airways flight began its descent over Moscow's flat, fir-dotted western plain towards Sheremet'yevo and obediently Charlie and Anne secured their seat belts.

"It's been a trip of discovery," declared Anne. Her legal briefing had been as Jeremy Simpson anticipated but she was excited at the drama of the defense to murder.

"In all sorts of ways," agreed Charlie.

The wheels snatched at the ground and they were pushed back in their seats by the reverse thrust of the engines.

"Thanks for showing me Liberace's piano."

"It's a must on every cultural visit."

"Readjustment of friendship now that we're back on home territory?" she suggested.

"It might be an idea."

"Let's see."

The impatient embassy chauffeur on the arrival concourse said Charlie was to contact Donald Morrison as quickly as possible, so Charlie used the car phone.

Morrison said, "President Yudkin died an hour ago."

18

The death of Lev Maksimovich Yudkin ratcheted up by varying degrees the pressure upon everyone and marked the beginning—although at the time unrealized—of eventual awareness of a few of them.

Sir Michael Parnell personally, unavoidably, reinvolved himself and was waiting with Richard Brooking when Charlie and Anne Abbott reached the embassy. The premature relief of both diplomats to their overeager, overinterpretative acceptance of the ballistics information was abruptly tempered by Anne's explanation that there still appeared a *prima facie* case of conspiracy against George Bendall. That explanation stretched to a detailed summary of accusations possible under Russian law up to and including terrorism, which, like conspiracy to murder, carried the death penalty. She hoped to be able to give them better guidance the following day, after her initial meeting with the Russian lawyer engaged to lead Bendall's defence.

Charlie used the same need-to-bring-myself-up-to-date escape finally to end the empty encounter, which he did with a hopefully self-benefiting assurance to both knicker-wetting—or perhaps more distastefully knicker-fouling—diplomats that he would alert them to anything professionally relevant. Charlie had actually left the embassy and was making his way past the zoo before he realized that in their totally consuming objectivity he and Anne had parted in the embassy as professionals, making personally disassociated arrangements for the following day, and not as lovers who had explored every sexual depth and height together.

It was at about the same time of the still unembarrassed return that Charlie remembered, too, he hadn't followed up his embassy arrival message on Natalia's personal Lesnaya answering machine that he was finally on his way home and by then there wasn't any point in calling. She was at the mansion apartment when he got there. She looked tired, positively careworn, the skirt of her suit creased from several day's wear. It was still water-pocked from bathing Sasha and her hair was straggled. For the first time Charlie was conscious that although there wasn't any gray Natalia's once lustrous auburn hair was fading.

She gestured towards herself and said, "I expected you to call again. Tell me you were on your way."

"I was . . . it was a heavy meeting . . . you look wonderful."

"I've had a heavy day, too. Sasha's asleep. I didn't tell her you were coming home in case you were delayed. She's missed you." It came out like a read-from-a-card statement.

"What about you?" demanded Charlie.

"What about you?" returned Natalia, in an echo.

"Do you have to ask that?" Bastard, he accused himself.

"It was your question."

"Yes I missed you. And worried about you. And missed and worried about Sasha, as well." Double—treble—bastard.

"I'm glad you're back."

"This is for you." It was a diamond bar brooch he'd bought from the don't-forget jeweller's shop in the Dorchester foyer.

She stared into the box for several moments. "It's lovely. And thank you. But I told you not to."

"I'll leave Sasha's beside her bed, to be there when she wakes up." As he positioned the ribbon-tied package Charlie saw an identical doll already perched on the edge of Sasha's toy box, one eye collapsed in what looked like a wink. "I forgot. It was from the last trip, wasn't it? Shit!"

Natalia, who'd come into the bedroom with him, said, "We can say it's a sister."

"Or that her father is an idiot!" To what—or involving whom—did that excoriation apply?

"It's a sister," insisted Natalia. Why was he so on edge?

The awkwardness between them wasn't entirely of his making, Charlie tried to assure himself. There was an over-politeness, two people who didn't know the other very well each anxiously waiting for the other's lead. He said, "We didn't kiss hello."

"No we didn't, did we?" she agreed. She sounded uninterested.

When they did kiss that was polite, too. Dutiful. Back in the main room he went through the familiar drink making ritual and as he handed Natalia her wine he said, "You'll have more to talk about than me."

She did and it was thirty minutes and another drink later before she finished, ending with the decision to arraign Bendall in open court.

"You've got the monkey, not the organ grinders!" protested Charlie.

"I don't know what that means."

"We haven't got the real assassins, just their performer."

"It's publicly—politically—necessary now that the president has died."

"Who's pushed for it to be so quick?"

"The militia, initially. Now the Kremlin's taken over."

"We know it wasn't Bendall's bullet that killed Yudkin," reminded Charlie, urgently. "In fact it doesn't look as if Bendall shot anybody."

"Doesn't look like it to whom?" demanded Natalia.

She listened to Charlie's account as intently as he'd listened to hers. When he finished she said, "I see what you mean."

"Then make others see!" urged Charlie. "It's going to be a show trial, like the show trials of the 1930s! But this time not just the outside world but Russia will recognize the staging, recognize that the people responsible aren't going to be accused. Politically it'll be a disaster!"

"Yes it will be," Natalia agreed, in further understanding.

"Argue against it!" insisted Charlie.

"It's not a decision in which I'm personally involved, have any part of."

"You're at the very center of everything!"

"Except this."

"You've got the ear of people! The Federal Prosecutor and Yuri Trishin, for Christ's sake! Who can be more involved that those two!"

"Maybe it needs rethinking," Natalia conceded.

"You told me Okulov backed you when you confronted Karelin," further reminded Charlie. "That strength—his confidence—will be known now wherever it's necessary to be spread. An empty trial, which this will be, will make Okulov look ridiculous."

"It's an independent legal decision."

"Bollocks!" rejected Charlie. "It'll be twisted by Okulov's opponents to be his decision, in his eagerness properly to take over as president."

Natalia offered her glass, to be refilled again. As Charlie was doing it she said, "We're talking politics, Russian politics at that. I thought our job—your job particularly—was to solve a crime."

"Okulov backed *you* against the FSB. I don't—we don't—want Okulov displaced."

Natalia was silent for several minutes. "I hadn't thought that far forward."

"Now we have."

"You have. I'll make the point."

"As strongly as you can," encouraged Charlie.

"As strongly as I can," promised Natalia.

They prepared dinner together—starting with the Beluga he'd bought at the airport—and halfway through Charlie realized that the polite reservation had gone. That night though, when he reached out for her, Natalia had turned her back. He changed the gesture into arranging the covering more closely around her before turning, sleeplessly, on to his back. Somewhere he'd professionally missed something, he decided, something that he was sure, even though he didn't know what or where it could be, was important. Vital even. Then he wondered what Anne was doing and wished he hadn't.

Arkadi Semenovich Noskov was a huge man, both in height and girth and made to look even bigger by the full, unclipped beard like a black canopy over his chest. The bass profundo voice rumble from low within the barrel chest and Charlie thought the man would have better occupied one of the opera stages Natalia had tried so unsuccessfully to convince him he should enjoy than a courtroom. Charlie hoped that in the theater Noskov had chosen he wouldn't be called upon to sing too many tragedian lament, although the performance in which Charlie had so far featured that day weren't encouraging Charlie's biggest frustration was not being able to disclose the Russian intention to arraign George Bendall, which made largely pointless this first conference with the lawyer. Charlie's dissatisfaction was compounded by the outcome of every telephone call he'd so far made, in attempted anticipation of the meeting.

The first had been to the incident room and after outlining the British ballistic opinion he said, "The rifle—and the bullets—aren't any longer at the American embassy. They were withdrawn—physically removed by Olga Melnik—when the militia walked out of the cooperation arrangements. Our ballistics experts will only provide a definitive opinion—testify if called upon to do so—if they can scientifically examine Bendall's weapon."

"And it's not usual for the prosecution to make physical evidence available for defense analyses, either," rumbled Noskov. "I'm surprised they did, in the first place." He looked directly at Anne. "And you know from your consultations in London that it's unlikely they'll limit themselves to one charge."

"Which brings us back to mental impairment," said Anne.

It was Charlie's cue to recount his London meeting with the Home Office psychiatrist, which he concluded with a forewarning from another of his unproductive calls. "I've tried to speak to Olga Melnik but was told she's unavailable. I've left messages, telling her we're going to the hospital."

"We've been officially told we won't be able to interview Bendall alone," reminded Anne.

"They're making simultaneous recordings," Noskov pointed out. "We'd hardly gain anything by being by ourselves with the man."

"Do we have Russian psychiatrists available?" asked Anne.

The huge man nodded. "But I want to see Bendall by myself— with just you two—first. I want to gain my own impression before getting theirs."

Charlie half expected Olga Melnik to be waiting for them at the Burdenko Hospital, but she wasn't. There was no attempted body search by the foyer protection squad but they insisted upon examining the briefcases that Noskov and Anne carried. Only Guerguen Agayan waited beyond the cordon.

At Bendall's ward Noskov said to the obviously alerted second group, "Two of you stay. The rest get out, to make room."

"I'll stay, too," insisted the psychiatrist. "I don't want another collapse."

Charlie was impressed by the lawyer's unchallenged command. Even with only two guards and the doctor remaining, Noskov's size meant the room was crowded, as the embassy car had been bringing them, Anne squashed into a corner of the rear seat with Charlie gratefully relegated to the front, beside the driver.

From the moment of their entering the solitary ward Charlie's concentration upon George Bendall was absolute, registering the man's consciousness of everything around him, instantly isolating the intentness with which Bendall's eyes followed the initial chair-shuffling uncertainty of accommodating themselves in the confined space. Charlie was very aware of how close to him Anne had to sit; he had to learn across her, physically touching, positioning the tape recorder carefully away from the already operating Russian equipment.

"Remember me, Georgi?" invited Charlie. Noskov had agreed during their cramped drive that Charlie should try to follow the London psychiatrist's direction.

Bendall didn't respond, his attention entirely upon the gargantuan Russian lawyer.

"It's good to see you out of bed," said Charlie, who hadn't imagined the man would have been fit enough to be put into a chair. The injured shoulder didn't look to be wrapped so heavily and without the head bandages the fair hair flopped, greasily.

Bendall continued to look unwaveringly at the bearded Russian.

Charlie said, "You've given us a hell of a lot of work, Georgi. And we're getting nowhere. You really planned everything very well, didn't you?" The attention faltered, briefly, Bendall's eyes flickering towards Charlie who went on, "I don't just mean us, the British. Everyone else, too. America. Russia. You're really leading us by the nose."

Bendall finally looked properly towards Charlie, a smile twitching at the corners of his mouth. The wailing hum was almost inaudible.

Charlie said, "I don't know what we're going to do. Admit we're beaten, I guess."

The dirge grew stronger. Noskov shifted, creaking his over-burdened chair.

Charlie said, "You knew you could do it, didn't you Georgi? Beat us?"

"Course I did."

"That's what everyone's going to recognize, how much better than anyone else you've been."

"I know."

"I wonder if that KGB guy will realize it; the one who talked to you with your father that time?"

Bendall frowned but said nothing.

"You remember that time?"

"Wasn't frightened."

"I'm sure you weren't, not someone capable of doing what you've done now."

"Wouldn't do what they wanted, when I got in the army."

Charlie thought he heard Anne's intake of breath. "What was that, Georgi? What did they want you to do?"

"Doesn't matter, not now."

"It would have mattered to them, if you refused."

"Thought they had me, but they didn't."

"Why would they think that, because of your father?"

"No!" rejected Bendall, loud voiced. "Didn't need him! Never needed him!"

"Always your own man," flattered Charlie. Could he chance it? "They helped you get in the army, though?"

"Didn't become their man because of it. Not like my father. Taught them a lesson."

This could be the opening of the gate, thought Charlie, hopefully. If the KGB had got Bendall into the army he would have had a Control. "They must have been pissed off at that, made life difficult. Had people argue with you, try to persuade you?"

"Tried. Didn't work."

"He must have got into a lot of trouble, the man who tried to persuade you?"

"Took him away."

The lead, at last! "There was a man who came to see you, like they came to see your father?"

"Yes."

"A soldier, like you. I bet he wasn't as good as you with a rifle?"

Bendall smiled at the continued blandishments. "Wasn't a marksman."

Charlie breathed in deeply. "What was his name, Georgi?"

"Don't remember."

The reply was too quick but it would be wrong to press, to risk the gates closing. The Control would have joined Bendall's unit around the same time as Bendall was installed, giving them a date from which the name could be deduced from the man's withdrawal.

"I suppose you had to use all the skills you learned in the army to set your White House operation up? It must have taken a lot of time, a lot of planning?"

"Clever."

"Certainly that. You're going to be very famous. They're going to know Georgi Gugin. There'll be books written."

Bendall's eyes moved back to the lawyer, who was sitting with his head slumped, beard flowing over his chest. Part of the preparation was for Noskov to remain unidentified. Charlie said, "No, that's not right. There won't be books."

The remark brought Bendall back to him, frowning. "Yes there will."

Charlie shook his head. "Not the way you've organized it. There's not enough known for anyone to write a book, a book needs all the facts and information. We do know about Vasili Gregorovich, though; know that he was killed, drugged and left to die in front of the train. I really don't understand that. Vasili Gregorovich Isakov was your friend: your special friend. Why did he have to be murdered? Wasn't he doing things properly, obeying orders?"

Bendall's uninjured arm began to twitch, violently, and Charlie tensed for another uncontrolled outburst. Agayan came forward, too. Bendall said, "The bastard killed him." The voice was uneven, snagging the words.

Agayan said, "Easy, Georgi, easy now." To Charlie he said, "You'll have to stop."

"Who's the bastard, Georgi? Tell me," encouraged Charlie, ignoring the warning.

"That's enough!" insisted Agayan.

"I know who," said Bendall, more controlled.

"He's all right," Charlie told the psychiatrist. To Bendall he said, "They should be punished, for killing Vasili, attacking your group."

"Have been."

Charlie knew he'd lose it—lose Bendall—with one wrong word but he didn't know how to go on. "People should be told, know what happens to anyone who attacks you."

"Yes."

There was movement from the doorway, where the two guards were, but Charlie didn't look, wanting to hold Bendall's eyes. Which were very clear and quite alert. The man knew what they were talking about, understood what was being said. By comparison Charlie felt he was blindfolded. Into Charlie's mind echoed the psychiatrist's words. *I got the impression that he wants to tell someone. After all his life being discarded and downtrodden he's suddenly someone, the focus of everyone's attention.* "The television of the shooting was incredible. It's been seen in every country in the world. Millions of people have watched."

There was a positive smile. Bendall didn't speak.

"A world stage, with you on it."

The smile stayed. "Yes."

Charlie saw a way to continue. "That's how it should go on."

"I want it."

"There'll be cameras at the trial. Everyone will be watching you: listening to you."

Arkadi Noskov stirred. There was more movement noise from the doorway. Bendall said, "That'll be good."

It was the prearranged time, determined Charlie. "Arkadi Semenovitch Noskov is your lawyer. He'll be with you in court, we all will be."

"To help you," came in Noskov, perfectly on time. "There are things you want to tell the court?"

"Maybe," withdrew Bendall, cautiously.

"You want them to know, don't you?" The earlier, ordering command had gone from the sonorous voice, it was coaxing now, inviting.

"Maybe."

"They'll have to know everything, to understand. And it'll be important not to miss anything out."

Able for the first time to break his total concentration Charlie saw that despite their tape recorder, Anne was hurriedly scribbling notes on a large legal pad. He couldn't see beyond the two remaining guards at the door. Agayan was sat back, seemingly content with Bendall's recovery.

"Nothing will be missed out," said Bendall.

"We'll have to prepare carefully. Make sure of that."

"Yes." Bendall's smile was back.

"That's my job," said Noskov. "Making sure nothing's left out. You want everyone to know about Vasili Isakov?"

"Yes."

"Then we'll need to talk about it, for me to know all there is. You understand that, don't you?"

"I suppose so."

Charlie was nervous of the obvious doubt, aching to reenter the exchange but that wasn't part of their car cramped rehearsal.

"It all has to come out, to make the impact you want," encouraged Noskov and Charlie relaxed.

"I want to think about it."

Charlie abruptly realized that Bendall was relaxing, too, formulating proper sentences instead of clippping his responses to one or two words.

"I'd like you to do that," urged the lawyer. "You've thought about it already, haven't you?"

"Of course I have."

"People will be surprised, won't they?"

"It'll be sensational."

"We know it will. We'll have to go through it before we get to court, though. So that I can guarantee we don't forget anything."

"I won't forget."

"It's best that we talk about it first. There might be things I'll have to do, evidence I'll have to find to confirm what you're going to say."

"I want to stop now. Think," declared Bendall.

"I'd like to talk a little further," tried Noskov.

"When I want to," insisted Bendall, exercising his imagined control. "Not when you want to."

"I don't want him pushed," said Agayan.

The British psychiatrist's assessment had been remarkable accurate, thought Charlie. Compared against all the other interviews, they'd made quantum leaps forward. But did he have a comparison against *all* the interviews, now that the Russians weren't sharing information anymore? The situation between himself and Olga Melnik had to be resolved as quickly as possible.

"We'll come again tomorrow. At the same time," Noskov was saying.

"I'll see," postured Bendall. "Go now. I want to think."

Charlie had to stand to reach across Anne again for their tape machine and as he did so he saw Nicholai Badim in the outer corridor. Olga Melnik was expressionless beside him.

They needed the large waiting room, not Badim's smaller office. From the way Olga went through the ritual of introduction to Arkadi Noskov, Charlie guessed she knew of the man's reputation, even if she hadn't met him before. Olga's attitude towards Anne Abbott was cursory to the point of being dismissive. No one sat. The hospital surgeon-administrator looked hopefully for guidance between everyone else in the room but was disappointed. Agayan sat quietly in a corner.

Charlie told Olga "I've been trying to reach you." He wondered what he could conjure from this encounter.

Olga said, "I got the message, that's why I'm here."

"You and I have a lot of operational things to discuss, apart from today," said Charlie.

"Those 'operational things' have changed."

"Not between you and I, our two countries."

"The investigation has moved on,"

"To what?" It was encouraging. Charlie thought.

"It's officially—legally—under the direction of the Justice Ministry."

"How can that be?" Noskov's voice was like a thunder roll.

"The facts have been laid for an official arraignment."

The declaration removed the restrictive frustration between himself and the two lawyers, but as always part of Charlie's mind was way ahead of the current conversation, looking for darkened alleys and hidden side tracks. He didn't believe Olga's being there was in direct response to his earlier attempted contact, although his messages was that he would be at Burdenko. Was she trying to separate him further from the Americans by the premature announcement? If she were there was every reason to go along with the invitation, even though he was sure by now that Natalia was not keeping anything back. As pivotal though they both imagined her to be, a lot could be withheld from Natalia: if not positive information, attitudes and intentions it was important for them personally, always protectively, to get indications of before they were instigated.

Noskov's attention was on the doctor. "Is Bendall fit enough to go to court?"

"For an initial arraignment," confirmed the man.

"And mentally he's capable," added Agayan. "He simply mustn't be crowded, pushed."

Responding to Anne's whispered aside, Noskov said, "I'll seek independent medical advice on that."

"There are restrictions on access," said Olga.

"I'll want those examinations to be in the presence of this doctor, a hospital panel if necessary."

"You can make your application," condescended Olga.

"I don't see how Bendall can be arraigned on what I understand so far to be the available evidence," protested Noskov.

"That's a matter for legal judgment and interpretation," avoided Olga, easily.

"What are the formal court charges going to be?" demanded Noskov, imperious voiced again.

Olga wasn't as cowed as the ward guards. "Again, a decision for the Justice Ministry and the federal prosecutor. The militia function has been to present the evidence."

Charlie saw the opening. "Evidence it is officially agreed between our two countries—between London and Moscow—should be shared. I know you have withdrawn material from the American incident room but I expect that agreement still to exist between the two of us."

"Again that is no longer a matter for me," said Olga. "All the evidence has been passed over to the federal prosecutor. It has to be his—and the ministry's—decision if the arrangement still exists."

"We will make formal, diplomatic requests," said Anne.

"Of course you will," patronized Olga.

Charlie gestured back along the corridor. "You have just duplicated the recording of a conversation between Bendall and his legal advisors."

"There is no legal prohibition upon our doing that."

Noskov nodding his head, in agreement. Charlie said, "Has there been any further interrogation—Russian interrogation—since the claimed injection."

"Medically *proven* injection," corrected the woman.

"Medical proven injections," gritted Charlie and waited.

"There may have been."

It was her first overconfident lapse. "Olga Ivanova! You are the chief investigating officer. You would personally have conducted any subsequent interviews!"

Color spread up from the Russian detective's throat. "Any subsequent interviews would form part of the evidence already filed on record and held by the federal prosecutor."

"And forbidden to us?" demanded Anne.

"I've no way of knowing what the ministry or prosecution response would be to an official request for access."

"Which will be legally filed," promised Noskov.

"And diplomatically made as well, according to the terms of our agreement," supported Anne.

Olga Melnik was a messenger boy—or girl—Charlie realized, answering his earlier uncertainty. But well briefed. By whom? he wondered. Don't get sore, get even, he reminded himself, invoking one of the axioms of life. "As our professional cooperation appears to be over you can't expect me to pass on the evidence that's been gathered in London?"

Olga's hesitation was so long it was as if the breath had been taken from her. At last she managed. "I most certainly would if it contributed to the further progress of the investigation!"

"Which I thought was being pursued independently now?" goaded Charlie. There'd been a miscalculation, he guessed. Briskly he said to the lawyers, "Let's go to make those representations as quickly as we can. Hopefully get things back on course. There's a lot else for us to do, as you know."

In the car Noskov said, "It's political."

Anne said, "But stupid."

"Or something," said Charlie. His feet throbbed, to a metronome beat. Espionage had been a fucking sight easier than this.

Charlie arrived at the American embassy just before noon, dropped off at Novinskij Bul'var by the two lawyers on their way back to their respective offices to file their respective protests, promising both as he got out of the car that he'd call if he thought there was anything relevant from the now isolated American investigation. The FBI station chief was waiting in the incident room, closely flanked by Donald Morrison. After the younger man's back-up during his London absence Charlie didn't have the heart to exclude the man now that he'd returned.

Charlie anticipated some sort of outburst from the crumpled, cigar-perfumed American at the news of the impending court appearance but John Kayley remained reflectively silent. He didn't initially interrupt, either, when Charlie began outlining the Bendall bullet disparity but then abruptly held up a stopping hand to lead the way through the linking corridor to the improvised laboratory and the American ballistics scientist.

Willie Ying said at once, "We've been waiting for your corroboration."

"Is that why it isn't computerized yet?" angrily demanded the ignored MI6 man.

"It's your defense, against a murder charge," said Kayley, in a smooth defense of his own. "You wouldn't have wanted the Russians knowing about it in advance if it had only been a temporary walk-out, would you?"

The don't get sore, get even philosophy was American, remembered Charlie: it would be good somehow to give Morrison his personal chance. But not now. And the man was soon going to learn how things were eked out. "Did you get actual test firings, before the rifle was removed?"

The Chinese smiled. "Twenty, fired at measured graduation from in front and from behind the measurable distance from which Bendall shot. Not a score mark on any of them. Not that distance has got anything to do with it. The best guess is that Bendall's bullets went off somewhere in the park, behind the White House."

"We've actually looked," said Kayley. "I had guys examine the most obvious trees—anything that might have stopped a bullet—in the line of fire. Came up with nothing."

There was a shift of increasing anger from Donald Morrison but before the younger man could speak Charlie said, "I need those test-fired bullets. From the runaround I got from Olga Melnik this morning I don't think I'll get the rifle for my people to test."

"You got it," guaranteed Kayley.

"We'll need testimony as well," pressed Charlie.

There was a shrugged, head-nodding exchange between the two Americans. Kayley said, "You got that as well. It'll be good to show the bastards how wrong they were, walking out on us."

Charlie couldn't quite adjust the reasoning but it wasn't something to dispute. He didn't physically need the rifle and Anne had her dramatic defense to at least one of the charges likely to be brought. One good turn deserves another, Charlie thought. Offering that morning's tape he'd brought to be copied into the evidence collection, he said, "George Bendall wants to tell us all about it." He wondered if Morrison imagined he was a team player or whether the man realized the rules were only applied one way: it might mitigate the humiliation of his being ignored by the Americans.

Kayley smiled as he listened. Halfway through he ignited an aromatic cigar. When the replay ended Kayley said, "He does, doesn't he?" Then he said, "You take Bendall just a little further down the road and we're going to have the others. *The* bastard, whoever he is. And the Russian militia will come crawling back."

The last part was further reasoning that Charlie found difficulty with but he didn't dispute that, either. "Let's hope I can take him further."

Kayley said, "I've got to go upstairs. There are people who'll want to hear this."

"They're bastards, too!" said Morrison, vehemently, as he and Charlie returned to the main incident room.

"Don't take it personally," soothed Charlie. "They'd have tried to fuck me if I hadn't come up with it."

"You sure?" demanded Morrison.

"Positive," said Charlie, who wasn't but wanted to help the other man.

"Hope I haven't disturbed your room too much," said Morrison, when they reached it.

To Charlie it didn't appear to have been occupied by anyone else. He settled into his place with its convenient foot rest and logged on to his computer to bring himself up to date, scrolling patiently through the alphabetically assembled files, stopping abruptly at the name Vasili Gregorovich Isakov. It had been compiled by three named FBI agents and ran to twelve pages, although it wasn't the written material that immediately interested Charlie. Three photographs had been scanned on to the disk.

John Kayley was again included with the ambassador and the secretary of state for the satellite link with Washington but only Walter Anandale and his chief of staff were waiting at the White House end. He'd have to wait, Kayley knew, but it was difficult.

"So we've got a new game," opened the president.

"Which we need to play very carefully," advised James Scamell.

"How?" said Anandale.

"I think you need to come back for Yudkin's funeral."

"You serious! There are still guys out there who tried to kill me!"

"As serious as it's possible to be, Mr. President. Your not attending will be read every which way, all of them bad. One spin will be that you're too scared. Another that you're abandoning Oku-lov, to be beaten by the communists. Who are, incidentally, de-manding an immediate election to confirm an elected president. Then there's the treaty. There's growing media speculation that there was a hidden agenda, that we never ever really intended to conclude it and that it was a cosmetic dance to go on until Yudkin got confirmed for a second term."

Wendall North admired the secretary of state's diplomacy. Sca-mell wasn't talking of Moscow's media pressure. He would have got from his own people at Foggy Bottom that morning's *Washington Post* story of a potential paper trail from oil contract firms finally being followed to Anandale's election funding. The chief of staff said, "I go along with Jamie's assessment, Mr. President. We're in a box here, with only one way out."

"What's happening with the investigation, John?" avoided An-andale.

Kayley had risked holding back from either the secretary of state or the ambassador the Russian decision to arraign Bendall, wanting to present it ahead of any official announcement as his personal discovery, despite the breakdown with the Moscow militia. He also explained the ballistic evidence as an exclusive detection of the FBI team he headed. He had to concede the British would be the source of any statement from Bendall from which it might be possible to locate the others in the conspiracy, but did so inferring that Britain needed Bureau manpower and scientific expertise to continue the investigation.

"*Find* the people who shot Ruth!" picked out the president, in-stantly.

"If we get the statement the Brits expect," backtracked Kayley.

"Now we're getting there!" enthused Anandale.

"I'm giving it to you as it's come to me," said Kayley, stressing the impression of urgency at the same time as shielding himself from questions he couldn't answer. "There's a lot I need explained fur-ther, pieces to fit together."

"We've got things to talk about when I get there, John," hinted Anandale. To the secretary of state he said, "Is it going to be a State occasion? World leaders?"

"I'd imagine so," said Scamell.

"Find out," ordered the president. "Here's how we'll run it. I'll come early, for meetings with the British premier and the French president. Overnight either in London or Paris, so I can be in and out of Moscow from either city the same day as the funeral."

"You need to meet with Okulov," insisted Scamell.

"Not to do so would be worse than not going at all," said North, in continued support.

"I'm not giving anything away for nothing," said Anandale. "You make it clear, whichever way it's necessary, that I won't meet Okulov if their damned investigators don't come back to the table." He hesitated. "Everything else stands. I'm out of there the same day, OK?"

"It's obvious the British are getting through to Bendall," insisted Olga, taking the Russian copy of the interview tape from the machine on the table between her and Leonid Zenin.

"And we're getting every word of it," the militia commander pointed out.

"If we do get a lead to the rest of them, arraigning Bendall will be premature."

"It's out of our hands now," said Zenin. "And it's not a trial. It's a public arraignment, for public consumption: the formal laying of the formal charges. The prosecutor can apply for adjournments as long as we ask him."

"You sure it's wise, shutting out the British as we're shutting out the Americans?" pressed Olga. "They've obviously got something."

"Or bluffing."

Olga shook her head. "I don't think he was bluffing."

"We'll see how their next interview goes," decided Zenin. "We can easily get back together if it turns out to be really productive." He was silent for several moments. "In fact it might be an idea if you were actually present, able to see as well as hear for ourselves. We're going to come out well from this, Olga Ivanova."

Olga smiled at his automatically talking in the plural, of both of them. "I think we already have."

"You got it, Charlie!" agreed Anne, excitedly. "An absolute defense to murder! An expert witness, even."

"I'd still prefer him to be British," said Charlie. He was distracted by the Isakov file. Like so many other unresolved impressions—frustrations—there was something in it demanding to be seen. But like all the others, he couldn't see it!

"I've filed the diplomatic protest. So's Noskov, legally." Anne was disappointed—curious even—at how subdued Charlie was.

"We're still short of too much else." He was glad he'd printed off the Isakov material to bring back to the embassy, to go over it further.

"There could be the breakthrough with Bendall if you continue teasing him along as well as you did today. And that could be as early as tomorrow."

Her ambition was making her over-confidence—or over-expectant—Charlie decided. "Then all our problems will be over. Or just beginning."

"Misery guts!"

"Realist," he corrected.

Anne put into its designated order the material Charlie carried into her office thirty minutes earlier and gestured vaguely in the direction of the embassy's residential apartment block. "The weary end to a long day. You fancy a Happy Hour drink?"

Charlie couldn't at that moment imagine anything he would have enjoyed more. "No."

"OK." Anne showed no offense, no anger at a rebuff, which Charlie hadn't intended it to be.

That night Natalia came to him in bed and the lovemaking was as uninhibited and passionate as he could ever remember, even from their first, excited, discovery days. Afterwards Natalia said, "I'm sorry, Charlie: sorry for too long being such a shit."

"We've both been shits," said Charlie and at last felt the overdue and searing guilt.

19

Viktor Ivanovich Karelin was the first intelligence chairman Natalia had ever personally met but the apparent diffidence was so alien to the lower hierarchy with whom she was familiar that she was vaguely disconcerted by it. Which, she acknowledged, she was perhaps supposed to be, although she didn't get the impression there was any affectation about the self-effacing demeanour. Another interpretation could be that Karelin was so sure of himself and the power he represented that he didn't feel the need to posture and intimidate.

"Thank you for returning to us so quickly," greeted Natalia. What would the man have managed to achieve in thirty-six hours compared to what their president-endorsed demand to the Defense Ministry had generated in less than twelve, five of those with the previous night intervening? It would be important for her—the tribunal—not to appear to try to trap the man.

"You stressed the urgency," reminded Karelin.

"We're indeed anxious to hear what you have to tell us," said Filitov, stilted in his eagerness to get himself on the ever-kept record.

"There has clearly been considerable, malicious interference—possibly destruction—of a substantial proportion of archival material concerning Peter Bendall and his family," admitted Karelin, at once. "I have instituted an enquiry, the results of which I will make fully available to this commission when it is completed."

Honesty or yet further prevarication? She was the trained interrogator, Natalia reminded herself. "This malicious interference? Is it indiscriminate, consistent with the haphazard pilfering by disgruntled former personnel, about which we talked earlier? Or is there a pattern?"

A smile wisped across Karelin's face. "There is unquestionably a pattern."

Had the smile been admiration or something else? Having been specific Natalia intentionally generalized. "Help us with that."

"No material whatsoever remains for what would have been the last five years of Peter Bendall's life."

"And the son?"

"Nothing."

"Which there would—should—have been?"

"Unquestionably." The woman, with her KGB background, was the only one who might be difficult. The lawyer and the politician were spreading their bets.

"So the interference has been calculated, carried out for a reason?"

"Obviously," agreed the FSB chairman.

"What reason?" demanded Yuri Trishin.

Karelin frowned. "That's what I've set up an internal enquiry to find out." The man looked fleetingly across the echoing Kremlin room towards the record-keeping secretariat. "There is clearly an attempt being made to discredit the organization I head by apparently implicating it in the assassination of the president. The FSB was, obviously, in no way involved. Its only culpability is a serious lapse of internal security, which has already been corrected as well as those responsible being punished."

The fulcrum upon which Natalia's early employment in the KGB had been balanced was her being able to judge whether the person she was interviewing was lying or being truthful. Karelin had conceded what they already knew. And had established internal enquiries, which was precisely what her outside commission had been created to prevent. Despite which Natalia's professional assessment was that the FSB chairman *was* telling the truth. Continuing to call upon her previous association and awareness of Russian intelligence working, Natalia said, "Peter Bendall's records would not have been concentrated. Archives would have been cross-referenced with Registry. While he was alive, even though his practical use might have become minimal, there would have been a current file maintained upon him?"

The shadowy smile came and went again. "It's the very fact that the removal has been from several different centers that *confirms* a pattern."

"Nothing whatsoever beyond that which has already been made available has survived?" persisted Natalia.

Karelin had his tidbit ready. "I have obtained from Registry the identities of four of Peter Bendall's Control officers, one of whom might, calculated from the son's age, have been the man who might have corrected George Bendall in his teens and obtained psychiatric help for him."

"The KGB would have had a copy of that treatment," insisted Natalia.

"I've checked. There is no copy," said the man.

There was a shift from the men either side of her but Natalia remained unmoving, curious at how Karelin was providing his information. He was unarguably cooperating but at his own careful pace, which she realized she was making easy for him. The occasional smiles were more likely to be self-satisfaction—just tinged with gratitude—at how he was manipulating her questioning than admiration of her technique. It would be as wrong too obviously to challenge the man as it would not to make him aware, as subtly as possible, that she recognized his skill. "I'd like to think that he particularly was available to help us. But I don't imagine that any of them are."

"They're all dead," the FSB chairman confirmed. She was *very* good, to have anticipated that: a loss to the service, in fact.

"How?"

Karelin, in his complete self-confidence, decided to test the woman. "The first, who took Peter Bendall over upon his arrival in 1972, died of cancer in 1975. His successor had a stroke, in 1981. The Control most likely to have put George Bendall back in line—briefly at least—was electrocuted by faulty wiring in his apartment and the fourth committed suicide by hanging himself. He was one of the officers made redundant during the restructuring of the old service."

"A disgruntled officer!" seized Filitov, overanxiously.

"Beyond which we've already extended the discussion," dismissed

Natalia. Karelin hadn't finished but wanted prompting, she guessed. "You didn't give dates, for the last two deaths?"

She'd more than passed the test, decided Karelin. "The man most likely to have lectured George Bendall died three months ago. The one who committed suicide did so last month."

"Both deaths were accepted for what they appeared to be?" came in Filitov, unexpectedly.

Karelin took folders from his briefcase, offering them across the table. "They are the personnel files on all four. The last two are marked. Both their deaths are now being investigated for possible suspicious circumstances. The result of those investigations, like the internal security breaches, will be made available."

Another intelligence-restricted enquiry, Natalia noted. "But there had to be other Controls after these—at least one—during the last five years of Peter Bendall's life?" She spoke looking down at the newly presented dossiers, needing the names. None fitted.

"Yes," agreed Karelin.

"And a case officer—or officers—for the son?"

"That's the system." There was no way an outside tribunal like this could breach the protection built up over so long by the succeeding intelligence services but it would be wrong for him to be complacent about this woman.

"We made another request, at our previous meeting," reminded Natalia. "About FSB presence at Burdenko Hospital?"

"There is no FSB—or long-established KGB—presence at Burdenko Hospital," asserted Karelin, positively.

It was time, Natalia decided. Despite the awkwardness with which Karelin had tried to ringmaster the encounter she still had to guard against appearing confrontational. "There is—or has been—some sharing between us, the Americans and the British, into the shooting of the presidential group; more particularly, perhaps, with the British who have consular access to Bendall. Their interview recordings are automatically duplicated . . ."

Karelin sat politely attentive, making no effort to anticipate what Natalia might say but knowing there was something for which he had not been able to prepare.

"At one such interview yesterday Bendall claimed the KGB maneuvred his admission into the Russian army. And that a Control was infiltrated to monitor whatever function he was expected to perform in the military," continued Natalia.

"I know nothing of this," said Karelin. His face was mask-like.

It was predictable but Natalia had still hoped for more. "From the interview it would appear Bendall's Control was withdrawn or discharged from his specialized unit after Bendall's persistent refusal to operate as he was instructed."

"It should be fairly simple to check personnel movement from military records, especially from a specialized unit," said Karelin, at once. He genuinely didn't know anything about it but it was quite likely to be the case. And if it was, it took the enquiry outside his— of FSB—containment.

Perfect, decided Natalia. "We realized that. This morning, unfortunately not in time to advise you in advance of your coming here, the Defense Ministry provided us with the names of fifteen men discharged, transferred or reassigned from Bendall's group during the first six months of the man's service . . ." She pushed the Defense file across the desk towards the intelligence chief. "The four Control names you've supplied are not among these. We'd like you to have Registry run a check, against the fifteen."

Karelin hesitated, then picked up the folder. "I cannot confirm the KGB had anything to do with arranging Bendall's army service."

Karelin felt himself tricked, despite her effort to prevent his thinking that. "We accept that, Chairman Karelin. It's not what we're asking you to confirm. We are asking you to compare the fifteen names through Registry, in an attempt to discover if any KGB personnel accompanied George Bendall into his military service. That should be very easily possible, shouldn't it? Within hours, even?"

"I would expect so," agreed the expressionless man.

"If one of them does appear in Registry, let's hope he's still alive," said Natalia.

The meeting had been convened solely because of the FSB chairman's approach to them and Filitov and Trishin appeared surprised that Natalia didn't move at once to suspend it until the promised-within-hours result of their new request to the man. But Natalia decided that she had sufficient excuse—if not the true reason—to argue against George Bendall's court arraignment.

There were other more self-protective points she felt necessary to establish, too. Virtually as the door closed behind Viktor Karelin, she said, "What's your feeling about what we've just been told?"

Each man looked to the other to respond first.

"Pavl Ivanovich?" pressed Natalia.

"It's positive confirmation of the conspiracy being within the FSB," declared the lawyer.

"Yuri Fedorovich?"

"I was surprised at the chairman's openness," said the presidential chief of staff.

"He has, though, taken all the enquiries away from us—kept everything internal—which we were specifically appointed to prevent," Natalia pointed out.

"He's undertaken to make them available to us," said Filitov.

"*Something* will be made available," qualified Natalia. "We have no independent way or method of knowing whether we are being told the truth. Or how much of any enquiry is being given to us. We've been very effectively and very cleverly neutered."

Trishin shifted, uncomfortably. "I wouldn't go that far."

"Think about it," demanded Natalia.

The silence lasted several moments before Filitov said, "What do you suggest?"

Natalia tapped Karelin's naming dossiers. "An independent, professional militia investigation into the two most recent and violent deaths. A presidential insistence upon there being an outside militia presence or monitor on the internal FSB enquiries. And an independent militia trace upon the fifteen names we received this morning from the Defense Ministry."

"That's directly challenging Chairman Karelin's integrity," protested Filitov.

"Not to do so is directly challenging ours, and by inference that of the acting president," insisted Natalia, acknowledging the repetition of the same argument as before but at that moment anxious to move on to what she considered the other, more important argument. "The Defense Ministry names opens the door into the conspiracy."

"Only if one of them is on the FSB Registry," insisted Filitov.

"No," refused Natalia. "We've got last known addresses as well as names. And every legal justification for having the militia fully investigate every one, as soon and as quickly as possible. Beginning today, in fact."

There was a pause from both men.

Filitov said, "Yes, I suppose that, specifically, would be the right course for us to take."

"I agree," said Trishin.

"Which surely creates something else to be considered?" suggested Natalia.

"What?" demanded Filitov.

"The court arraignment of George Bendall."

"What consideration is that of this commission?" demanded Filitov.

"Quite separately from anything with which Chairman Karelin might return, from the Registry check, we are providing the militia with a source which could lead us to others involved in the conspiracy, could greatly affect the charges and prosecution against George Bendall," said Natalia. Directly addressing Filitov, she said, "Surely the prosecution doesn't know enough for an arraignment, this early? Aren't you risking a flawed case, not giving the investigation more time."

"The arraignment isn't the trial," rejected Filitov. "That's weeks away, time enough for all the conspirators to be identified and arrested and co-joined in a prosecution upon whatever additional charges need to be proffered."

"World attention will be upon us, for the funeral of President Yudkin," said Trishin. "Politically it is necessary for there to be a publicly witnessed court appearance . . ." He hesitated. ". . . And there has been some overnight communication from the Americans that make that even more essential."

She was wasting her time, Natalia acknowledged: she didn't have either logic or law on her side, quite apart from political necessity which more often than not wasn't affected or influenced by either.

"The order is from the Kremlin, from Okulov's office itself!" said Zenin. He was red-faced, pacing his crumbling office, needing movement to exorcise his fury.

"Why?" asked Olga. She pushed the indignation into her own voice but was secretly glad at the instruction to resume cooperation. What little progress had been made—far too little though it was—had been through association, particularly with the Englishman. There was more professionally—by which she meant career enhancing—to be gained than sacrificed by linking up again.

"No reason was given." Zenin slumped in his seat. "It's a personal rebuke, to me."

Olga had momentarily forgotten the withdrawal had been Zenin's decision. "No it's not. If it had been considered a mistake it would have been overruled immediately; you were actually supported. Something's happened, to change things."

Zenin's smile was as brief as it was reluctant. "Yes, I suppose you're right."

She was the person who had to crawl back, Olga abruptly realized, her own anger surfacing. "Am I expected just to walk into the incident room, as if it was all a big misunderstanding!"

"I'm sorry," said Zenin, unhelpfully.

"So am I!" It wouldn't be as difficult with the Englishman, despite the previous day's argument at the hospital. Her personal difficulty would be openly descending into the American embassy basement with everyone's eyes upon her.

"Today's hospital meeting . . ." Zenin started to remind but stopped at the tentative entry of his personal assistant, a uniformed major.

The man extended the package he carried and said, "It's been couriered from the Kremlin. For immediate and personal delivery."

Olga saw the smile, no longer reluctant, settle on Zenin's face as he read. It remained when he looked up. "We've got names of people from Bendall's unit who could have been his KGB case officer. The commission wants us to trace every one. It's your entry back. I'll assign the investigators, you provide the list as part of the combined investigation. And we'd already decided you should be at the British interview this afternoon."

It wouldn't make any easier her humiliating embassy reentry, thought Olga. She said, "The militia will be directly and identifiably investigating the FSB, what we agreed would be dangerous."

Zenin's smile faltered. "Not our decision. Provably ordered, by the presidential enquiry."

"We're still being sucked in too close," warned Olga.

She was waiting directly outside George Bendall's ward when Charlie arrived, with the two lawyers. Five chairs were set out in readiness in the room already emptied of guards who hovered further along the corridor. Beyond the woman Charlie saw Bendall was in a chair, too. Charlie was sure the bandaging on the man's leg as well as the swathe around his shoulder and arm was less than the previous day.

Handing Charlie the list Olga said, "Names you might want to put to him, they're the men moved out of Bendall's unit in the first six months of his army service."

"You haven't put them to him already?" demanded Charlie, at once. They had to have been. Perhaps they had but she wanted Bendall's failure or refusal to respond to be on his recording, not on their no longer shared duplicate.

"I've only just got them," Olga replied, honestly. "Only just arrived here myself."

Would she risk the lie being exposed by Bendall protesting he'd already been asked? It wasn't important, Charlie dismissed. He had them, to put to the man. He nodded further into Bendall's room. "Have you interviewed him today?"

Olga shook her head, speaking more to Arkadi Noskov. "Professor Agayan and two colleagues conducted their psychiatric assessment this morning—I'll see you get them, of course. But I haven't taken my questioning any further."

Charlie saw Anne's eyebrows lift at the name familiarity but didn't give any reaction himself. He wouldn't have imagined the previous day's British protests would have brought about such a total reversal. Another reflection that wasn't important. He ushered the two women into the room ahead of him and set up his tape. Noskov overflowed beside him.

"You're looking better, Georgi." The schedule was again for Charlie to lead the questioning, although for the lawyers to come in at once if there was something they wanted to pick up upon.

The man's eyes went to each of them in turn but he didn't respond. Assessing his audience for the latest performance, Charlie decided. "You feeling OK?"

Bendall shrugged.

"Can't imagine someone like you found this morning's meeting too difficult?"

"Didn't know what they were talking about: rubbish, most of it."

"That's what I told you before, you're cleverer than any of us. But we do need to understand more ourselves, to make it easier for others to get the complete picture of what it's all about."

"They'll find out."

"It's the complete picture that's important," joined in Noskov. "We mustn't leave anything out."

"I don't intend to."

It had been a useful interruption, judged Charlie. "It just could happen. Your not being able to remember the name of the man the KGB put into the army with you, for instance. People might not believe that if you can't recall a name, think you were making it up." Bendall's face darkened and his mouth opened for the shout but before he could Charlie said, "We don't think that, of course. That's why we've done what we can to help you."

Bendall's mouth closed but the expression remained suspicious. He needed to be aware of every expression, Charlie realized. Which he couldn't do and read out the fifteen names at the same time. Without looking at Anne he passed the list across the bed to her, at the same time saying, "We've got some names that might jog your memory. People who were in the army with you."

Anne's take-over was seamless. "Kirril Semenovich Kashva?" she began.

Bendall remained blank faced, blank eyed.

"Yevgenni Iosifovich Ibrimacimov?"

No reaction whatsoever.

"Sergei Leonidovich Golovkin?"

"Lost his nerve," broke in Bendall. "Was good at first, had a good eye. But then he developed a shake. Can't be accurate if you shake."

"Not like you," flattered Charlie, wanting to break the recitation.

"No, not like me," smiled Bendall.

"Ilya Aleksandrovich Dolya?" resumed Anne.

Bendall shook his head, swirling the lank hair. There was no grimace of discomfort from the injury.

"Boris Sergeevich Davidov?"

There was a recognition! Almost imperceptible, a fraction of a second, but Charlie was sure he'd seen the movement in Bendall's eyes, the vaguest tightening around the man's mouth.

"Igor Mikhailevich Amosov?" continued Anne, her concentration entirely on the list.

"Had a breakdown, like Sergei Leonidovich. Weak," sneered Bendall.

"Yakov Ivanovich Lomakin," persisted Anne, to Bendall's further head shake. After the following two identities the man stopped bothering even with that rejection, listening but giving no response. The only exception was with the last of the fifteen—Vladimir Grigorevich Pigorov—whom Bendall once more dismissed as weak, unable physically to endure the training.

"So the man the KGB put in with you isn't one of these?" pressed Charlie.

"Not that I recognized."

Charlie was sure that both Olga and Anne stirred, at the qualification. He said, "You would have recognized it, if he had been among them, wouldn't you?"

"Maybe."

"Do you want us to go through the list again?" offered Anne.

"Not so soon."

Wrong to push him, remembered Charlie. "Would you like a copy of the list, to look through on your own?"

"Yes," accepted Bendall at once. "Let me have a copy to take my time over."

"There's something that we can't understand, need you to help us with," said Noskov. "You only had two bullets and we know that five were fired. So there had to be someone else. Did you know there was to be someone else?"

Charlie tensed for the outburst, remembering the hysteria of the American interview, but instead of answering Bendall softly began the dirge, his eyes fixed somewhere above their heads. Hurriedly Charlie said, "Tell us about February 18, Georgi. The Thursday night Vasili Gregorovich died. You were with him that night, weren't you?"

The humming stopped. "All of us."

"The brotherhood?" prompted Charlie.

"Drinking. Singing."

"Where were you drinking?" Don't anyone interrupt, try to take over, thought Charlie.

"It was a good night. All there."

"All six of you?" chanced Charlie.

"Felt good," avoided Bendall.

"Everyone drunk?"

"Everyone drunk," agreed Bendall. "Anatoli Nikolaevich's birthday."

Charlie wished the others in the room would stop shifting, not wanting Bendall's reverie broken by the slightest distraction. Keeping his own voice an even, dull monotone, wanting only to stroke the strings, Charlie said, "A lot of toasts?"

"Smashed the glasses, the first time. Traditionally."

"Vasili Gregorovich was all right to drive, though? Knew how to drink?"

"Best drinker among us."

"Why didn't you go home to Timiryazev with Vasili? You often did, didn't you."

"Don't remember. I was drunk. Someone did."

"Who! Give us his name," abruptly demanded Olga Melnik, strident-voiced.

Bendall physically jumped and blinked, several times, as if being awakened and the fury surged through Charlie. Anne groaned, audibly, and that annoyed Charlie too. Bendall looked carefully, alertly, from one to the other, smiling, and Charlie's anger went as soon as it had come.

It was Noskov who tried to retrieve the mood, the thunderous voice soothing, encouraging. "You're doing well, Georgi. We're getting somewhere. Tell us about the funeral. You all went to that, didn't you?"

"How do you know?" Bendall was still smiling.

"I don't," said the lawyer. "I want you to tell me about it."

"Not the time."

"We've got all the time in the world, I told you that," misunderstood Noskov.

"Not the place," corrected Bendall.

"Of course you'll be able to tell everyone in court," accepted Noskov, quickly recovering. "That's what I *want* you to do. Tell me and then we'll tell everyone again, in court. Make sure everyone understands."

"No," refused the man. "I decide."

"I know you do," said Noskov. "Everything's your decision. Will you see me tomorrow?"

Bendall appeared to consider the request. "All right."

Outside in the corridor Olga said at once, "I'm sorry. It was . . ."

"It's all right," stopped Charlie. "We didn't lose anything."

Both lawyers looked at him in surprise. Anne said, "We were going like a steam train in there!"

"Bendall was driving," said Charlie.

Olga's request to come back to the incident room with him precluded the Noskov-crowded embassy car. Charlie hailed a taxi and rode to Novinskij Bul'var without asking about the apparently renewed cooperation and Olga didn't offer an explanation. The attention at their entry wasn't as obvious as Olga had feared and Kayley greeted the Russian as if there had been no interruption in her being there.

Charlie held up the tape like a prize and said, "It's the best yet."

Olga matched Charlie's gesture with what she carried and said,

"We've got a list of names that possibly includes Bendall's KGB minder, in the military. We've assigned individual teams to trace each one."

"Let's hope to Christ that this is lift-off at last," said Kayley.

That night Zenin took Olga to bed early and was more demanding than he'd been before and afterwards she lay exhausted beside him, wondering how much longer it could possibly last, unsure for the very first time how well—or badly—she would be able to cope when it ended. Whenever it did—again for the very first time—it wouldn't be by her choice.

"It's not proof," he said, picking up the earlier dinner table conversation. "You're reacting to instinct."

"I know," admitted Olga. "But I'm *right*! I can feel it. The lead we want is among those fifteen names."

"If he's there, we'll find him."

"We should allow ourselves more time, not worry so much about media timing," persisted Olga.

"You know the answer to that."

"Will we share?"

Zenin was quiet for several moments. "*After* we've got him: got everything."

"What if he's still serving in the FSB? It's more than possible."

"But we've got the authority of the presidential commission."

"Will we invoke it?"

"If we have to."

"Be careful, darling. Personally careful, I mean."

"How was it for you, going back today?"

"Better than I thought it would be."

"You think the Americans, with all their manpower, will try to trace all the fifteen?"

"Without a doubt."

"That could be our protection," suggested Zenin. "Maybe we will share. Give the Americans the name, if we think we've discovered it, let them take on the FSB."

Olga turned, moving her hand over his hair-matted chest. "Do that! It'll be safer."

"The FSB's wrecked. And Karelin with it."

"All the more reason—*every* reason—for not being associated with its destruction. Russian intelligence changes its face but not its memory."

"I'll look after you," said Zenin.

"For how long?" asked Olga, wishing she could have bitten the words back as she uttered them, stiffening beside him. She lay with her eyes closed, as if by not seeing she shut out the embarrassment. She felt him turn towards her.

"It's something for us to talk about—think about—isn't it?"

"Is it?" she said, breath tight in her chest.

"How would you feel about having me as a husband as well as a lover?"

"I'd feel very happy. How would you feel having me as a wife?"

"Very happy. And very proud."

It wasn't going to end! It was going to go on, forever and Olga couldn't imagine anything she wanted more. "Now we've got even more reason to be careful. I don't want to lose this, to risk anything."

"You think you would have got more?" asked Natalia.

Charlie shook his head. "Bendall wasn't lost in memories. It was an act, feeding us a bit at a time and making us dance to his tune . . ." he smiled at the unintentional pun. "And it's a bloody awful tune, too."

"You achieved a hell of a lot, though."

"As much as Bendall wanted to give." He hadn't told Natalia—discussed with anyone—what he believed to have been Bendall's recognition of the Davidov name. Totally unoffended by Charlie's disbelief and anxious to earn the offered fifty dollars, the concierge of the dilapidated block on Fadeeva Ulitza had two hours earlier let Charlie into Davidov's listed apartment address to prove the man was no longer there, unprotestingly watching Charlie explore the few pieces of furniture that allowed the place to be described as furnished. Davidov had lived alone and hadn't been friendly, complained the man. Davidov had been about thirty-five years old and looked fit, as if he trained, running or swimming or something like that. On the few occasions the concierge even remembered seeing him, Davidov had worn a suit, with a collar and tie, so the caretaker assumed he worked in an office. Three militiamen and some Americans who'd said they were detectives had already been there so he guessed Davidov had done something pretty serious. Charlie agreed it might have been and left with the promise of another fifty dollars if the man called his embassy number to tell him Davidov had reappeared, hoping he'd outbid the Americans to whom, along with the militia, he decided to leave the legwork involved in trying to trace Davidov further, at least until the following day.

"How long do you think it will take?"

"I've put to him the idea of the court being his stage. I wouldn't be surprised if he kept a lot back until he appears in public."

"You might not have to wait long," said Natalia. "I ran into a brick wall arguing the court hearing should be postponed. Then this afternoon Okulov's ordered the arraignment should be the same day as the funeral."

"That's in two days!" said Charlie.

"Can you imagine the media coverage?"

"Not when we enter a plea of not guilty, after everyone's seen the television film," said Charlie.

"There's something else."

"What?"

"The Justice Ministry have decided there's insufficient evidence of foul play for a militia investigation into Vera Bendall's death."

"Where's the fix from, the Justice Ministry or the FSB?"

"Lefortovo is ultimately under FSB control," reminded Natalia.

20

Natalia accepted she had been outmaneuvred with almost child-like ease but bruised pride was the least of her several concerns. Her need was to adjust Charlie's don't-get-sore-get-even philosophy, the only guide she had from all the half-remembered conversations and anecdotes to reverse the ambush Filitov and Trishin had trapped her into, just thirty minutes before Viktor Karelin's arrival. She was on her own and in those first suspended minutes she couldn't see a way to do it.

There were no smiles, wisped or otherwise, from Karelin. The face of the FSB chairman was as fixed as the way he sat, facing them, the only movement the slight tremor in the hand in which he held her initiated recommendation for militia involvement in the FSB internal investigations.

"We felt you should be advised in advance, as a matter of courtesy," improvised Natalia. It had been Filitov's insistence, backed by the chief of staff, that there should be a vote upon advising Karelin before forwarding the suggestion to the Kremlin, ridiculous though the pretense had been with the two men so determinedly against her. The point, as always, had been to establish a provable, safety net record. From which the most glaring, and worrying, inference was that the federal prosecutor—but more importantly Yuri Trishin—seriously doubted Aleksandr Okulov's formal election chances and were taking out insurance against the overthrow of the new regime, with the inevitable resurgence of the omnipotent intelligence service of which the man himself had once been such an integral part.

"By a majority decision," hurriedly added Filitov, in unnecessary confirmation of Natalia's reasoning.

"I believe the problems that have been uncovered within my organization can be very adequately dealt with internally," said Karelin. "One, in fact, already has been. Your recommendation there has been overtaken by events."

She could come back to that later, gauged Natalia. A vague idea was formulating but she didn't know how to carry it through to the end. "We're not questioning the adequacy of your organization. The intention . . ." She paused, unsure at the risk but then recalling Filitov's blatant entrapment "is to protect it." They had to commit themselves—from their own mouths—if she was going to turn their maneuvre back upon them. She needed a response—any response—she could use.

"Protect it!" demanded Karelin. He always had an escape, to keep his service inviolable, but he was intrigued by their even imagining such an intrusion was possible. Not "their" imagining, he corrected, the woman who'd once been in the service. It was as difficult to understand as Okulov appointing an investigating commission in the first place, with her as its chairman.

Good enough; very good, in fact. Natalia was conscious of Filitov and Trishin twisting sideways towards her, matching Karelin's bewilderment, and just as obviously turned herself to the chief of staff. "You would agree, wouldn't you Yuri Fedorovich, that one of the essential remits of this Commission is to ensure *external* transparency, particularly as far as the United States of America is concerned?"

Trishin sat trying to anticipate towards which abyss he was being prodded. Unable to, he reluctantly said, "Yes."

"And there's also the undertaking, personally announced by the acting president, to make public the findings of this enquiry?"

"Yes," agreed Trishin again, even more entangled.

It was going better than she'd hoped but it would be wrong for her to read too much too soon into their confusion. She went back to Karelin. "One of your first remarks to us was to deny emphatically any FSB part in an assassination conspiracy?" Natalia thought some of the stiffness had gone from the nondescript man.

Karelin said, "Which I just as emphatically repeat."

"And which will be set out very specifically in our conclusions, all of which are to be made fully public," said Natalia. That hadn't been agreed—discussed even—and she waited for Trishin's challenge, but it didn't come. Having allowed the wait, Natalia went on, "Aren't we limiting ourselves by *only* discussing an assassination conspiracy?"

"I'm not sure what you're talking about," complained Karelin.

Natalia could see her way now—actually realizing there was something positive to learn—and was not in a hurry, the longer she strung it out the further Filitov and Trishin would be stranded. "Public, international perception," said Natalia.

"I still don't understand," protested Karelin, who believed he did but was unwilling to risk a mistake.

"There has been considerable ill feeling between us and the Americans over some aspects of the overall investigation," reminded Natalia. "It's reflected—clearly through informed and official leaks—in the highly critical media attacks in the American press. You have been remarkably open with us, conceding that the FSB has been seriously embarrassed. Wouldn't you agree, Viktor Ivanovich, that such an honest admission exposes you and your service to international media accusation—speculation at the very least—of complicity?"

"An accusation I am totally refuting!" insisted Karelin. She was right, he admitted to himself.

Natalia abruptly switched back to Trishin, intercepting as she did so the look of concern passing between the men on either side of her. "Denied or not, it is the sort of hostile analysis the international media will make and against which it is necessary for the FSB to guard, wouldn't you agree, Yuri Fedorovich?"

"Not if the denials were made strongly enough," tried the politician.

"Are you, Viktor Ivanovich, prepared to take that chance with the reputation of your organisation at stake?" demanded Natalia, moving between the intelligence chairman and the chief of staff before switching to the prosecutor. "Are you, Yuri Fedorvich?" She had them! Boxed and tied with ribbon.

"Isn't this escalating out of proportion?" said Filitov, recognizing how totally their intended isolation of Natalia had been thrown back at them.

"Answer your own question," Natalia returned at once. "Outside militia participation will show the FSB and its chairman willing to be totally transparent, to international opinion and judgment. *Prove* it has nothing to hide." It wouldn't prove anything of the sort—the FSB, like its predecessor, were adept enough to conceal anything they didn't want found out—but that wasn't the point. At that precise moment the point was justifying any sort of outside monitor.

"It's a convincing argument," said Karelin. "I'm glad it's been made."

"And I'm personally glad you've acknowledged it," said Natalia.

Neither Filitov nor Trishin would be so happy with the secretariat transcripts now. She wondered how much more benefit there was to be achieved.

Karelin lifted and let drop the no longer agitated hand that still held the proposal for militia involvement. "And I appreciate the courtesy. And the consideration." There was even, finally, a fleeting smile.

"You have no problem with the idea?"

"I need to consider it further. Which I will do keeping your arguments very much in mind, Natalia Fedova."

"You said one of the uncovered problems has already been dealt with?" prompted Natalia.

"Colonel Spassky was held responsible for the internal security breach," disclosed Karelin. "He has been dismissed and a new directorate chairman appointed to instigate an entirely redesigned system. It is conceivable that during that reorganization there might emerge some further information on the interference itself."

Natalia acknowledged that Spassky had to be the most likely and available scapegoat. That had been the ineffectual man's role from the very beginning. "You left yesterday to carry out a Registry search for us?"

"None of the names from the Ministry of Defense with which I was supplied appear on any Registry or Archive documents of the current FSB or the KGB which preceded it," said Karelin, formally.

"That would seem to bring to an end any further assistance you might be able to give us?" said Trishin.

"Does it?" came in Natalia, sharply. "The identity of any who might be involved could be among material intentionally removed as part of the conspiracy, couldn't it?"

"Most certainly, if any of them were part of it," agreed Karelin.

Everything had to end on her personal terms, decided Natalia, or perhaps more essentially to her personal benefit. "We've no other witnesses, unless you can suggest anyone else."

"There's no one," confirmed Karelin, at once.

"At the moment the FSB is inextricably—and inescapably— linked with a very carefully planned treason because of which it can only be discredited," Natalia spelled out.

"Until we prove otherwise," said Karelin.

There it was, the top-to-bottom investigations Karelin hadn't disclosed and into which he wouldn't for a moment admit outside investigators! "Such very careful planning wouldn't have been possible by disaffected personnel abruptly dismissed your service?"

"I don't think so," agreed Karelin.

"Could there be factions still *within* the FSB that might want to discredit you personally and the organization as a whole?"

"If there are, they will be discovered," insisted Karelin, in further confirmation of the undisclosed purge.

"Can you suggest to us who—or what—else might be responsible?" asked Trishin, anxious to restore himself.

"Not at this moment," said Karelin. "I'm discounting a foreign intelligence service. One could not have infiltrated to this degree."

"I've used the word discredit," reminded Natalia. "If this conspiracy isn't totally explained and the conspirators—*all* the conspirators—brought to justice, couldn't we be talking about the *destruction* of the FSB? Certainly about the need for yet another but more complete restructuring?"

"All of these difficulties have been realized and are being acted upon," assured Karelin.

The unbreachable confidence was wavering, thought Natalia. "They are also difficulties that we will necessarily have to recognize, in our report to the acting president."

"Are you warning me you believe the FSB *is* actively connected with this outrage!" demanded Karelin.

"I'm certainly not!" said Filitov.

"I am advising you of the evidence—and the observations—with which we have to work," said Natalia. "With the hope of further contact and cooperation between us."

Charlie judged it so far to be a day more confusing than most—too many of which had already been confusing enough—couldn't see how it was going to get any better and wished now he hadn't responded to instinct by returning to Fadeeva Ulitza instead of going back to Burdenko Hospital with the lawyers, defense psychiatrists and Donald Morrison. The initial uncertainty was the concierge's disclosure of the arrival at Boris Davidov's abandoned apartment, within an hour of his having been there the previous night, of an FSB squad. According to the caretaker they'd asked similar questions to everyone else and appeared to be trying to locate the man, which they wouldn't have had to do if he was still a serving officer but certainly would if he'd served in the past and needed to be removed from awkward questioning. Another perhaps far more feasible thought—countered only by Charlie's impression of Bendall's reaction—was that the FSB had joined the game of musical chairs and were chasing each of the fifteen names, in the footsteps of the FBI and the militia.

To test that possibility Charlie went directly from Fadeeva Ulitza to the American embassy and was further frustrated. Nowhere, in any of the FBI reports, was there a reference to their overlapping with either the intelligence or police service. Of the fifteen, eight—including Davidov—were logged as being not immediately traceable but with enquiries continuing. Two were serving prison sentences and another had died four years earlier, shot by the militia in an attempted armed robbery in an Arbat jewellery store. Three were working for security firms offering protection to Western businessmen in Moscow from organized mafia and the last was an instructor in the gymnasium at the Balchug Kempinski hotel. None of the security men nor the gym instructor remembered Georgi Gugin as serving with them in the army, despite the television and newspaper pictures. Nothing of the militia efforts to trace the fifteen was yet logged on the centralized system.

John Kayley came down into the incident room from the upstairs embassy as Charlie finished his fruitless computer scroll. The American was in shirtsleeves dark with sweat across his shoulders and beneath his arms.

Kayley said, "You want to guess how many Secret Servicemen we got coming here with the president?"

"No," refused Charlie.

"Seventy-five! They hear a sound louder than a sparrow's fart they'll open fire and there'll be another massacre."

"You part of it?"

Kayley shook his head. "I got a court hearing to attend and ex-soldiers to find."

"How's it going?"

Kayley gestured to Charlie's blank computer screen. "What you see is what we got. Which so far is fuck all. You all set for tomorrow?"

"Short of just about everything I'd like," said Charlie, honestly.

"You think we're ever going to get it?" asked Kayley, kindling one of his cigars into a perfumed cloud.

Charlie considered for several minutes before he replied. "No," he said, confronting the doubt properly for the first time. "I don't think from the way it's going at the moment that we stand a chance in hell."

Charlie's seriousness appeared to concentrate Kayley's mind. "And I believe you're probably right. I don't think we are, either." Thank Christ, he thought, for the Teflon protection of Paul Smith's over-reactive e-mail.

Charlie seized upon Anne Abbott's unexpected, car phone requests for a preparing, pre-hearing review—eager for a sounding board after the brief exchange with Kayley—without waiting for Morrison's return to the incident room. Arkadi Noskov was already tightly wedged into the largest available chair—which would have enveloped anyone else—in Anne's embassy office, vodka glass contentedly resting on his tablecloth of a beard. Charlie accepted the offered scotch, even though it was a mix. Anne wasn't drinking.

"So how'd it go?" Charlie asked.

"It would have been better if you'd been there," said Anne.

Charlie detected the edge to her voice. "I'm sorry?" he queried.

"So are we," she said. "Bendall went through the routine with our psychiatrists but said he wouldn't cooperate with anything else if you weren't there. Which you weren't."

A serious oversight, acknowledged Charlie. It really was spiralling into a totally fucked up day. The refusal wouldn't do anything to restore Donald Morrison's confidence, either. Charlie said, "You really think he had any intention of saying anything today?"

"We're never going to know, are we?"

"What about the psychiatrists?"

"He was impeccable," replied the deep-voiced lawyer. "His behavior virtually amounts to proof of his sanity, without our needing to be professionally told."

"Is that what the psychiatrists did say, that he was fit to plead?" demanded Charlie.

"They've promised qualifications in their written assessment but they're unanimous on the deciding factor, that he's mentally capable of understanding a criminal charge," said Noskov.

"And that he's mentally aware of what he's done, capable of distinguishing between right and wrong," finished Anne.

"What are the qualifications?" said Charlie.

"Delusory, to the point of severe fantacism," Anne set out. "Fluctuating schizophrenic paranoia, susceptible to mental manipulation."

"What's that give us?" asked Charlie.

"At best, psychiatric mumbo jumbo for a plea of mitigation," said the Russian lawyer, cynically. "And we've got the intended charges."

"Which are?"

"Conspiracy to murder, murder, membership of a terrorist organization, terrorism, espionage and discharging a weapon with intent to endanger or take life," enumerated Noskov.

"Espionage?" isolated Charlie, curiously.

"They've trawled through the statute book and will probably come up with some they haven't got to yet," said Noskov, with continued cynicism. "Don't forget it's only the initial, legally required arraignment. The prosecution will formally lay the charges, I'll formally enter a plea of not guilty to each and that'll be that for the next ten or twenty or however many custodial remands the prosecution ask for."

"Perhaps," said Anne, offering their individual bottles to each man for refills.

"What's that mean?" questioned Charlie.

"Bendall's demanding to address the court," she said. "When we told him tomorrow wasn't the time or the place he threatened to dismiss us and defend himself." She hesitated. "That's when we could have done with you most, to calm him down."

Charlie accepted the persistent criticism. "We're here to review. Let's do just that, assemble what we've got."

"Or rather what we *haven't* got," said Anne. "Give us your analysis against ours."

On his way to Protocnyj pereulok Charlie had believed he had everything neatly compartmented in his mind but almost as soon as he began to talk the doubt arose. The undoubted conspiracy was brilliantly conceived by people with sufficient power, influence and knowledge to penetrate KGB-era material and come literally within a hair's breadth of a sniper's rifle sight to assassinating two presidents. As it was, they'd killed one and by a fluke of an instinctive movement maimed the wife of another. Anne cut in, impressively advocatorial, when Charlie talked of a brotherhood and listed what they'd believed he'd extracted from Bendall about it, even managing a passing imitation of the man's wailing dirge.

"Delusory, to the point of severe fantacism," she reminded. "And that's from our *own* experts! OK, we know from the number of shots fired and the different caliber of the bullets that there *was* a conspiracy but any half decent prosecution with a television film like they've got will cut us to pieces if we start talking of stupid bonding songs and blood brothers."

"We've got an irrefutable defense to murder," said Noskov. "The rest only just helps with a mitigating defence on the evidence of mental instability."

"He'd have believed it, though, wouldn't he?" said Charlie, slowly. "Someone who was easily deluded, retreated into fantasy in preference to his own shitty existence, would grab at the blood brother nonsense."

"Where's that take us?" asked Anne.

Charlie didn't know but his feet throbbed, which was a good sign. "What are the inconsistencies! The things that don't fit?"

"Most if it," said Anne, despairingly.

"No!" refused Charlie. "Let's go through it again, to find what doesn't fit. Unarguable facts. It's brilliantly . . . No!" Charlie stopped himself. "It's a *professionally* conceived operation, the sort of assassination that would have needed the expertise of an organization trained and equipped to carry out authorized killings . . ."

"The FSB and before them the KGB," interrupted Anne.

"And before them all the rest," agreed Charlie. "We know from the different calibration of the *two* different rifles that there were *two* different marksmen, each capable of firing a total of five shots in under eight seconds. Professional marksmanship but not professional planning. If it had been truly professional, the rifles would have at least been of the same caliber . . ."

"An inconsistency," recognized Noskov.

"Let's mark it," Charlie agreed. "Now let's look at all the others. George Bendall, a dysfunctional, mentally unstable—but mentally malleable—man who was long ago trained as a marksman. A third rifle but only two bullets, because they know he can't hit the intended targets and if he hits anyone else—which he fortunately didn't—it doesn't matter. Purpose? The dupe who is intended to take the blame. His cowed, frightened mother who doesn't appear to know anything, yet is murdered in a jail for which the organization with the capability to commit assassination is responsible. And his apparent—his *only*—best friend, also possibly murdered in what was made to look like an accident on a level crossing. Anything I've missed out?"

"Bendall's mystery pentathol injection," reminded Anne.

"OK, let's add that," accepted Charlie. "Anything else?"

"Orkulov and the KGB," said Noskov, simply. "Where's that slot in?"

"It doesn't, if its successor service is involved; whatever the changes, they rarely shaft their own . . ." Charlie hesitated again, remembering the number of times he'd been strung out to dry. "Not often, anyway."

"Okulov appointed a presidential commission *into* the FSB," argued Anne.

"*After* the shooting and with the finger pointing at them and him," said Charlie. "Politically he didn't have any alternative." Into his mind's eye came the two taunting photographs of Vasili Gregorovich Isakov: what the fuck was it he couldn't see! With everything else so fragmented this discussion wouldn't be taken forward by his getting the prints from his office and inviting the lawyers' examination. "Is that it?"

Both lawyers nodded their heads.

"So what's there that shouldn't be?"

"Like I said, most of it," remarked Anne.

"That's not helping," threw back Charlie, balancing her earlier criticism.

"You know the impression I'm increasingly getting?" invited Anne.

Both men looked at her, waiting.

"I don't find it difficult to imagine that there's someone on the inside of this investigation manipulating the whole bloody lot of us, just as they manipulated George Bendall."

There was a long silence.

"One of the conspirators?" said Noskov, finally.

"Maybe even more than one," suggested Anne. "Think about it. Nothing adds up. Every move we've made—every move anyone else has made, as far as we're aware—always runs into a brick wall."

"Are you suggesting someone at our level?" pressed Charlie, feeling the beginning of a chill at his recognition of how much sense Anne's remark made.

"I'm just pointing out that we've been made to dance around in circles and for that to happen so consistently it would be useful for the bad guys to have someone very close to the investigation."

"You think Okulov *is* masterminding it to get the presidency? That's the only level with a link to the FSB—or rather the KGB before it—that makes sense."

"I'm not sure what I think," said Anne, uncharacteristically careless.

Okulov—through Trishin being on the commission—wasn't the only one who fitted, thought Charlie. He ran the rest—their faces even—through his mind, desperate for a more likely suspect. And failed. Which didn't prove anything. Nothing *was* provable. The whole thing—the entire speculation—was based upon a casual, throwaway aside that just, only just, might have sinister implications. But from her chairmanships of both the Russian coordinating groups and the presidential commission Natalia perfectly fitted the incriminating profile. Which was absurd. What reason—what possible purpose—could there be for Natalia even to be remotely connected—the ultimate of unacceptable absurdities—with the killing and maiming of people. And yet . . . ?

It had been a working dinner and the recalled James Scamell had, only minutes before, quit the Regents Park official residence of the United States ambassador to England, leaving Anandale and Wendall North alone together.

Anandale said, "You sure the plug will hold?"

"They're short eleven documents, three the minutes of the meetings at which the decision was made to contribute the soft $750,000 to your campaign and in which you were specifically named," assured the chief of staff. "I've got the chief exec's personnel guarantee they're shredded. What's left is a general discussion, about election funding. As far as the paper trail goes, it was a discussion upon which no action was taken, no names mentioned."

"How many of the board know?"

"Five."

"What if they're subpoenaed?"

"They'd fall too. Diverting company funds without stockholders— and the full board's—approval is fraud, a criminal offense."

"They could plea bargain. Cop an amnesty for turning State's evidence."

"They're firm. There's insufficient to pressure any of them."

Anandale swirled the brandy in his snifter. "How long before the Grand Jury's concluded?"

"Two weeks. And from now on it's the dregs, no one who can hurt us," guaranteed North. "You're still high on the sympathy wave and the media are taking the duty-before-personal-safety line of your going back for the funeral."

"Three specialists have so far decided there's nothing that can be done for Ruth. Only two to go."

"I'm very sorry to hear that, Mr. President."

"Find more doctors, Wendall. Better qualified. We can't let her stay like she is. She's too proud."

The chief of staff looked unnecessarily at his watch. "Donnington will still be up at the hotel. I'll call him right away."

"Let's go outside the country—Europe's fine—if he gets the name of the right man."

"I'll make sure Donnington understands."

"You really think I should do what Scamell wants in Moscow after all the speculation?"

"Kayley doesn't buy it. And we've been through the protection arrangements with a finetoothed comb. Aston says it's safe. It's been rehearsed so many times everyone can do it in their sleep." Wendall North had ensured that this time there wasn't a single security provision or objection in which he was a named participant.

"I want everyone with their eyes wide open," said Anandale.

Charlie stayed late into the evening, alone in his own embassy office, going through everything—even the CNN film—knowing it was ridiculous but having to acknowledge that Anne Abbott's suggestion deserved consideration and that when it was considered, Natalia was the best placed of any possible suspects to be an inside source. He couldn't—wouldn't—contemplate her being involved—aware in advance—in the actual murders. That was totally unthinkable. But examined closely—and Charlie's examination was microscopic—that wasn't what the lawyer had theorized. Anne Abbott had been referring to the almost orchestrated confusion afterwards. Which still didn't make sense. Wasn't it as unthinkable that she'd become inveigled afterwards? Knowing complicity after the crime would be as bad—as criminally culpable—as knowing of it before. He asked himself if she could have acted *un*knowingly and decided that was impossible: Natalia was far too astute to allow herself to be used unknowingly. It was only when he spread the reflection to honesty and integrity, trying to imagine any conceivable situation in which she'd be prepared to sacrifice either, that Charlie felt the first real flicker of unease. He didn't doubt that Natalia would abandon honesty and integrity—even contemplate breaking the law—to protect Sasha. And the risk to Sasha—the upheaval to their daughter more than anything that might happen to her—had been Natalia's constant, corrosive fear ever since she'd moved into Lesnaya. Still not enough; still unthinkable. There wasn't even circumstantial evidence. It was circumstantial—*very* circumstantial—hypotheses at best. Or worse.

It was past nine when he finally got home, going directly to the drink's tray when he entered the apartment.

Natalia said, "I could have kept something. Waited so we could have eaten together if you'd called to say you were on your way."

"I'm not hungry."

"A development?"

Charlie shook his head. "Complete review for tomorrow."

"Tomorrow's only a formality, surely?"

It was obvious she'd know that, Charlie accepted. "Lawyers wanting to know we're prepared for the unexpected."

"Are you?"

Charlie hesitated, wondering if he were good enough to make their conversation a test, remembering he'd once before been able verbally to trick her. "We don't know enough to be prepared for anything, expected or otherwise. What happened with you today?"

Natalia said, "I came closer than I ever want to come again to being washed away," and Charlie's feet twitched and he wished they hadn't.

Charlie listened with a divided mind, assessing her account as she wanted him to but at the same time unsuccessfully searching for any nuance that might resolve the doubt created by Anne Abbott. When Natalia finished he said, "Did you think you could manage it?"

"Not at first."

"Now comes your report," said Charlie. Would there be any indication now?

"Filitov and Trishin said they needed time to read all the statements, which is ludicrous. There's only Karelin."

"What's your opinion?"

"Serious maladministration within the FSB."

"But not complicity?"

"Someone with access has to be part of it."

She'd personally gone to the Lubyanka, supposedly to pressure Spassky, had actually talked to him afterwards about how lapse internal security was. And she'd knew her way around the building. "You going to say that?"

"It's obvious. We'd make ourselves look stupid not to."

"What if Filitov and Trishin don't agree?"

"I don't see how they can disagree. If they do I can record a dissenting opinion."

"Will you?"

Natalia frowned. "What else can I do?"

How would she confront the actually suspicion? "Something curious came up during our review."

"What?"

"The thought that someone connected with the investigation might be part of the conspiracy: misleading or blocking things." Charlie spoke looking directly at Natalia who looked directly back.

"Who?" she demanded.

"It was a general remark. You've probably got the widest overview of anyone. What do you think?"

Natalia shook her head. "I don't see it. If we chase that we'll confuse ourselves even more than we're confused now."

Charlie decided he knew her too well—had spent his entire life spotting deceit—not to have detected something in that reply, which he hadn't. And yet. . . .

21

Two planes were needed in addition to Air Force One to carry the number of Secret Service personnel, the travelling White House, Surgeon Admiral Max Donnington's mobile hospital facilities and virtually every nationality of every accredited White House journalists, television as well as print. A carefully selected group of correspondents—the TV majors, commentators as well as political reporters from what was considered America's national press and all the Texas media—travelled on the president's aircraft. Anandale, word perfect from the secretary of state's briefing papers, spent a full thirty minutes in the back of the presidential jet talking unattributably on the European Union trade protectionism scheduled for discussion with British and French leaders. Despite limiting to hours the amount of time he would be in Moscow, he also intended to meet acting president Aleksandr Okulov. Because of the circumstance of the visit, it was inappropriate to go into any detail of the Star Wars treaty negotiations but as they all knew Secretary of State James Scamell had remained in Moscow, apart from this short trip to London. It was, quite naturally, a difficult personal return to Moscow for him. He had no safety concerns whatsoever, having complete confidence and trust in the joint security measures of the American Secret Service and the Russian presidential protection service. As its former and forever proud governor he deeply regretted the pointless time, money and effort being wasted by the politically hostile Texas legislature, time, money and effort that would these past months have been spent better and more properly governing the best state in the Union. He was pleased to say that the First Lady was responding to treatment and there was every reason to hope she would make a full recovery.

Back in his separate, private section of the aircraft, Anandale said, "OK?"

"You gave them enough for a whole month's coverage," judged Wendall North.

"I'll have public affairs circulate it to the media on the other plane," said Scamell. "Don't want to leave anyone out."

"You know what they'd rather see?" demanded the president, rhetorically. "They'd rather see me shot by the sons of bitches who missed me last time because it's a better story."

"They're not going to get it," assured North. "You're coming back like this is good enough."

"You speak to Donnington?"

"He talked to people in England, before we left. We'll have names when we get back tonight."

Jeff Aston, the head of the Secret Service detail, appeared from the flight deck. "We're on our way down. The advance planes are already there. Everything's set up."

Anandale looked out of the window as the aircraft descended through the clouds and the flat, tree-tufted plain came into view.

He said, "God awful place. No wonder no one smiles."

They landed as before at the same military installation on the eastern outskirts of the city. There were three television positions, none elevated, and five still camera places. Between them and the arriving aircraft was an outwardly facing wall of Secret Servicemen through whom there were minimal gaps for unimpeded pictures. The specially-flown in bullet and blast proof Cadillac was hard topped, with darkly tinted windows, and drew up to within ten meters of the steps even before they were secured into position. At the same time Aleksandr Okulov and Boris Petrin emerged from their waiting, smoke-windowed Zil, to make their way forward in a greeting line with individual interpreters. There was a second, shielding line made up equally of Russian and American protection officers.

Walter Anandale emerged the moment the doors of Air Force One opened for the required, top-step photo opportunity but was dwarfed almost at once by Jeff Aston. Two more similarly-sized Secret Servicemen covered the president from the back and side, making awkward the crowded descent to the ground. Okulov was several inches shorter than Anandale and appeared even smaller against the American guards when he came forward to embrace Anandale, Russian bear-hug style. Anandale barely responded, anxious to be released.

The group moved so quickly towards the waiting vehicles that Scamell and Wendall North had to hurry down the steps to avoid being left behind. The American chief of staff supervised the transportation, ushering Aleksandr Okulov and Walter Anandale into the Cadillac, alone but for their interpreters. Anandale and Okulov sat side by side, their translators facing them from the jump seats. Lev Lvov, the Russian presidential protection chief, was crammed into the front seat alongside Jeff Aston, the raised glass partition closing them off from the rear of the vehicle.

Okulov said, "How's the First Lady?"

"Recovering," said Anandale. "Thank you."

"Fully, I hope."

"There's still a lot of specialist treatment necessary."

The armor plating, which extended from the sides down to the underside of the car, brought its weight up to nine tons but it was still travelling at ninety m.p.h. down the central reservation of the cleared road. There were two ranks of escorting motorcycles, the outer line closing off any space left by the inner. It was impossible to hear the overhead helicopters, through the steel-reinforced roof.

Orkulov said, "I trust all the misunderstandings are resolved between us, over this investigation?"

"I believe they are. But the progress is slow," said Anandale.

"The Englishman is appearing in court today."

"Slow in detecting the others with whom he is involved."

"I understand that immediately prior to the outrage no substantive difficulties remained between our two sides over the missile defense system?"

"There were some. There had been no independently confirmed statistics for nuclear holdings."

"They have now been exchanged between our foreign minister and your secretary of state."

"There remain uncertainties with China. And North Korea."

"Uncertainties that existed—and stayed parallel—before and during our negotiations."

"According to our intelligence North Korea is increasing its nuclear capacity, with Beijing's assistance."

There was a momentary silence. They were entering the city now, along barriered streets this time totally devoid of people apart from regularly distanced uniformed militia officers.

Okulov said, "That is not our information."

Anandale shrugged. "You'll accept, of course, that I have to make judgments upon the best advice I receive."

"An enormous amount of time and even more commitment has gone into bringing our two sides to where we are now. It would be very unfortunate if at this stage it were to fail."

"My secretary of state has remained in Moscow," reminded Anandale. "We have publicly travelled into the city together today."

"Does that mean our negotiations are going to be concluded with the signing of the treaty?" demanded Okulov, directly.

"It means our negotiations are continuing to a hopeful conclusion, that hope being that no unexpected, insurmountable difficulty arises," said Anandale, as the cavalcade swept across the cleared Red Square for the televised entry into the Kremlin.

American television had a simultaneous feed from the Russian coverage of Anandale, flanked by Scamell and North, solemnly filing past the open coffin of the assassinated Russian president. Aleksandr Okulov was already in place by the time they reached the receiving line, in the center of which stood a black-suited Raisa Yudkin, her two sons either side of her. She smiled at his approach and Anandale leaned forward to kiss her.

"How's Ruth?" said the woman, her voice heavily accented.

"Getting better." He gave a slight movement towards the coffin. "I'm so sorry." He shook the hands of both boys and moved off.

There was a preinterment reception, also televised, in an adjoining state room and Anandale allowed Scamell to steer him into two appropriate groups—German and Italian—before settling briefly with the British. Anandale said he was looking forward to the following day's working lunch and the prime minister said he was, too.

It was not until they were back in the armored Cadillac, slotting into their prescribed position in the cortege, that Wendall North said, "You happy how it went?"

"Hear for yourself," invited Anandale. Through the now lowered separating screen he said, "You get it all, Jeff?"

"Loud and clear, Mr. President," assured the Secret Service chief, slotting the recording of Anandale's conversation with Okulov into the Cadillac's cassette deck.

Everyone's concentration was totally inside the vehicle, oblivious to everyone and everything outside. When the tape snapped off Anandale said, "Well?"

"Couldn't be better," said Scamell.

"Thank you, Jeff," said Anandale, pressing the control to raise the screen. "You know what I'm thinking? I'm thinking that now we've got the Texas problem out of the way, we don't need the goddamned treaty, we'd do better carrying on perfecting the shield technology."

"Let's take pause on that, Mr. President," advised the chief of staff.

"OK," agreed Anandale. "But carry out some very discreet soundings: see how further developing it plays on the Hill."

Charlie was able to see the first five minutes of Anandale's televised arrival at the military airfield before leaving for the hospital and watched with an impression of *deja vu*, wondering what emotion the American president would be having. The reflection went at once driving to the hospital with Anne beside him, responding perfunctorily to the occasional remark from the lawyer bent over her case papers in final preparation, his own concentration fully upon the lingering doubt about Natalia. She'd come to him the previous night, wanting him, but he hadn't been able to respond which had never happened before. The only excuse he'd been able to think of was tiredness from the investigation and she'd turned away tight with frustration and the tension had still been between them that morning.

Impossible though it was—ridiculous though it was—what if Natalia had been drawn in, not in the actual shootings but in some cover-up afterwards? George Bendall had unchallengably been involved in a murderous conspiracy but they had a guaranteed defense against the murder charge itself, so there was no risk of an innocent man being wrongly convicted. She would be obstructing justice, certainly, but how many times had he done that—and worse—any means always justifying a practical end? A lot, although always with more of an episode resolved and more of the opposition punished. What ever, he had no moral or integrity grounds from which to criticize or question. Which wasn't his problem, he forced himself to admit. His problem was entirely personal, the thought of her holding a distorting mirror in front of him. Which was the most absurd of all. But not all, he thought on, relentlessly. His doubt wasn't solely about the investigation: maybe not even a major part of it. He was stirring into the mix all his own uncertainties about himself and Natalia: changing the metaphor, holding up his own distorting mirror in front of himself.

"Charlie!"

He started at her demand, realizing he'd missed a question the first time. "Sorry. What?"

"You think you can keep Bendall quiet?" repeated Anne

"That's what we're going to the hospital for, but I don't have a magic formula."

"Do you really want to keep him quiet?" she demanded, turning to Charlie in the back of the embasssy car. "He promised sensation, remember? He could unlock everything."

"I want it for myself first, not for a herd that would include the world's press," said Charlie.

Olga, Nicholai Badim and the psychiatrist, Guerguen Agayan, were outside the ward when Charlie and Anne approached after passing through the entrance check, which Charlie noted to be as stringent as it had been on the first day, minus only the disputed body check. The regular three-man team was inside Bendall's room, but there was a much greater number—a lot in militia uniform— further along the corridor, waiting to escort the man to the court.

Anne said, "We need prehearing consultations."

"A condition was made, about a protective presence," said Olga.

"Which you can be," said Charlie, curtly. "There is no need for the guards within the room or for any medical attendance."

"That's for us to decide," said Agayan.

"Is he fit to appear in court?" asked Charlie.

"Yes," said Badim.

"Can he stand?"

"Sufficiently. There's a crutch."

Looking more closely into the room Charlie saw there was an old fashion, T-shaped support propped against the side of the wheelchair in which Bendall was already seated. "Then you've fulfilled your function. We want the room empty except for attorney Abbott, myself and militia colonel Melnik."

Agayan moved to protect further but Olga said, "That'll be all right. We haven't a lot of time."

There was a shuffle of passing people. Inside Charlie recognized that Bendall was dressed in the jeans and long-sleeved sweater the man had been wearing during the tussle on the TV gantry, although they appeared to have been cleaned. He didn't recognize the faded fabric windcheater in which Bendall only had his right arm, the left side pulled over the man's injured shoulder. There was scarcely any bulge from the bandaging and Charlie guessed it had been further reduced. There didn't appear to be a particularly thick dressing at the man's hip, either. The routine of arranging their own recording was practically automatic.

Charlie said, "Sorry I wasn't here yesterday, Georgi. You had something you wanted to talk to me about?"

"No," said Bendall.

"You kept asking for Charlie," reminded Anne.

"Not important anymore."

"It might be," said Charlie. "Why don't we just talk it through."

"I don't want to."

"There aren't the facilities for us to talk in a court cell," said Anne. "That's why we're here."

"OK," said Bendall.

"I mean we've got to talk about anything here," said Anne. "There won't be another chance."

"There's nothing to talk about."

"You remember our telling you yesterday that this isn't the full trial? It's just to formally list the charges."

"I know." There was a tinge of irritation in Bendall's voice.

"You'll have to stand, for a few moments, while the charges are put."

"I can do that."

"Arkadi Semenovich will enter the plea. You don't have to say anything. You'll be allowed to sit when that's over. The prosecution will ask for an adjournment and that will be that, OK?"

The faintest smile pulled at the corners of Bendall's mouth.

"You don't say anything, Georgi," stressed Charlie. "You let your lawyer say it all. You got anything to say, say it to me here, now."

"Changed my mind."

"Don't!" urged Charlie, the frustration burning through him.

Bendall said, "I want to go now. I'm ready."

"Let's talk about it some more."

"No!" refused Bendall, his voice raised.

There was movement from the outside corridor. Olga said, "The prison transport's waiting."

Charlie said, "We don't want any outbursts in court, Georgi.

You'll get your chance to say all you want, but not today. You understand?"

Bendall said, "I want to go."

"We'll come here afterwards," promised Charlie. Back in the embassy car, he said, "I fucked up yesterday."

"Badly," agreed Anne, at once.

So many roads were closed or restricted because of the funeral security that they had to make an elaborate, looping detour to get to the Central Criminal Court building. There was a bristled hedge of television cameras, stills photographers and sound and print journalists blocking its front and Charlie too late regretted the identifiable embassy car. He shouldered a path for Anne, wincing at the klieg light and flashbulb glare, both of them ignoring the shouted demands, in English, for them to identify themselves. None of the uniformed, lined-up militia officers made any effort to help them. The yelling, jostling scrum pursued them into the pillared vestibule and Charlie only picked out Noskov because the man towered over everyone else.

When they reached the Russian lawyer Charlie, to whom public identification was anathema, said, "Let's get into court, out of this!"

It was a comparative oasis of calm and quiet beyond the heavy doors. It was the first time Charlie had been inside a Russian court and his initial impressions was that it was very similar to those he knew from England, apart from the more functional raised bench for the five examining judges being necessarily longer but without any carved canopy. The centrally positioned dock was raised the same as in England, topped with a familiar surrounding rail, and to its sides and rippled out in front were benches for lawyers, their support advisors and court officials. Two rows were cobwebbed with headsets for simultaneous translation and at the second sat the six-strong American legal team, selecting their channels and testing the sound. The rest of the court was already nearly full. A stenographer was at his table, beside the one facing row directly beneath the judges' bench. To one side was the press enclosure, from which reporters were overflowing into a standing line in front. There was a lot of noise coming from an overhanging balcony into which Charlie couldn't see but which he assumed to be the public gallery. The glassed booth from which the proceedings were being televised was at the same height as the public gallery, adjoining the translators' pod. Olga was seated next to a tightly bearded, impressively uniformed and medalled man, with other officers attentively around them. At his entrance Charlie saw her bend to the man, who turned expressionlessly to examine him. Olga gave no facial reaction, either. There were two uniformed militiamen at every door into the well of the court and a further two at each of the two doors leading on to the judges' bench. John Kayley was away from the rest of the Americans, in one of the shorter rows to the side of the dock. When he saw Charlie he gestured that there was a seat beside him.

Noskov said, "Anything?"

"He'd changed his mind," said Charlie.

Noskov sighed. "You warned him about histrionics."

"As well as I could."

Noskov led Anne to the first row facing the bench and Charlie eased himself next to the American. Kayley said, "What's new?"

"Nothing," said Charlie. "You found any of those missing from our fifteen?"

"Not a one."

"Have the militia added any?"

"Nope. Going to talk to Olga about it, later. You coming straight back?"

"Returning to the hospital first, to talk to Bendall."

The noise abruptly increased and there was a turning of heads and Charlie turned too, to see Bendall's wheelchair being lifted from an unseen stairwell into the dock. Seated, the man's head scarcely came level to the rail. Bendall looked alertly around him, smiling up at the television position, and Charlie thought, an actor. He was sure Bendall would attempt his promise to be sensational, which it probably would. From the slight smile on Kayley's face, the American guessed it too.

There was the usher's demand, in Russian, to stand for the crocodiled entry of the five judges. The dock warders supported Bendall until he got his balance on the single crutch beneath his right arm and prodded him to remain upright, after everyone else sat, for the charges to be read. Bendall stood tight against the dock edge, showing no discomfort.

The clerk set out the charges in both names, the chosen Russian identity first, beginning with the conspiracy to murder and finishing with the intent to endanger or take life. Throughout Charlie sat twisted towards the dock, waiting, although he was aware from the corner of his eye of the huge lawyer levering himself to his feet for the equally formal pleas. He saw, too, that Anne was turned completely towards the dock, as expectantly as he was.

Noskov got as far as, "My client's pleas to these . . ." before Bendall's shout drowned him out.

"I want to tell . . ." started Bendall but then Anne screamed, "No!" and from behind Charlie there was an ear-ringing explosion and then another and the side of Bendall's head burst in a cloud of scattered red debris.

Charlie swivelled to see a man already running, lowered pistol still in hand, from the first of the continuous rows back towards the door through which Charlie and Anne had entered, fifteen minutes before. And then he saw one of the guarding militiamen with his Markarov drawn, crouching and now Charlie shouted, "No! Don't . . ." but the policeman fired, jerking the running gunman to a complete stop and in the split second in which he remained like that, frozen, the court guard fired a second time to send the man crashing backwards.

Charlie and Kayley instinctively moved together, and reached the gunman at the same time. Both shots had hit him in the chest, smashing so much into a pulp there was nothing left to show if he were capable of breathing, which he wasn't.

So deafened was he by the shots that Charlie lip-read more than heard Kayley say, "Now what the fuck have we got?"

"Nothing," said Charlie, not able to hear his own voice, either.

22

The initial panic was only slightly less than the aftermath of the presidential shooting. There was a pandemonium of shouting—screams even—and a melee of people milling without direction apart from getting away from the killer now lying harmlessly dead. Every militiaman had his weapon drawn and were adding to the noise, shouting to each other for instructions, and briefly—frightened—Charlie became conscious that the officer who had killed the gunman had the Makarov trained upon him, as if about to shoot and Charlie yelled for the man to turn the gun away.

It was Leonid Zenin who restored order. The bearded militia chief clambered up on to one of the benches, to become the focal point of the court, and bellowed for quiet and when the noise began to subside bawled again for order. By the time he achieved it the judges were being bustled out of the court. Zenin told all his officers to holster their weapons before calling upwards, for those on duty upstairs to empty the public gallery ahead of gesturing others to shepherd lawyers and officials from the well of the court.

Still partially deafened, Charlie lip-read more than heard Anne ask if there was any reason for her to stay and shook his head and told her to leave. Anne smiled and nodded. Arkadi Noskov and the American attorneys were anxiously filing out without protest. Charlie felt a prod against his shoulders from another officers clearing the court and shook his head again, now in refusal, identifying himself as an investigator. There was another shove, with the order he did hear to leave, as Olga arrived and told the policeman Charlie could remain. Kayley was arguing with another uniformed man by the dock and Charlie walked with her as Olga crossed to them, to repeat the permission. Olga gazed without any emotion at the nearly headless body of George Bendall crumpled in one corner of the dock. The man lay with the bandaged arm oddly thrown up, as if to protect himself. The warder over whom most of Bendall's brain debris had scattered had been sick and was slumped in the furthest corner from the body. Caught by a thought, Charlie turned and looked towards the television position, realizing that these killings would again have been caught on camera.

"We back to square one?" wondered Kayley.

Charlie was relieved to begin hearing properly at last. "I wish I knew." There was, he thought, too much he wished he knew.

They all turned, at Zenin's approach. Olga made the introductions. When Kayley offered his hand Olga said, "No! You don't shake hands in the presence of death, it's bad luck."

Charlie saw that Zenin had held back from responding. "Everyone's getting more than their fair share of that, George most of all."

Zenin looked between the dock and where three uniformed officers—one a major—were standing in a semi-circle around the dead gunman and said loudly that nothing was to be touched or moved until forensic examiners got there.

Beside Charlie the American said, "What's that saying about stable doors and bolting horses?"

Charlie recognized how immediately Zenin had adopted command. He even followed the man himself as they went back to the body. The gunman, blond-haired and heavily moustached, was lying on his back, his eyes still open. His left leg was folded beneath his right and both arms were spread out. His gun, a Makarov, was about three feet from his right hand. Both militia shots had caught him fully in the chest, caving it in. His shirt, red to begin with, was totally soaked in blood that was seeping into the lapels of an already crumpled fawn suit.

"I'd like to include my forensic people," said Kayley.

Zenin's hesitation was momentary. "Of course. I think that would be a good idea."

The American smiled to find battery power on his cell phone within the confines of the court. The staccato conversation with the embassy incident room was very quick.

"I want every guard officer assembled," Zenin told the major. As the uniformed squad began filing back into the court Zenin said, "Who called out 'No'?"

"Alive he might have given us something. Dead he can't," said Charlie.

"A gun . . ." stumbled the militiaman who'd shot the assassin. "He had a gun . . . in his hand . . . I thought he was going to fire again. . . ."

"You behaved totally correctly," reassured Zenin. "I'll approve a commendation." He looked around the assembled officers. "How the hell did an armed man get into the court!"

There was no reply.

"I asked a question!" demanded Zenin.

"He had authority. A shield," said a man half-hidden at the rear of the group.

"Come forward. Say that again," ordered Zenin.

The officer was young, his face still actually pimpled with youth. "He had a shield. Authority."

"What shield!"

"*Federtnaia Sluhba Bezopasnosti.*"

"Search the body!"

It was Olga who instantly stooped, not repelled by the gore and careless of her formal militia dress uniform getting blood-smeared. It was an expert body search. She lifted the jacket pockets open with a pen tip, more easily for her fingers to go inside with the minimum of displacement. She found the FSB shield in the left side pocket. The congealing blood made it difficult to get the jacket away from the body. She found the wallet in the inside, right pockets, using the pen to flick it open. The photograph was official, the man front facing according to regulations, his name neatly printed beneath it.

"Boris Sergeevich Davidov," she read out, unnecessarily.

"Knew he had to be around somewhere," said Kayley.

Air Force One was just clearing Russian air space when the news was patched through from the embassy, relayed by the American lawyers.

Anandale said, "I was right! It *is* Dallas, November 1963. Oswald kills Kennedy, Ruby kills Oswald, Ruby dies. . . ."

"And no one ever finds out what it was all about," said Wendall North, finishing the historical comparison.

There was a babbled surge when they emerged from the court. John Kayley was swallowed up by the waiting American attorneys and Charlie once more found Anne by using Arkadi Noskov as a marker visible above all the rest.

Charlie identified Davidov as the killer and said, "Don't ask me where that leaves us because I don't know." Don't know, don't know, don't know, he thought. It was a constant mocking chant.

"Bendall's dead?" queried the Russian lawyer.

Charlie thought Noskov would have been able to see into the dock as he'd passed. "Very dead." Charlie's ears had cleared completely but they ached.

"I want formally to place on the court record—and publicly announce—the absolute proof of Bendall's defense to murder," declared Noskov. "Left as it is the prosecution have an assumption of guilt."

"Does it matter now?"

"That's how it will be left on file," said Anne. "We know—and can prove—he didn't do it so the consideration is natural justice."

"You're the lawyers," said Charlie. Justice, natural or otherwise, scarcely seemed to fit any of his most pressing considerations. Natalia would hardly be able officially to conclude her enquiry now, although with Davidov dead he couldn't see how it could be taken any further: how anything could be taken any further. Which was, of course, the intention. *The* intention? Or Natalia's intention? It seemed very easy—automatic even—for the suspicion to be part of every thought now.

"I can't professionally act," Anne reminded Noskov.

The Russian nodded, understanding her point. "I'll call you later."

In the embassy car, Anne said, "I know you told me not to ask where this leaves us but where does this leave us?"

"Beaten," said Charlie.

"That sounded personal."

"It is."

"With Bendall dead—and with the Russians determined that Vera's death was suicide—there's nothing more officially for me to do; everything's down to the Russians," Anne pointed out. She hesitated. "Isn't it all over for you, too, Charlie?"

"I don't like being beaten."

"Come on, Charlie!"

"I missed something. Two more people are dead."

"We went through it all," she said.

"Not properly. I'm going to do it again and again until I find what it is."

Charlie insisted that Richard Brooking's demand for an immediate meeting at Protocnyj pereulok could only concern legal matters, which Anne could easily handle by herself, nodding in agreement when she called him a bastard, and actually locked the door of his office against any interruption. He'd been right about the court television, although he hadn't expected it to be made available so quickly or to every Moscow television channel. It was even on CNN, which used the new footage as an excuse to rerun—sometimes side by side on a split screen—their film of the presidential shooting. Charlie's initial, total concentration was on the courtroom film, feeling an odd discomfort as his own very clear and visible part of it. He saw himself flinch at the first explosion, his head swivelling between the dock and the gunman. Davidov's shooting was very quick and accurate, the bucking of his hands the clearer definition between the two shots than the noise itself, which virtually merged into one sound. There didn't appear to be any separate impact, either, Bendall's head simply disappearing in one burst. Charlie was turned towards Davidov, facing the camera, when he shouted, able clearly to see his lips form the word, his memory was of calling "No" only once but there were two separate utterances before Davidov was shot by the militiaman.

At that moment CNN split their transmission again between the two films, running the courtroom killing of Davidov against the camera pod struggle between Bendall and the NTV cameraman, Vladimir Sakov, for possession of the sniper's rifle.

And at that moment the awarenesses engulfed Charlie. He was physically chilled, although the shiver was more in frustration at what he'd missed for so long than from the feeling of coldness.

His internal telephone momentarily distracted him but Charlie ignored it, strained forward for a repeat of the comparison between the two films, sure that he was right, sure that he'd seen things properly for the first time—had most certainly for the first time seen what was most important but which he'd consistently overlooked—and allowed the scourging personal annoyance. It had been there all the time, like a banner in the breeze, and he'd missed it and it didn't matter that everyone else had missed it as well: what mattered was that it had taken him so long—too long—and too much *still* remained unexplained. The rerun began and Charlie looked now at what he knew there was to see, the annoyed chill of belated awareness changing to a warmth of satisfaction as it unarguably showed on the screen. And then he remembered how, momentarily deaf, he'd had to understand what people had said in the court in the initial minutes after the shooting and saw something else he should have recognized. But hadn't.

London had the film. It would only take an hour, two, three at the outside. The photographic evaluation shouldn't take any longer. But with an addition, Charlie thought, as his problem with Vasili Gregorovich Isakov finally slotted into its long overdue place. Charlie snatched up the internal telephone on its third demand, talking over Richard Brooking's demand that he come at once to the chancellery. He would, Charlie promised, when he'd finished liaising with London, which at that moment had the higher priority. He depressed the receiver, to disconnect the protesting diplomat, but left the handset off its cradle to prevent the man intruding a fourth time.

Charlie had the FBI-collected photographs of Vasili Isakov before him for the next rerun—determined against any wrong or misconstrued assumption—and afterwards, quite positive, he gave himself thirty minutes to compose the fax to London to ensure there could be no misunderstanding about what he wanted.

Richard Brooking was tightlipped, white with fury, when Charlie eventually reached the man's office. Anne Abbott sat quite relaxed on the other side of the desk. Brooking said, "You were specifically told to report to me the moment you entered the embassy."

"I'm not permitted to report operationally to you, to avoid any awkward diplomatic crossover," reminded Charlie. "I report to London, which is what I've been doing."

"About what?" insisted Brooking.

"Hasn't Anne told you?"

Brooking's face became a mask. "I meant what, precisely, have you discussed with London."

"Getting everything ass about face for far too long," admitted Charlie. "But now I think we're on the right track." Track was the apposite word, decided Charlie. He still needed a hard, metalled road, preferably stretched out in front in an uninterrupted straight line.

The assembled men sat quietly around the communal table, the identical photographs and transcripts in front of them. Before each place was a photo-analysist's magnifying glass but only Jocelyn Hamilton had found the need to use it. He kept it in his hand when he looked up and said, "It's a great pity it took so long to discover."

"We've each of us had it here, practically from day one," said Patrick Pacey. "A great pity that you didn't pick it up for us and saved everyone a lot of time."

"I think it's a brilliant deduction of Charlie's," said Sir Rupert Dean, coming in as a buffer between the two other men. "Everything he suggested has been confirmed."

"We're in an even more jurisdictional quagmire than we were before," warned Jeremy Simpson, the legal advisor. "I'll need definitive guidance, of course, but with Bendall dead—and the case against him dying with him—I don't see we've any legal claim to remain associated with the investigation."

The director-general gestured with the Arkadi Noskov's news agency statement of George Bendall's bullet caliber defense to murder. "There's still an unsolved case of conspiracy. I would have thought we have every justification to remain involved, despite Bendall's death. We don't even know if there are other Britons involved."

"I don't want to know, if there are!" said Patrick Pacey.

No one laughed. Simpson made his own gesture to the material in front of him. "Charlie's only got one lead and it's Russian. He hasn't got the authority to pursue it. And as he points out in today's messages, there's a high mortality rate among people who become identified."

"I propose that Muffin is positively ordered to do nothing—to take no further part in the investigation, even if he's permitted to do so—until we have the necessary jurisdictional guidance," said the deputy director. "Of course the court episode is deplorable but objectively it's the least difficult outcome there could have been for us. Things should be allowed to settle, not be stirred up."

"As cynical as that is, I think it may well be the government attitude," said Pacey, uncomfortable at politically having to side with a man with whom he almost invariably disagreed and whom he did not personally like.

"It's Charlie's breakthrough," protested Dean. "I'd like to let him run with it. We still don't know what the hell it's all about. Our primary remit is to forewarn the government against the unexpected. We can't do that putting Charlie on hold."

"It's my advice—and my political opinion—that we should," urged Pacey. "Particularly with the legal uncertainty. We should at least wait until that's clarified."

"All right," agreed the director-general, reluctantly.

"And let's not give Muffin any excuse for intentionally misunderstanding," said Hamilton.

Charlie didn't misunderstood but he discarded the do-nothing instruction after the first reading, intent upon the technical evaluation which confirmed everything he'd asked to be checked. He hesitated, unsure which call to make first, finally deciding upon Natalia's personal answering machine at Lesnaya. She'd be able to guess just how much there was to do, after what had happened, he dictated. He didn't know how late he was going to be but it would probably be a good idea to eat without him and if he was very late to go on to bed.

To Anne Abbott Charlie said, "You want to hear just how ass about face it all was?"

"I've got Islay malt at the apartment. I checked with the embassy commissary to find out what you preferred."

"What about a video player?"

"State of the art."

"Thirty minutes," accepted Charlie. There was nothing wrong—nothing he should feel guilty about—in his having a drink while he talked these new developments through. And Anne was the most obvious person to do that with, the lawyer who knew every facet of the investigation.

"I could have postponed moving in," said Olga.

"Everything's organized and under control," insisted Zenin. "There was no need. I want to find out what sort of wife I'm going to have."

"Apart from my clothes there's not a lot more to bring."

"The important thing is that you're here," said Zenin.

23

After what seemed to be an eternity of constantly not knowing, Charlie knew this was very definitely wrong; knew that despite every snatched-at justification—and there *were* official and legal justifications for his choosing Anne with whom to discuss the analyses—it should have all been kept strictly professional, which was how they'd agreed by her rules things should be restored after their return from London. So why had he changed the rules, hinting a situation that shouldn't arise, certainly not in the insular claustrophobia of an embassy in which everyone knew before it lowered its hind leg when a mouse peed? Self-flattery? he wondered, answering his own question with another: Anne being interested in him while Natalia wasn't? Not good enough by a million miles, Charlie rejected at once: juvenile, an even worse self-accusation. Or, alternatively, the arrogance that had been the life raft to keep him afloat for so long? Closer but still not sufficient. Adventure happened, as it had with him and Anne, to be taken and enjoyed but as no more than that, a shared adventure to end when it ended, as unexpected adventures always did. Or should do.

So why was he threading his way through the lesser-used passages between the functioning embassy and its residential compound, until this moment so determinedly avoided that it took all his concentration to negotiate? A lawyer's question, although hardly appropriate: never ask a question—even to yourself—to which you don't know the answer. Back—responding to Kayley's earlier question—to square one. Don't ask, don't get a reply you don't want. Go, for the moment, with the flow: wherever it goes. He was copping out, Charlie honestly acknowledged at last; hoping for something without being the provable instigator.

Anne was barefoot, in a sheer beige silk and cashmere sweater beneath which she obviously wasn't wearing a bra and jeans, and which didn't betray a panty-line, either. The Islay malt, properly offered without either ice or water, was alongside the Stolichnaya, which did have an ice bucket, on a low table between matching piece of leather furniture too large correctly to be described as easy chairs but just slightly too small to be miniature settees. The apartment was pastel-shaded modern, grays and blues, which was hardly a choice considering its newness, and the curtains were drawn back for the ships' marker river illumination and the lights of unseen traffic necklacing Tapaca nabereznaja beyond.

Anne said, "You pour for yourself, I'll pour for me. Sorry I couldn't manage Liberace's piano; you didn't give me time to ship it over."

As he generously served himself Charlie said, "It wouldn't have gone with the decor, too much glitter."

"Do you want to eat? I could fix something with the miracle of microwave."

"That's not why I'm here."

Anne hesitated. "The foreplay's been tantalizing. Shall we get to the point of whatever you *are* here for?"

Now it was Charlie's turn to pause. He decided against picking up on the sharpness. Holding up the cassette as he crossed to Anne's VCR, Charlie announced, "The entire film of the presidential shooting. Don't look at anything but the struggle between Bendall and Sakov." He was defending himself against his oversight, Charlie recognized, and wanting to impress her, at the same time. "And here's this morning's: the very moment that Bendall, then Davidov was shot. . . ."

"We've watched so much so often that there's nothing more to see," dismissed Anne.

"Which was my problem—our problem," admitted Charlie. He passed her a transcript. "I'll play the White House shooting again and this time follow it with what Bendall and Sakov are yelling at each other, which I've had London extract verbatim with Russian-speaking lip readers . . ."

"*What!*"

"Watch."

"Jesus!" exclaimed Anne, staring down at the paper in advance of the film being run. "You're . . ."

"Watch," repeated Charlie, taking up the commentary. "They're on the camera platform. They're fighting, for possession of the rifle: Sakov's preventing Bendall shooting again, fire at anybody. That's what we all thought. But he wasn't doing that at all. Read what Bendall's saying. 'Stop shoving. . . . Got to get away, you cunt . . . ! You know I've got to get away. . . . ! They're waiting for me. . . . ! Stop pushing . . . shoving me. . . . ! Too near the edge. . . . ! Can't hold on . . . Stop!' But that's what Bendall was doing—*holding on* to prevent himself being thrown over the edge . . ."

Charlie glanced across at the lawyer, who was coming up and down between the film he was describing and the transcript of what the struggling men were saying to each other. "And here's Sakov, when they swing around as he's hit by the swivelling camera and what he's saying can be lip-read. 'You're dead, Georgi. Done what you're here for . . . down you go, like Vasili Gregorovich . . . no use anymore . . . let go the fucking rifle . . .' Here's the helicopter marksman. 'Get the fuck out the way . . . need a clear shot . . .' and you see that Sakov tries to do that and Bendall says 'No, you fucker. You're coming with me, everyone's coming with me.' And that's when the bodyguards get to him up the ladder but that's something else I missed. Bendall doesn't fall, not really from the true height from the pod. He slips under the rail, grabs at the edge and for a second hangs suspended before his hands are kicked away, kicked away by Sakov. But Bendall's lessened by a good two meters, maybe more, how far he's going to fall. So the drop doesn't kill him. . . ."

"Which it was intended to," came in Anne, understanding.

"Which it was intended to," agreed Charlie. "Instead it badly hurts him."

"But leaves him alive, the *holder* of the smoking gun, to tell all when he gets his moment in court," said Anne, with her customarily quickness.

"Which he thought he had this morning," continued Charlie "Here's today's transcript . . ." He scrolled through, for the moment he wanted. "Here! Here's Davidov, turning away from killing Bendall. The gun's by his side, not in any firing position. He sees the militiaman for the first time, standing in front of him. Now look at the words. 'Not me. . . . Get out of the way. . . . That's the door . . . get out of the way of my door . . .' Not *the* door. *My* door. The door he'd been told he'll be able to use to get away. Just like Bendall had been told he'd be able to get away from the camera platform and lose himself in the crowd—helped by whoever it was waiting for him below—before anyone properly realized what had happened. Which he would have been able to do if Vladimir Petrovich Sakov hadn't grabbed him and tried to throw him over the edge."

There was a long silence. Then Anne said, "That it?"

"No," said Charlie. He slid across the table towards her two of the photographs the FBI obtained in their background investigation of Vasili Gregorovich Isakov. The clearer showed the young man in shorts and a singlet, smiling into the sunlight at a beach bar with a wine glass half-raised towards his lips, as if he were responding to a toast. "Bendall's closest—only—friend who died on the Timiryazev level crossing too drugged and drunk literally to know what hit him. Look at his left arm—the one holding the wine—just above his wrist . . ."

"I can see it," said Anne.

"Now look at this," said Charlie, restarting the presidential shooting tape but very quickly into the struggle pressing the pause button and pointing with his finger right against the screen. "The same tattoo, two parallel lines with an arrow, like a fulcrum, in between them, on the same place on Sakov's wrist. London's done the comparison, although it wasn't really necessary. They're identical."

"You any idea what we're talking about here?"

"Some," said Charlie. Her admiration was obvious and he enjoyed it.

Anne insisted on stopping to get crackers and cheese and changed to wine, although Charlie stayed with scotch, and asked for both films to be shown again against their transcripts.

"Why let Bendall live!" Anne demanded, when the transmission finally stopped. "Sakov fails, the first time. But they—whoever 'they' are—have got Bendall at their mercy, in hospital. . . ."

"Maybe they tried, with the injection," reminded Charlie. "Pentathol *and* alcohol: alcohol we thought—because we were supposed to think—was residual in an alcoholic. An abnormally high level, injected directly into a vein, into the blood stream, to kill a man suffering advanced cirrhosis. Except that it didn't. And afterwards he was under heavier guard, surrounded by doctors and nurses. It was too dangerous to try again."

Anne shook her head. "I think you're close but not close enough."

"Where am I going wrong?" demanded Charlie, unoffended, glad she was questioning with a lawyer's mind.

"I don't know but it's too loose an end. It always was," insisted Anne, bent forward in total concentration. "Bendall was *alive*, uncontrolled and liable at any moment to tell us—tell anyone—what it was all about! Compared to that, the risk of trying a third time to kill him wouldn't have been a consideration."

"I said *maybe* the injection was another attempt to kill him," said Charlie. "You want another scenario?"

"What?" prompted Anne, bringing her head up to him.

"He wasn't *un*controlled! The very opposite. He was controlled. What *weren't* we—haven't we—been given!"

"You've lost me, Charlie."

"There aren't any taped records of George Bendall being treated: talking to doctors but probably more importantly to a psychiatrist."

"Agayan?"

"Not necessarily but Agayan told us himself that he'd had several sessions with Bendall. Remember him saying something about Bendall being a classic, textbook case?"

Anne nodded, doubtfully.

"It's Agayan's voice on the tape closing Kayley and the Americans down, when their one interview blew up in their faces," said Charlie. "And Guerguen Agayan was always around at every interview we had with Bendall . . . interviews that Arnold Nolan, our own psychiatrist, said at the beginning were entirely wrong, misdirected, to get a proper response from anyone with the mental condition Nolan suspected Bendall to be suffering . . . the mental condition Agayan would have known how to govern when he wanted to and manipulate when he wanted to. I talked to you in London about what Nolan told me—that people with Bendall's condition are totally susceptible to directional suggestion . . ." Charlie paused, at the further recollection. "Totally susceptible to directional suggestion particularly under the administration of drugs like pentathol. How about Bendall being kept total controlled by an injected drug his medical doctor chanced upon finding just that once?"

"I don't want to piss on the fire you're stoking up here, Charlie, but there are so many holes it's threadbare. You're suggesting Guerguen Semonovich Agayan is in this conspiracy right up to his neck, right?"

"It's a possibility. Or another psychiatrist."

"And that he's the mind manipulator who got George Bendall up on a TV platform with a gun in his hand to be held responsible while others carried out the assassinations?"

"We know that's what Bendall was there for. We just don't know who put him there."

Anne held up her hand. "Let's keep it simple. Bendall's supposed to be pushed over and killed but instead he's just badly injured. Now for the coincidence! Of all the hospitals in Moscow Bendall gets taken to, bingo, it's the one to which his puppet-master, Guerguen Agayan, is attached and, double-bingo, gets assigned to care for the guy whose strings he's been pulling. I believe in coincidences but I don't believe in this one."

During Anne's dismissal Charlie had sat staring down into his glass, locked into the sort of concentration she'd shown earlier. When he looked up he was smiling. " 'I never knew how or why it happened but George stopped stealing ever so suddenly,' " he quoted. " 'It was a long time before he told me he was seeing a doctor, a friend, who was helping him. I don't remember his name. I'll try. I'll really try.' There it is, Anne. Why Vera had to be killed in Lefortovo, *before* she could remember."

"You're forcing the bits into the jigsaw because they look the right shape."

"It fits."

"You'll have to do a lot more to prove it. And whether there's a need to prove anything is another debatable point, isn't it?"

Instead of answering, Charlie said, "I need to see Bendall's body. I'd like to see Davidov's, too, but even though he's dead we've got the right of consular access to see Bendall's body, haven't we?"

"I haven't got a clue," admitted Anne. "But what are you looking for?"

"Tattoos."

"I wouldn't have believed that if I hadn't seen it with my own eyes. I'd have dismissed it as kids' stuff," conceded Anne.

Charlie shook his head. "Remember how George reacted at belonging to an elite? Elite groups—societies—have often used tattooes as a sign of elitism. The praetorian guard of the Roman emperors marked themselves out like that. So did the Nazi SS. It's the sort of shit George would have gone for."

"And so did Vladimir Petrovich Sakov," picked up Anne. "You think there's a chance in hell of making him tell you about it . . . ?" She waved towards the VCR. "You've got evidence there of his being part of the conspiracy! He's not going to incriminate himself by admitting anything else."

"I'm working on it." Which wasn't true. Charlie thought there was a way to turn Sakov but it could also be the way to expose Natalia if she'd become part of an intelligence service cover-up. He was already officially on hold. Why push it any further?

Anne topped up her glass and leaned back in her encompassing chair, tucking her bare feet beneath her. "We could have done this in the office."

"I know." He'd forgotten the directness.

"How did your daughter like her doll?"

"She already had one just like it."

"London was good. A lot of fun."

"Yes."

"I'm not looking for commitment, Charlie. Or to pick up other people's pieces."

"I wasn't going to ask you to."

"You sure about microwave magic?"

"Yes. But thanks."

"Another time. When it's right."

"Yes, when it's right."

Natalia had eaten but was still up when Charlie got back to Lesnaya, watching the only story being covered on the late night news.

Charlie said, "I thought you'd already be in bed."

"I stayed up to watch this again. Do you want anything?"

"No." He nodded to the newscast. "How's that change things?"

"I'm not sure. We're recalling Karelin, obviously. What about you?"

"I'm waiting for London's instructions. Until then I'm not to do anything."

"It took until now to be told that?"

Charlie frowned. "What?"

"I'm surprised it took until now to be told that. It all happened this morning."

"And I had to go back and forth to London and go through God knows how many conferences and discussions at the embassy, so of course it took until now!"

Natalia froze the transmission at the exodus from the court. "And there you are, on TV!"

"Looking as if I'd shit myself. I almost did a little later, when I saw the militia officer had his gun on me."

Natalia didn't smile. "And there's the British lawyer."

Charlie frowned again. "Yes."

"The one you went back to London with?"

"Yes."

"You didn't tell me she was a woman."

"I didn't think it was relevant."

"She's attractive."

"I don't think that's relevant, either." Where the fuck was this intuition coming from!

"Was she at tonight's meetings?"

"She was at *today's* meetings. With a lot of other people. What is this!"

"I'm just surprised you didn't tell me your lawyer was a woman, that's all."

"Natalia, you spend every minute of your day working more with men than with women. Does it ever occur to you to tell me about them?"

"It probably would, if I went on an overseas trip with them."

"Well it didn't with me. And if you're reading something into it, which I wish you wouldn't because there's nothing to be read in, then I'm sorry. Sorry things are breaking down between us as badly as they seem to be doing."

"Yes," agreed Natalia, solemnly. "I'm sorry about that, too."

24

When Charlie answered Anne Abbott's internal voice mail message she at once announced, "I know where Bendall's body is! And how you might get to see it!"

"Where? How?"

"Back at Burdenko. They've called, expecting us to handle the funeral arrangements, by which they really mean the cost. Brooking's apoplectic."

"He usually is. Are we going to?"

"Bendall was still officially a British subject: legally there's a liability. But we need a declared death certificate. Brooking doesn't want to sully his hands by asking for it and says we know the people there. You volunteering?"

The hospital vestibule seemed oddly empty without its challenging guard detail but the receptionist recognized Charlie and located Nicholai Badim on her second attempt. She said, "You're lucky he doesn't have a theater list."

After the preceding twelve hours his luck deserved to change, Charlie decided. He had a lot of bridges to rebuild and leaving Lesnaya without bothering with breakfast was scarcely the way to begin the reconstruction. He wasn't sure he yet knew where or how to start but running out of the house wasn't the way: if anything it was an unspoken admission of what Natalia suspected him of having done in London. Even Sasha had detected the frigid atmosphere, asking why they weren't talking and why he was leaving so early. The previous night they'd laid—almost theatrically—stiffly apart, Natalia jerking away when she'd relaxed into a half sleep and accidentally touched his leg with hers.

The balding, quickly blinking surgeon-administrator came curiously into the foyer, frowning at Charlie's reason for being there. "We could have arranged that by telephone."

The man was anxious to reestablish the authority that had been too often overridden during the questioning of Bendall, Charlie decided. "I've also got to satisfy myself that it is Bendall's body. Formal identification."

The frown—and irritation—deepened. "See it! There's hardly anything left of the face to identify!"

"It's a necessary formality. You must surely know what bureaucracy is like."

The other man shrugged, gesturing for Charlie to follow as he thrust off deeper into the hospital. "If it will hurry things up. We need the mortuary space. I've told the militia I want to get rid of the other one."

"Davidov's body is here as well!" His luck was definitely changing.

"We're the nearest mortuary to the court. It's inconvenient, an imposition."

The corridor along which they were walking was littered with dirty laundry, predominantly sheets, some abandoned on the floor and some piled up on a row of empty, metal-framed beds. A lot were bloodstained. There were also equipment cartons and boxes, mostly empty but a few were still sealed and unpacked. There was even a stack, sealed, in the lift in which they descended into the basement. Badim seemed oblivious to it all.

All the mortuary drawers appeared to have name designations on them. Boris Davidov's was next to Bendall's. There was only one attendant in the room, who half straightened at Badim's entry but then decided not to bother with the respect. The surgeon ignored him, too, hauling Bendall's drawer out himself and flicking the covering sheet back from the near headless body. It was made bloodlessly white by the refrigeration.

"OK?" the Russian demanded, impatiently.

The sheet still covered most of the dead man's torso. Charlie quickly lifted it, uncovering the left side. The upper part of the injured arm was still bandaged almost down to the elbow but the wrist was bare. On it was the parallel line tattoo separated by the arrow fulcrum.

"What are you looking for?" said Badim, at Charlie's shoulder.

Charlie lowered the sheet. "I'd like to see Davidov's body, too."

"Why?"

"I'm not sure how much information London will want in my report. They might have a query about Davidov and I don't want to have to bother you a second time."

The adjoining drawer was withdrawn even more impatiently. Badim said, "I don't want to be bothered again either."

The entire upper part of Davidov's body appeared crushed. No attempt had been made to clean up the bullet wounds. There was the same matching tattoo on the man's left wrist. "Are you carrying out autopsies?"

"The cause of death is self evident in both cases."

"They haven't been asked for?"

"No. Finally satisfied?"

"Thank you," said Charlie, falling in step with the man as they left the mortuary. "All I need now is the certificate."

"How quickly can you have the body removed?"

"I'll try to have things moving as soon as I get back to the embassy." Charlie wondered upon whom Brooking would unload that chore; the man had actually smiled his gratitude when Charlie had offered to collect the certificate.

"Today, if possible," urged the Russian.

"I can understand how glad you and Dr. Agayan are to get the hospital back to normality."

Badim turned to Charlie in the elevator, frowning again. "Agayan? He's not attached to my staff."

Charlie's tell-tale feet throbbed. "But he was here . . . part of your team . . . ?"

The surgeon-administrator made a disparaging gesture towards the cardboad litter. "We aren't funded sufficiently for cleaners, let alone a resident psychiatrist. Agayan is at the Serbsky Institute."

Which was the principal KGB psychiatric institute in which Soviet dissidents were incarcerated and many made mad to justify their imprisonment at the height of the communist oppression, Charlie instantly recognized. "How did he come to be involved?"

"Seconded in, as part of the emergency when Bendall was admitted."

"Seconded in by whom?"

Badim humped his shoulders, uncertainly. "The militia, I suppose. He would have been the obvious choice."

There was another foot twinge. "Why the obvious choice?"

"He knew Bendall's case history. Had treated him in the past, apparently."

It only took minutes for Badim to complete the certificate. "Are you sure you've now got everything you want?"

"More than sufficient," thanked Charlie. Once the floodgates opened, things usually seemed to come in a surge. But did he want it to anymore?

Her KGB career had been based on psychology and Natalia was sure she psychologically knew Charlie intimately and wished for once that she didn't. He hadn't denied it. If he had, positively, she would have accepted it because she wanted to accept it—believe it for herself and for Sasha and for *them*—but he hadn't. So he hadn't wanted to lie to her personally and by not lying he'd confirmed what had only been the vaguest of suspicions, predicated upon nothing more than the television-captured look and whatever the lip-moving exchange had been between the woman and Charlie as she'd left the court. *He hadn't denied it.* The four words were a continuing mantra in Natalia's head, distracting her—deflecting her—from the reconvened meeting, which had just ended as inconclusively as every other session with Viktor Karelin. Now all she wanted to do was end it, to get away from these two men and their verbal carousel of avoidance. So enclosing was her despair that Natalia felt something close to the need to run—like Charlie had run from Lesnaya that morning—which was absurd because there was nowhere mentally or physically to run. But didn't she have to? Didn't she have to make some move, either physically or mentally, to end her impossible, perpetually conflicting situation with Charlie Muffin? What about loving him, which despite everything she still did? She at once acknowledged the much more important question. What about his loving her? He hadn't, sufficiently, when he'd abandoned her in London all those years ago and he clearly didn't now. So there was no point in going on with the pretense, convincing herself it was better for Sasha and better for her. There were too many risks, too many dangers, and she'd fooled herself into believing there was some way she could handle it. *He hadn't denied it.* Now it was time for her to deny there'd ever been a chance of their making a life together.

Natalia forced the reflections back, willing her concentration entirely upon the more impending demands, almost as unsettled by the behaviour of the two men supposedly conducting the enquiry with her. Federal Prosecutor Pavl Filitov had tried as hard that morning as on every other occasion to be conciliatory and nonconfrontational towards the recalled intelligence chairman but Yuri Trishin's attitude had been quite different and she still didn't understand it. "It's time to finalize our opinion and make our recommendations to the president, agreed?"

Yuri Trishin didn't respond to Filitov's inviting look. It was the chief of staff who said, "Yes."

"Were either of you better satisfied with Chairman Karelin today than on previous occasions?"

"I was not impressed at all," said Trishin.

Natalia felt the slightest lift of satisfaction at what, small though it might be, was the first positive opinion Trishin had volunteered since the commission had opened. Which he wouldn't have offered if there hadn't already been some discussion between the man and the acting president whom he represented. "Pavl Yakovlevich?"

"I believe there has been serious infiltration—sabotage—of which the disappearance of any details of Boris Davidov having once been an officer in the KGB or the FSB is a part," said the Federal Prosecutor, stating the obvious—but avoiding a commitment—with a lawyer's pedantry.

"That wasn't the question, but let's explore your answer," said Natalia. "It isn't simply records of Boris Davidov that disappeared from the federal intelligence archives! The man got into court using official identification from the *Federalnaia Sluzhba Besopasnosti* and shot dead with an officially issued weapon a man accused of murder. Wouldn't you agree that's an appalling lack—and breach—of internal security?"

Filitov stirred uncomfortably at the pressure. Before the lawyer could speak, Trishin said, "That's very definitely my assessment."

Further guidance from another Kremlin suite, Natalia recognized. From the quick look he gave the other man, she suspected Filitov at last realized it too. The lawyer said, "There are unquestionably grounds for criticism."

"Not censure, for maladministration?"

Filitov waited for the chief of staff's lead but Trishin remained silent. Finally Filitov said, "That might be an extreme judgment."

"We've been made to look internationally ridiculous," said Trishin. "And throughout these hearings we—and the acting president—have been treated with contempt by everyone we have summoned from the intelligence community."

Now it was Natalia who hesitated, surprised at the virtual confirmation of pressure from Aleksandr Okulov. But it was more than that. They were being told which way to go but the responsibility would be theirs, not Okulov's. "What about an external investigation?"

"I do not believe the situation can be left to an internal FSB enquiry, which is very obviously and clearly Chairman Karelin's intention," declared Trishin.

"What recommendations do you propose?" invited Natalia, intent on the answer. She'd never expected to get this strength of argument, from Trishin's earlier prevarication: wasn't sure she wanted it after her earlier doubts about her and Charlie.

"What are your suggestions, Pavl Yakovlevich?" retreated the chief of staff, at the moment of commitment.

The Federal Prosecutor looked across the room at the note-taking secretariat.

"There should be criticism, for the lapses. And a request to Chairman Karelin to publish the result of the internal enquiries."

"And yours, Yuri Fedorovich?" said Natalia, quickly, before the chief of staff could identify her as the proposer.

"There should be a totally independent, external investigation, with its result published," set out the portly chief of staff. "It should be made clear to Chairman Karelin that he and his officers are legally required to respond to every enquiry, a requirement that has been blatantly ignored here. And our findings should also be that the existing senior command structure of the *Federalnaia Sluzhba Besopasnosti* is guilty of serious failings in its administration and that steps necessary to correct it should be made public."

Was it conceivable that his political ambitions had turned Aleksandr Mikhailevich Okulov so totally against his former colleagues? Or was the determination to reject the speculation that the same ambition implicated him in some way with the attack upon the two presidents? Or something altogether different, an agenda she couldn't guess at? She said, "What's your feeling upon those proposals, Pavl Yakovlevich?"

The Federal Prosecutor stared for several moments at Trishin. "I believe they are too draconian. And you haven't responded yourself yet?"

"I believe the attitudes and the events justify them."

"Which gives you a two to one majority in favor," acknowledged Filitov.

"Unless you care to make it unanimous?"

"I don't," said the lawyer. "I also wish to register a minority disagreement."

"That's your right," recognized Natalia.

"I know it is."

Charlie reached his decision—the only one there realistically could have been—long before he got to the American embassy. It was going to be the first time in his never-lose, never-be-beaten life that he'd turned his back on a half-finished operation. And he didn't give a shit. Integrity was Natalia's problem, not his. He didn't care if she was even peripherally, unwittingly, involved: the suspicion was probably an aberration, like so many other bloody stupid things he'd done in the last few days. But he couldn't take the chance. The only consideration was bridge building: keeping himself and Natalia and Sasha together. And to do that he was prepared to make any compromise and every concession.

Anne Abbott would expect an explanation. Which would be easy. He'd simply lie and insist that Bendall didn't have a tattoo. Not tell her about Davidov or Agayan at all. Which only left Vladimir Sakov, whom she did know about. Easy again. She was more aware than he was that he had no legal authority to arrest or interrogate the cameraman. He'd tell Anne he'd done the only thing possible, alerting the Russians, and leave it at that. It wasn't important anymore to impress Anne. Madness to have tried—wanted to—in the first place, to have been flattered by the adventure.

Should he admit it to Natalia? Confess to the madness that it had been and plead her forgiveness: flagellate himself, if that's what it took? What if she couldn't forgive him? Consider it his final betrayal, to go with all the rest. Too dangerous a strategy. Safer to say nothing, neither deny nor confirm. It was, after all, only intuition, remarkable though that had been. The next few days—he hoped not the next few weeks—weren't going to be the best fun he'd ever had but he'd brought the ashes on his own head so he'd have to live with it. Just as long as Natalia was living it with him.

There was an atmosphere of flatness—of everything being on half power—about the American incident room. John Kayley came odorously from his side office and said, "Tell me you've come up with something to keep this investigation on the road."

"Like what?"

Kayley shook his head, in defeat. "We're stymied. I've got everyone carrying out a total review but we've done that already, days ago. Now everything's under Russian control."

"Where is Olga?" asked Charlie, looking into the empty office.

"Hasn't shown. I've got calls in. What are your people saying in London?"

"I'm to sit and do nothing, until told otherwise. Yours?"

"I've still got a murder and the maiming of the president's wife, by a person or persons unknown. And until I find who those persons are, my ass is being burned every hour on the hour. Scamell's gone to the Foreign Ministry, to try diplomatic pressure to get us actively involved but all we'll get is the runaround. I'm fucked, Charlie. For the first time in my life, I don't have a lead to follow or a path to take. After the fuck up with the director I thought I was fireproof but not any longer. This could be goodbye John Deke Kayley. So all suggestions will be gratefully received."

The way to take everything forward—probably solved it all—burst upon Charlie with complete clarity. He said, "Sorry, mate. I'm as stymied as you are."

Charlie bypassed both Richard Brooking and Anne Abbott, once more locking himself away in his riverview office and actually standing at the window, running the idea through his mind for problems and finding none. Except one: causing difficulties for Natalia if she was being manipulated in some way, which was as high as he was any longer prepared to consider her being an unwitting inside source. And the danger of which was, after all, why he intended lying to Anne Abbott and doing nothing about what he'd discovered that day.

Turning his back, Charlie reminded himself again, for the first time ever. It irked him, like the nagging, persistent pain from an abscess that was going to go on hurting until it was lanced. Whatever compromise or concession, he thought in further reminder. His personal difficulty was that giving up had always been the one compromise he'd never been prepared to make. So now was the time to learn. At least he knew himself he could probably have brought everything to a conclusion although examined as closely as he was examining now it wasn't one hundred percent certain that he and Kayley could have instilled sufficient fear.

Brooking agreed to see Charlie at once and said again how grateful he was when Charlie delivered the death certificate. A complication had arisen with the Russians arguing the embassy was responsible for Vera Bendall's burial as well but at least in her case they had a certificate. The housing officer was arranging it all. They were hoping Peter Bendall's plot would be big enough to accommodate two more coffins. With luck they'd manage the interment without the media learning about it.

Anne said it was bad luck that George Bendall hadn't been tattooed but that it had been worth checking and agreed that they had no jurisdiction whatsoever to investigate Vladimir Sakov. She wondered what Olga would do with the information about Vladimir Sakov and Charlie said he didn't know but the militia colonel had promised to keep him informed.

"So what's that leave you to do?" she asked.

"Wait for London's instructions," said Charlie.

They were waiting for him on his personal fax machine when he got back to his office. With Bendall—and his killer—dead the enquiry became entirely one between Russia and the United States of America. He was to take no further active part in the investigation, merely to maintain a liaison role to enable the file to be closed when it was satisfactorily concluded.

Now he'd been officially told to turn his back, Charlie recognized. It still irked him because he'd never done that when officially ordered, either.

25

Charlie called out for Sasha, which he always did if he got home to Lesnaya at a time she would be up, but there was no scurried response. Natalia was sitting in one of the large lounge chairs, facing the door, as if she were waiting.

Charlie said, "I hoped you'd be home."

"Did you?"

"Where's Sasha?"

"Sleeping over at Marina's."

"She's only five." Marina was Sasha's closest friend at preschool.

"Five and a half. Which is old enough."

Retreat, Charlie warned himself. "Of course it is. We could go out to dinner if you like."

"No."

He'd poured the ashes over his own head, Charlie reminded himself. "I'm getting a drink. Would you like one?"

"No."

From the drinks tray he said, "London's told me to stand away from the investigation. Leave everything to the militia and the Americans."

"Have they?" She shouldn't have packed the cases waiting in the bedroom because she didn't want to do it. Now that the moment had come—now that she'd made the plans—Natalia wanted to pull back but knew she couldn't. Or could she? It was only the cases, really. Couldn't she hide them in a closet, stay after he'd left the following morning and unpack them?

Charlie sat on the matching couch, close enough to reach out and touch her but not doing so. From the attitude so far it was going to be a long time before he'd be touching her. "How did today go?"

Was it fair to seek his advice? There was no one else—another, finally accepted professional although now cynical reason for changing her mind—and Charlie had a bat-like protective antenna. "Not the way I expected."

Better! seized Charlie. "Let's go through it."

Natalia did, hesitantly to begin with, and Charlie didn't once interrupt hoping he'd found the first bridge. When she finally finished he said, "I think you're right about pressure from Okulov: he's got to do something to impress Washington to get the treaty he needs for the election. And purging the FSB—which needs purging from what you've told me—would be a hell of a way publicly to do it."

"With the commission, which recommends the purge, the casualty of any battle between the communist-leaning FSB and the existing group in the Kremlin."

Natalia was right, Charlie accepted. And at risk if the presidential shooting was left to run inconclusively into the ground. So what about his own rock and a hard place, trying to protect Natalia by not using what he knew against endangering her if he did? According to everything she'd told him it had been Natalia—provably, on secretariat tapes and in secretariat notebooks—who had been consistently critical of the FSB from the outset of the official enquiry. With Yuri Trishin, the president's chief of staff, unpersuaded until today. Which showed Natalia—arguably (although she wasn't) a disenchanted former KGB officer—the prime instigator of any FSB overhaul. An obvious and unavoidable target. It could also be the unproven, unproveable evidence of Yuri Trishin—never Natalia, even unwittingly—being the internal source to the conspiracy. A new mantra echoed in Charlie's mind: unproven, unproveable. "I want to talk something through with you again."

"I want to go on talking about this," misunderstood Natalia, deciding at the same time that there were several closets in the unused bedrooms in which she could hide the cases until the following day.

"That's what I *am* thinking about."

"I'm sorry . . . I thought . . ." she stumbled. Shit, shit and double shit! Even Charlie's frustration cursing was automatic for her.

Good, thought Charlie. She was on the defensive: a footplank if not a bridge. Every little helped so he'd push it as far across the gulf as he could. "Don't try to think ahead of me. *Talk* with me. What reason was there for Trishin's u-turn today?"

"Karelin stonewalling, as always."

"As always," echoed Charlie, snatching at the response. "He's stonewalled at every encounter, even sent sacrifices at the beginning."

"Yes?" Natalia accepted, questioningly.

"Do you remember our conversation about there being an inside source—a leak—for every move in the investigation to be sidetracked or misdirected?"

"Yes?" she questioned again. She couldn't follow him, see the point towards which he was going.

"Could it have been Trishin: *be* Trishin?"

Natalia's mind was in a turmoil, too many unconnected thoughts fluttering in a wind-blown paperchase. "Doing what?"

"Using you . . . manipulating . . . ?"

"*No!*" Natalia's mind cleared, the paperchase wind abruptly blowing away the uncertainty. "You didn't mean using me . . . manipulating me. You thought it *was* me! Suspected *me*! Imagined I was part of something . . . !" She was forward in the chair, eyes bulged in outrage.

"No!" frantically denied Charlie, despairing of her psychology-tuned intuition. "I'm frightened you've been used . . ."

"I have, haven't I Charlie? Used for such a very long time!"

"Stop it, Natalia!" he shouted. "Stop this going wrong . . . getting any worse. I can help . . . there's a way . . ."

She jerked up but having done so didn't know what to do, thrusting forward but then coming back, to stand over him to stare down contemptuously. "Sasha is staying with Marina's family because I asked if she could. I didn't want her to be here tonight. To see. I'd even changed my mind. Was going to try to forget whatever you did with that woman because it could have been a mistake . . . something you didn't think about. But you don't do anything without thinking about it, do you, you bastard! You're even ready to think I'd cheat on *you*: be prepared to mislead your fucking precious professionalism . . ."

"Stop it!" Charlie shouted again. "This is stupid . . . shouldn't be happening . . ."

"I'm not part of anything . . . a conspiracy or a cover up or whatever else it is your contorted, convoluted mind imagines. You want to know what I'm guilty of! I'm guilty of believing that you could change and love me and trust me and dear God, wasn't that a mistake! You did it very well, Charlie. You got a posting here and you realized how useful I'd be and you managed to make it work for all this time . . ."

She was hysterical, beyond immediate reason. "Sit down. Please sit down and listen to me, Natalia. You're wrong. All the way wrong. Sit down and listen to me: *listen* to what I have to say. What has to be said."

"I'm leaving, Charlie," announced Natalia, shaking her head as she walked away. "It's over. Should never have begun." She emerged at once from the bedroom with a case in either hand.

"I'm asking you not to leave." Charlie was standing, his hands out.

"You should learn to trust someone sometime, Charlie. But you never will."

"Where are you going?"

"An hotel, initially."

"Which one?"

"Don't become a nuisance."

"What about Sasha?"

"What about her?"

"What are you going to tell her?"

"How about the father who didn't want to see her for the first three years she was born had to go away again?"

"That's not fair. Or true."

"Let's not get into a discussion about fairness or truth."

"I love you!" Charlie called after her.

Natalia quietly closed the door behind herself.

Charlie waited at the British embassy entrance to authorize John Kayley's admission. The American said: "You look rough. Bad night?"

"Kind of," said Charlie. Wallowing in a lake of self-pity and Islay malt hadn't been the best idea. "You mind passing on the cigars for a while?"

"Not if you tell me what I'm here for."

"Pictures and moving lips."

Kayley followed the video struggle between Bendall and Vladimir Sakov with the lip-read transcript before him and did the same directly afterwards with the courtroom killing but on this showing Charlie freeze-framed the tattoo comparison between the NTV cameraman and the FBI-collected photograph of Vasili Isakov. Charlie said, "Bendall and Davidov have the same tattoos in the same place. Their bodies are at the Burdenko mortuary but the hospital wants to get rid of them."

"We need photographs."

"London's taken responsibility for Bendall's body. We might be able to bluff the hospital about Davidov but at the moment the priority is with the living more than the dead, before he gets dead."

"You've done good, Charlie. Damned good. You worked it out to the very end already?"

"Not yet," Charlie admitted. "But I think I know how to." Would Natalia ever learn what he'd done, to keep her safe? He already had the list of Moscow hotels to call later, to find out where she was. "How's this measure for size?"

Once, as Charlie talked, Kayley's hand strayed to his cigars but the American remembered in time, smiling apologetically. When Charlie finished Kayley said, "We swing a trick like this, I'm permanently in the Bureau's Hall of Fame and you're a to-die-for friend for life. But we'll never get it to work."

"That mean you don't want to give it a try?"

"Sure as hell no! But we'll only get one hit."

"You think Washington will go for it?"

"The president's wife was shot, for Christ's sake! By a bullet meant for him! And you ask if they'll go for it!"

"You going to ask them, first?"

Kayley snorted the rejection. "It doesn't work, my tit's in the ringer for failing. If it does work, I'll announce it and wait for the presidential congratulations."

"Officially I'm on watch and listen, no active participation."

"It's my call, anyway."

"And there's no jurisdiction."

"Now you're trying to talk me out of it!"

"Just getting the rules of engagement clear between us," insisted Charlie. "Like you said, we only get one hit. So where?"

"The station says he's off sick. I called without saying who I was."

"Let's hope he's not too sick."

Vladimir Petrovich Sakov didn't sound too sick but there wasn't the belligerence there had been in the mess room of the NTV studios. The muffled demand to identify themselves was shouted through the chipped door of the apartment in a crumbling block on Kazakova Ulitza gradually being shaken off its sand-ballasted foundations by the perpetual shuddering traffic of the inner peripherique behind and the reverberating railway line in front. When they said who they were the voice came back stronger. "Fuck off!"

"Relieved it's us?" Kayley shouted back.

There was no reply.

"We know, Vladimir Petrovich," said Charlie. "We've got all the proof we need, too. We even know about the tattoos."

Kayley gently pushed Charlie out of the direct firing line through the door, pulling himself to the opposite side. The American said loudly, "You worried? I'd be, if I were you. I'd be shit scared."

There was still no response from inside.

"I just realized something," said Charlie. "This railway line is the one on which Vasili Isakov was murdered, further up at Timiryazev, isn't it? You think they might try that again?"

"Why not?" said Kayley, responding to Charlie's nodded invitation. "You got away with it well enough last time, didn't you Vladimir?"

"What's it like, knowing you're going to die and that there's nothing you can do about it?" asked Charlie. "You really must be shit scared."

"You want your life saved, you open the door, Vlad old buddy," advised the American. "We're your only chance, so stop being an asshole."

The shuffling was audible on the other side.

"We're waiting," said Charlie.

"But not for much longer," added Kayley.

There was the grating of more than one lock being released ahead of a longer clattering sound. Vladimir Sakov put himself to one side, for a warning view of several meters along the outside corridor, head-nodding them into the room. The long sleeves of the well-pressed blue woollen shirt were buttoned, hiding the body markings, and the jeans were much cleaner than those at his meeting with Charlie at the TV station. The apartment was surprisingly neat and well furnished, in contrast to the outside neglect and there were photographs—one of instant interest was of a much slimmer, younger Sakov in army uniform—but Charlie didn't get the impression of permanence. The impression he did get was of a very different man from the gut-rot swigging slob of the TV mess room.

Charlie turned at the repeated clattering and saw there was a cat's cradle of chains criss-crossing the inside of the door. The dead lock and mortise looked new. A Makarov lay on a table which was totally hidden from the outside when the door was open.

Kayley gestured to the handgun and said, "You're going to need more than that to keep you alive, once everybody knows what we know."

"So it's only the two of you who do, at the moment?"

This man's training had involved more than being taught how to use a camera, Charlie thought. Pushing the pained condescension into his voice he said, "Vladimir Petrovich! Do we look as if we just drove in from the steppes in a hay cart? We said we *know!* And one of the things we know is that your job was to kill George Bendall, not save him. Do you think we'd come here and confront a willing killer without insurance? Come on!" Charlie hoped Sakov hadn't seen the tension twitch through the bulged American. They'd all three been standing but now Charlie walked casually, as if he had the right, to a chair closest to the photographs. Beyond the one showing Sakov in army uniform was another of the man in swimming shorts. None showed Sakov with either male or female companions. Kayley found himself a chair and finally Sakov sat down.

Very slowly, enabling the Russian to see what he was doing, Kayley extracted the lip moving transcripts from the manila envelope he carried. "Let me read something to you. 'You're dead, Georgi. Done what you're here for . . . down you go, like Vasili Gregorovich . . . no use anymore . . .' Recognize those words: your words? And what Bendall said back? 'No, you fucker. You're coming with me, everyone's coming with me.' If you'd pushed him properly, not let him see you coming, it would have worked and he would have been over the top, head first, before that CNN lensman heard the commotion and turned his camera on you . . . saw everything. That was real bad luck, wasn't it?"

"How?" said Sakov. There wasn't the slightest belligerence in his voice any more.

"That favorite phrase of politicians," said Charlie. "Read my lips!"

"Now you've got to read ours," said Kayley. He went into the envelope again, taking out Isakov's picture and the CNN freeze frame. "Just so you know what there is. By tonight we'll have the match from the mortuary with Bendall and Davidov."

So far Kayley hadn't put a foot—or rather a word—wrong but Charlie hoped the American properly realized they were dealing with a professional. Could he risk a wrong word, taking things on as he wanted? "How'd you feel, after Bendall survived? After 'you're coming with me, everyone's coming with me?' I know he's clever—that's why he was moved in at once—but you were putting a hell of a lot of trust in just one very clever man to keep Bendall from talking, weren't you? What a pity you didn't have someone on the theater staff at the hospital. Bendall could have died under surgery and the problem would have been over, wouldn't it? You'd have got him the second time."

"Guerguen Semonovich could do anything he wanted with the idiot!" said the Russian, his uncertainty deepening. "He had Bendall trained like Pavlov's dogs, responding without question to any instruction, any guidance. Isakov too, to an extent. Isakov trusted him, believed he was curing Bendall of his demons."

Got it! thought Charlie, triumphantly. All they needed was that little extra nudge: one wrong word, he thought again. He was about to speak when Kayley began, "Even though . . ." but Charlie urgently talked over the American. "But Guerguen Semonovich Agayan didn't train you: the KGB did. And you were the link between the idiots and the real planners. That's why I don't understand why they've let you live."

"The court was the end: that closed it down."

"But it didn't, did it?" pressed Charlie.

Kayley came back on track, again indicating the Makarov and the chained door. "And you didn't believe that it did yourself, did you, Vlad old buddy."

"For fuck's sake stop calling me Vlad old buddy!" erupted Sakov.

"You'd better believe it," said the American. "We're your way— your *only* way—to stay alive now."

"You said that before."

Both Charlie and Kayley recognized the half question as the beginning of the capitulation. Kayley said, "Here's how it is, the toss of a coin. Only in your case, Vlad old buddy, heads you lose—the moment we make public what we know, with all the photographs and the lip read transcripts—and tails you lose again, because they can't afford to let you go on living, telling all you know. So here's what you do. You run. To me. To America. I get you out of here, on an American flight on a phony passport, like we've got a lot of Russian defectors out before. You testify before a Grand Jury, telling us all about the conspiracy, so that we can issue legal indictments against everyone who's part of it, to enable Moscow to make all the arrests. Then we put you into the Witnesses' Protection Program. New identity, new citizenship and a U.S. government pension. And you live happily ever after."

"What guarantee have I got you'll do all that?"

"A better guarantee than you've got staying alive here when we go public," said Kayley. "But think about it. You think the president of the United States of America isn't going to be grateful for you telling everyone who tried to kill him and so badly hurt his wife!"

"I get full amnesty?"

"That's the deal."

"When?" asked Sakov, his voice almost inaudible.

"How much time do you think you've got?"

"None," Sakov finally conceded.

"I don't think so either," agreed Kayley.

"Don't call me Vlad old buddy anymore."

"I won't," promised the American.

Ruth Anandale had her good hand to her face, sobbing, and it was a mistake to reach out for the useless one because she screamed hysterically, "Dont! Stop it! Don't touch it: it's dead!"

"There's progress all the time," insisted Anandale, a worn out assurance. "The moment there's a breakthrough, we'll have it. I told you you'd get better and you will. I promise!"

"Stop it, Walt. Stop it! Stop it! Stop it! I'm a freak, always going to be a freak. Can't dress anymore as I want. Swim as I want and ride as I want and play tennis like I want. I can't even cut my own fucking food anymore or drive a car anymore. Or write my name anymore. A freak, Walt! What's it like to be married to a fucking freak!"

It had been Max Donnington's suggestion to be discreetly in the background when Anandale told his wife that the two European brachial plexus specialists had unanimously agreed with the American surgeons that there was no treatment or surgery possible to restore any use to Ruth Anandale's arm. The admiral came quickly forward, already prepared. "Come on, Ruth. Take these, they'll make it easier . . ."

Ruth Anandale was calm when she looked up at the man. "These aren't the pills—the tranquilizer—I need, Max. What about some pills to make it really easy?"

Anandale remained for another hour in the private quarters of the White House, waiting until his wife finally fell asleep and when he was sure she had and wouldn't hear he said to Donnington, "You think we've got an additional problem?"

"Unquestionably. Trauma of some sort was inevitable. The only uncertainty was the degree."

"Does this degree needs specialist treatment, too?"

"I think it would be wrong *not* to consider psychiatry. As I told you before, your wife is going to need all the help she can get."

Anandale looked up irritably at the butler's hesitant entry. "I told you I was off limits."

"I think you'll want to hear Mr. North," said the man.

"What!" demanded Anandale, emerging into the outer dressing room.

"Kayley's got one of the guys involved: the cameraman on the gantry with Bendall. He's defected and agreed to go before a Grand Jury. Kayley's on his way with him now."

For a moment Anandale stood with his head bowed, savoring the moment. Then he looked up, smiling. "I don't want a single rat to run. The security blackout on this is absolute. Tell Justice I want a Grand Jury empanelled at once, starting today. And I want to see Kayley the moment he hands the guy over."

It took Charlie less than an hour to locate Natalia's booking at the Radisson Slavjanskaya Hotel, on Berezhkavskaya naberezhnaya. Having done so he sat uncertainly in his embassy office for a further thirty minutes, finally deciding against a personal encounter, particularly in front of Sasha whom he was sure would be staying there with her.

The longest time of all was spent composing the letter because Charlie always had the greatest difficulty openly expressing personal feelings. Which was probably the root cause of all his problems with Natalia, he acknowledged. He wrote, finally, that he loved her and he loved Sasha and wanted them both back with him at Lesnaya. He was sorry how badly things had collapsed but that it wasn't irreparable. All they needed to do was to talk: to get the misunderstandings out of the way, the compromises accepted. He was certainly ready to make compromises and hoped she was, too. There also might be another reason for them to speak very shortly. She knew the number at which he'd be waiting.

Charlie took the metro to the Kievskaya stop and was careful entering the foyer, not wanting any accidental meeting. He waited to see the receptionist put the envelope in the pigeonhole for room 46. There was no key displayed, which meant she had to be there.

He was back in the Lesnaya apartment by eight. No message had been left on the answering machine during the time he was away. The telephone didn't ring during the rest of the night, either.

26

John Kayley was pouch-eyed, bristle-chinned, and the always-crumpled suit in which he'd lived for close to forty-eight hours looked like the dustbin liner a bag lady would have rejected. Around him hung the sourness of curdled cigar odor. Charlie had snatched at the outside line, hope flaring that Kayley's call from Sheremet'yevo had been Natalia. He again waited at the embassy entrance for the American's arrival direct from the airport.

When he did get there Charlie said, "Now you're the one looking rough."

"But happy," said Kayley.

The telephone warning had given Charlie time to have the Islay malt and glasses ready. Pouring, Charlie said, "We got all the reasons we want to celebrate?"

Kayley offered his glass towards Charlie's, to make the toast. As the glasses touched the American said, "You're not going to believe it: any of it!"

"I've heard that a lot of times."

"Never like this."

"How much did you get before handing him over?" Charlie was glad the other man appeared to have sickened himself of his scented cigars: the riverview office was becoming clogged by the aromatic residue.

"Enough to get almost the whole of the conspiracy. The Grand Jury should get the rest. What they don't will come out of the woodwork here once we issue the indictments. It'll be Christmas wrapped."

Charlie refilled their glasses, leaving the bottle within easy reach between them. "So what am I not going to believe?"

"It's a KGB stalwarts' conspiracy but it's not a KGB conspiracy. It's also an FSB wrecking cabal—to rebuild the old style KGB—

by the communist party who see it as their red carpet back into the Kremlin . . ." Kayley paused. "And who would most probably have got there if you hadn't got in the way, Charlie."

"My problem's not disbelieving," protested Charlie. "It's understanding."

"To understand you've got to hear it in sequence," insisted Kayley. "Be patient. Sakov's a KGB—now FSB—colonel. Career officer, originally working out of the Third Chief Directorate—responsible for monitoring the armed forces, which the armed forces resent to the point of eliminating anyone they discovered doing it—with two functions. He's an agent-in-place, a spy within the Russian army, reporting back to Lubyanka anything and everything. The second function is as a spotter, isolating potentially useful and usable people for what was, at the time he was in Afghanistan, the KGB . . ."

"OK, here's the first thing I can't believe because I never could!" broke in Charlie. "I can't believe any espionage service worthy of the description would isolate Bendall!"

"*Usable*," repeated Kayley. "That's how Bendall was described to Sakov by the Lubynka. Unpredictable, mad, drunk, whatever, he was still the son of a British defector. He had to have a use somehow, somewhere: they'd had him pinned to the board, like a specimen, since childhood. Sakov's instructions are not to get too close—he says he doesn't know who the kid's immediate KGB Control was, within his army unit—but constantly to watch and assess. He doesn't go for it at first, defector's son or not, but he does concede one thing. Sober—and under daily training—Bendall's a hell of a shot, able to take the eye out of the ace every time. And he likes killing, psychotically: in Afghanistan he used to volunteer, always out in front with his hand up. It's an ability—and a tendency—that gets registered, like everything gets registered: remember what the wise man said about knowledge being power? That's the watchword every espionage service in the world learned from Russian intelligence . . ."

"So what do they do with it, as far as Bendall is concerned?"

"File it, of course. We're talking an *old time* KGB faction, total control freaks who keep records on everyone. Sakov's army cover is as a movie and television cameraman. Gives him all the excuses to move around—*film*—everything and anything he wants. Another of the official divisional propaganda photographers is Vasili Gregorovich Isakov, who likes as often as he can to attach himself to Bendall's sniper unit . . ."

"His Control?" anticipated Charlie.

Kayley shook his head. "You know how the saying goes, boys will be girls. Seems that the military record we got was tightened down a lot. According to Sakov, who was there, the only time Bendall showed any stability—became normal—was when he and Isakov were a couple. Bendall didn't get drunk and he didn't fight and he hit everything he shot at, right in the middle. But being gay in the military—any military—isn't a good career move. They weren't particularly discreet about it and military intelligence just arrived one day, unannounced, and took Isakov away, never to be seen again. Bendall just flaked off the wall. He became virtually suicidal: like an animal, according to Sakov. That's when he drank diesel fuel and almost died."

Charlie accepted that he needed the chronology for perspective—to understand—but he was impatient to get to something he didn't at least have partial knowledge of. Even without Kayley smoking his office was going to smell like a humidor for days. "So they throw him out?"

"And he continues to freefall. Poor, want-to-be-blind Vera convinces herself he's stealing Western visitors' cases at Sheremet'yevo—which he does, occasionally—but Georgi-boy's bigger income is working as a male hooker around the tourist hotels. And how do we know? Because Russia's now redesigned and renamed internal security service, the FSB, has an attachment on Bendall's militia rap sheet and know every time a foreign gay has the balls to file a complaint after waking up from a night of passion to find his wallet and jewellery gone. . . ."

"The militia are in on it?" clarified Charlie.

"Just wait until I get to the cast list," confirmed the American, topping up their glasses again. "Now we get to the broader picture. The president of the United States gets some domestic difficulties and needs a diversion. The president of Russia doesn't look as if he'll make second term unless he gets a big one. A marriage made in heaven. But the *Kommunisticheskaya Partiya Rossiiskoi Federatsii* see an even greater potential. The American secretary of state commutes back and forth forever, dangling a treaty banning the U.S. Nuclear Missile Defense System. An American presidential visit was trailed for months, time enough to organize the assassination of two world leaders, ensure a communist reentry into the Kremlin and wreck, to and for the communist benefit, all Russia's intelligence organizational reforms. Everything goes back as it was before 1991, with Gorbachov a blip in Russia's history and Yeltsin the joke he always was . . ."

"That's not a broader picture," complained Charlie. "That's a panoramic screen."

"Sit back and listen to the coup of the century," promised Kayley. "Colonel Sakov's out of the army by now. Working for NTV—still the ideal posting to roam with a TV identification where he wouldn't be permitted otherwise—and where Vasili Gregorovich Isakov is chief cameraman and delighted to help an old army photographer colleague."

"But Sakov thinking there isn't a coincidence?"

"It isn't a coincidence," agreed Kayley. "As chief cameraman Isakov gets all the plum assignments and has even better access to places. He's singled out for positive FSB approach to become a source before the treaty shuttling starts. When it does our conspirators find a very different use for the guy."

"When do I get names?" demanded Charlie, finally giving way to the impatience.

"Two that Sakov positively knows are Nikolai Ivliyev and Aleksandr Kashva, both Communist Party deputies in the Duma. But there'll be more when the shit hits the fan," set out the American. "The Lubyanka traditionalists are General Gennardi Nikolaevich Mittell, first deputy director of the FSB, and General Boris Andrevich Lvov, commander of the presidential protection division. Real jewel in the crown—keeping them in front of every turn in the investigation—is Militia General Leonid Sergeevich Zenin: he's the bearded guy in court. And Sakov also told me that although he's not sure he thinks Pavl Filitov is in there. Zenin told him it was

Filitov, not anyone in the Justice Ministry, who rejected a murder investigation into the death of Vera Bendall. And you already know about Agayan. How's that for having a king in every castle?"

"In theory, unbeatable," said Charlie. Mittel was the deputy with whom Natalia clashed on the first day of the commission hearings, he remembered. "How was it supposed to work?"

"*Did* work, almost completely," insisted Kayley. "Sakov stages an accidental encounter with Bendall, who's cruising his favorite hotel, the National. During the reminiscences, Sakov drops the fact that Vasili Isakov is the chief cameraman at NTV. The tearful reunion takes place that same night. Isakov's got a lot of pull: it's easy to get the long-lost Bendall the gofers job. It's happy families again. The conspiracy need is to get Bendall under some sort of manipulative control. He starts to settle down again but Sakov suggests to Isakov that his boyfriend will benefit from seeing a psychiatrist. Enter Guerguen Agayan, Mr. Mind Bender himself from the Serbsky Institute. In less time that it takes to say labotomy, they've got their Pavlov dog . . ."

"Who's planning all this?" broke in Charlie.

"Sakov isn't clear on that. He thinks there's a group, a committee, in the Duma. Mittel's the liaison, with Lvov—who's supposed to keep the president alive!—ready to supply the route details when the time comes. But let's get back in sequence . . ."

"Sorry."

"Sakov says they can't believe their luck when the presidential summit is announced, knowing they're going to get the top prize. It's the signal to press the well-prepared button on Bendall, by killing Isakov . . ."

"*Who* killed him?" interrupted Charlie, again.

"Sakov says he doesn't know but I think he does. Maybe it was Sakov himself. He was certainly involved, admits to being with them both the night Isakov died. Bendall is distraught—inconsolable, which is what he's supposed to be. Agayan starts putting in the fix. Convinces Bendall, whom he can apparently make jump through hoops, that Isakov was murdered on the orders of the president, Lev Yudkin. Sakov works hard to cover his ass here: claims not to know where Bendall got the rifle but I can't see how it could have been anyone but him. To know so much about everything else and have a blank here doesn't make sense. He also says he doesn't know how Agayan kept the pressure up on Bendall but that doesn't square with me either. Like I said, a lot of the gaps are going to be filled by the Grand Jury and the outcome back here. He certainly doesn't deny— because he can't—knowing that Bendall was going to shoot, because his job was to kill Bendall afterwards, as we know and can prove: Sakov says that had he got Bendall over the edge but he'd survived, the intention was for the waiting Lvov to shoot him on the ground. But that Lvov couldn't, because of the delay of the fight alerting everyone to what was happening."

"Now it's all falling apart around them?" accepted Charlie, adding to their glasses.

"Panic time, because of what Sakov's said during the fight," agreed Kayley. "But these guys are resilient. They know from Lvov, who's right there literally on top of Bendall, that the guy's unconscious. By the time he comes round in Burdenko after surgery, Agayan is there, authorized to surgeon-administrator Badim's satisfaction by General Leonid Zenin, in over-all charge of the militia investigation . . ."

"Why doesn't Agayan kill him?"

"Sakov says he doesn't know how Agayan managed it—it'll certainly be a hard question for Badim—but no one else at the hospital apart from Agayan was ever totally alone with Bendall. If Bendall died we'd have demanded an autopsy. Agayan would have put himself in the frame, slipping him some unauthorized drug. And obviously he couldn't do it in front of Badim or the nurses or the guards. It was just always too busy."

"Jesus!" said Charlie. "And we thought only Sakov would be shitting himself!"

"I told you Agayan was Mr. Mind Bender. The way Sakov understands it Agayan convinces Bendall he's got a second chance of revenge against Lev Yudkin, in public. By making the exposing declaration he was trying in court when Davidov shot him . . ."

"Now there's a lot of questions here," stopped Charlie. "Bendall knows Sakov tried to kill him."

"Because all along, according to Agayan, Sakov was in on the plot to kill Isakov. Which he *was*! But Agayan convinced the poor bastard that Sakov was working *for* the Kremlin, under Yudkin's orders! That was going to be part of the courtroom denunciation."

"Which gets us to Davidov. How's he get into the picture?"

"Panoramic screen," corrected Kayley, smiling. "According to Sakov a KGB department unaffected by the supposed reforms and still maintained within the FSB is the Executive Action Department—Department V—to organize and carry out assassinations. Davidov served in it. He was simply ordered by Deputy Director Mittel to carry out the killing. Davidov *was* heading for a particular door because he'd been told his escape was arranged: actually there was another shooter outside—probably one of the gunmen who shot at the presidential group outside the White House—waiting to take Davidov out. But the militiaman put him down first."

Charlie shook his head. "Davidov had the same tattoo. I saw it!"

"It's not an arrow between two lines: it's supposed to be a bullet, in the barrel of a gun. It's traditional for marksmen, in Russian army sniper units, marks them out as an elite. Which I remember you getting close to unscrambling. Davidov was a sniper, although Sakov doesn't remember him being a contemporary of Bendalls. He must have been 'spotted' by someone and brought into Department V when he left the army. His KGB records are lifted, along with everything else that was taken, probably to be embarrassingly 'found' when he's identified from his army records."

"Isakov and Sakov were both cameramen," challenged Charlie.

"It was a love symbol for Isakov, when he and Bendall were together in the army. Made them elite—special—together. It was Agayan who insisted Sakov have it done, to make him part of the group—a blood brother—when they all got together at the TV station. Sakov had all the other shit put on his arms to make him one of the boys in the army: his father was actually a career office, a major in the KGB. It was Agayan who guided Sakov organizing their special evenings, drinking and singing that wailing song, which again was some fraternity crap they went in for in Afghanistan."

Charlie was glad he had more Islay malt in the office closet. The bottle they were drinking was almost empty. "Mittel lifted all the missing records and files, totally to incriminate the FSB?"

"Every one, he and whoever else he's working with at the Lubyanka," agreed Kayley.

"Making it—and Viktor Karelin's chairmanship—look ridiculous?"

"Karelin could never have survived."

"Neither could Okulov," recognized Charlie, remembering the recommendations of Natalia's official enquiry. "Whatever the outcome of the commission—or whether Okulov accepted its findings or not—there would have been no way Okulov could have convinced anybody the assassinations weren't orchestrated with the help of old KGB friends, to get his presidency confirmed. It would have been a walk-over for the communists."

"Even with their problems with the commission, it was a brilliant game plan," said Kayley, emptying the last of the bottle between them. "The communists win by a landslide, Okulov, Karelin and reforms vanish into oblivion and the communists regain the Kremlin and hold the Duma. Gennardi Mittel gets the chairmanship of the FSB and Leonid Zenin transfers as his deputy. Vladimir Sakov goes back into the fold, his field life over, to become chairman of whatever FSB Directorate he wants and Boris Lvov is appointed head of the militia. And finally Washington is given the stiff middle finger to its Son of Star Wars treaty in the hope of making things awkward for the American president, even if he's not killed."

Charlie heard the other man out but said at once, "What problems with the presidential commission?"

"Mittel apparently persuaded Karelin to let him represent the FSB, so he could really stir the shit. But the chairperson was a fiesty gal who sent him packing and insisted on Karelin appearing personally. And Zenin expected to get the commission chairmanship: imagine that as a destructive duo!"

Fiesty gal, picked out Charlie. Natalia was still in danger if the Grand Jury hearing didn't evidentially produce everything Kayley had just told him. "They'll run, make some move when they know Sakov's gone!"

Kayley looked curiously at the bottom of his empty glass. "Anticipated it!" he said, triumphantly. "Mittel was Sakov's direct contact. I had Sakov call him—recording it, obviously—to say he was going out of town. Got Mittel on tape ordering him—a supposed television cameraman, don't forget!—to stay in Moscow and wait to be told what to do next, that everything was under control. Sakov comes from Gorkiy: that's where they'll be looking for the next few days, not Washington."

"How quickly will the Grand Jury return the indictments?"

"Sakov's the only witness. It only took me about four hours to get what I've told you."

"What's the route then?"

Kayley shrugged. "Anandale talks to Okulov direct, to fix their simultaneous prime slot television appearances, giving Okulov time to brief Karelin to get everyone in the bag first. And you know the best bit?"

"What?"

"Okulov gets his sweeping election victory when the communists are exposed. And Anandale gets the sons-of-bitches that maimed his wife, maybe even the actual guys from Department V who pulled the trigger. But without having to suspend or cancel America's missile defense system, which guarantees his second term, too. Ain't that the prettiest thing?"

"And you?"

"I was called by the president into the Oval Office and with the acting head of the FBI and Wendall North as witnesses got told I could choose whatever internal Bureau division I want. You really have got me into the Hall of Fame, Charlie."

"You're welcome." It might have been by proxy but he'd maintain the never lose, never be beaten philosophy. He got the second bottle from the corner cupboard.

"All we've got to do is keep up the frustrated act over the next few days," said Kayley.

"It'll be a walk in the park," insisted Charlie. Who did he have to walk with? he wondered.

"That's what both the American and the Englishman are saying?"

"According to Kayley, American newspapers are openly saying that it's a conspiracy between Okulov and his old friends," said Olga.

"What about official investigation?" asked Zenin.

"They say there's nothing positive they can do, they're waiting for the result of the commission, like we are." Olga cleared the table while Zenin carried the remains of their dinner wine into the lounge.

"I've been talking to people," said Zenin. "There's no way Okulov or Karelin can survive."

"Do you think a change of government will affect us personally?"

"Who knows?" smiled Zenin.

Olga sat at Zenin's feet, her arm looped over his knees, her wine glass in her other hand. "Can I ask you something?"

"What?"

"You're not unhappy, are you: not thinking things aren't working out between us?"

"Of course not! Things *are* working out! Why do you think they're not?"

"In the last few days you've just seemed . . . I don't know . . . distant, I suppose."

"A man can't make love every night!"

"I didn't mean that."

"I've been considering a lot of options: trying to find a way to move forward. I want to get it over with. Finished."

"It will be, soon," said Olga, emptily.

Charlie waited four days before going to the Radisson Slavjanskaya hotel again, carefully allowing two hours from the end of Sasha's schoolday. The immediate anger would have gone by now. He certainly wouldn't lose his temper—he had nothing to lose his temper about—and hoped Natalia wouldn't, either, certainly not in front of Sasha. If Natalia insisted, he'd even keep it a telephone conversation, although he'd have more chance of persuading her if they could meet, face to face. Alternatively she might agree briefly to leave Sasha in the room, so they could talk in the hotel lounge or bar, although he thought that unlikely. He didn't want to leave Sasha alone in a hotel bedroom himself, no matter how briefly.

Charlie found the house phone in a corner of the foyer, glad it was an enclosed booth. The man who answered in room 46 said Charlie must have the wrong extension: he was a computer technician from Kiev who'd only arrived that morning. The receptionist told him Natalia Fedova and the little girl had booked out the previous day, without leaving a forwarding address.

Back at Lesnaya Charlie walked aimlessly around the echoing rooms, as he had every night since Natalia left. That night, though, he stopped in Sasha's room, properly seeing for the first time that there were still things of Sasha's that Natalia hadn't taken, particularly toys. Then he saw that the doll he'd bought back from London was there but the previous, forgotten sister with the droopy eye wasn't.

27

The perfectly coordinated seizures were filmed, to be shown directly before the simultaneous telecasts by both presidents. Anandale personally pressured Okulov during his alerting telephone call after the Grand Jury indictments for FBI agents to be visibly present at each arrest, which took place at four A.M. At each, doors were jackhammered off their hinges. Everyone named by Sakov was confronted before they could get out of bed. John Kayley, who was with the loyal FSB officers who took deputy chairman Gennardi Mittel into custody, was identified during the president's address to the nation as the officer who had broken the case. Olga Melnik was taken manacled from the apartment with Zenin and held for a week before being released. The detentions were announced—simultaneously again—five hours before the televised appearance of the two leaders, and in mid-afternoon Petr Tikunov, the communist party presidential candidate, put a gun into his mouth and pulled the trigger. In his broadcast Anandale spoke of a plot that could have destabilized world peace, which was now strengthened and more secure because of the cooperation between two great nations. Okulov even more grandiosely talked of Russia being pulled back from reentering the dark ages and of a cancer being excised from an organization and a political party which sought to subvert the new Russian democracy.

He echoed Anandale's insistence on a strengthening between the two countries and said he was looking forward to officially becoming Russia's leader in the forthcoming elections. Neither referred to a missile defense treaty.

Charlie Muffin watched alone in his echoing apartment, smiling at the sight—repeated after the president's identification—of John Kayley for the first time in a freshly pressed suit and laundered shirt. There was, inevitably, a cigar.

Charlie had turned to CNN for their quickly assembled documentary on the entire investigation—dominated once more by the gantry fight between Bendall and Sakov—when the telephone rang. His stomach hollowed at Natalia's voice.

"You?" she anticipated at once.

"Yes."

"Why did you give it away to the Americans?"

"That's the way it worked."

"And now that Filitov's been arrested you know I wasn't the leak."

"I said I was sorry. I'm glad you've called." He could persuade her. Not easily, perhaps, but now they were talking he could convince her to call the whole nonsense off.

"There are some things I need to collect."

"Come back, Natalia. Please." He'd let her have her pride.

"Clothes. And some stuff of Sasha's."

"How is she?"

"Fine. She asks after you."

"I miss her and I'm lost without you and I want you both to come back."

"Can I come by tomorrow, to pick them up."

That's when it would be best, when they were in the same room together. "What time?"

"About now?"

"I'll be waiting."

He was.

He opened Volnay but left it in the refrigerator to stay chilled and abandoned the idea of canapés because it would be trying too

hard. He did put cornflowers in a vase, though, because they were
her favorite and it was quite normal for him to buy them for her.
He poured himself scotch, which he would normally have done at
that time but left it untouched on the low table. Illogically he had
expected her to ring, from the street, and started at the sound of
her key in the lock, only just getting to his feet as she entered. She
had a case in either hand!

Charlie went towards her but looked beyond, for their daughter.
"You're back! Where's Sasha?"

Seeing his look and realizing his misunderstanding, Natalia easily
lifted both empty cases and said, "To carry what I've come to collect."

Charlie stopped, uncertain whether to go on to try to kiss her.
Not a good idea, he decided. "I've opened some wine."

"No thanks. I've got to get on." She couldn't let him talk her
round.

"You got my note at the hotel?"

"Of course."

"I went again but you'd moved out?"

"I've got a temporary ministry apartment, until I can find something."

"I want you to come back here."

"You said." It would be so easy to say yes but she really wasn't
sure if she wanted to, not totally.

"I made mistakes. Let's not make any more."

"It's too claustrophobic. We're not happy together." He had to
agree with that!

"We can be! Not all the time but most of it. People aren't, not
all the time. Let's learn from this, not suffer from it."

"I don't feel I'm suffering. I need space, to breathe." Which was
what she felt she'd been doing, breathing. Feeling free.

"Sit down. Please. Let's talk."

"I need to pack. Sasha's staying at Marina's again but I said I
wouldn't be long."

"You sure about this?"

"Yes."

"Now you're making the mistake."

Natalia walked around him and disappeared into their bedroom, saying nothing.

Charlie went to follow but stopped again. It would be wrong to crowd her. *I need space.* Leave her alone: let her see—feel—what it was she was abandoning. He stayed standing but sipped for the first time at the neglected drink. Natalia crossed from their bedroom into Sasha's without looking sideways along the corridor towards him. When she emerged with the two cases he said, "Do you need help with them?"

"No."

"I want to be able to see Sasha."

"Yes."

"So I need an address."

"I'll let you have it, when I get one."

"What about now?"

"It'll only be a few days." Stay strong, she told herself, don't give in.

"Don't do this!"

"Keep safe, Charlie."

He remained standing after the door closed behind her, quietly again, the drink forgotten in his hand. He put it down abruptly, angrily, spilling it, and at once wondered why—for whose benefit—he was performing like someone in a B movie. He went into their bedroom, seeing that this time Natalia had cleared everything from her closets. He thought at first she'd only left one thing in Sasha's room, the doll he'd brought back from London. Then he saw, beside it, the diamond bar brooch he'd also bought there for Natalia.